and the
TURKISH LIEUTENANT

First Second

Copyright © 2013 by Tony Cliff

Published by First Second
First Second is an imprint of Roaring Brook Press,
a division of Holtzbrinck Publishing Holdings Limited Partnership
175 Fifth Avenue, New York, New York 10010

Cataloging-in-Publication Data is on file at the Library of Congress.

ISBN 978-1-59643-813-2

First Second books are available for special promotions and premiums.
For details, contact: Director of Special Markets, Holtzbrinck Publishers.

First edition 2013
Book design by Colleen AF Venable

Printed in China
10 9 8 7 6 5 4 3 2

Delilah Dirk

and the
TURKISH LIEUTENANT

Tony Cliff

:01

First Second

New York

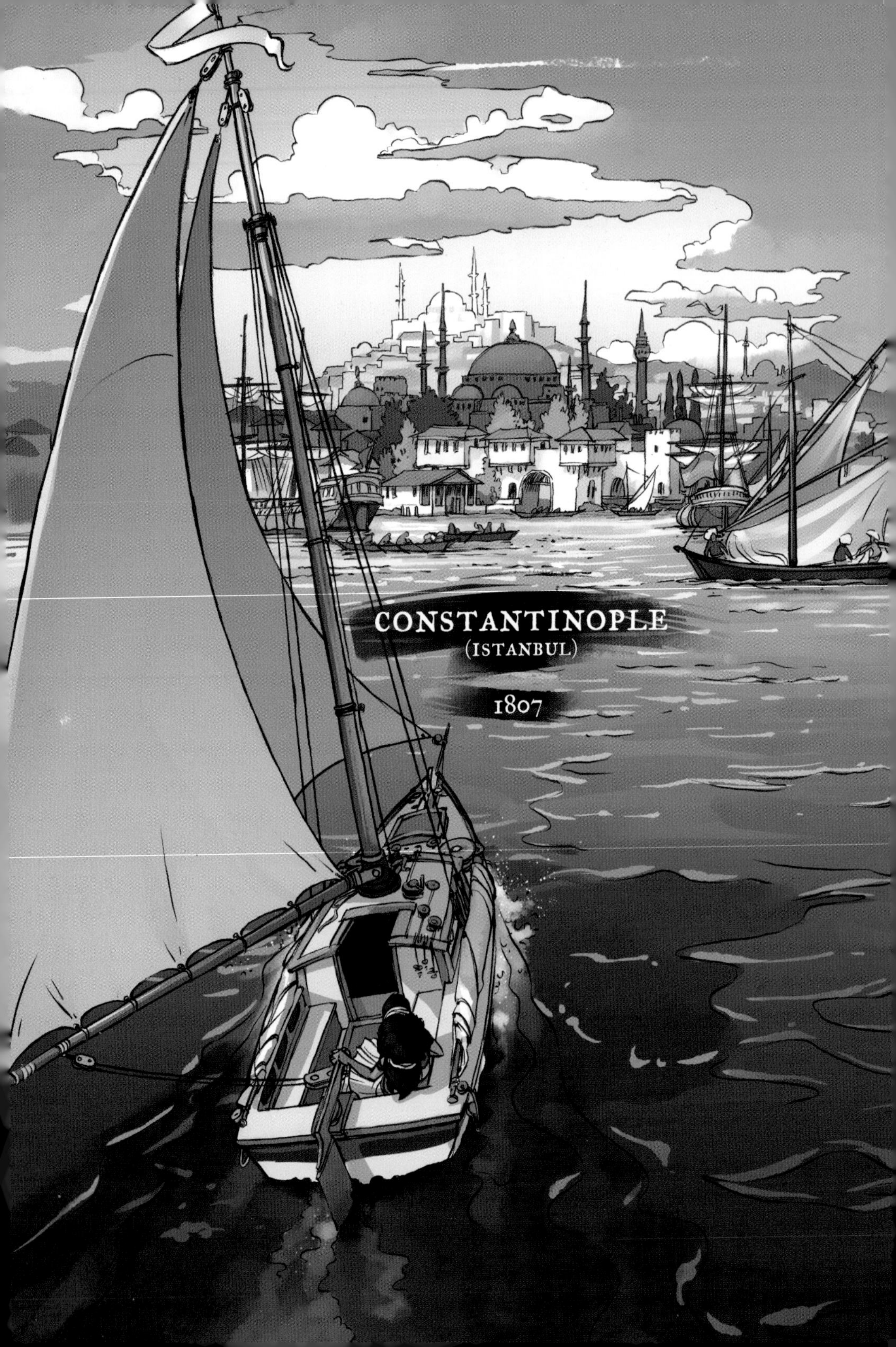
CONSTANTINOPLE
(ISTANBUL)
1807

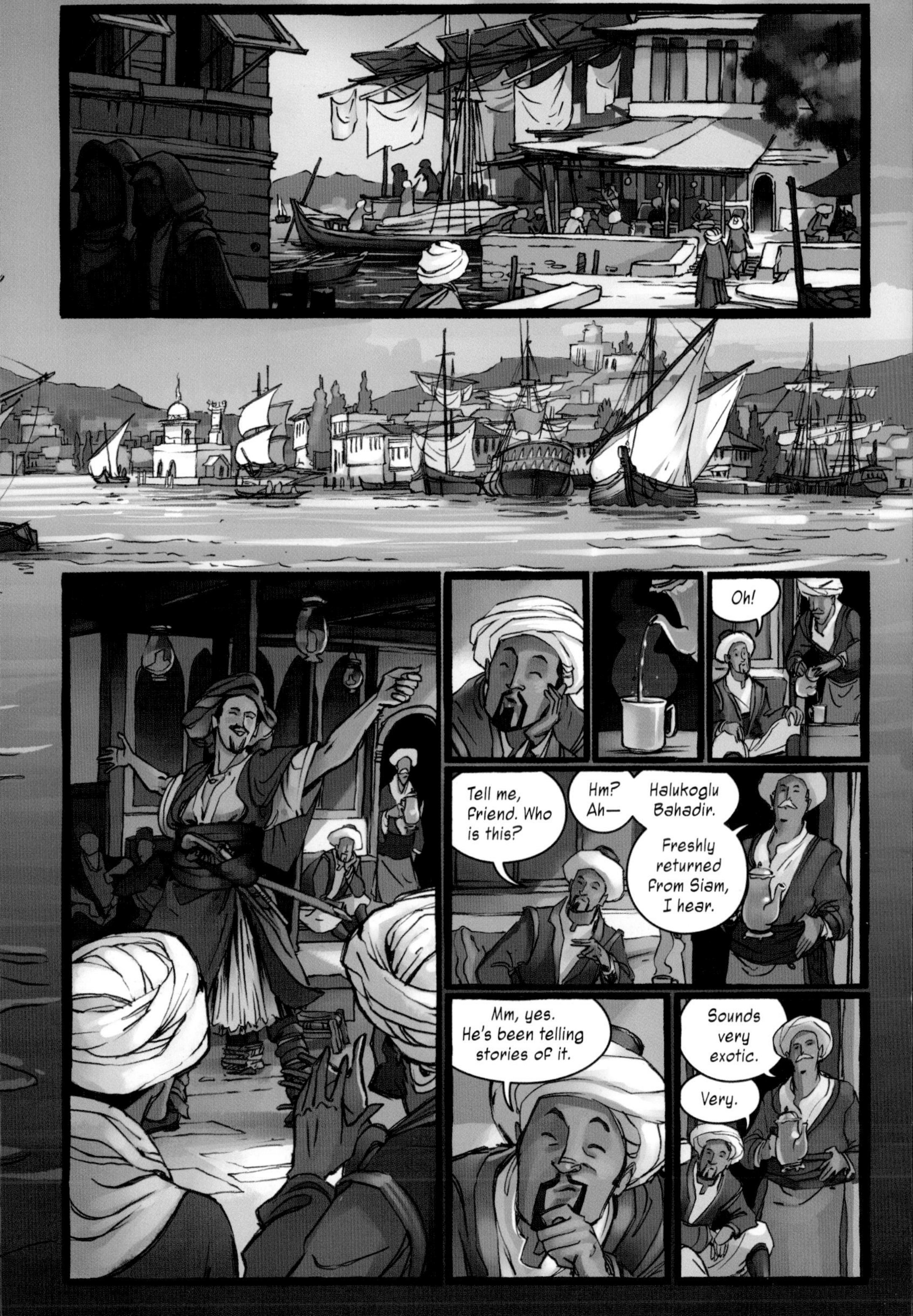
Oh!
Tell me, friend. Who is this?
Hm? Ah—
Halukoglu Bahadir.
Freshly returned from Siam, I hear.
Mm, yes. He's been telling stories of it.
Sounds very exotic.
Very.

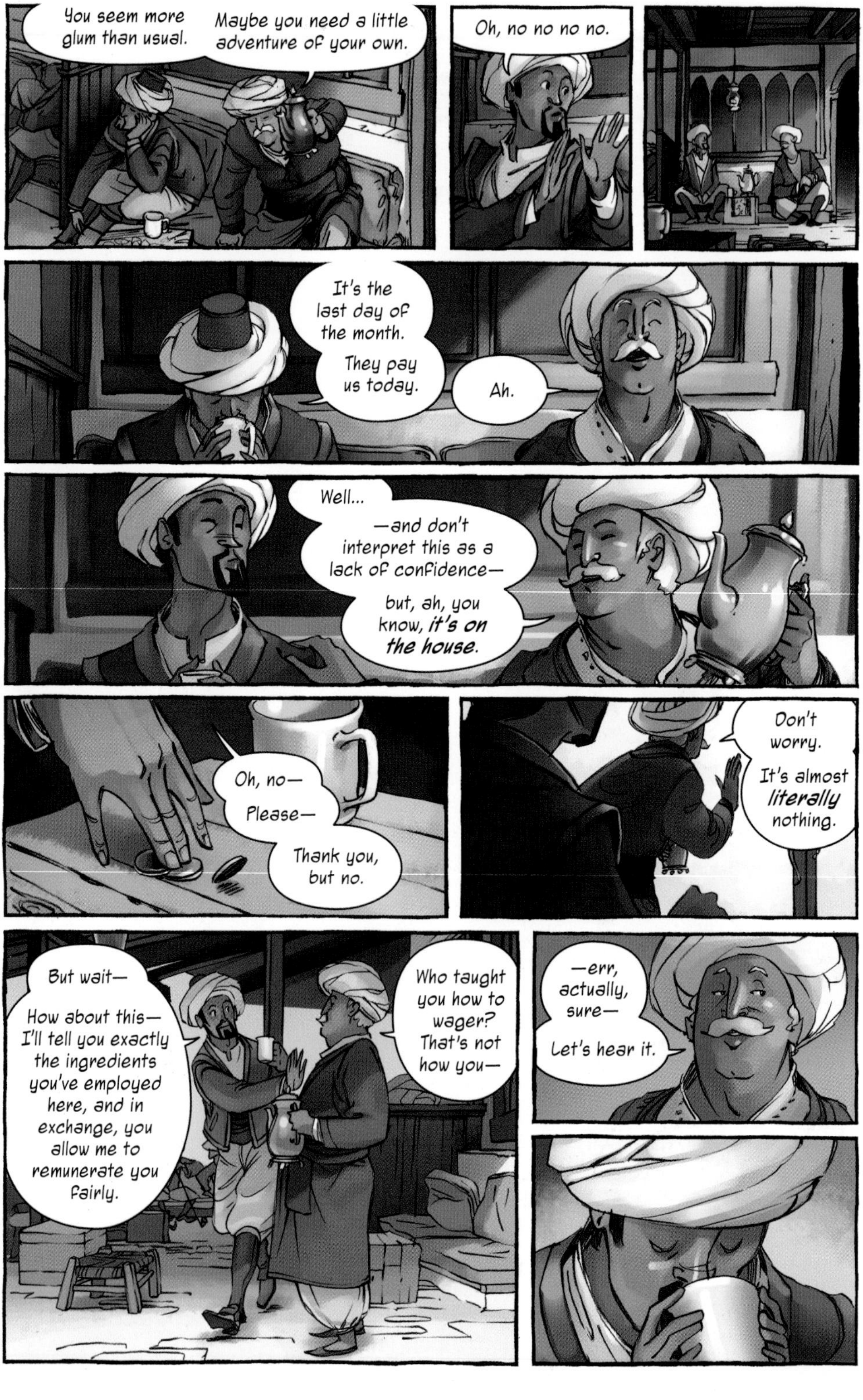
You seem more glum than usual.
Maybe you need a little adventure of your own.
Oh, no no no no.
It's the last day of the month.
They pay us today.
Ah.
Well...
—and don't interpret this as a lack of confidence—
but, ah, you know, it's on the house.
Oh, no—
Please—
Thank you, but no.
Don't worry.
It's almost literally nothing.
But wait—
How about this—I'll tell you exactly the ingredients you've employed here, and in exchange, you allow me to remunerate you fairly.
Who taught you how to wager? That's not how you—
—err, actually, sure—
Let's hear it.

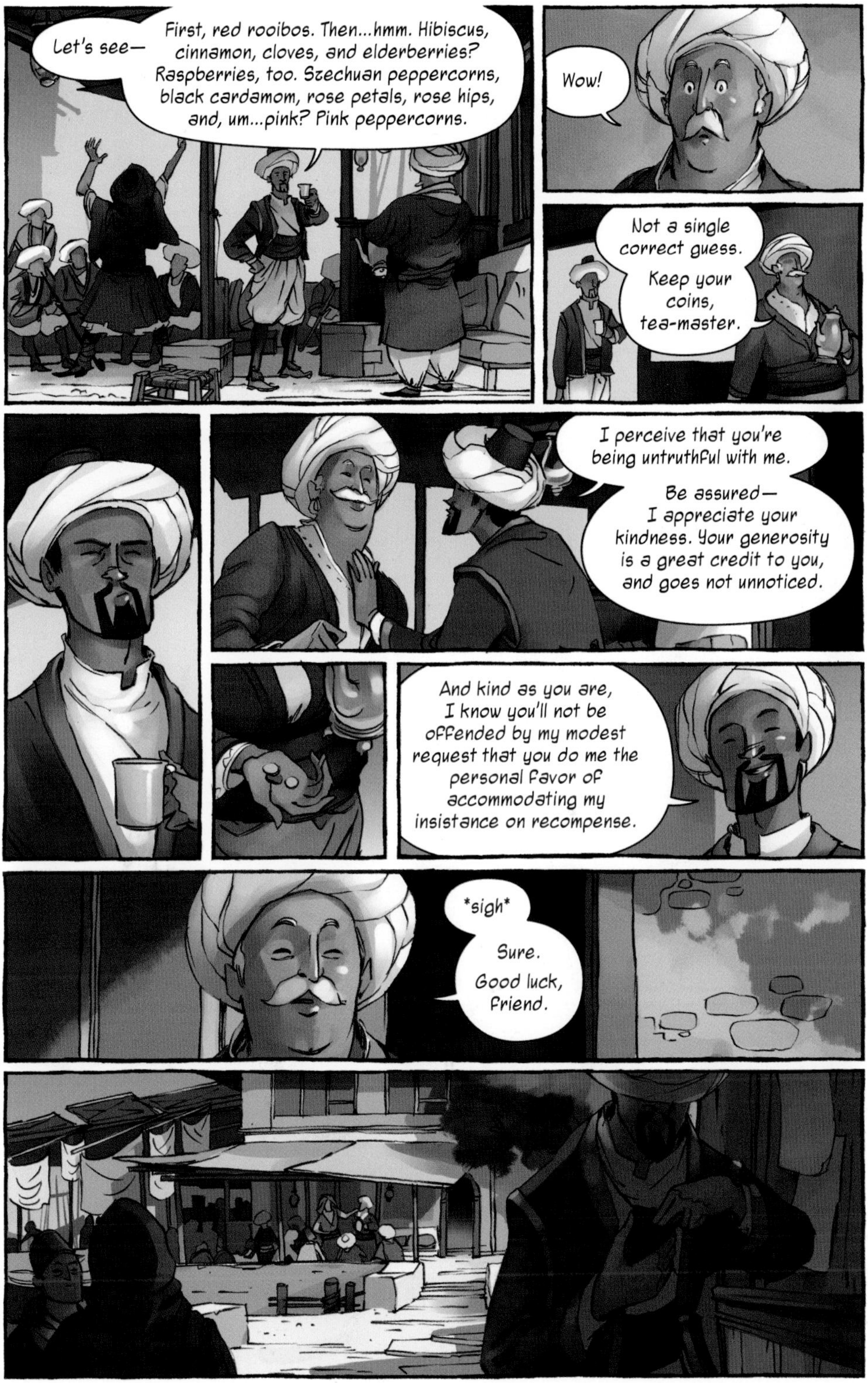
Let's see—
First, red rooibos. Then...hmm. Hibiscus, cinnamon, cloves, and elderberries? Raspberries, too. Szechuan peppercorns, black cardamom, rose petals, rose hips, and, um...pink? Pink peppercorns.
Wow!
Not a single correct guess.
Keep your coins, tea-master.
I perceive that you're being untruthful with me.
Be assured— I appreciate your kindness. Your generosity is a great credit to you, and goes not unnoticed.
And kind as you are, I know you'll not be offended by my modest request that you do me the personal favor of accommodating my insistance on recompense.
sigh
Sure.
Good luck, Friend.

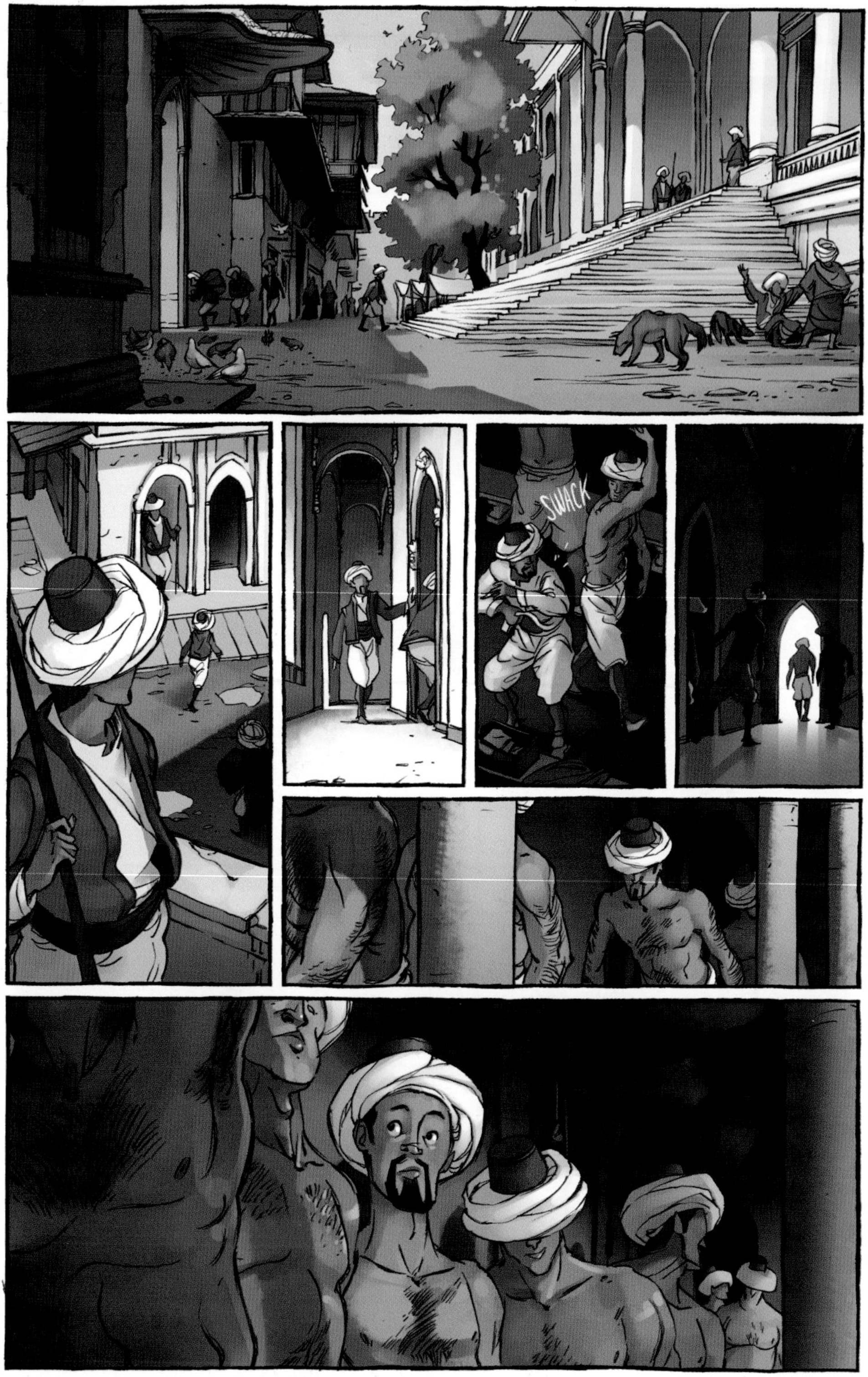
SWACK

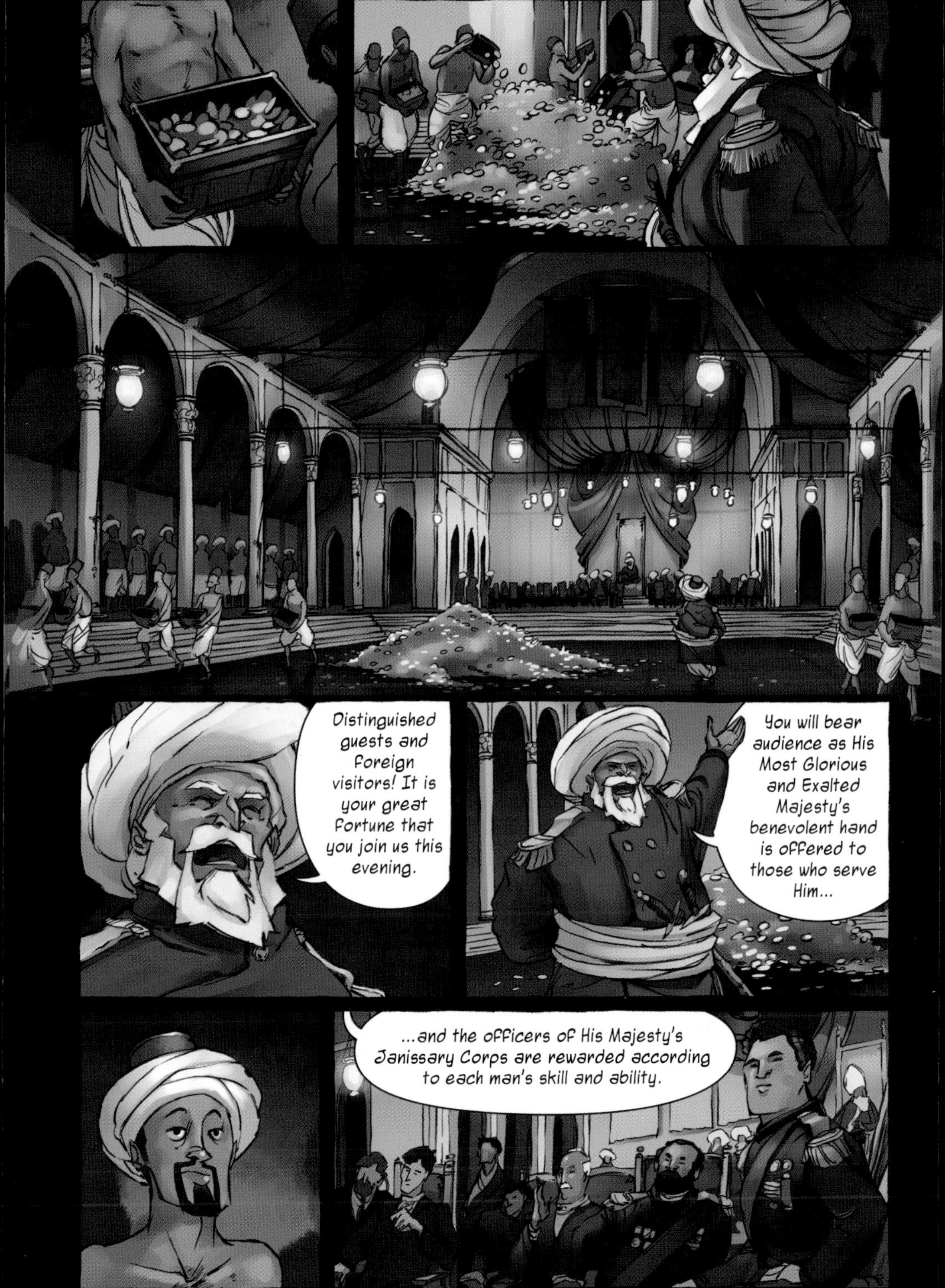
Distinguished guests and foreign visitors! It is your great fortune that you join us this evening.
You will bear audience as His Most Glorious and Exalted Majesty's benevolent hand is offered to those who serve Him...
...and the officers of His Majesty's Janissary Corps are rewarded according to each man's skill and ability.

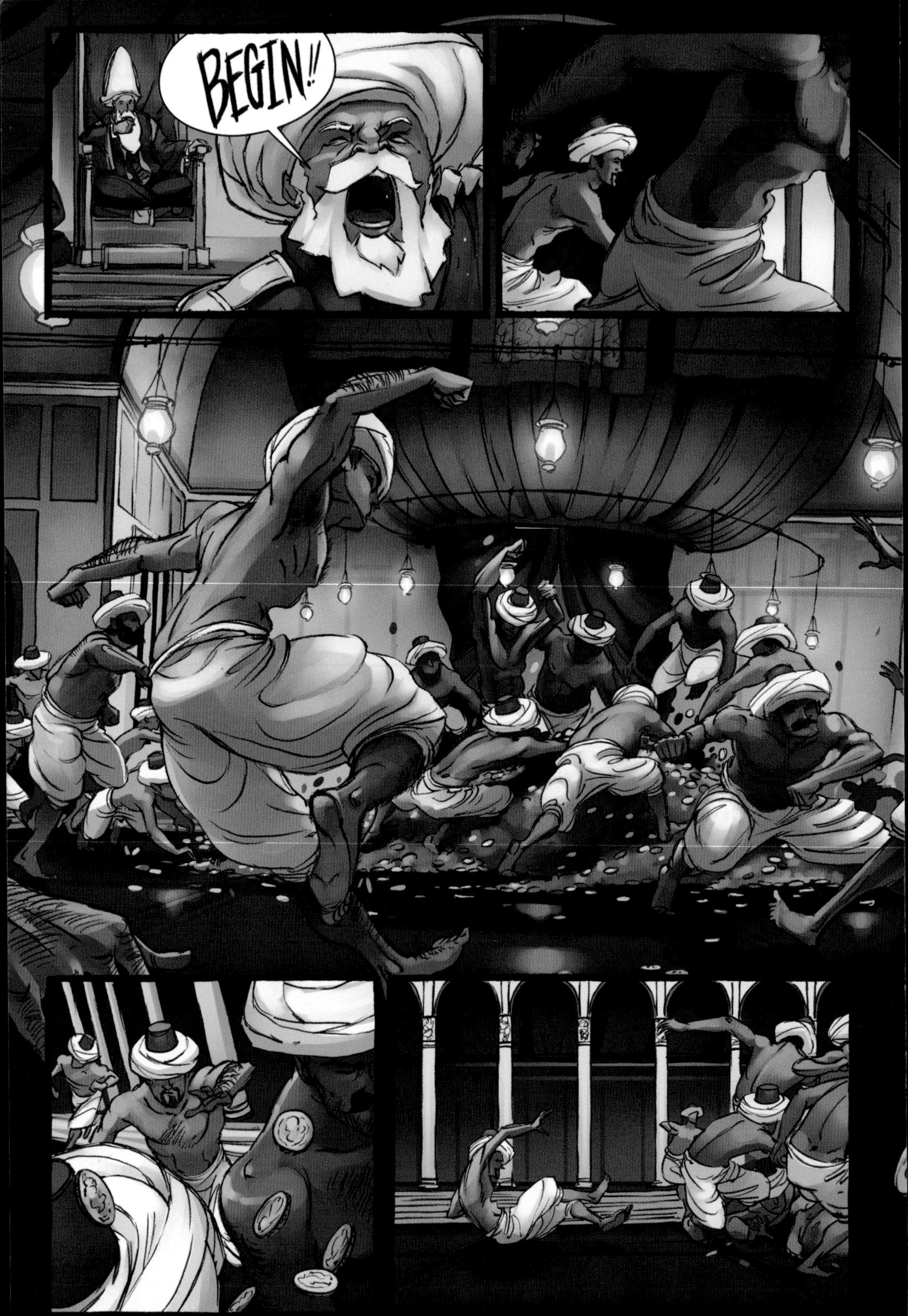
BEGIN!!

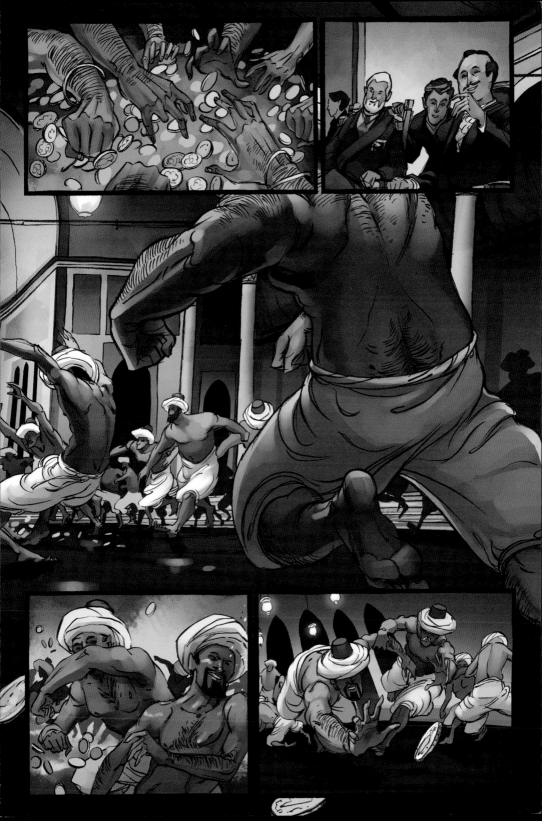

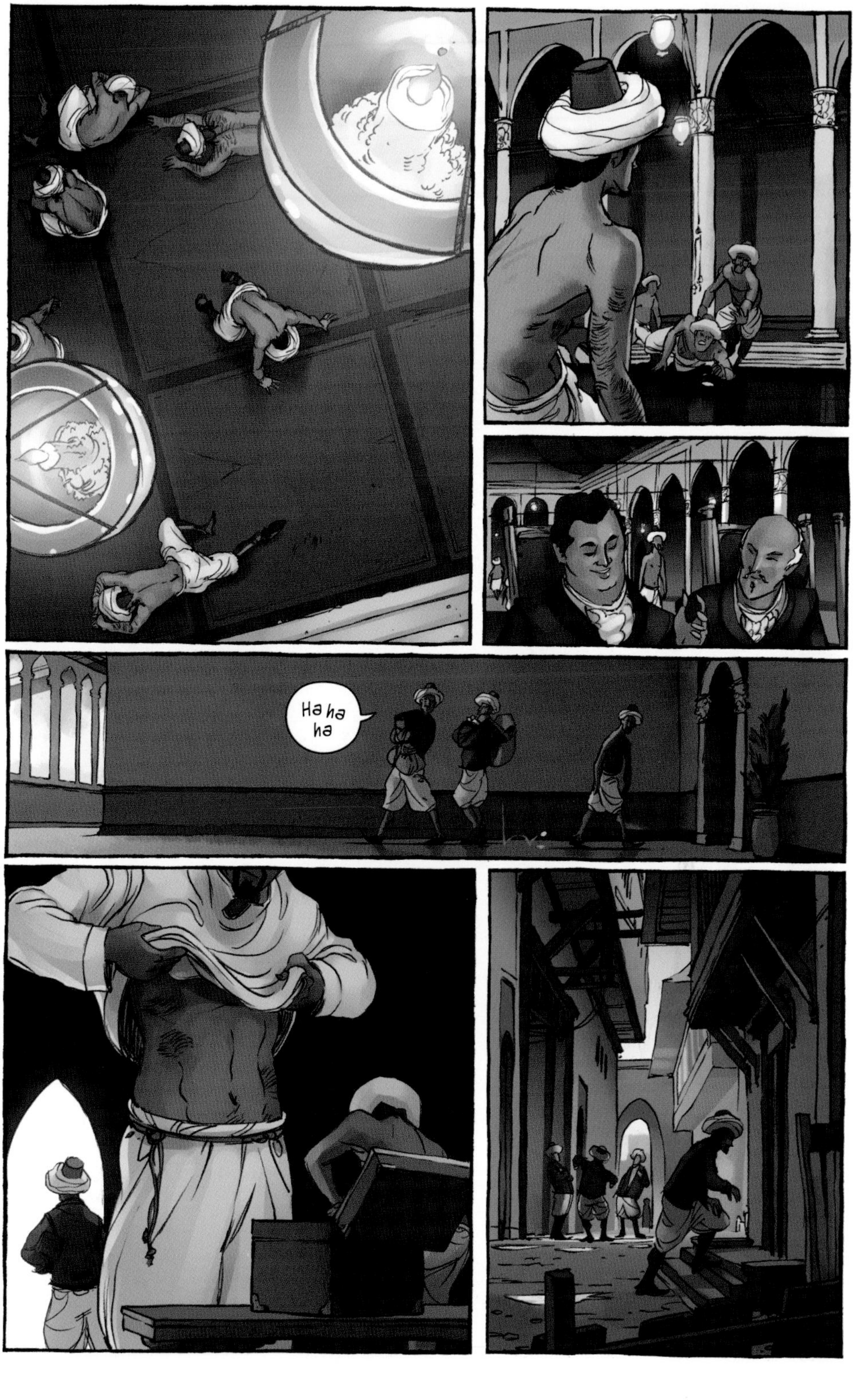
Ha ha ha

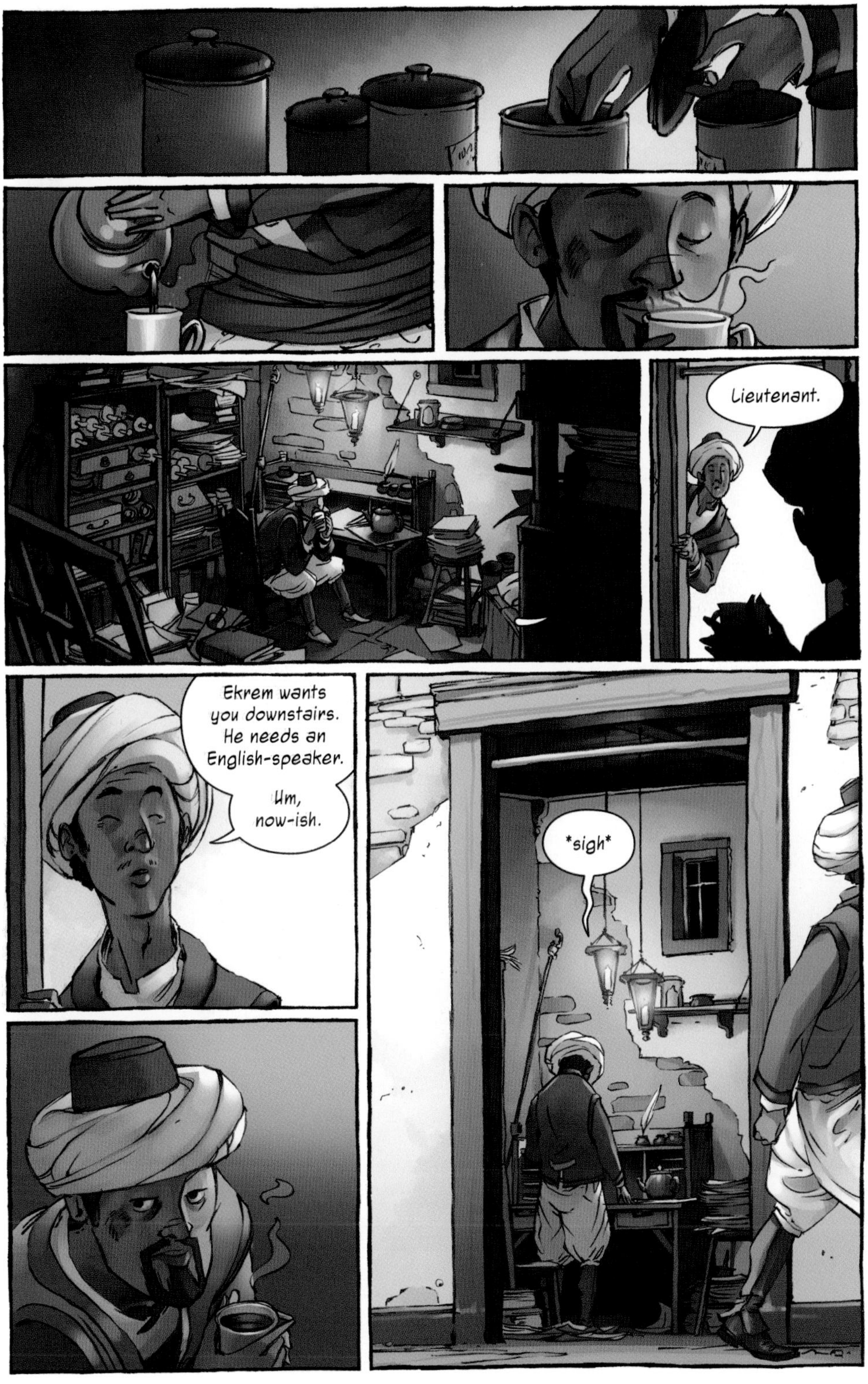

Lieutenant.
Ekrem wants you downstairs. He needs an English-speaker.
Um, now-ish.
sigh

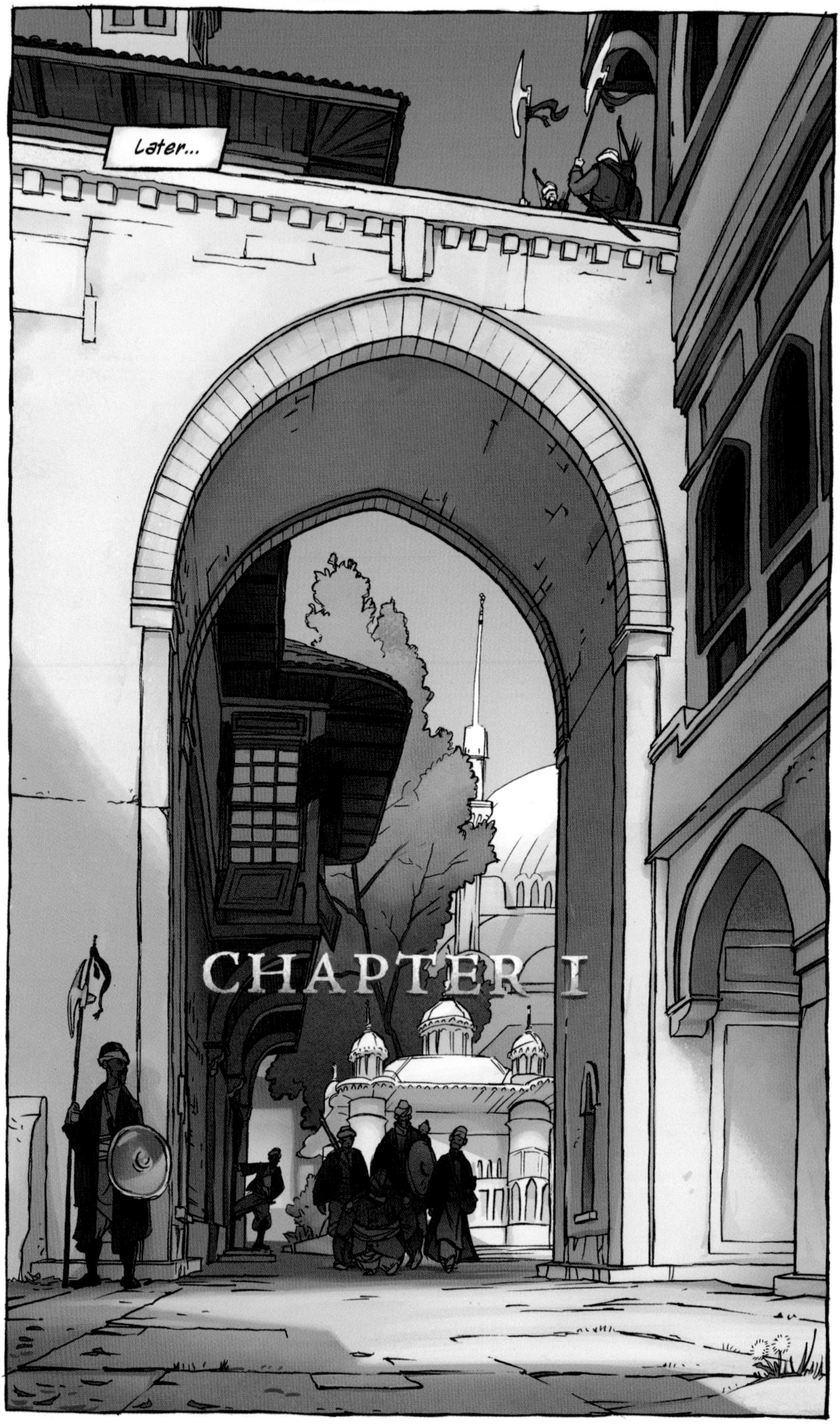
Later...
CHAPTER I

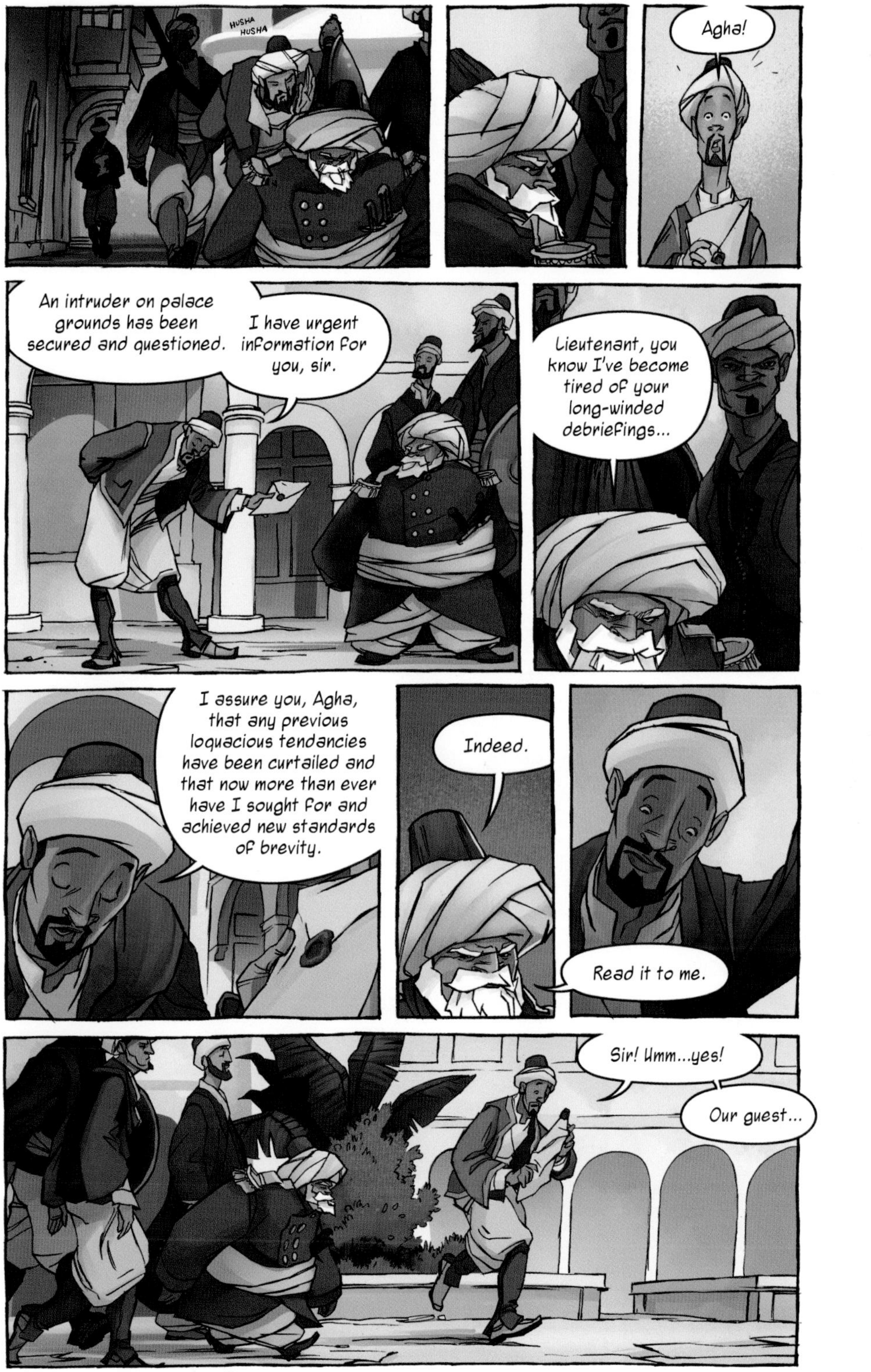
HUSHA HUSHA
Agha!
An intruder on palace grounds has been secured and questioned.
I have urgent information for you, sir.
Lieutenant, you know I've become tired of your long-winded debriefings...
I assure you, Agha, that any previous loquacious tendancies have been curtailed and that now more than ever have I sought for and achieved new standards of brevity.
Indeed.
Read it to me.
Sir! Umm...yes!
Our guest...

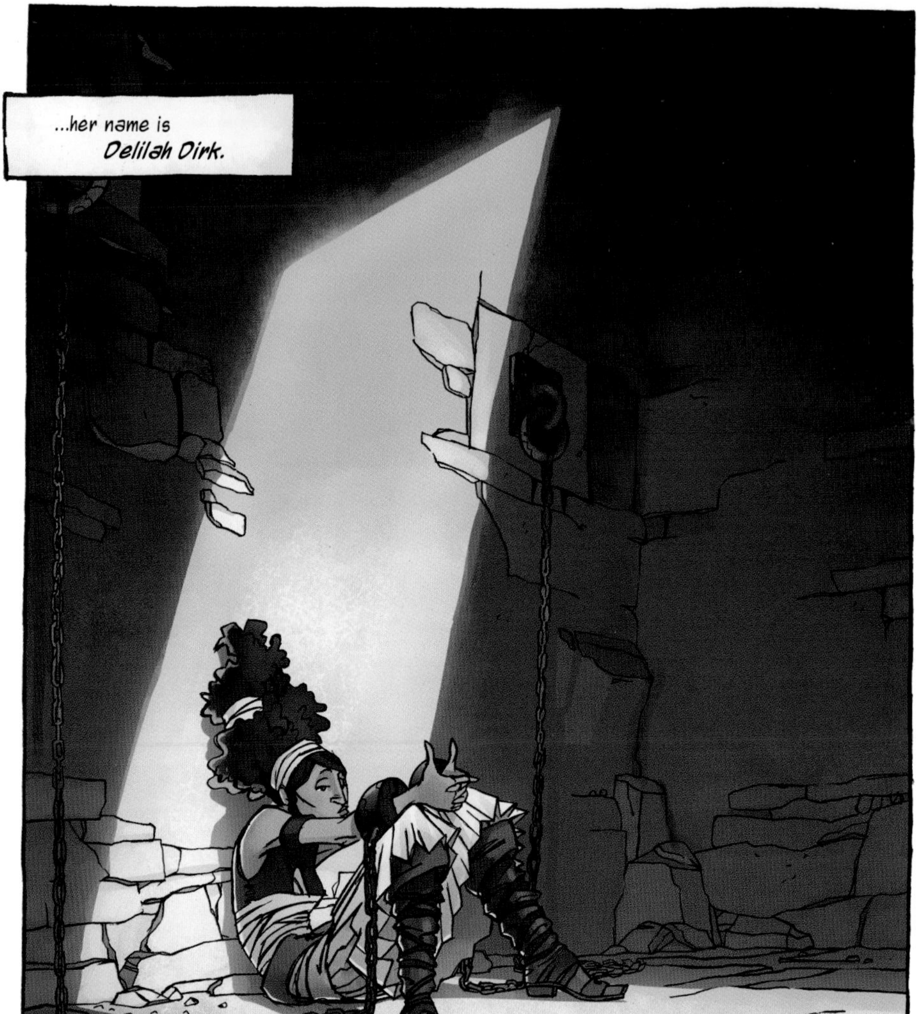
...her name is
Delilah Dirk.

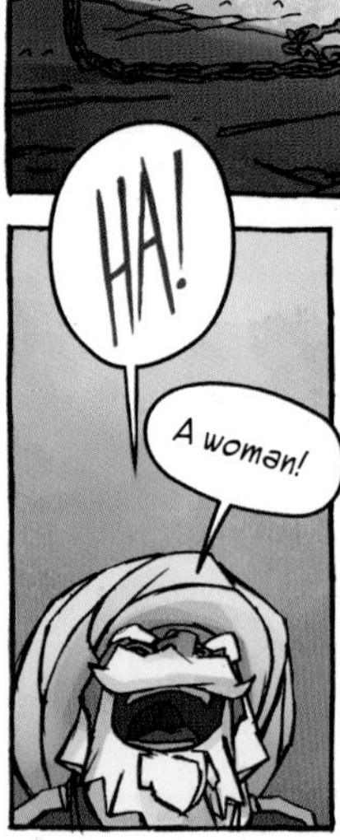
HA!
A woman!

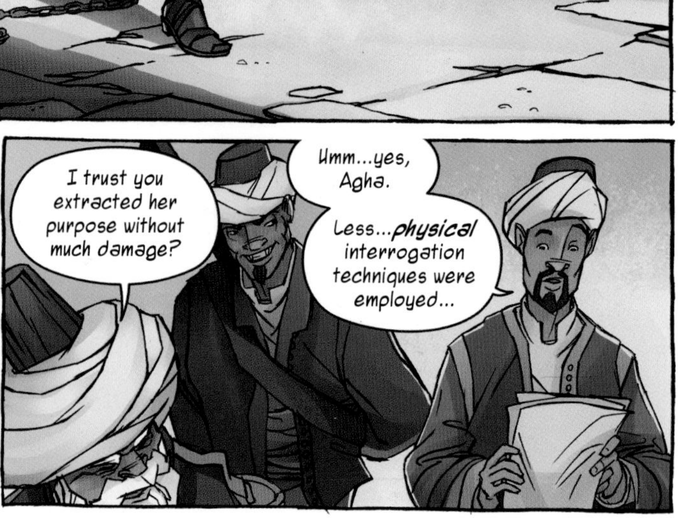
I trust you extracted her purpose without much damage?
Umm...yes, Agha.
Less...physical interrogation techniques were employed...

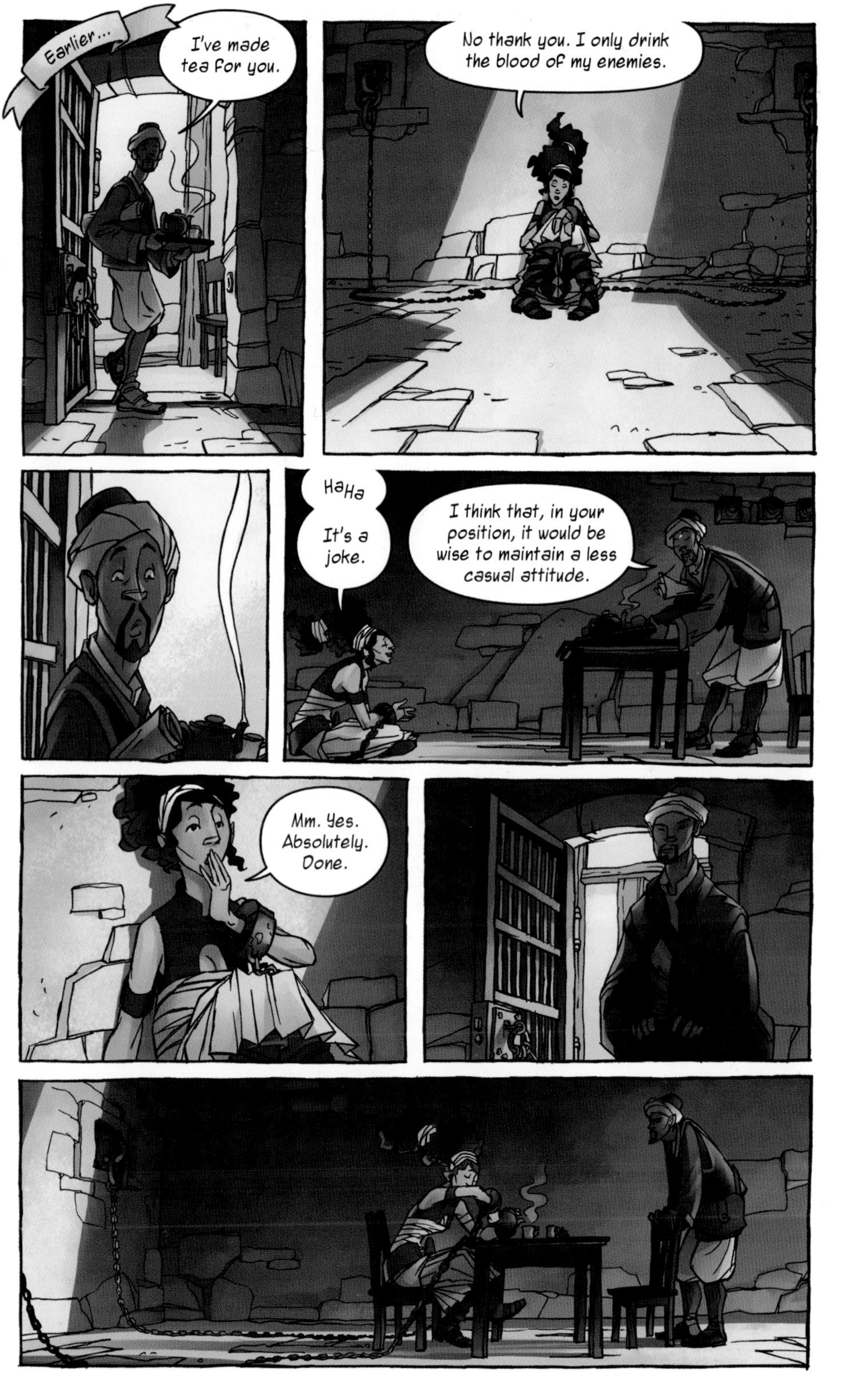

Earlier...
I've made tea for you.
No thank you. I only drink the blood of my enemies.
HaHa
It's a joke.
I think that, in your position, it would be wise to maintain a less casual attitude.
Mm. Yes. Absolutely. Done.

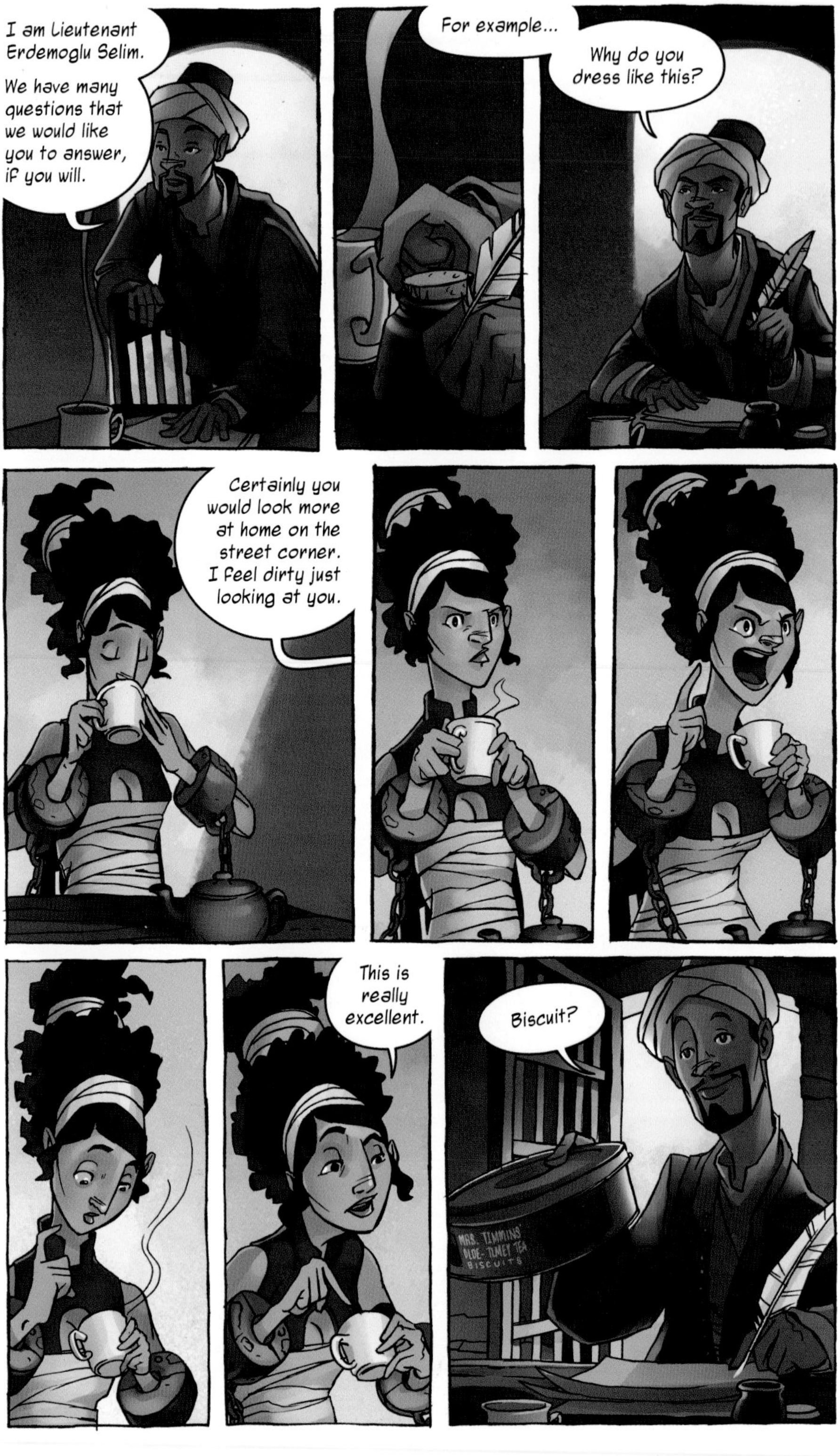
I am Lieutenant Erdemoglu Selim.
We have many questions that we would like you to answer, if you will.
For example...
Why do you dress like this?
Certainly you would look more at home on the street corner. I feel dirty just looking at you.
This is really excellent.
Biscuit?
MRS. TIMMINS' OLDE-TIMEY TEA BISCUITS

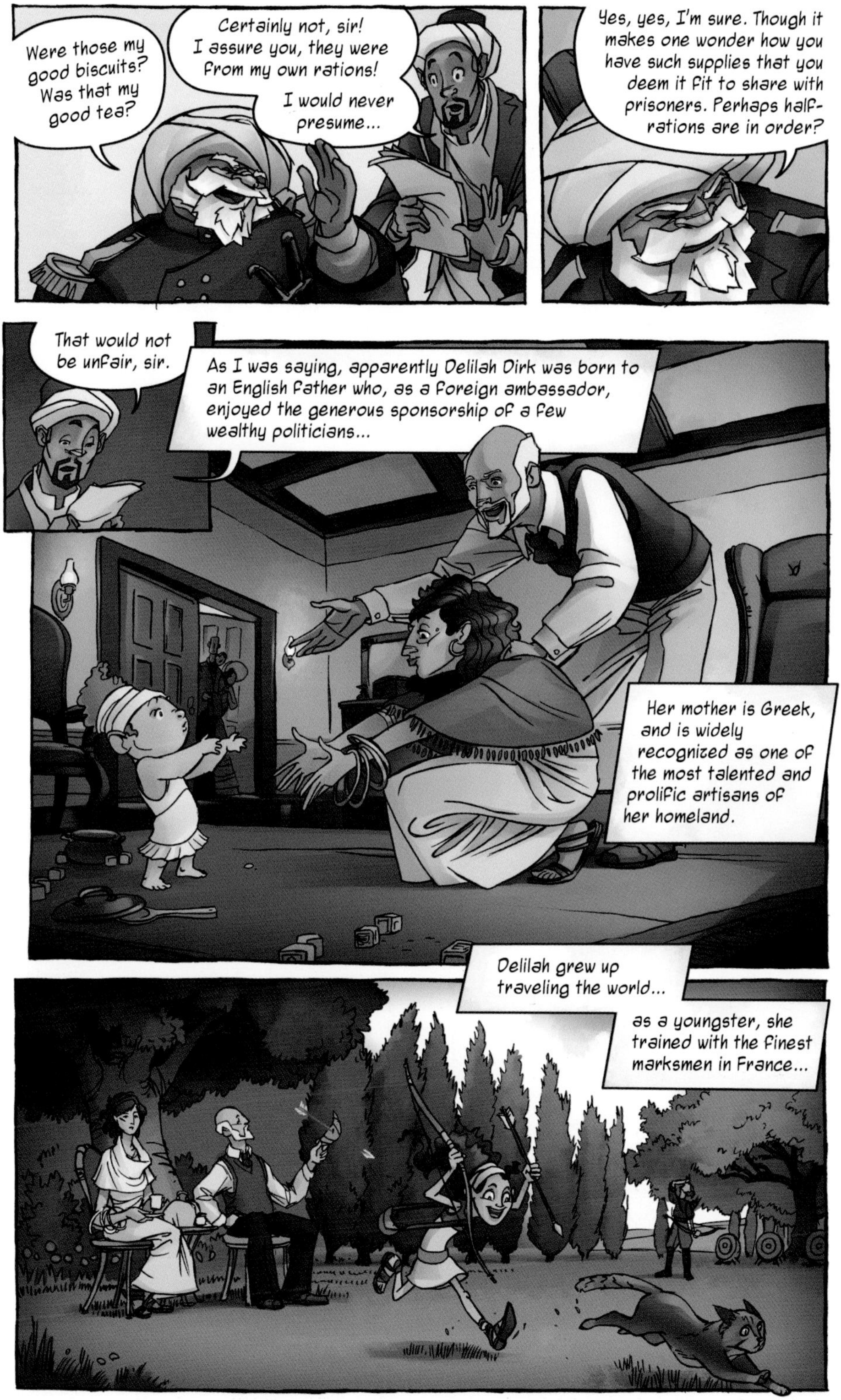

Were those my good biscuits? Was that my good tea?
Certainly not, sir! I assure you, they were from my own rations!
I would never presume...
Yes, yes, I'm sure. Though it makes one wonder how you have such supplies that you deem it fit to share with prisoners. Perhaps half-rations are in order?
That would not be unfair, sir.
As I was saying, apparently Delilah Dirk was born to an English father who, as a foreign ambassador, enjoyed the generous sponsorship of a few wealthy politicians...
Her mother is Greek, and is widely recognized as one of the most talented and prolific artisans of her homeland.
Delilah grew up traveling the world...
as a youngster, she trained with the finest marksmen in France...

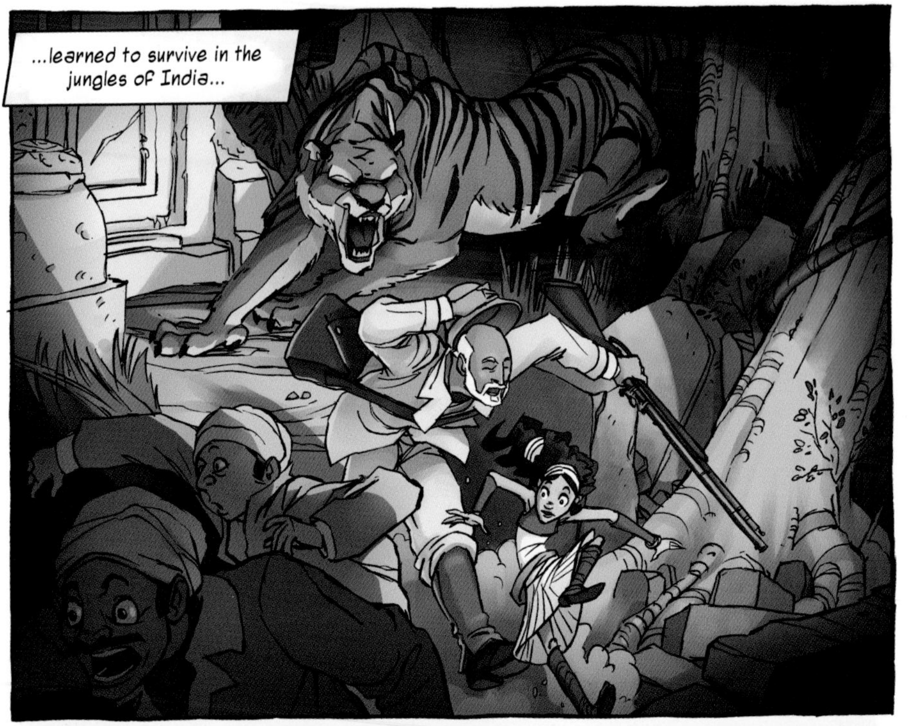
...learned to survive in the jungles of India...

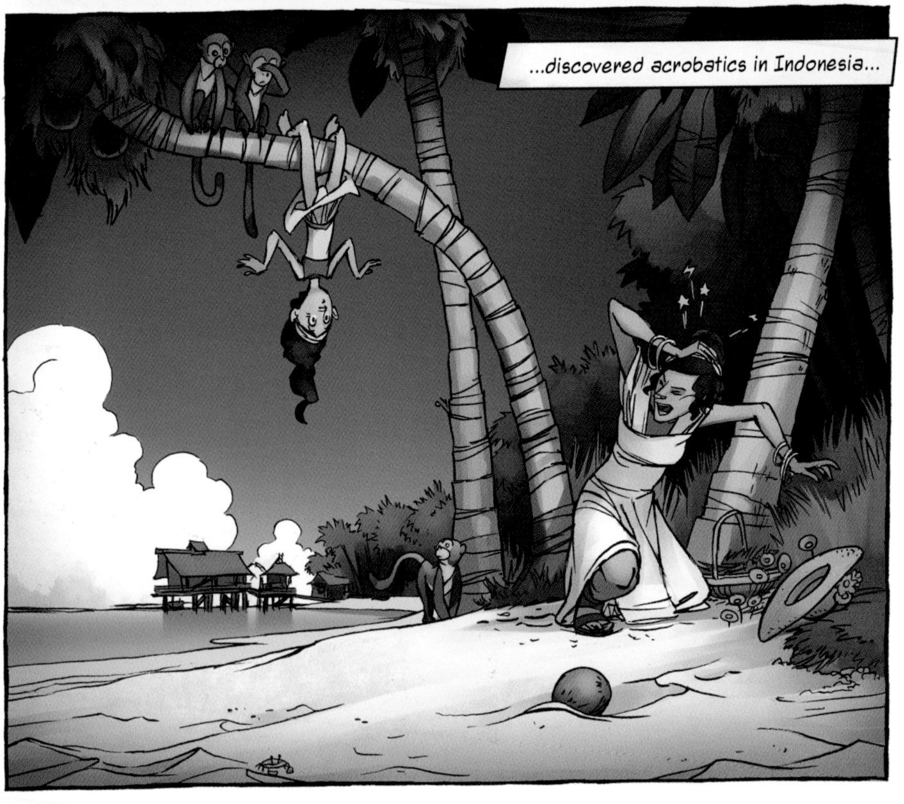
...discovered acrobatics in Indonesia...

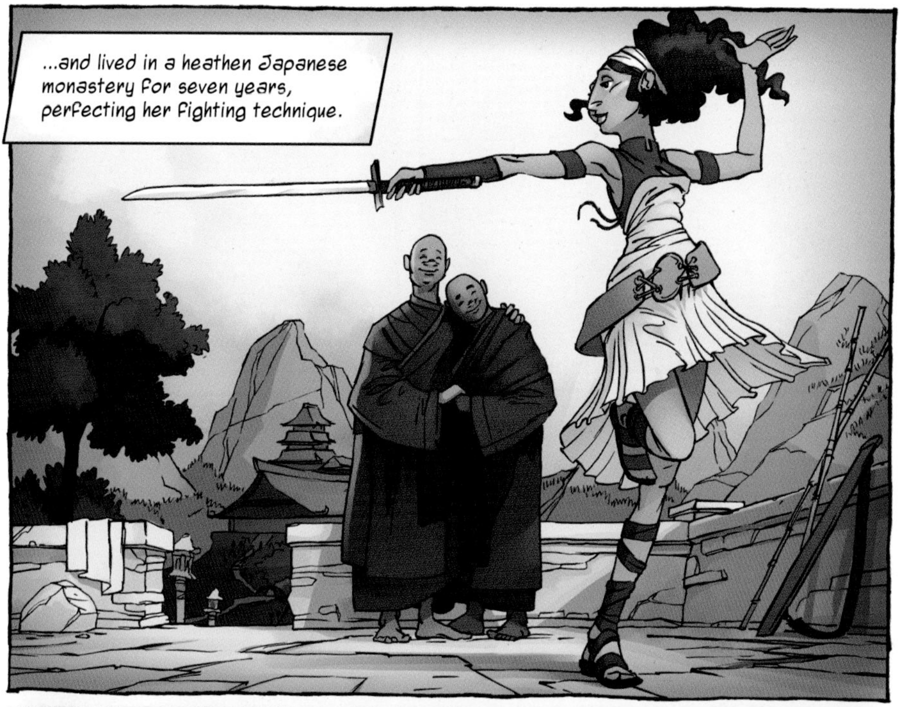
...and lived in a heathen Japanese monastery for seven years, perfecting her fighting technique.

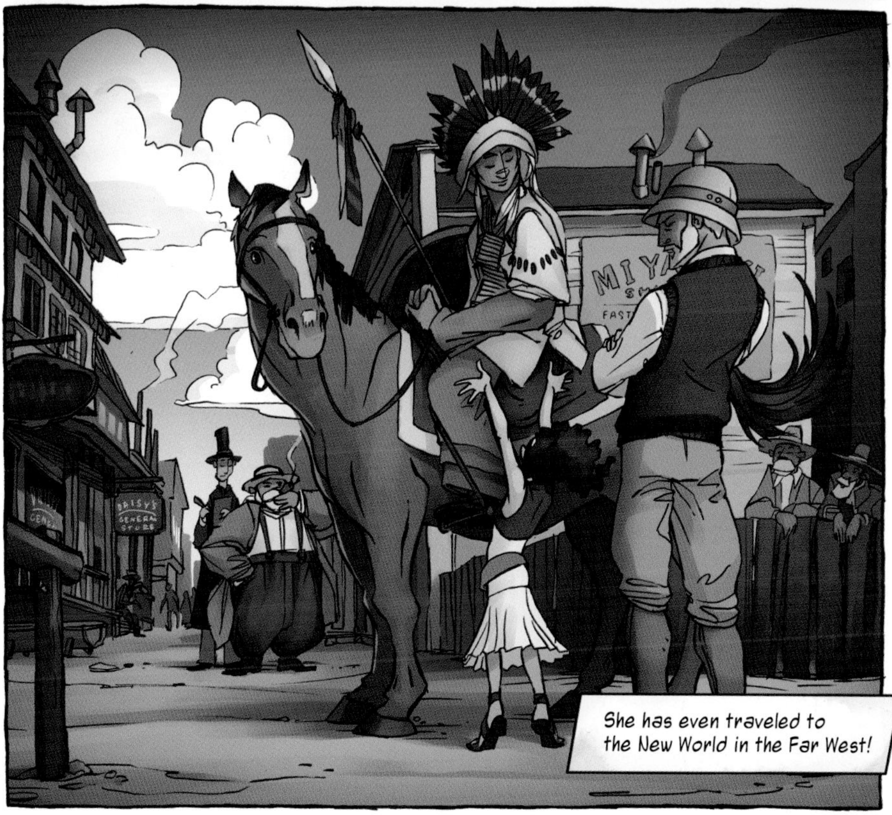
She has even traveled to the New World in the Far West!

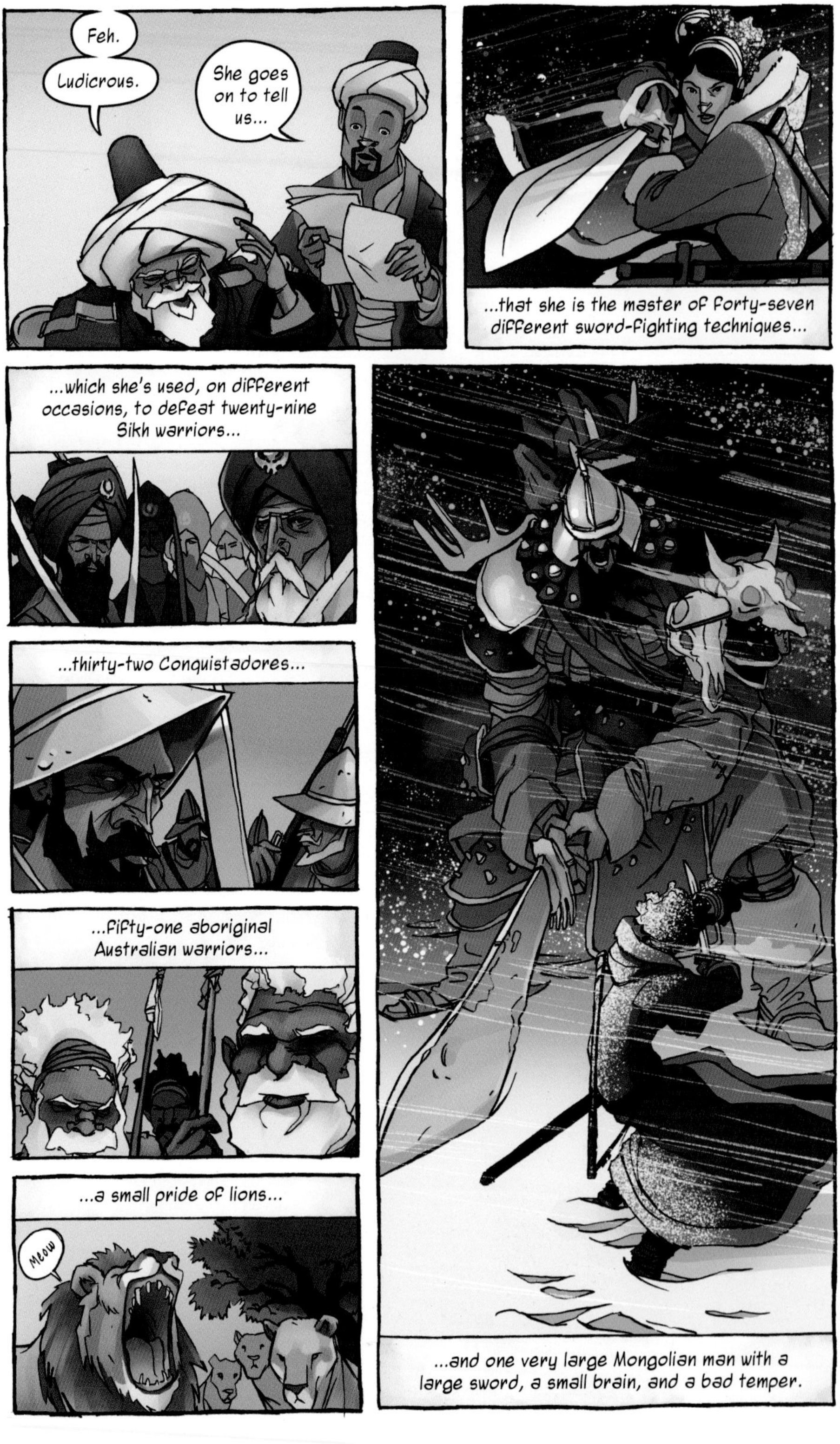
Feh.
Ludicrous.
She goes on to tell us...
...that she is the master of forty-seven different sword-fighting techniques...
...which she's used, on different occasions, to defeat twenty-nine Sikh warriors...
...thirty-two Conquistadores...
...fifty-one aboriginal Australian warriors...
...a small pride of lions...
Meow
...and one very large Mongolian man with a large sword, a small brain, and a bad temper.

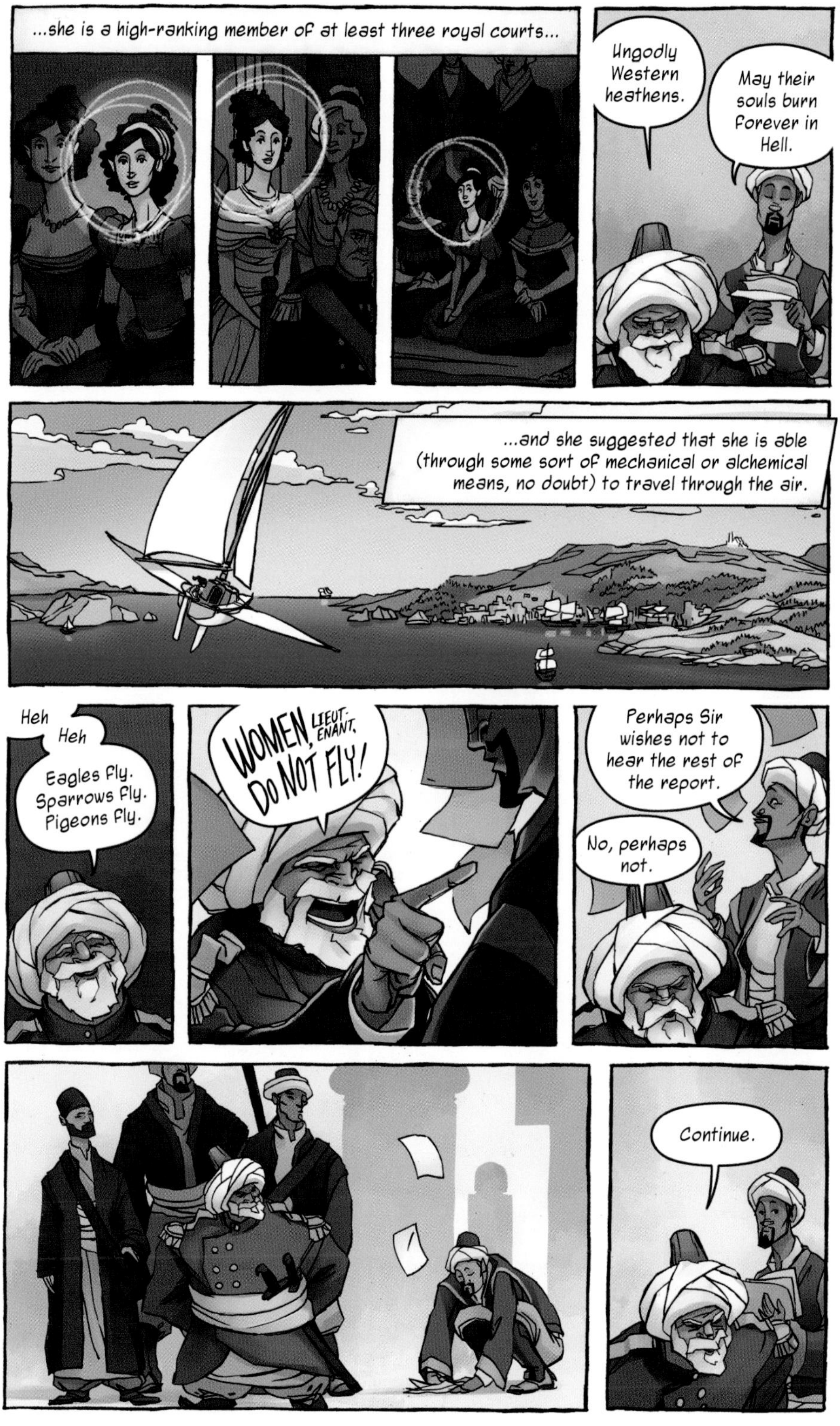
...she is a high-ranking member of at least three royal courts...
Ungodly Western heathens.
May their souls burn forever in Hell.
...and she suggested that she is able (through some sort of mechanical or alchemical means, no doubt) to travel through the air.
Heh
Heh
Eagles fly. Sparrows fly. Pigeons fly.
WOMEN, LIEUTENANT, DO NOT FLY!
Perhaps Sir wishes not to hear the rest of the report.
No, perhaps not.
Continue.

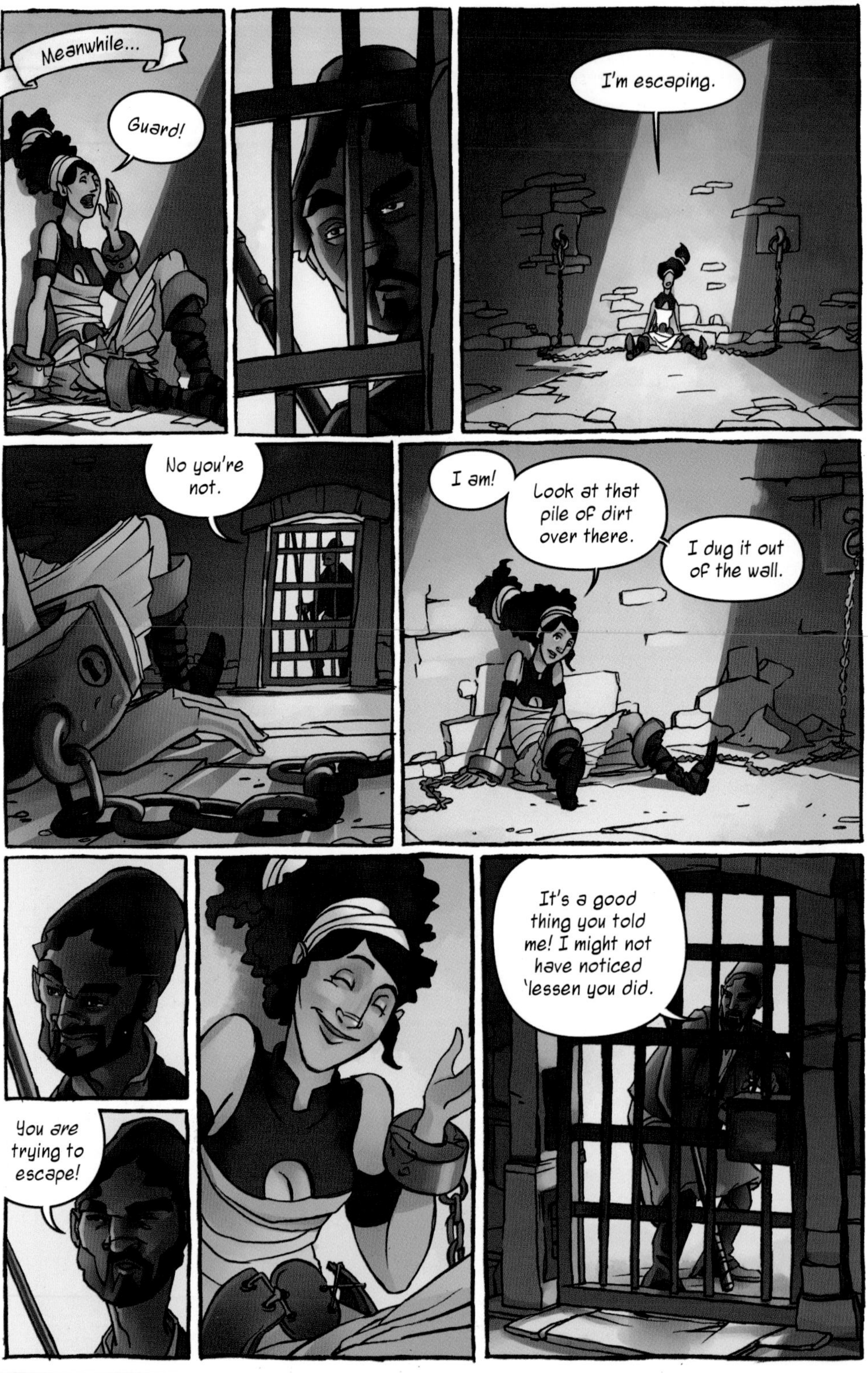
Meanwhile...
Guard!
I'm escaping.
No you're not.
I am!
Look at that pile of dirt over there.
I dug it out of the wall.
You are trying to escape!
It's a good thing you told me! I might not have noticed 'lessen you did.

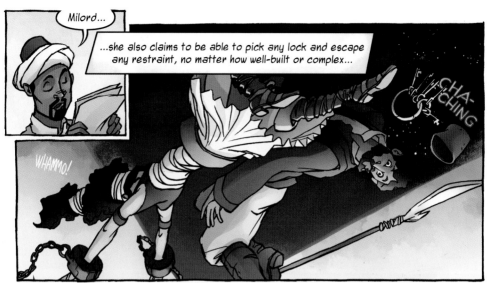

Milord...

...she also claims to be able to pick any lock and escape any restraint, no matter how well-built or complex...

CHA-CHING

WHAMMO!

...she can dismember a man in mere seconds,

BONK!!

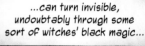

...can turn invisible, undoubtably through some sort of witches' black magic...

SMASH!

...and she claims to be able to walk through perfectly solid walls.

HA!

A woman!

A skilled fighter!

Indeed, sir.

But ludicrous as it may sound, she has revealed that her intention within these walls was to...erm..."repatriate" (as she put it) several of His Majesty's prized ancient scrolls.

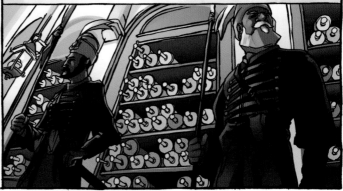

Well, if that is what she thinks, it will be a very slow, unpleasant death for her.

I have made sure our guard is reinforced where appropriate.

Reinforcements? Surely that isn't necessary, considering that she's already been well secured...

You don't...

Believe her, do you, Lieutenant?

I...

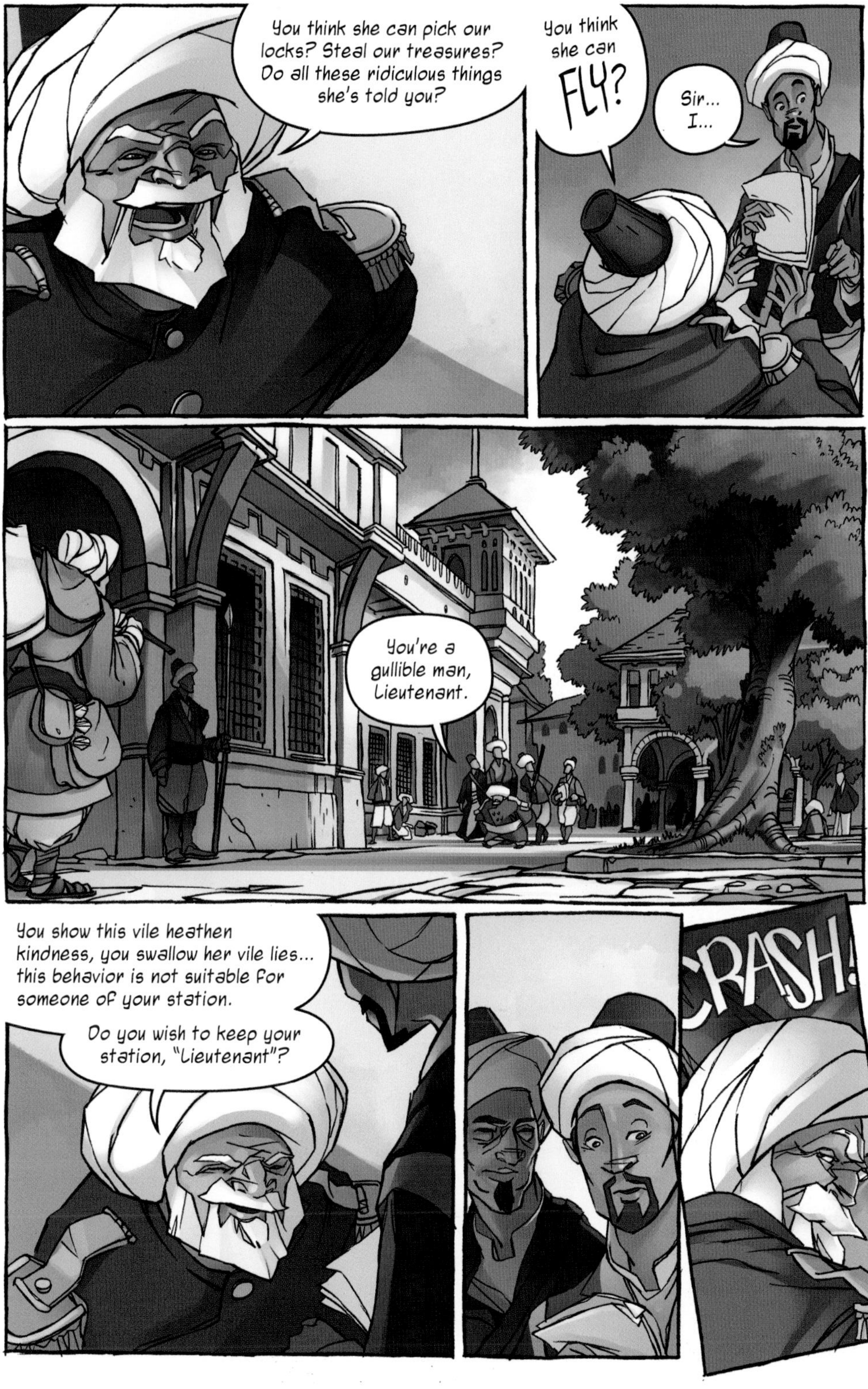
You think she can pick our locks? Steal our treasures? Do all these ridiculous things she's told you?
You think she can FLY?
Sir... I...
You're a gullible man, Lieutenant.
You show this vile heathen kindness, you swallow her vile lies... this behavior is not suitable for someone of your station.
Do you wish to keep your station, "Lieutenant"?
CRASH!

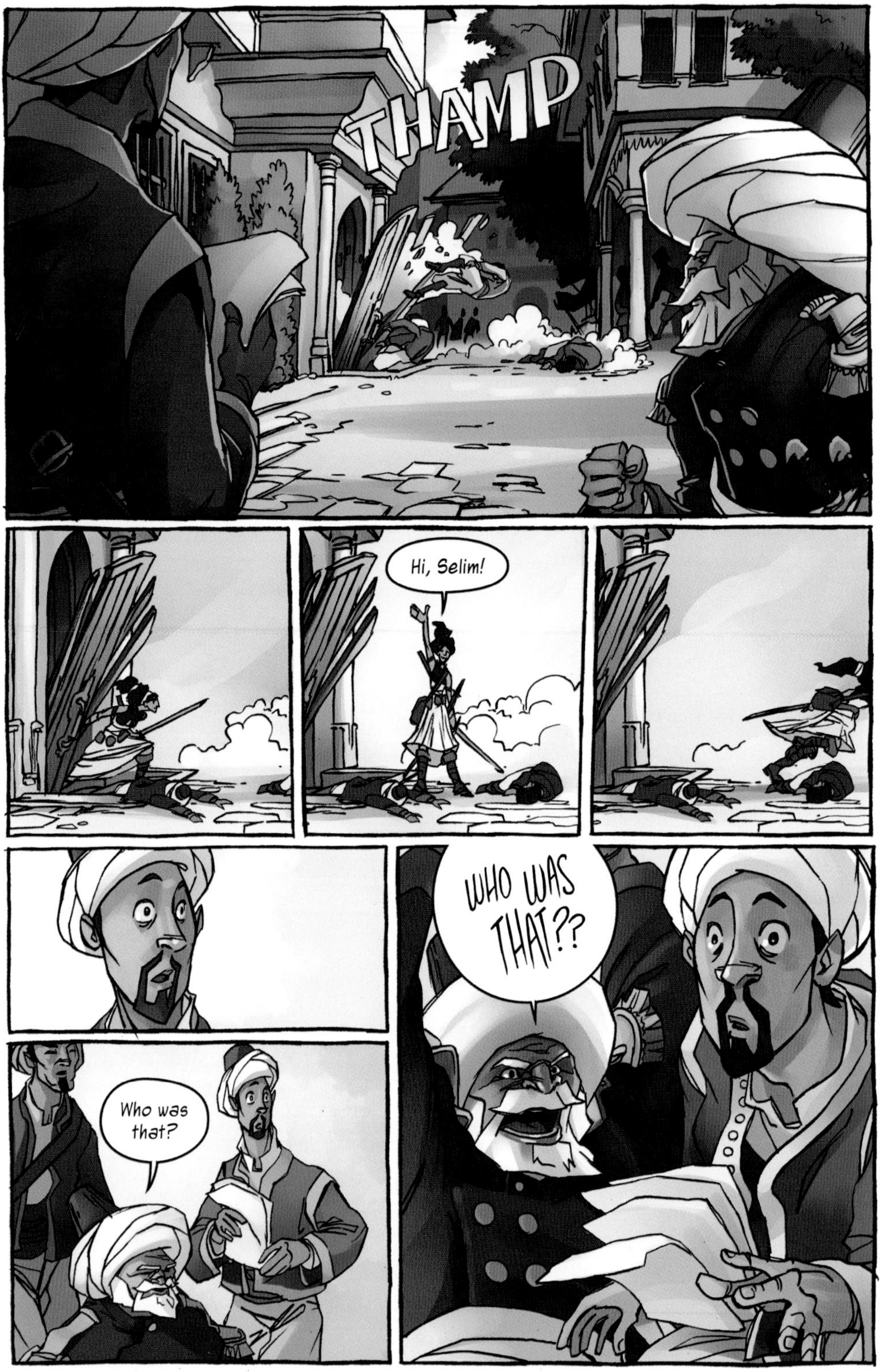
THAMP
Hi, Selim!
WHO WAS THAT??
Who was that?

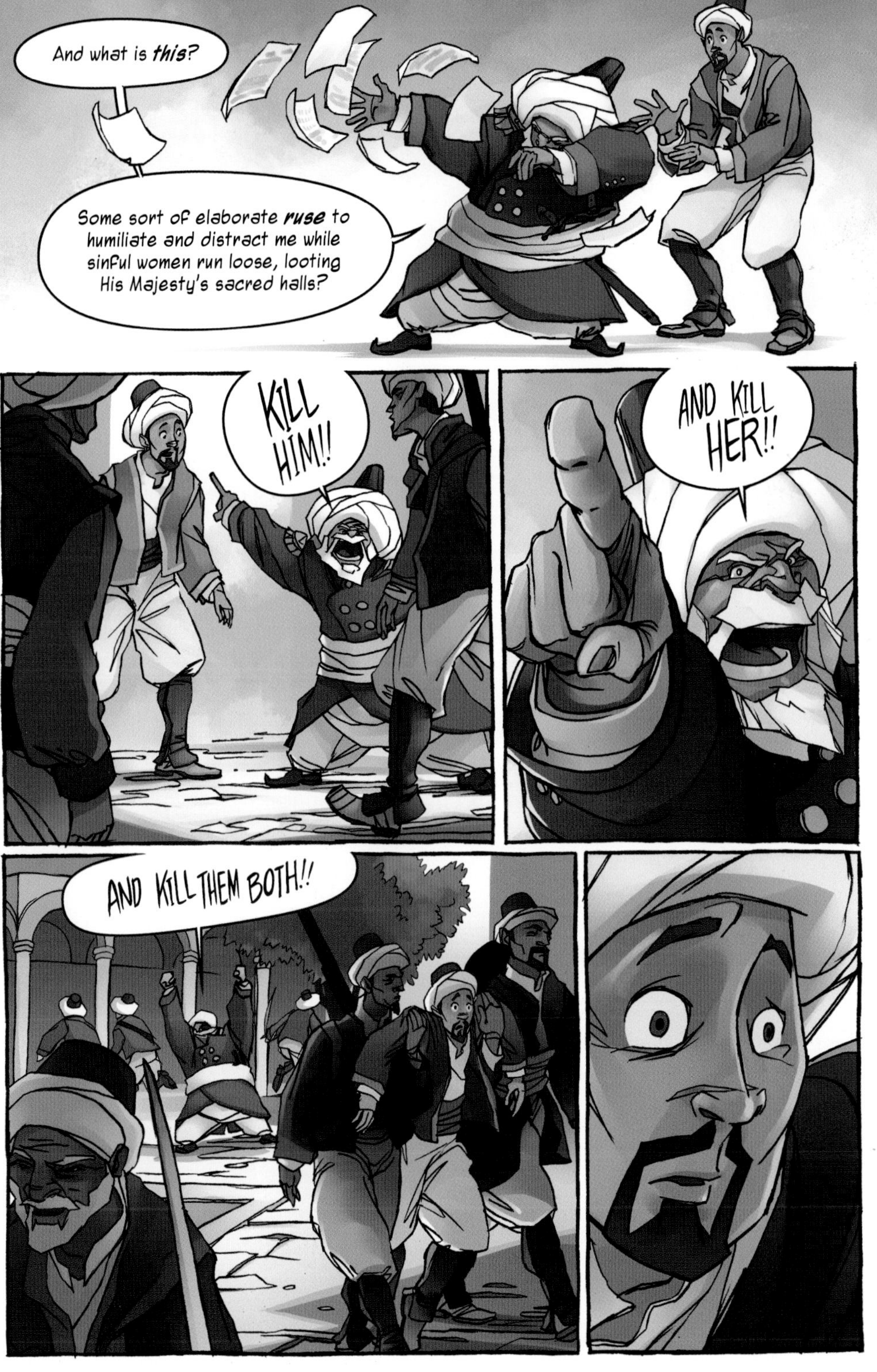
And what is ***this***?
Some sort of elaborate ***ruse*** to humiliate and distract me while sinful women run loose, looting His Majesty's sacred halls?
KILL HIM!!
AND KILL HER!!
AND KILL THEM BOTH!!

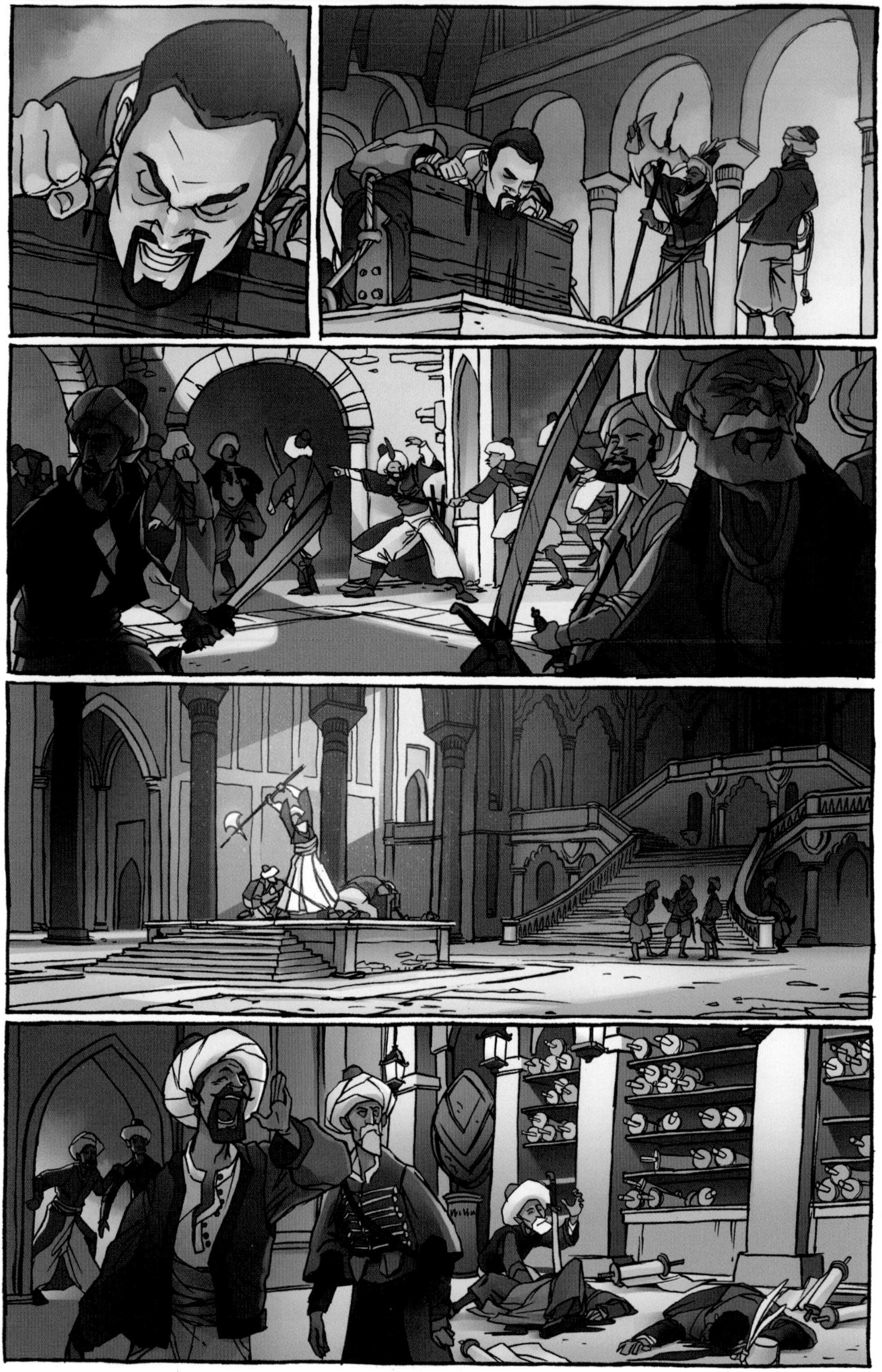

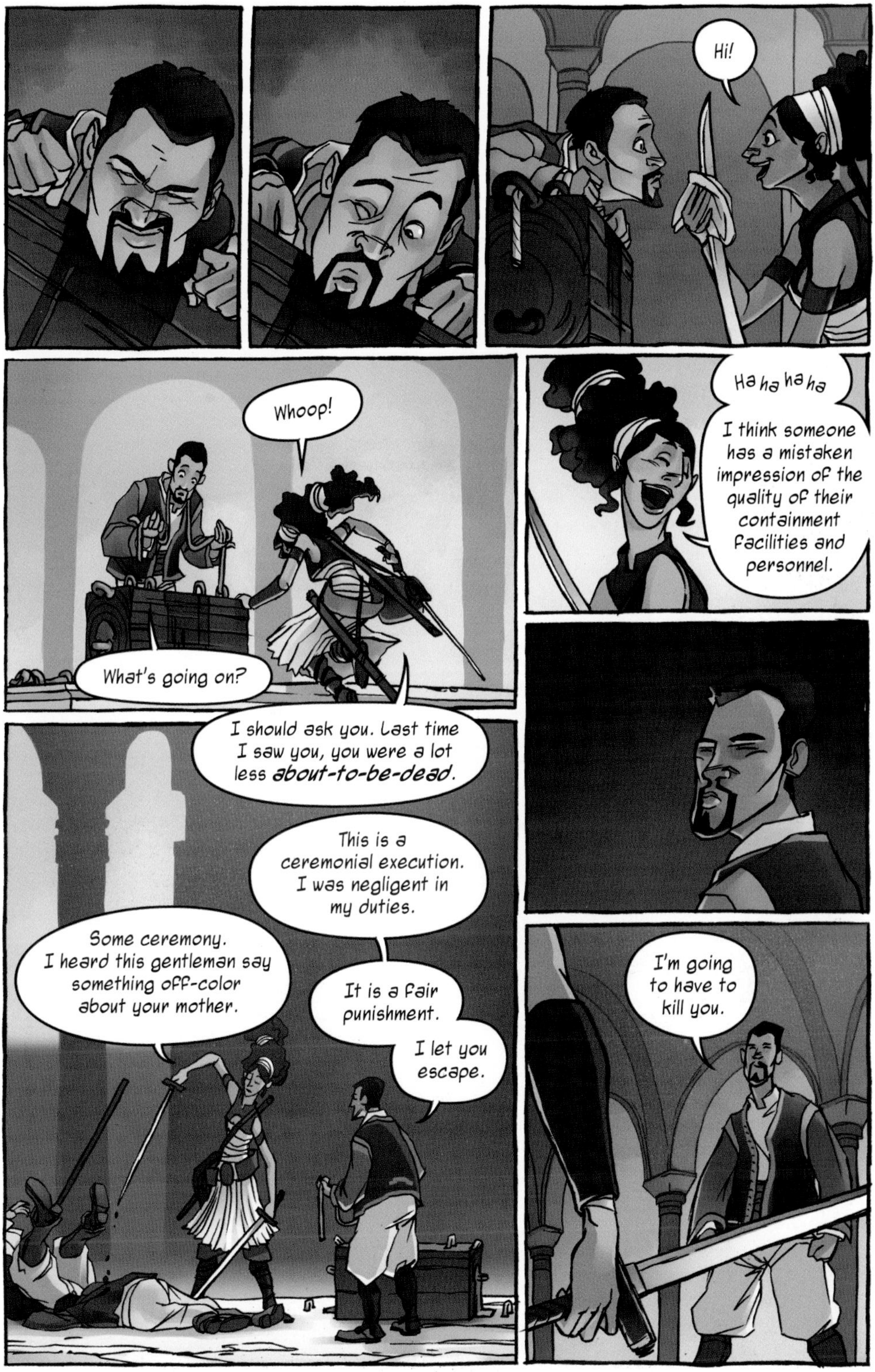

Hi!
Whoop!
What's going on?
Ha ha ha ha
I think someone has a mistaken impression of the quality of their containment facilities and personnel.
I should ask you. Last time I saw you, you were a lot less *about-to-be-dead*.
This is a ceremonial execution. I was negligent in my duties.
Some ceremony. I heard this gentleman say something off-color about your mother.
It is a fair punishment.
I let you escape.
I'm going to have to kill you.

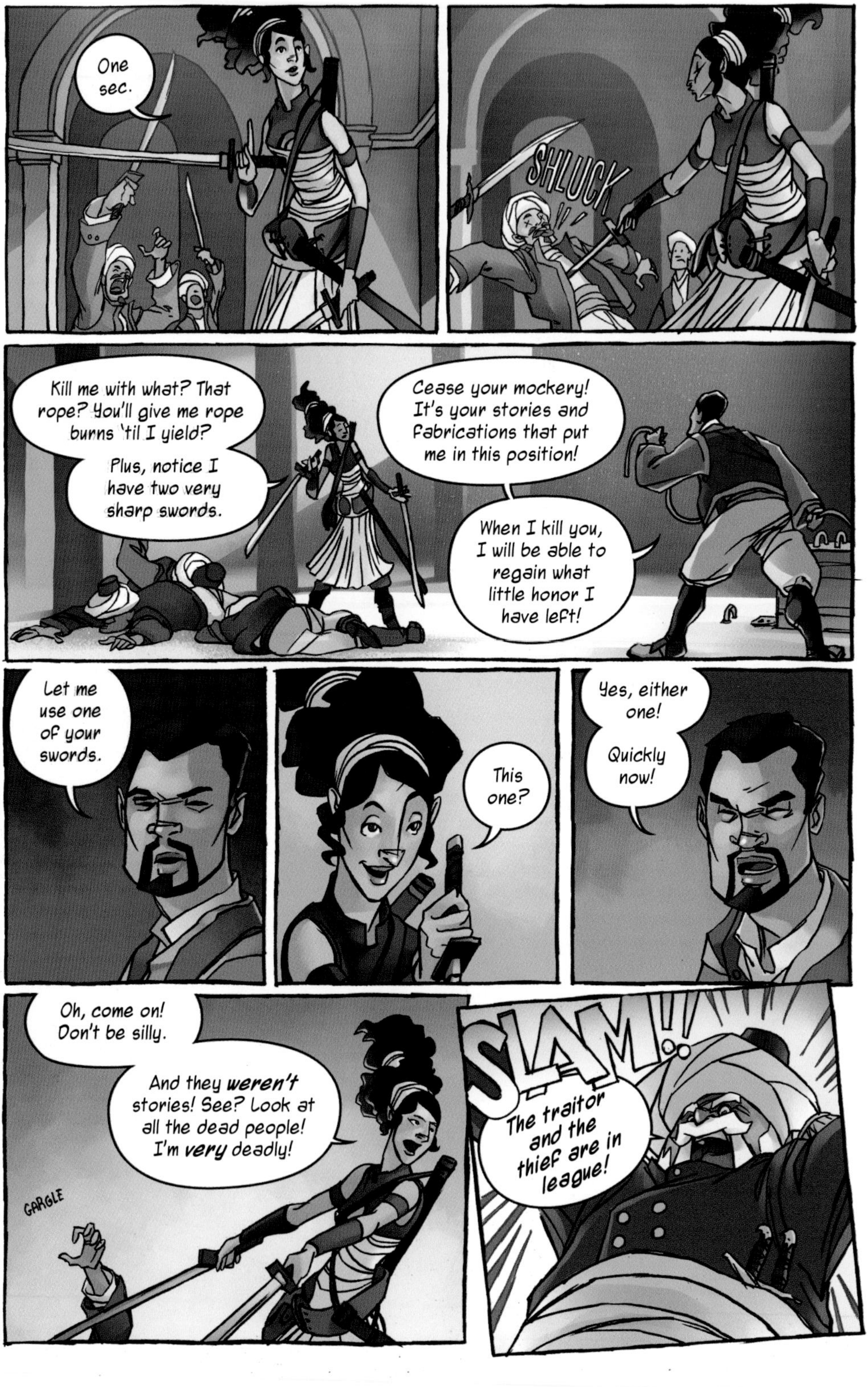
One sec.
SHLUCK
Kill me with what? That rope? You'll give me rope burns 'til I yield?
Plus, notice I have two very sharp swords.
Cease your mockery! It's your stories and fabrications that put me in this position!
When I kill you, I will be able to regain what little honor I have left!
Let me use one of your swords.
This one?
Yes, either one!
Quickly now!
Oh, come on! Don't be silly.
And they *weren't* stories! See? Look at all the dead people! I'm *very* deadly!
GARGLE
SLAM!!
The traitor and the thief are in league!

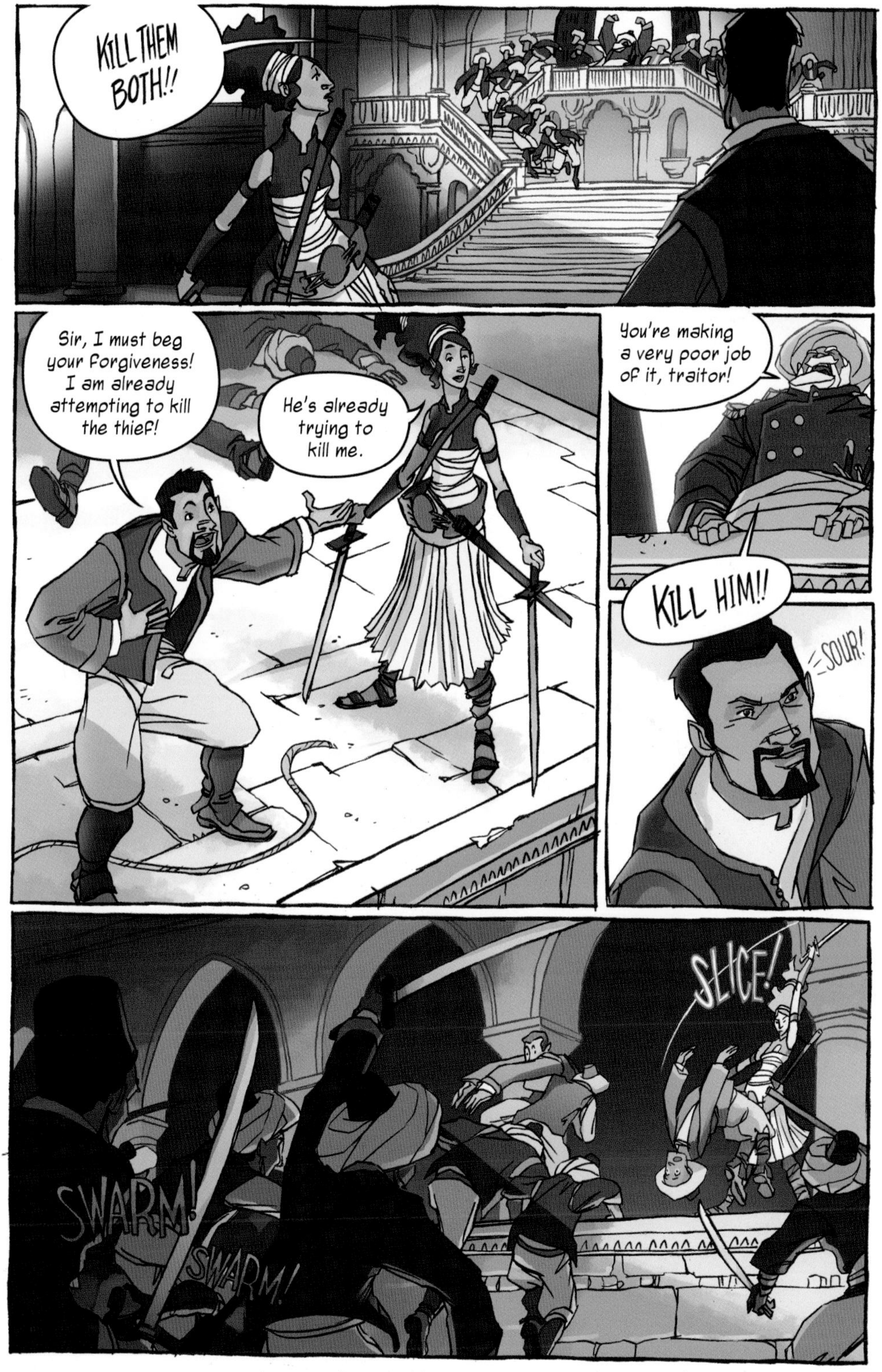

KILL THEM BOTH!!
Sir, I must beg your forgiveness! I am already attempting to kill the thief!
He's already trying to kill me.
You're making a very poor job of it, traitor!
KILL HIM!!
SOUR!
SLICE!
SWARM!
SWARM!

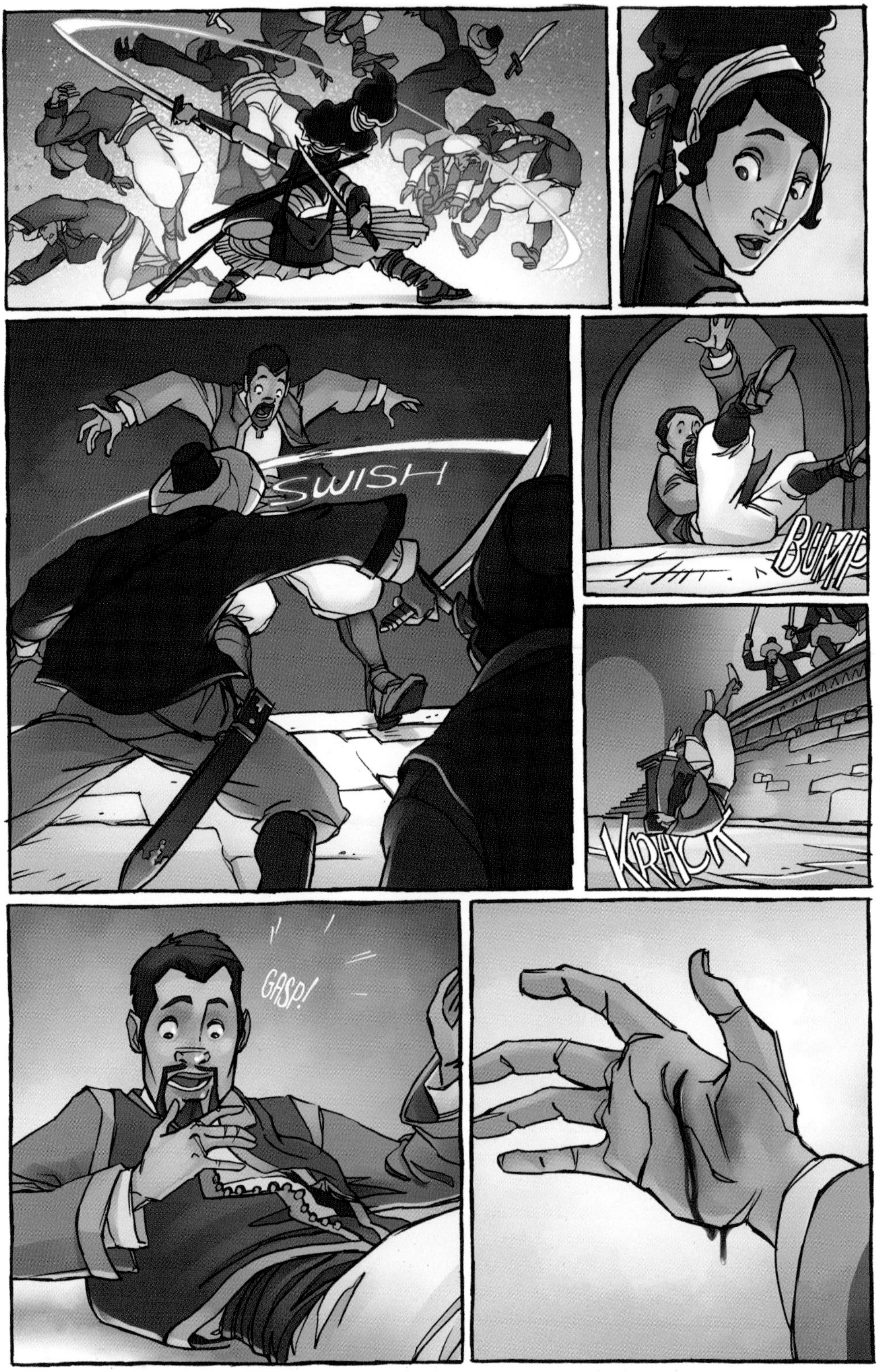
SWISH
BUMP
KRACK
GASP!

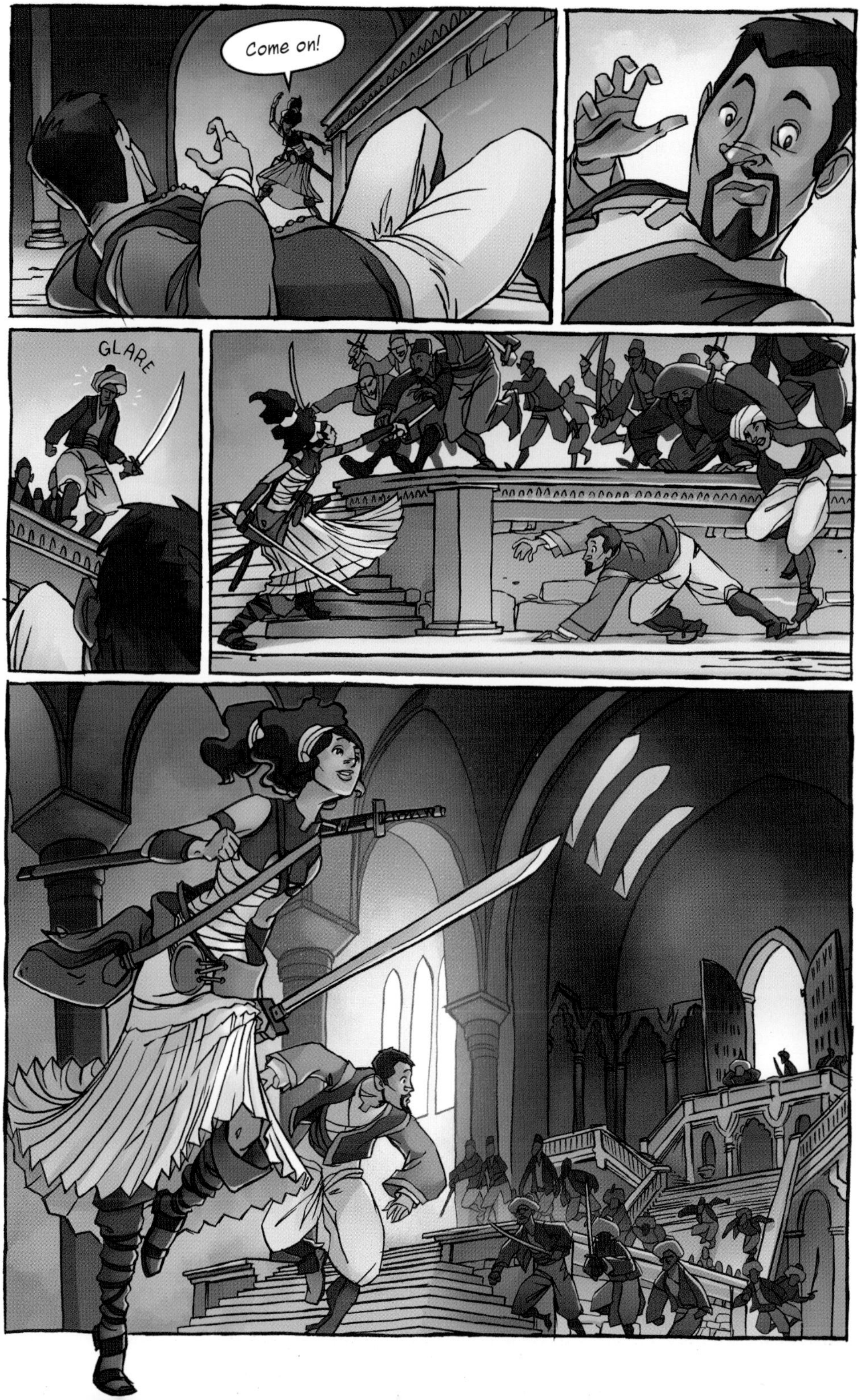
Come on!
GLARE

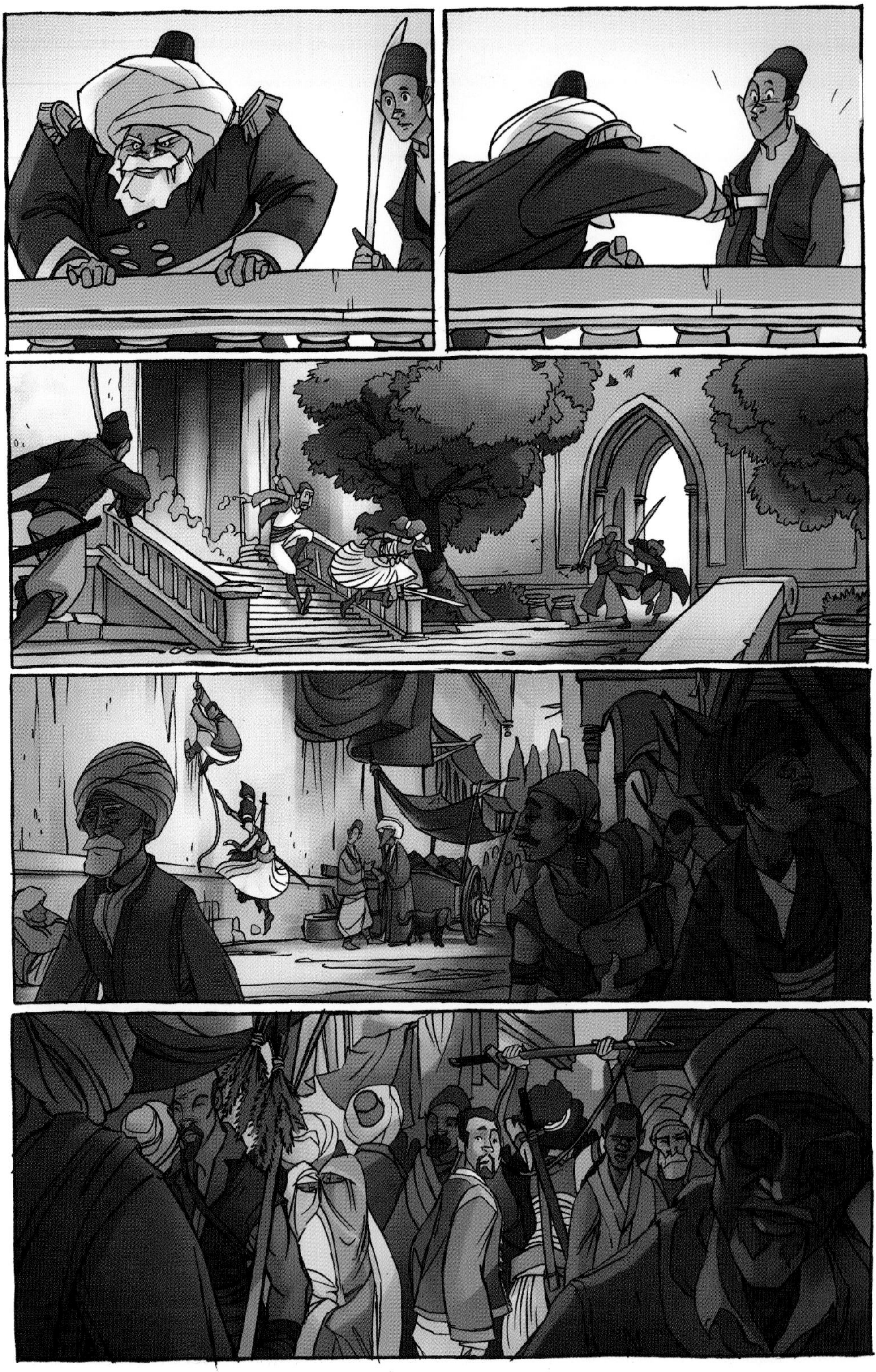

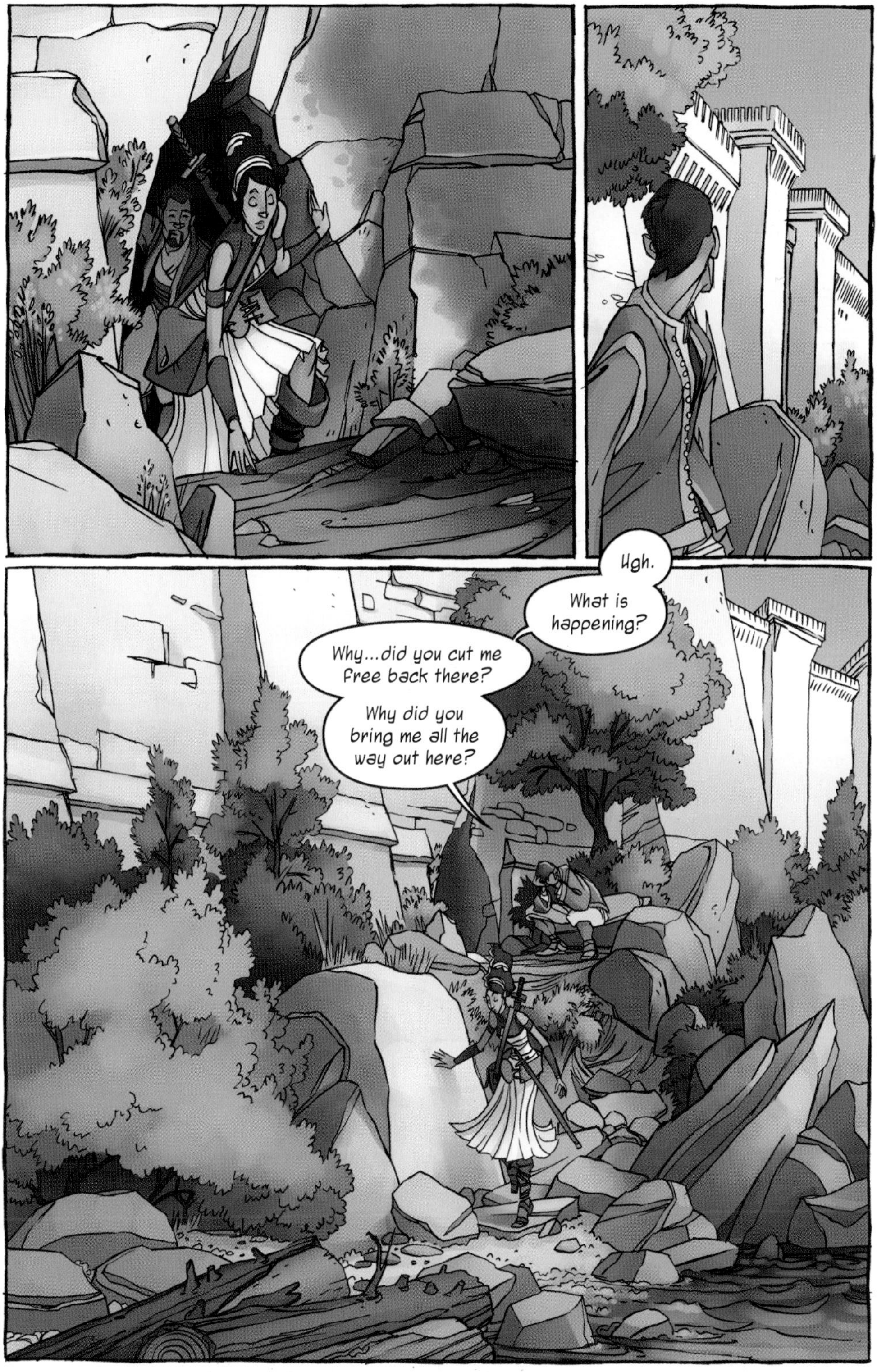
Ugh.
What is happening?
Why...did you cut me free back there?
Why did you bring me all the way out here?

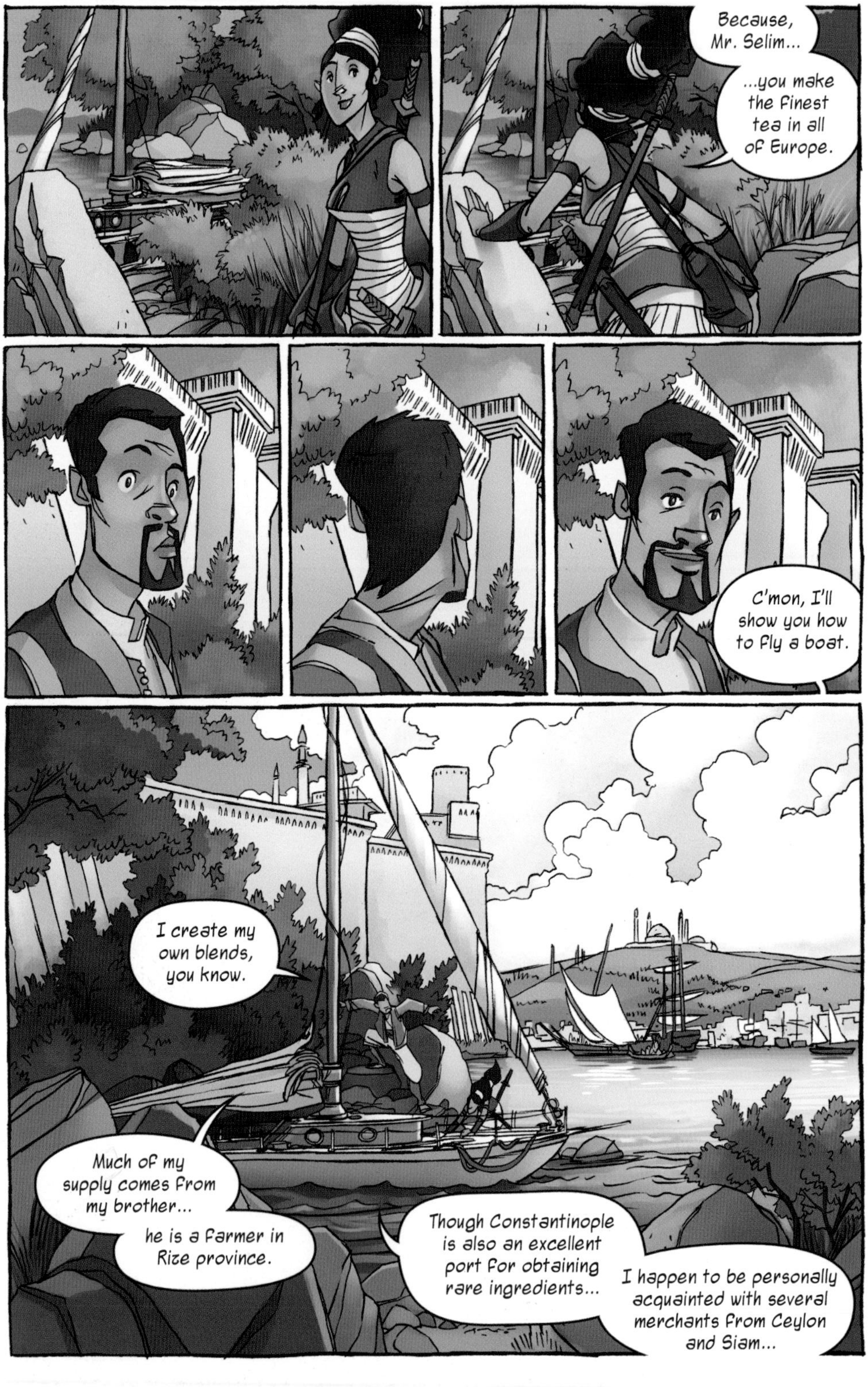
Because, Mr. Selim...
...you make the finest tea in all of Europe.
C'mon, I'll show you how to fly a boat.
I create my own blends, you know.
Much of my supply comes from my brother...
he is a farmer in Rize province.
Though Constantinople is also an excellent port for obtaining rare ingredients...
I happen to be personally acquainted with several merchants from Ceylon and Siam...

CHAPTER 2

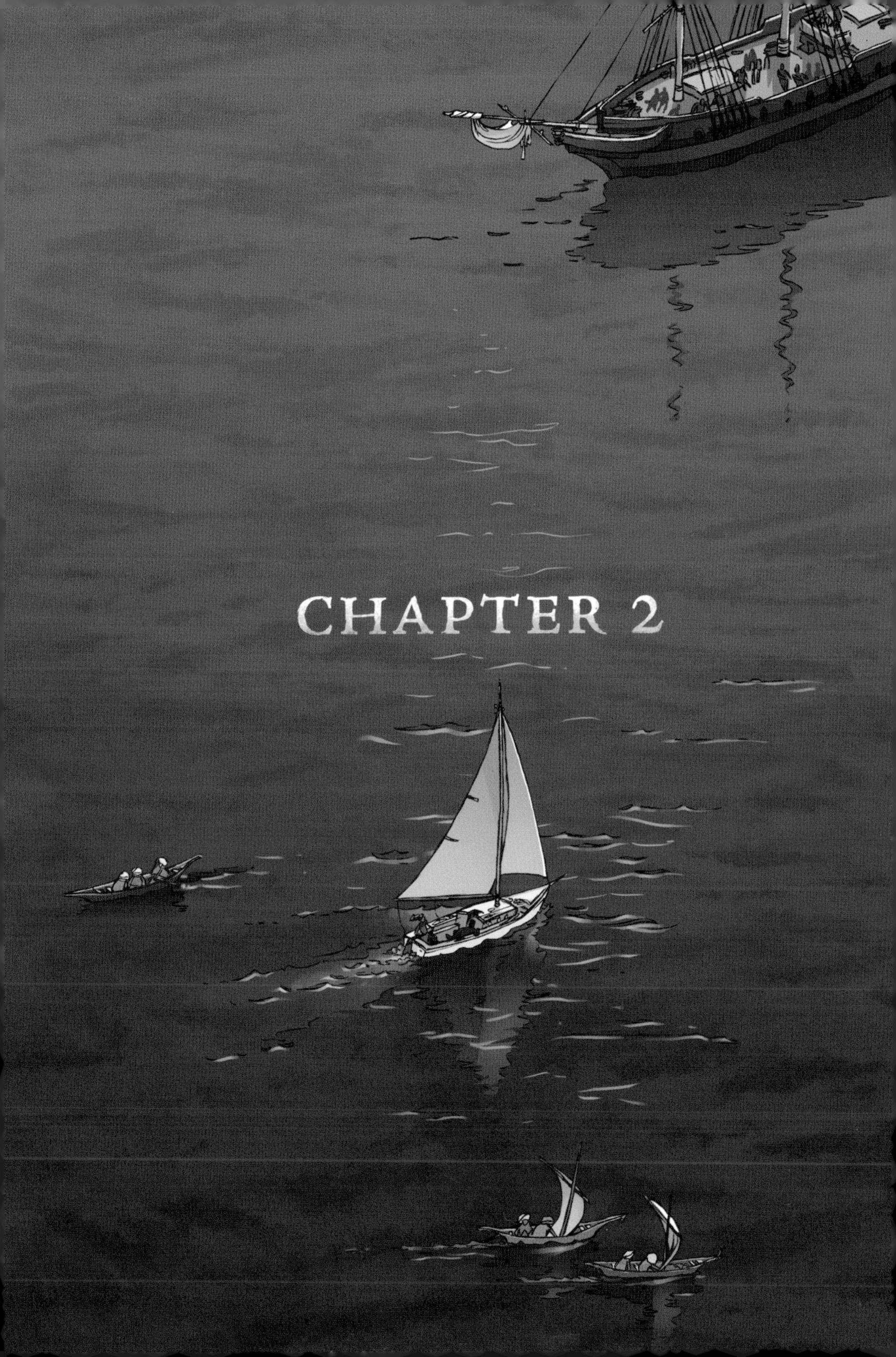

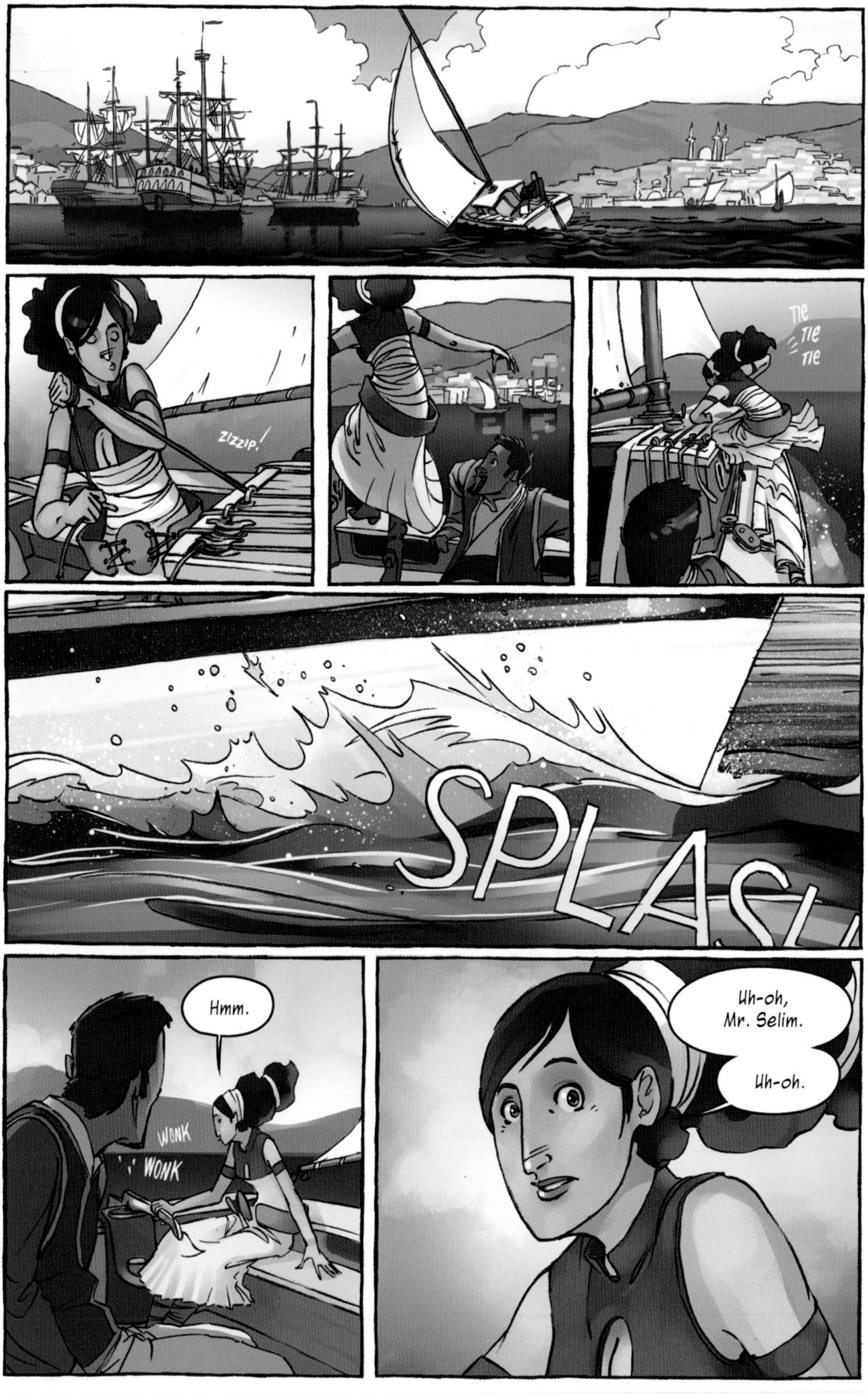
ZIZZIP!
TIE
TIE
TIE
SPLASH
Hmm.
WONK
WONK
Uh-oh,
Mr. Selim.
Uh-oh.

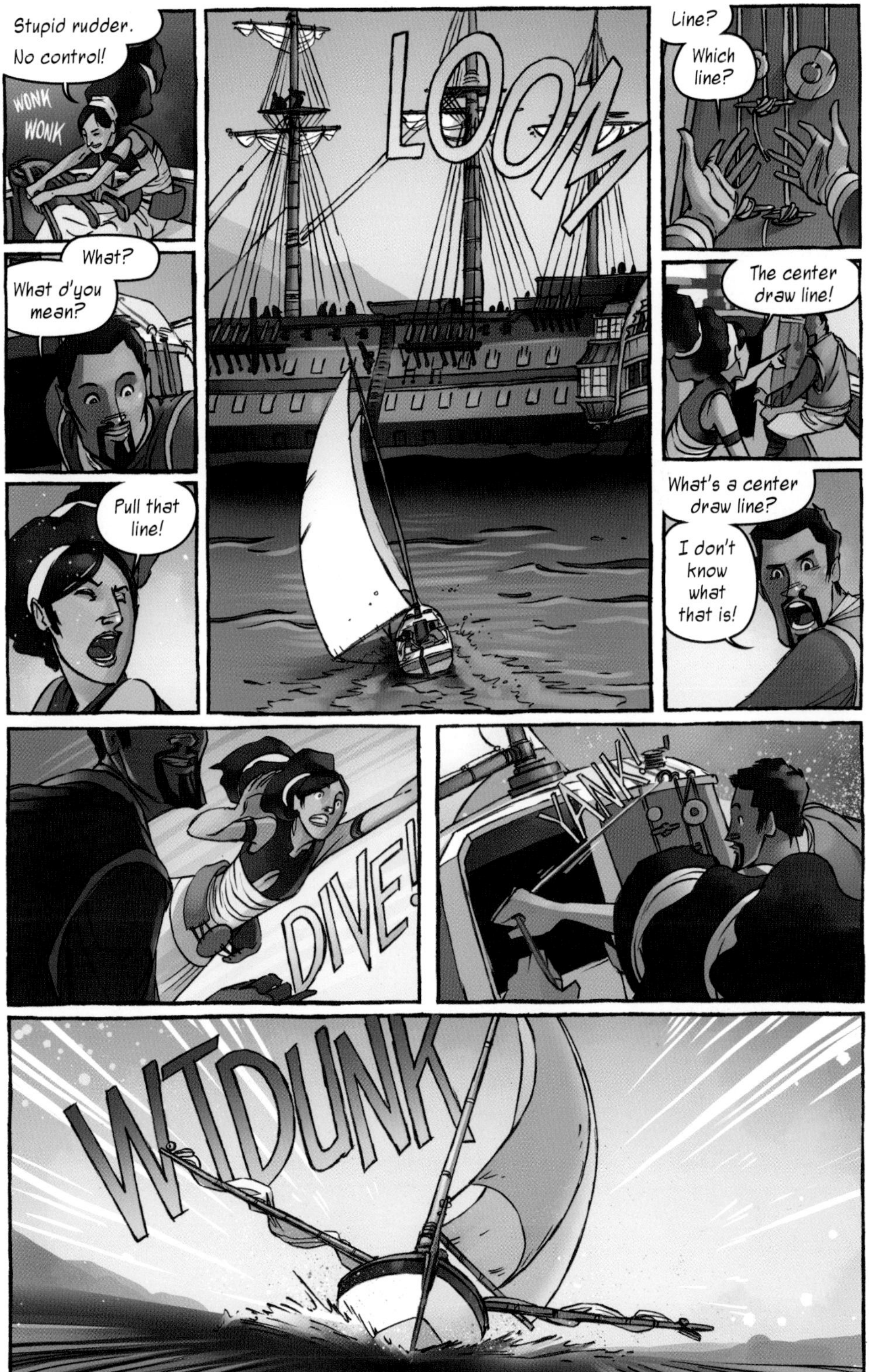
Stupid rudder.
No control!
WONK
WONK
LOOM
Line?
Which line?
What?
What d'you mean?
The center draw line!
Pull that line!
What's a center draw line?
I don't know what that is!
DIVE!
YANK!
WTDUNK

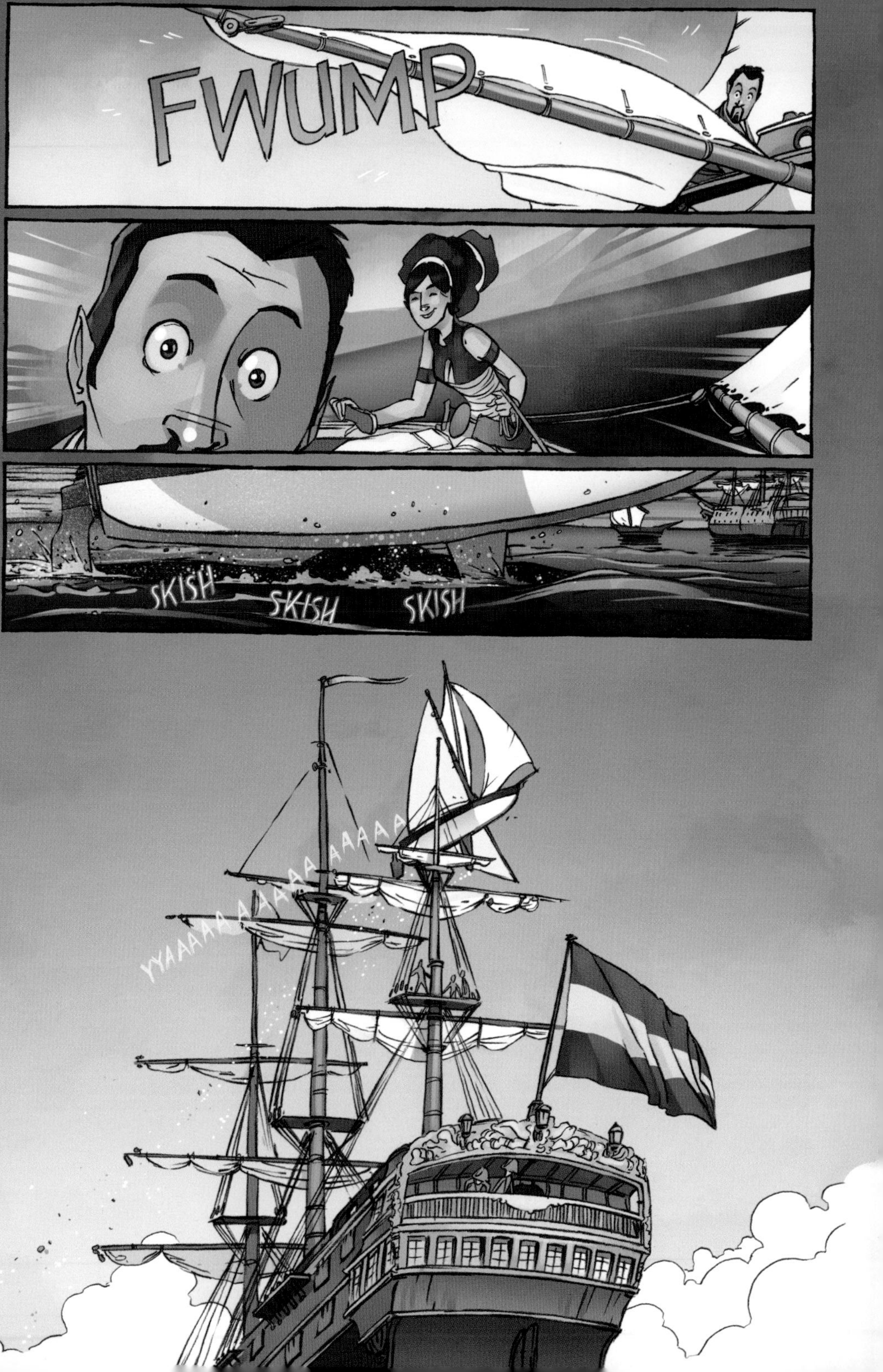
FWUMP
SKISH
SKISH
SKISH
YYAAAAAAAAAAAAAAAAAAA

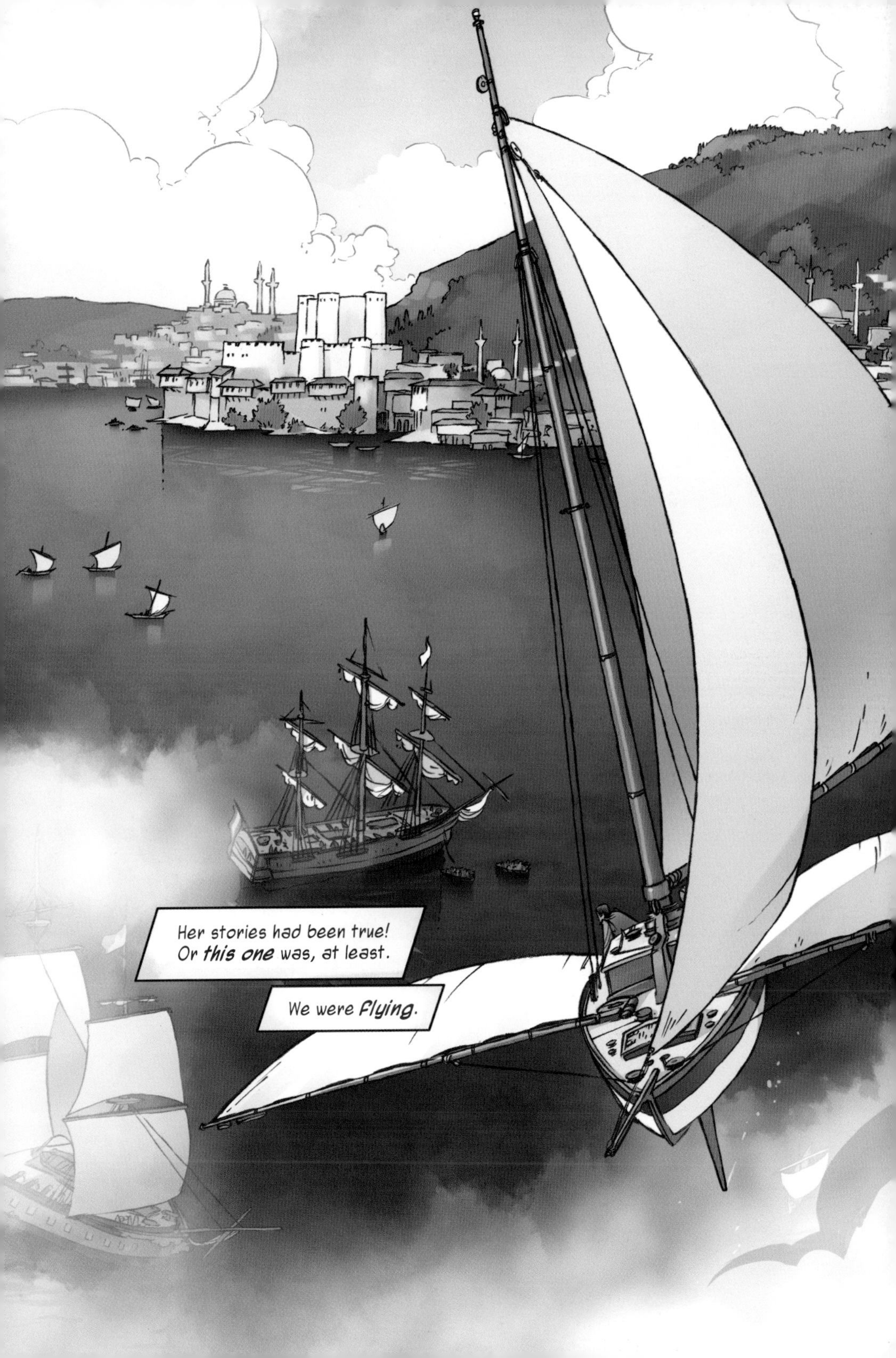
Her stories had been true! Or *this one* was, at least.
We were *flying*.

At the time, I hadn't bothered to question her "flying boat" claims. I just wrote them down.

And now here I was, with the sea dropping away, realizing how completely and utterly preposterous that must have sounded.

Is that how you would have reacted in a real emergency?

What? Why? Are you putting me through some sort of evaluation?

If I were, I wouldn't tell you.

Why?

Because then it wouldn't be a fair evaluation.

No—why are you evaluating me?

Just curious.

I like to know who my traveling companions are.

I understand.

And will there be many more tests of this sort?

If there were—

and there might be—

again, I wouldn't tell you ahead-of-time.

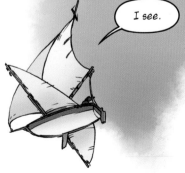

I see.

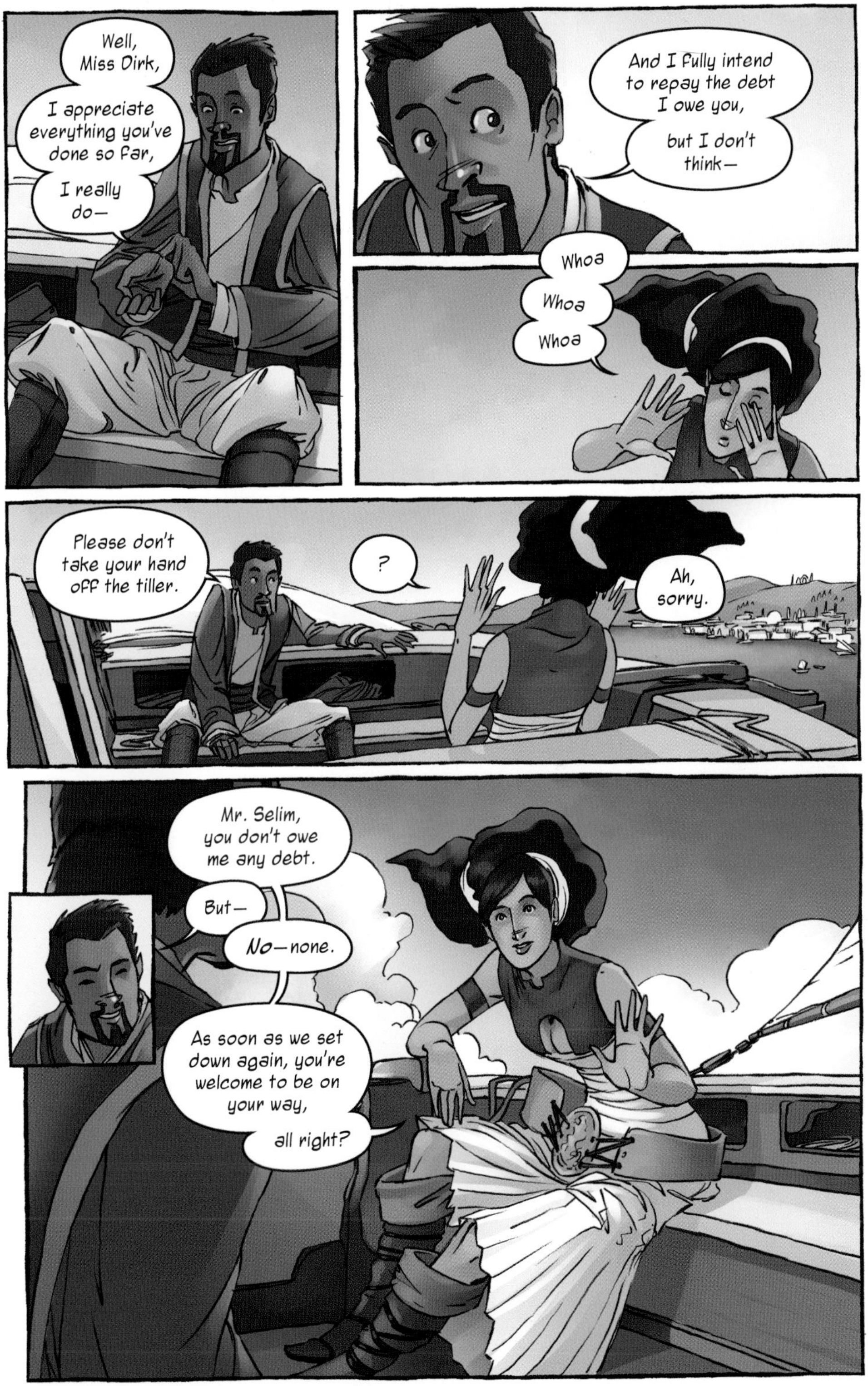
Well, Miss Dirk,
I appreciate everything you've done so far,
I really do—
And I fully intend to repay the debt I owe you,
but I don't think—
Whoa
Whoa
Whoa
Please don't take your hand off the tiller.
?
Ah, sorry.
Mr. Selim, you don't owe me any debt.
But—
No—none.
As soon as we set down again, you're welcome to be on your way,
all right?

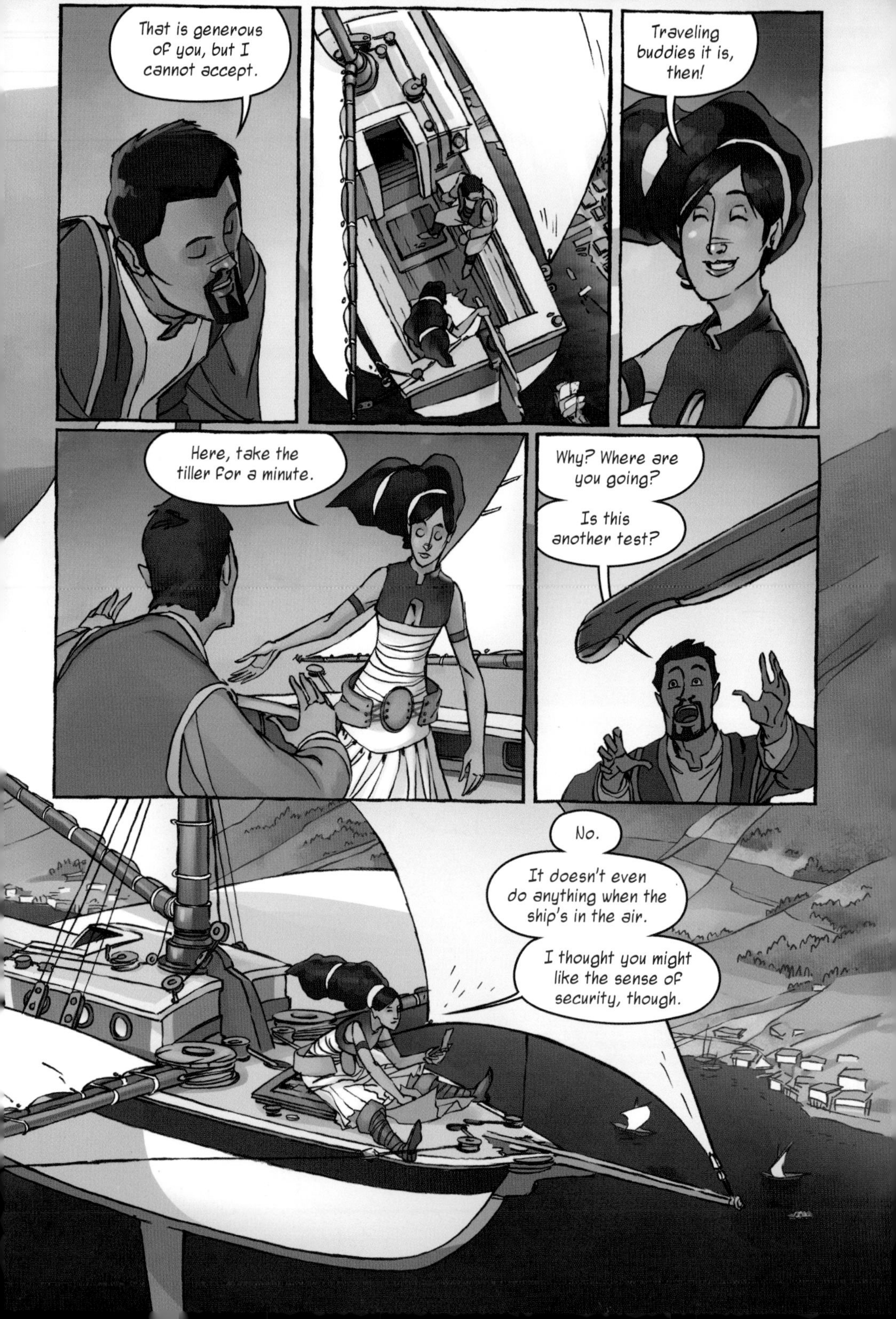
That is generous of you, but I cannot accept.
Traveling buddies it is, then!
Here, take the tiller for a minute.
Why? Where are you going?
Is this another test?
No.
It doesn't even do anything when the ship's in the air.
I thought you might like the sense of security, though.

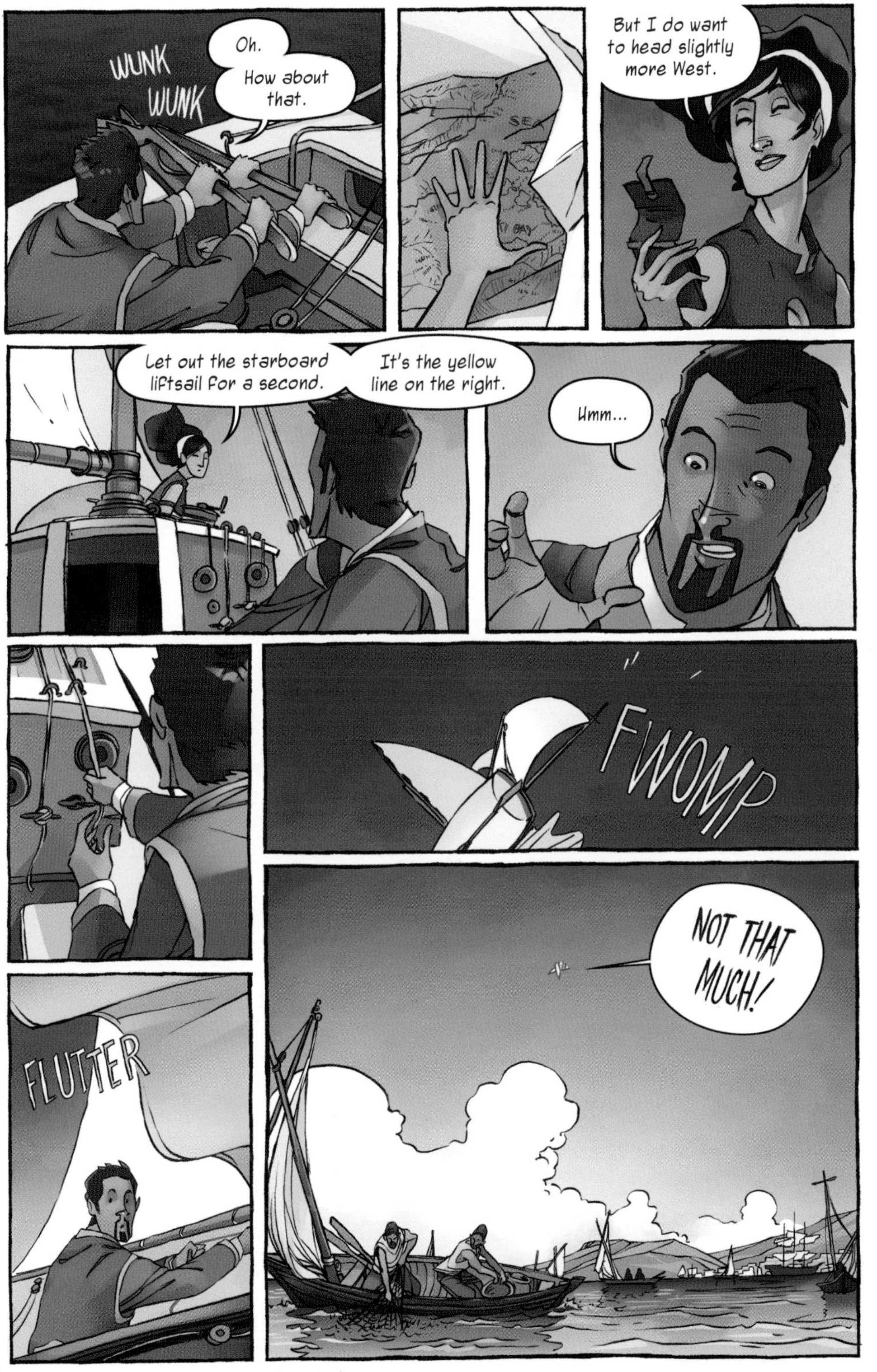
WUNK WUNK
Oh.
How about that.
But I do want to head slightly more West.
Let out the starboard liftsail for a second.
It's the yellow line on the right.
Umm...
FWOMP
FLUTTER
NOT THAT MUCH!

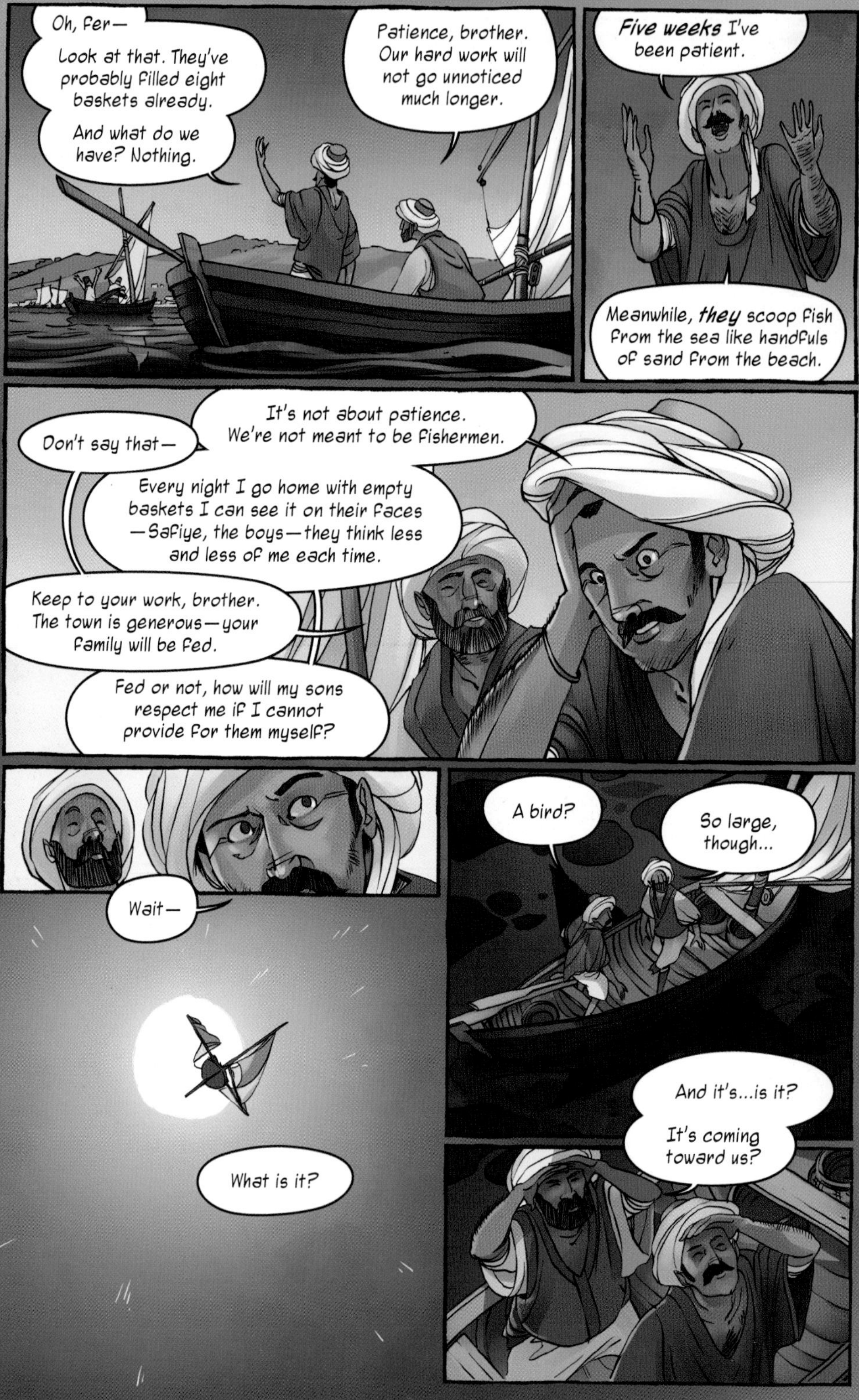
Oh, fer—
Look at that. They've probably filled eight baskets already.
And what do we have? Nothing.
Patience, brother. Our hard work will not go unnoticed much longer.
Five weeks I've been patient.
Meanwhile, *they* scoop fish from the sea like handfuls of sand from the beach.
It's not about patience. We're not meant to be fishermen.
Don't say that—
Every night I go home with empty baskets I can see it on their faces —Safiye, the boys—they think less and less of me each time.
Keep to your work, brother. The town is generous—your family will be fed.
Fed or not, how will my sons respect me if I cannot provide for them myself?
Wait—
What is it?
A bird?
So large, though...
And it's...is it?
It's coming toward us?

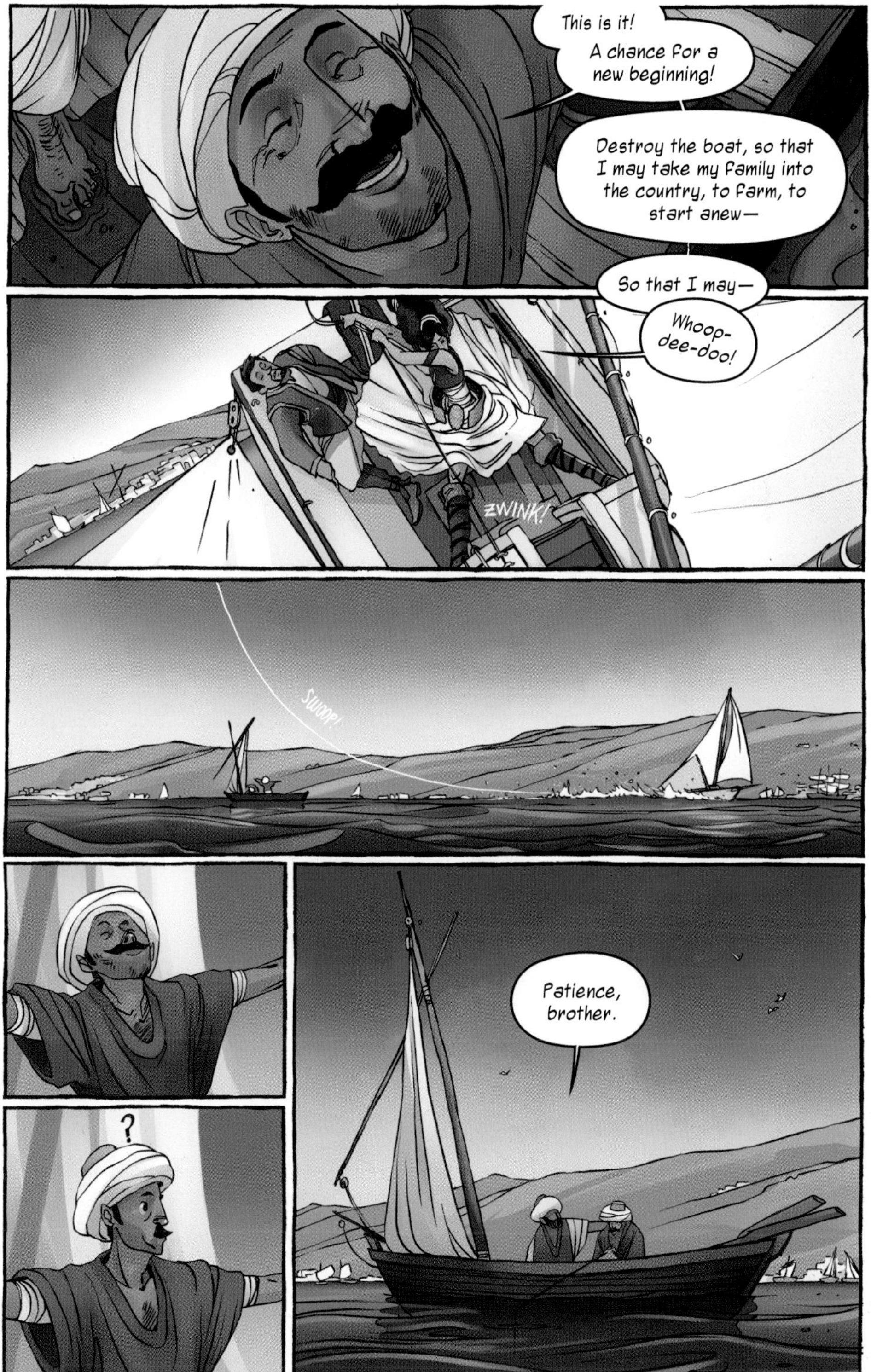
This is it!
A chance for a new beginning!
Destroy the boat, so that I may take my family into the country, to farm, to start anew—
So that I may—
Whoop-dee-doo!
ZWINK!
SWOOP!
?
Patience, brother.

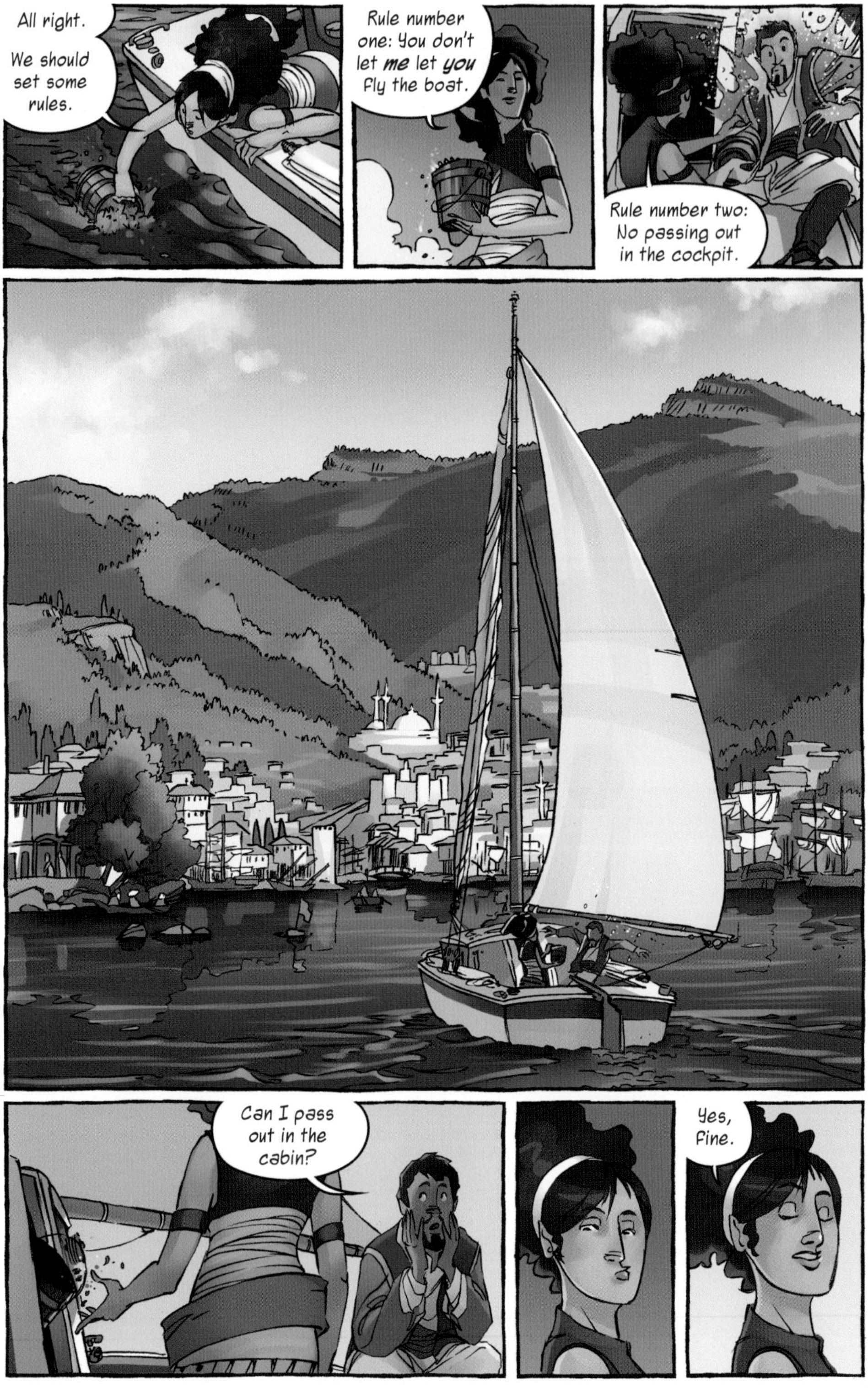
All right.
We should set some rules.
Rule number one: You don't let *me* let *you* fly the boat.
Rule number two: No passing out in the cockpit.
Can I pass out in the cabin?
Yes, fine.

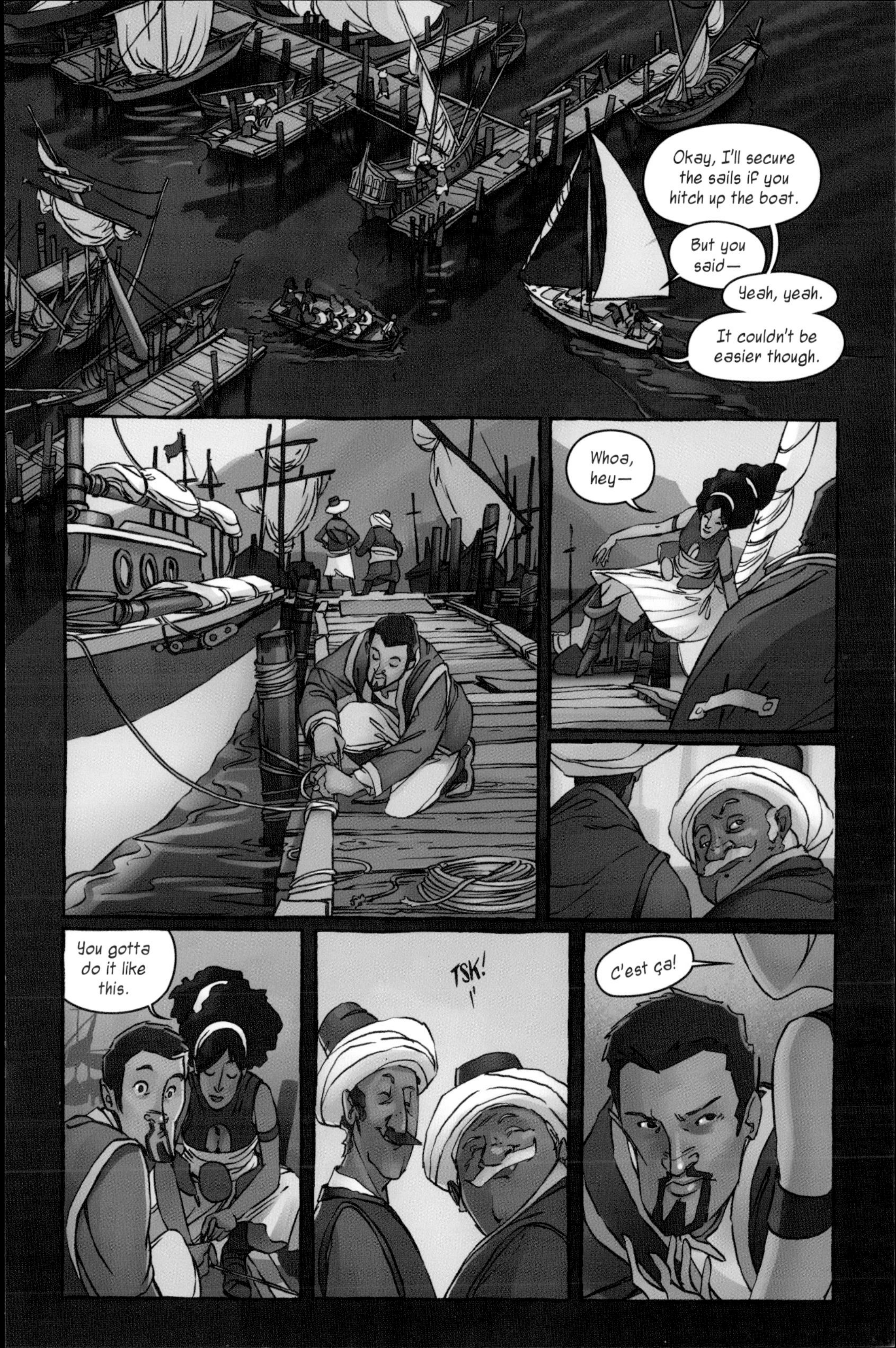

Okay, I'll secure the sails if you hitch up the boat.
But you said—
Yeah, yeah.
It couldn't be easier though.
Whoa, hey—
You gotta do it like this.
TSK!
C'est ça!

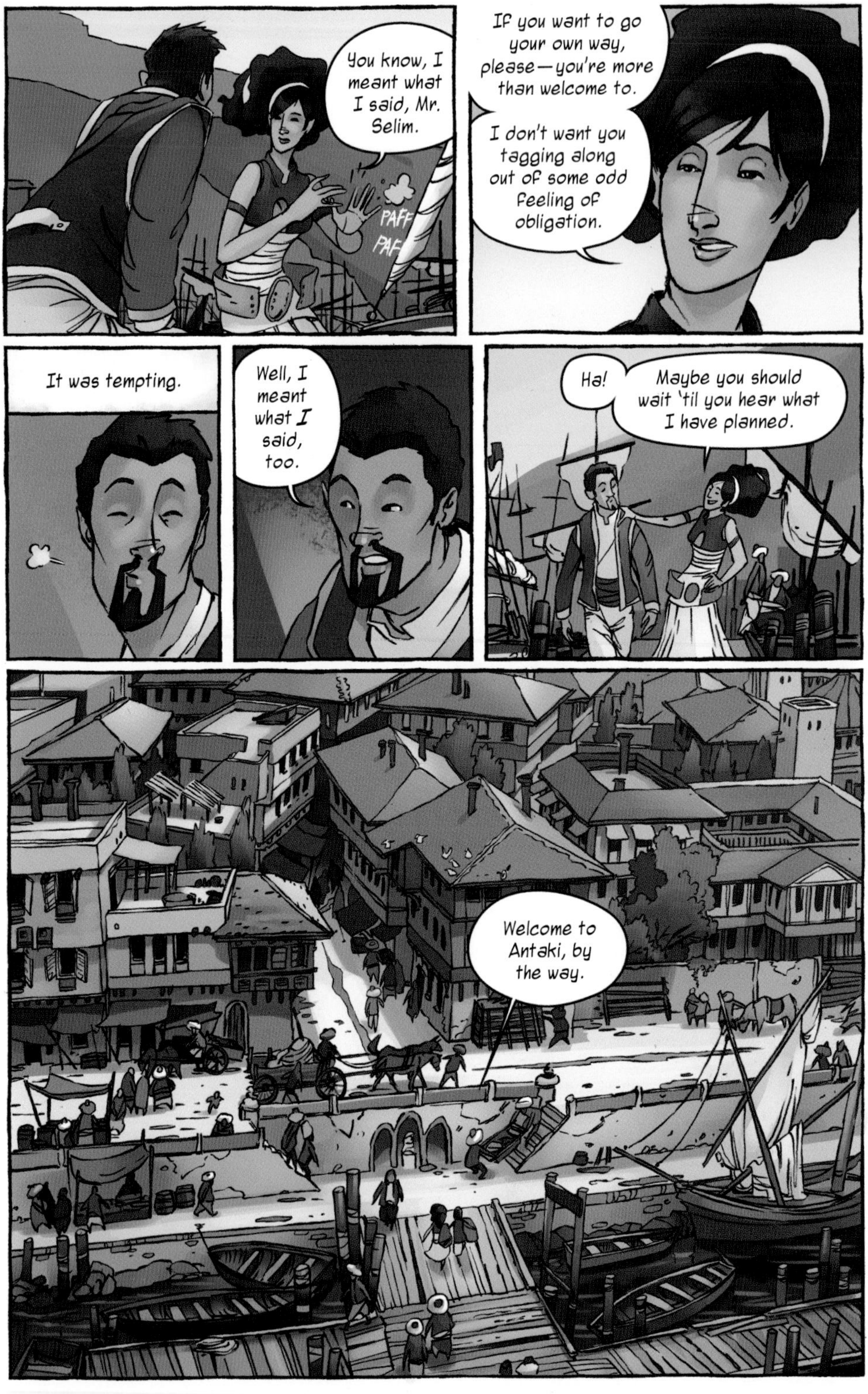
You know, I meant what I said, Mr. Selim.
PAFF
PAFF
If you want to go your own way, please—you're more than welcome to.
I don't want you tagging along out of some odd feeling of obligation.
It was tempting.
Well, I meant what *I* said, too.
Ha!
Maybe you should wait 'til you hear what I have planned.
Welcome to Antaki, by the way.

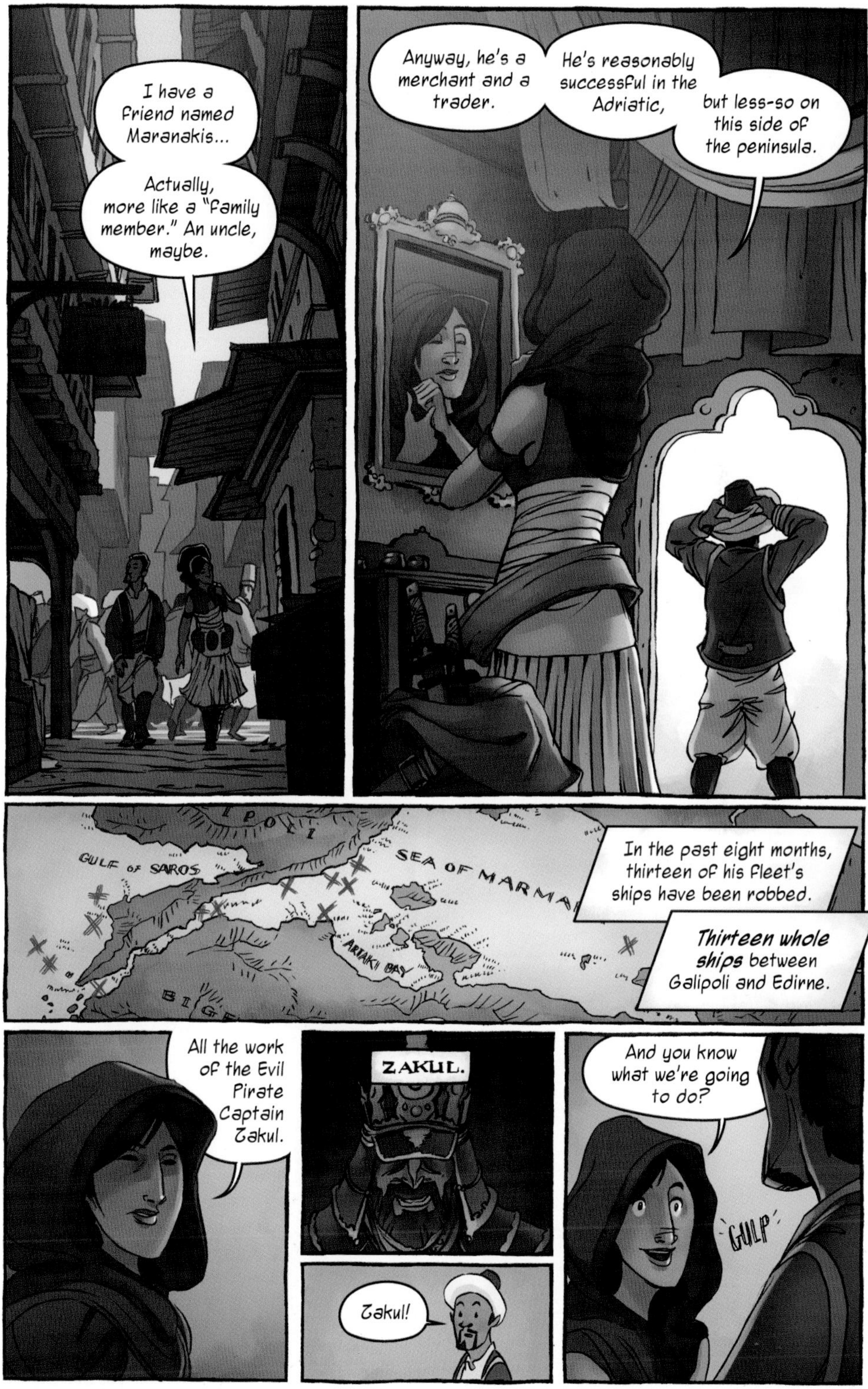

I have a friend named Maranakis...
Actually, more like a "family member." An uncle, maybe.
Anyway, he's a merchant and a trader.
He's reasonably successful in the Adriatic,
but less-so on this side of the peninsula.
GULF OF SAROS
SEA OF MARMA
ARTAKI BAY
In the past eight months, thirteen of his fleet's ships have been robbed.
Thirteen whole ships between Galipoli and Edirne.
All the work of the Evil Pirate Captain Zakul.
ZAKUL.
Zakul!
And you know what we're going to do?
GULP

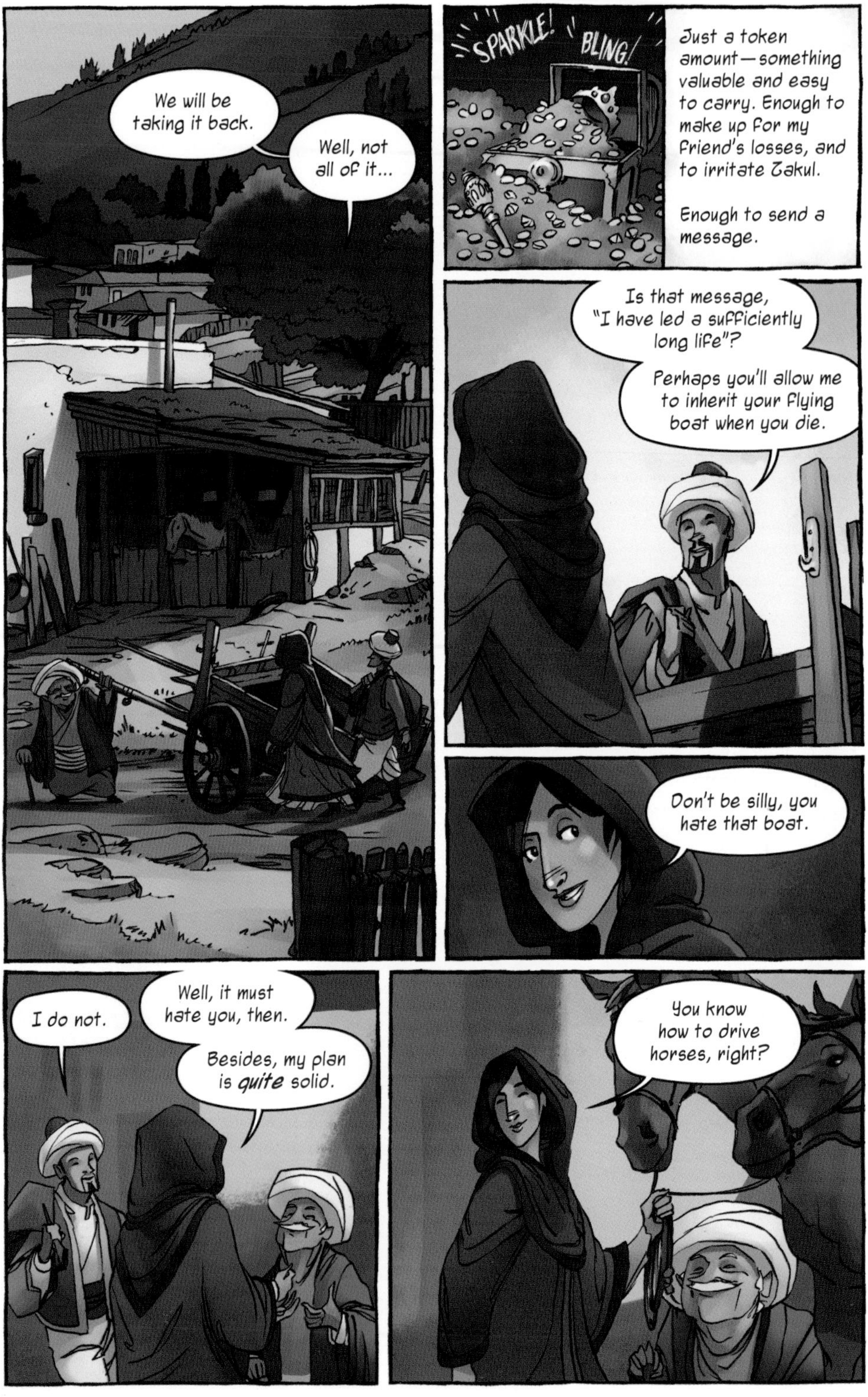
We will be taking it back.
Well, not all of it...
SPARKLE!
BLING!
Just a token amount—something valuable and easy to carry. Enough to make up for my friend's losses, and to irritate Zakul.
Enough to send a message.
Is that message, "I have led a sufficiently long life"?
Perhaps you'll allow me to inherit your flying boat when you die.
Don't be silly, you hate that boat.
I do not.
Well, it must hate you, then.
Besides, my plan is *quite* solid.
You know how to drive horses, right?

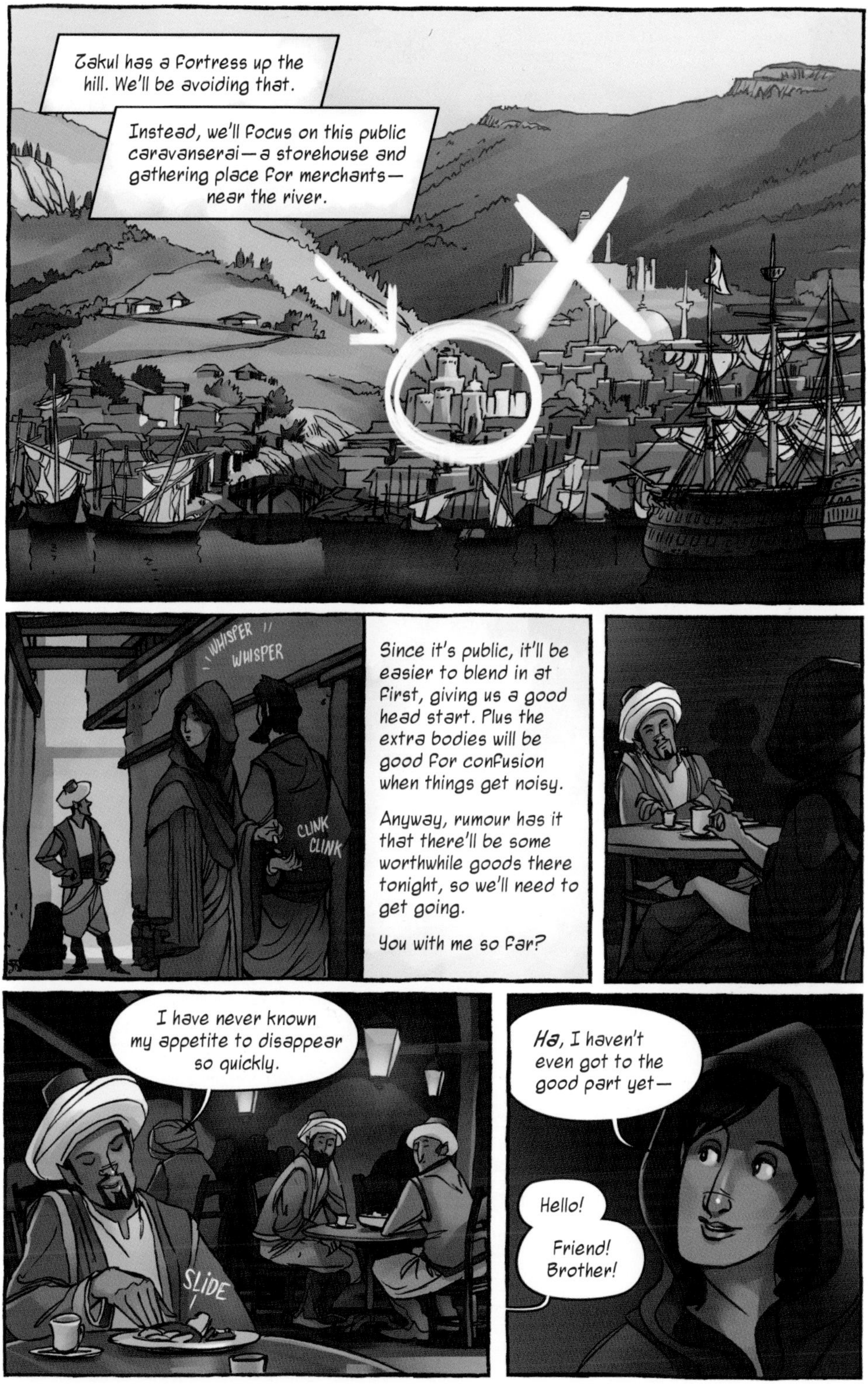
Zakul has a fortress up the hill. We'll be avoiding that.
Instead, we'll focus on this public caravanserai—a storehouse and gathering place for merchants—near the river.
WHISPER WHISPER
CLINK CLINK
Since it's public, it'll be easier to blend in at first, giving us a good head start. Plus the extra bodies will be good for confusion when things get noisy.
Anyway, rumour has it that there'll be some worthwhile goods there tonight, so we'll need to get going.
You with me so far?
I have never known my appetite to disappear so quickly.
SLIDE
Ha, I haven't even got to the good part yet—
Hello!
Friend! Brother!

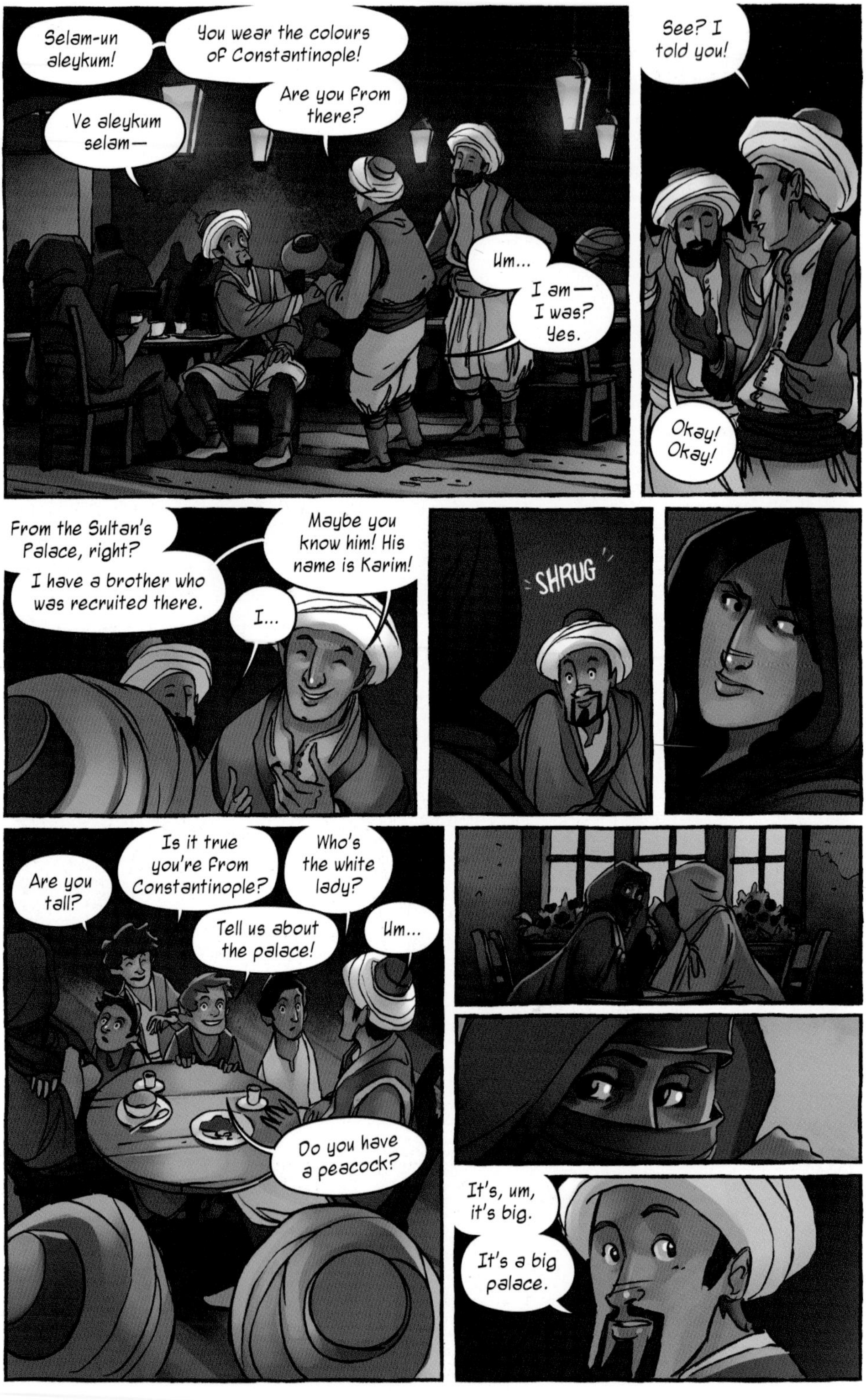
Selam-un aleykum!
You wear the colours of Constantinople!
Ve aleykum selam—
Are you from there?
Um...
I am— I was? Yes.
See? I told you!
Okay! Okay!
From the Sultan's Palace, right?
I have a brother who was recruited there.
Maybe you know him! His name is Karim!
I...
SHRUG
Are you tall?
Is it true you're from Constantinople?
Who's the white lady?
Tell us about the palace!
Um...
Do you have a peacock?
It's, um, it's big.
It's a big palace.

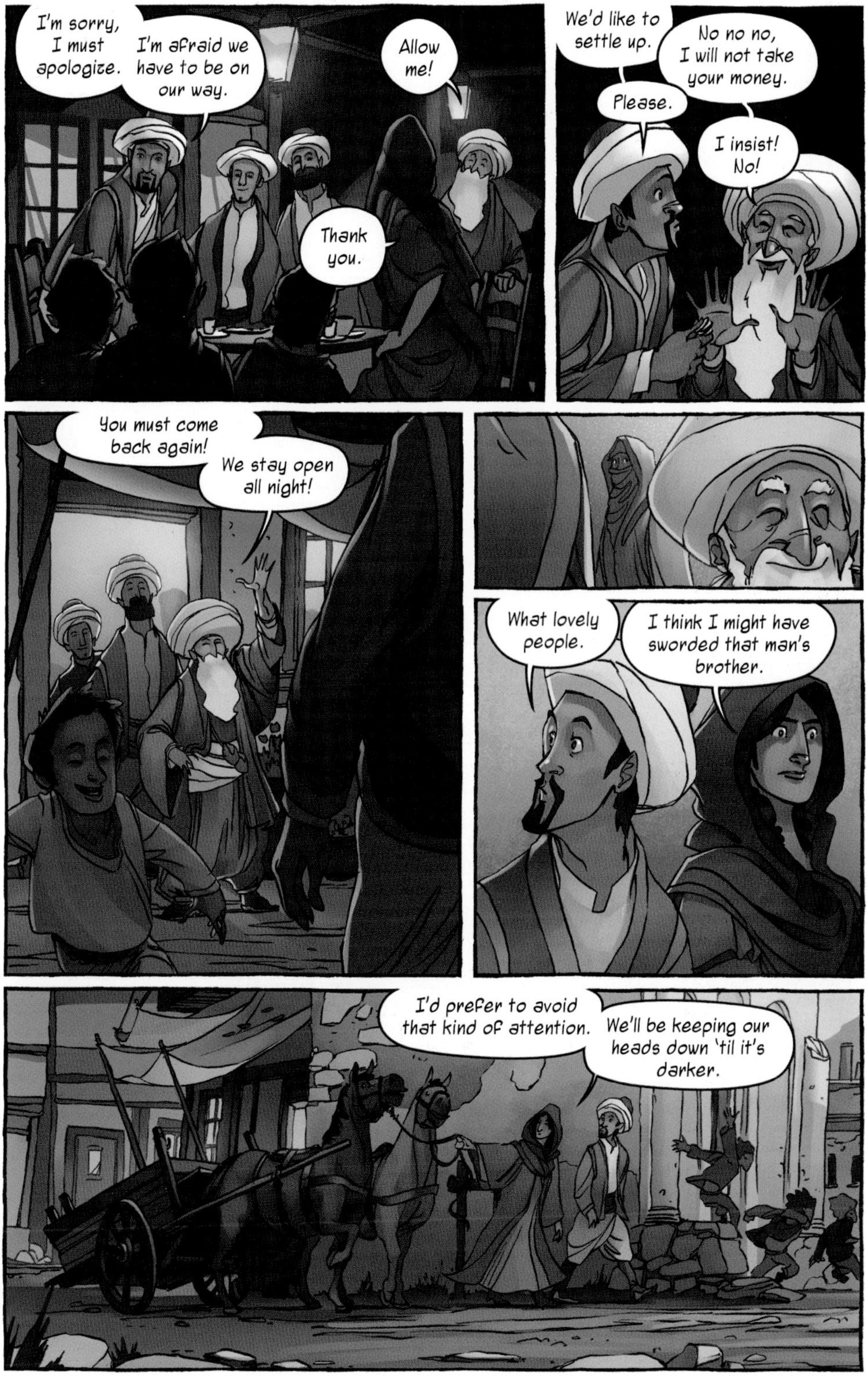
I'm sorry, I must apologize.
I'm afraid we have to be on our way.
Allow me!
Thank you.
We'd like to settle up.
No no no, I will not take your money.
Please.
I insist! No!
You must come back again!
We stay open all night!
What lovely people.
I think I might have sworded that man's brother.
I'd prefer to avoid that kind of attention.
We'll be keeping our heads down 'til it's darker.

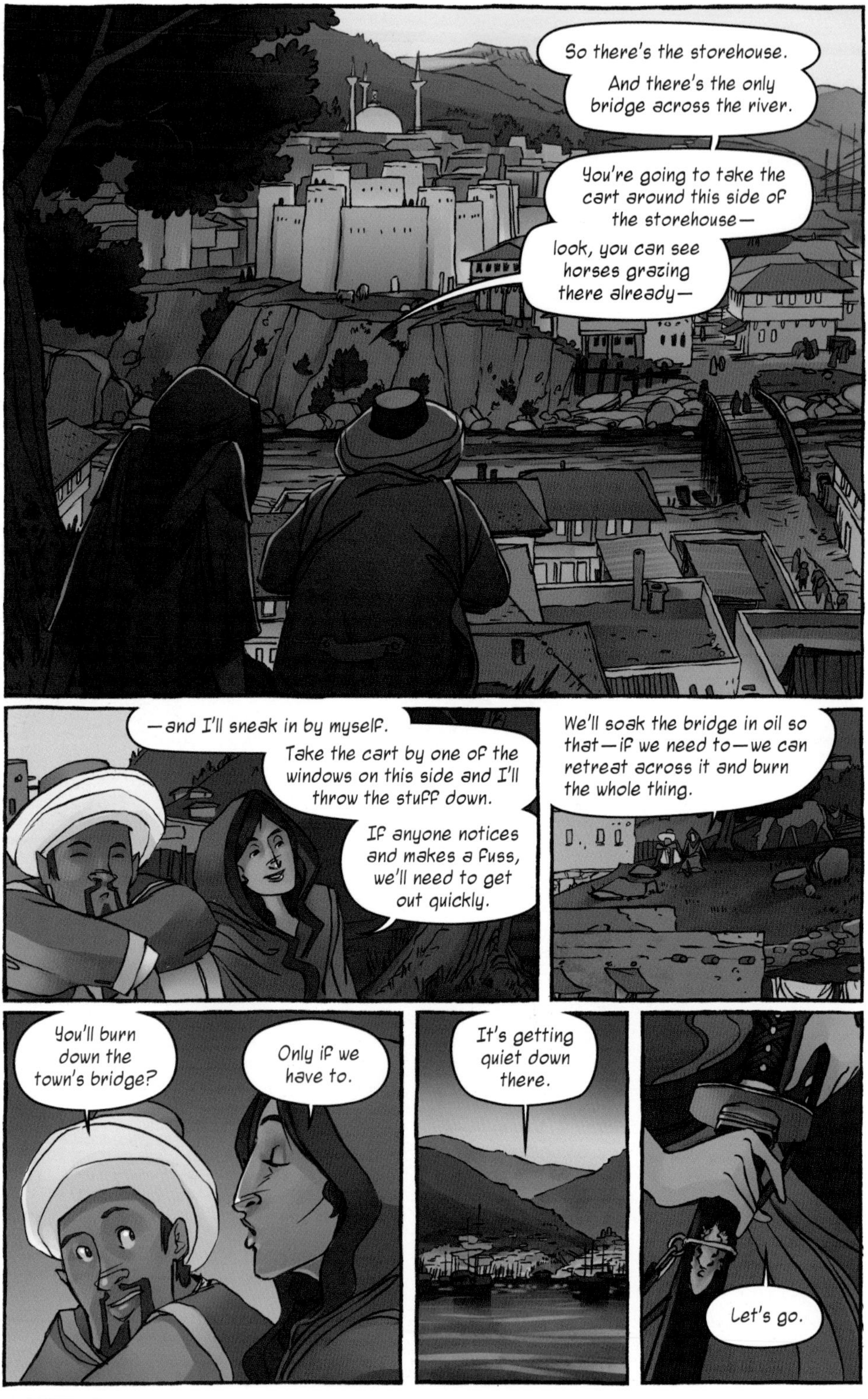
So there's the storehouse.
And there's the only bridge across the river.
You're going to take the cart around this side of the storehouse—
look, you can see horses grazing there already—
—and I'll sneak in by myself.
Take the cart by one of the windows on this side and I'll throw the stuff down.
If anyone notices and makes a fuss, we'll need to get out quickly.
We'll soak the bridge in oil so that—if we need to—we can retreat across it and burn the whole thing.
You'll burn down the town's bridge?
Only if we have to.
It's getting quiet down there.
Let's go.

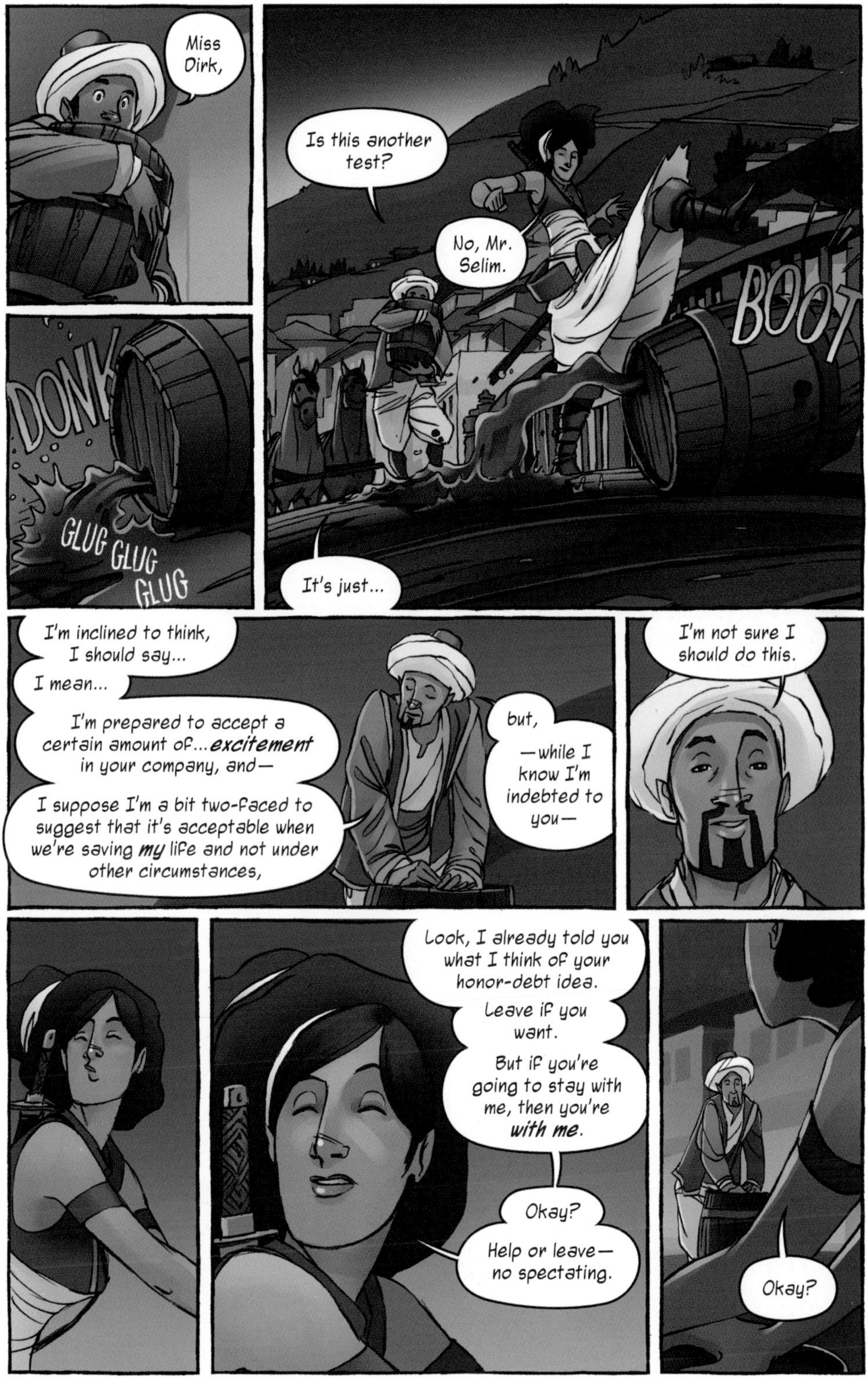

Miss Dirk,
Is this another test?
No, Mr. Selim.
BOOT
DONK
GLUG GLUG GLUG
It's just...
I'm inclined to think, I should say...
I mean...
I'm prepared to accept a certain amount of...*excitement* in your company, and—
I suppose I'm a bit two-faced to suggest that it's acceptable when we're saving *my* life and not under other circumstances,
but,
—while I know I'm indebted to you—
I'm not sure I should do this.
Look, I already told you what I think of your honor-debt idea.
Leave if you want.
But if you're going to stay with me, then you're *with me*.
Okay?
Help or leave—no spectating.
Okay?

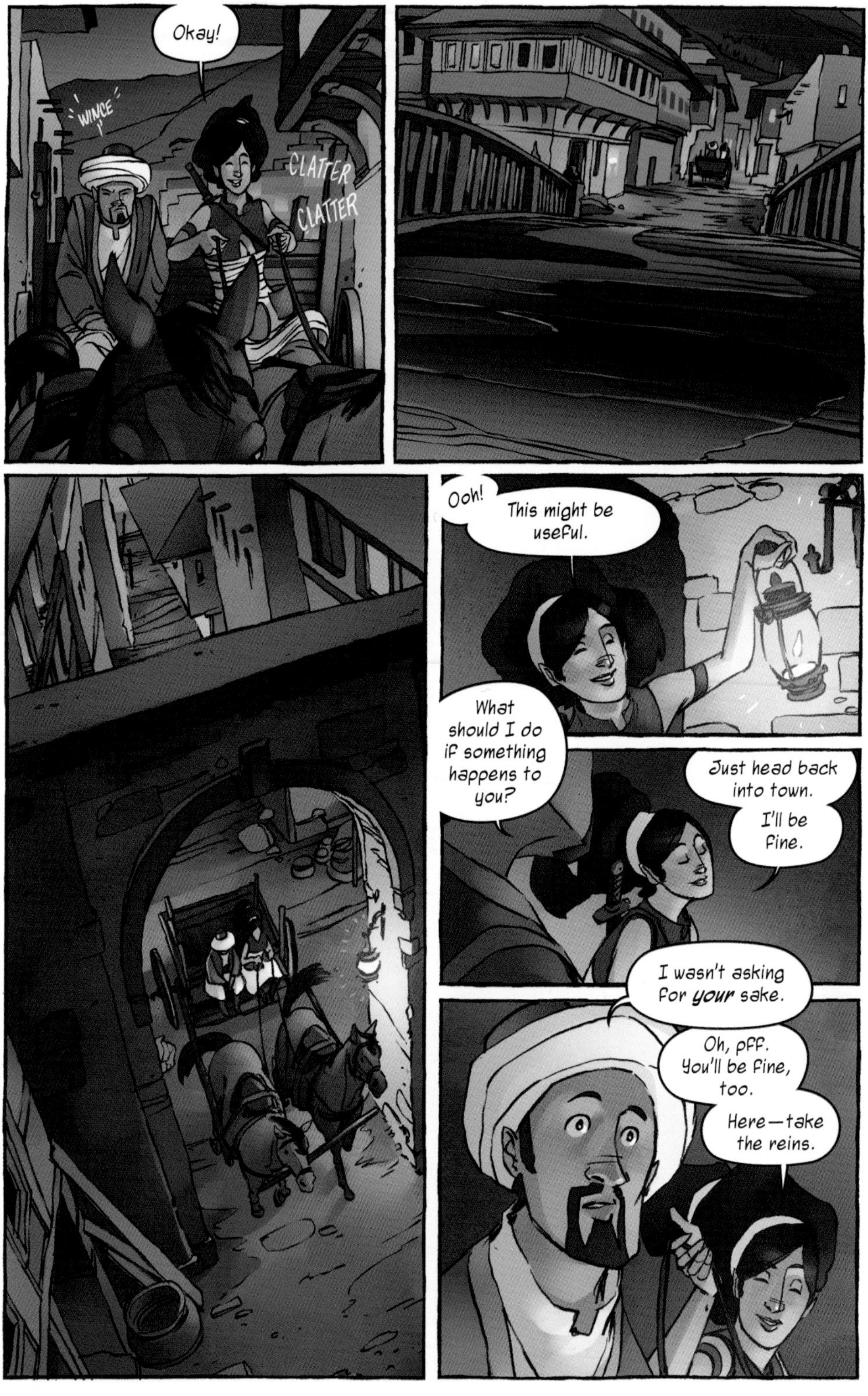
Okay!
WINCE
CLATTER
CLATTER
Ooh!
This might be useful.
What should I do if something happens to you?
Just head back into town.
I'll be fine.
I wasn't asking for *your* sake.
Oh, pff. You'll be fine, too.
Here—take the reins.

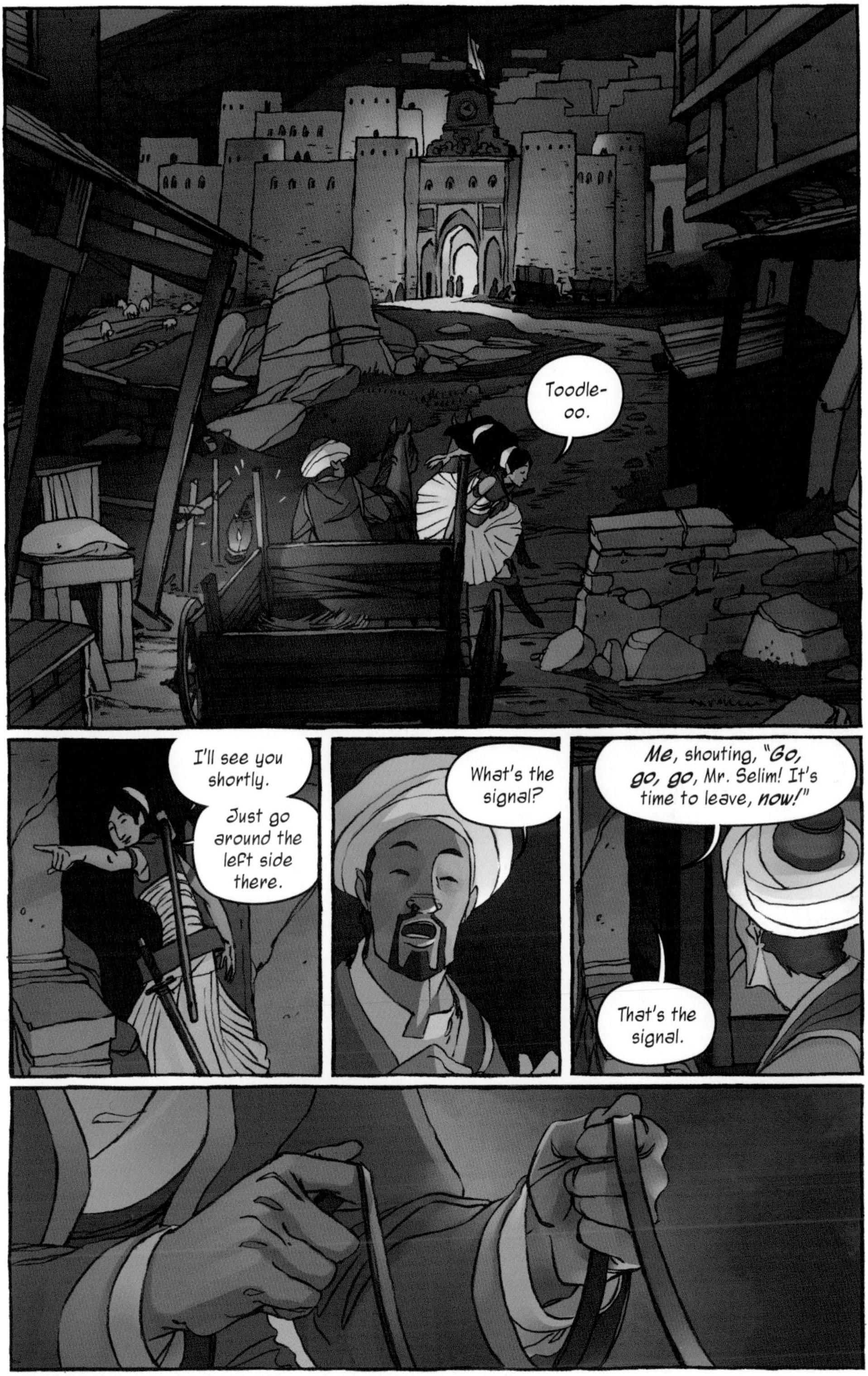
Toodle-
oo.
I'll see you shortly.
Just go around the left side there.
What's the signal?
Me, shouting, "*Go, go, go*, Mr. Selim! It's time to leave, ***now!***"
That's the signal.

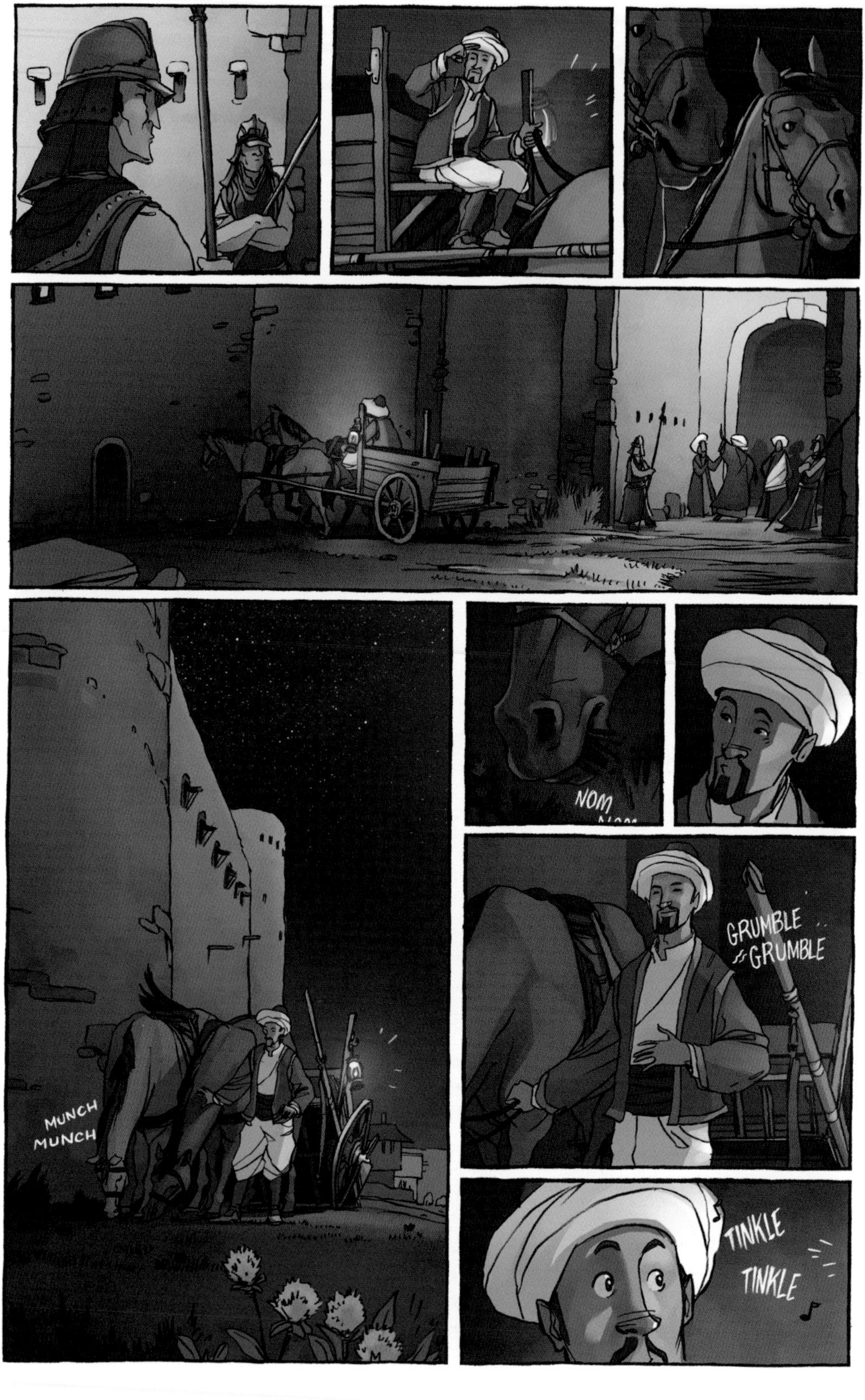
MUNCH
MUNCH
NOM
GRUMBLE
GRUMBLE
TINKLE
TINKLE

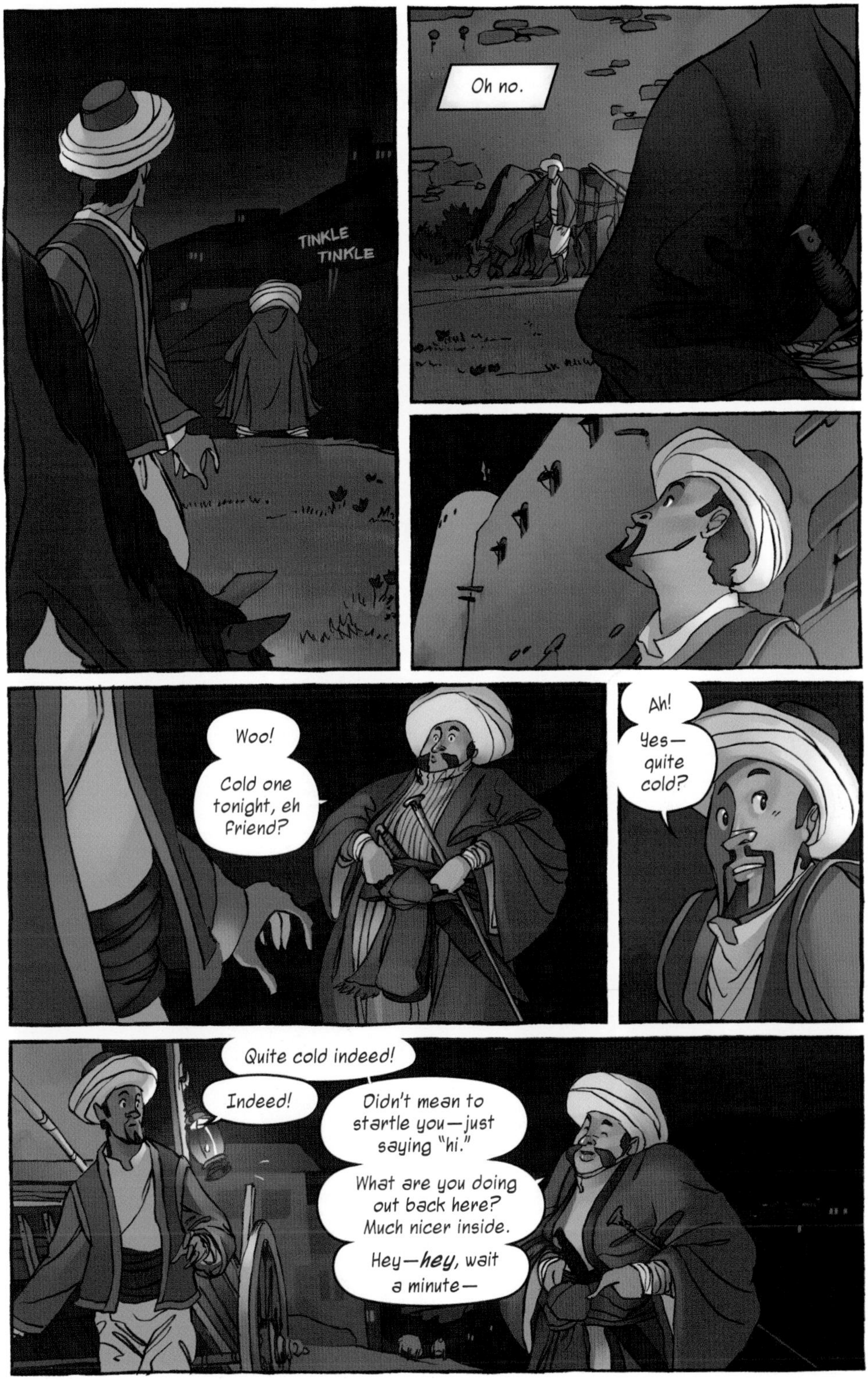
TINKLE
TINKLE
Oh no.
Woo!
Cold one tonight, eh friend?
Ah!
Yes—quite cold?
Quite cold indeed!
Indeed!
Didn't mean to startle you—just saying "hi."
What are you doing out back here? Much nicer inside.
Hey—**hey**, wait a minute—

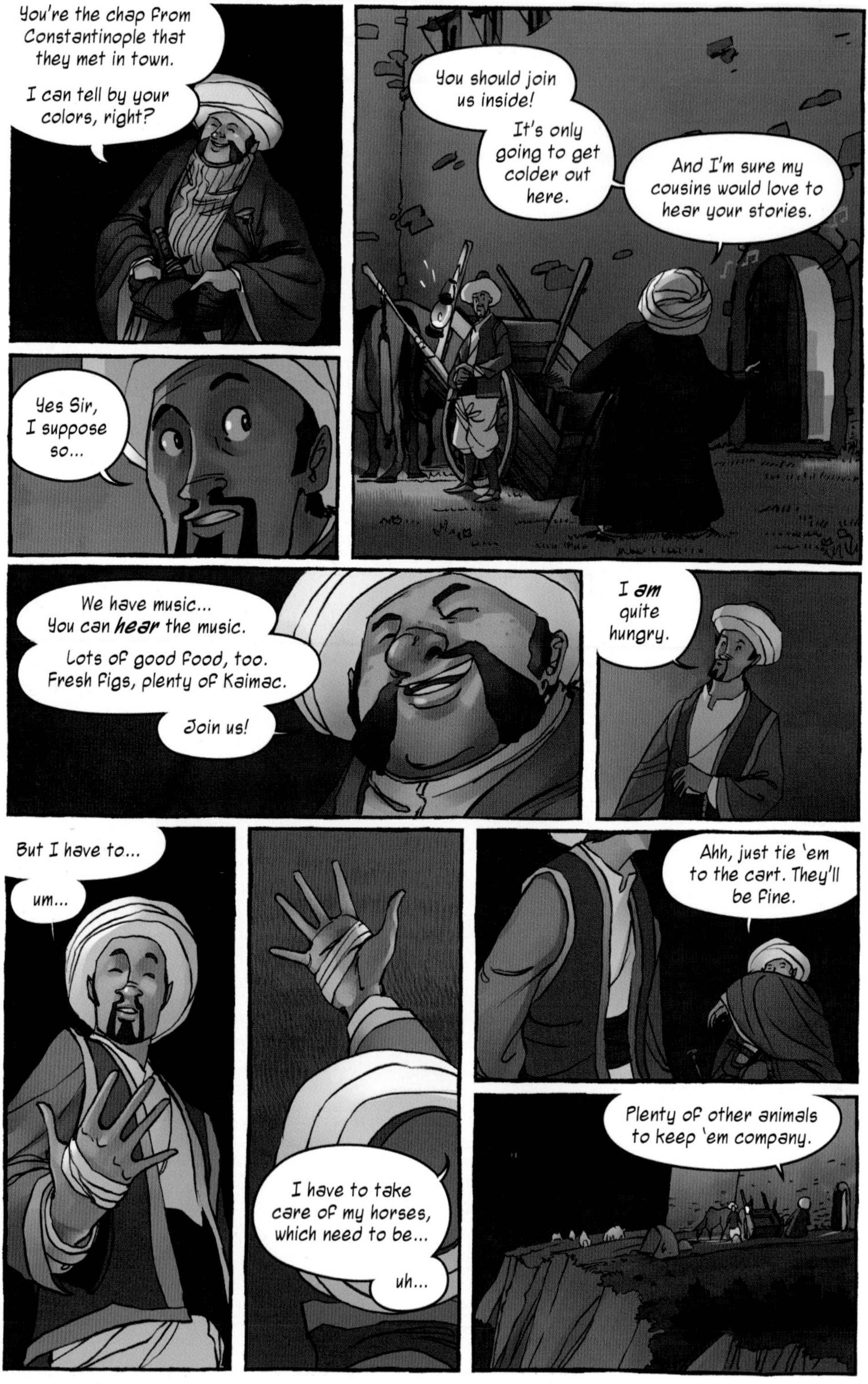
You're the chap from Constantinople that they met in town.
I can tell by your colors, right?
Yes Sir, I suppose so...
You should join us inside!
It's only going to get colder out here.
And I'm sure my cousins would love to hear your stories.
We have music... You can *hear* the music.
Lots of good food, too. Fresh figs, plenty of Kaimac.
Join us!
I *am* quite hungry.
But I have to...
um...
I have to take care of my horses, which need to be...
uh...
Ahh, just tie 'em to the cart. They'll be fine.
Plenty of other animals to keep 'em company.

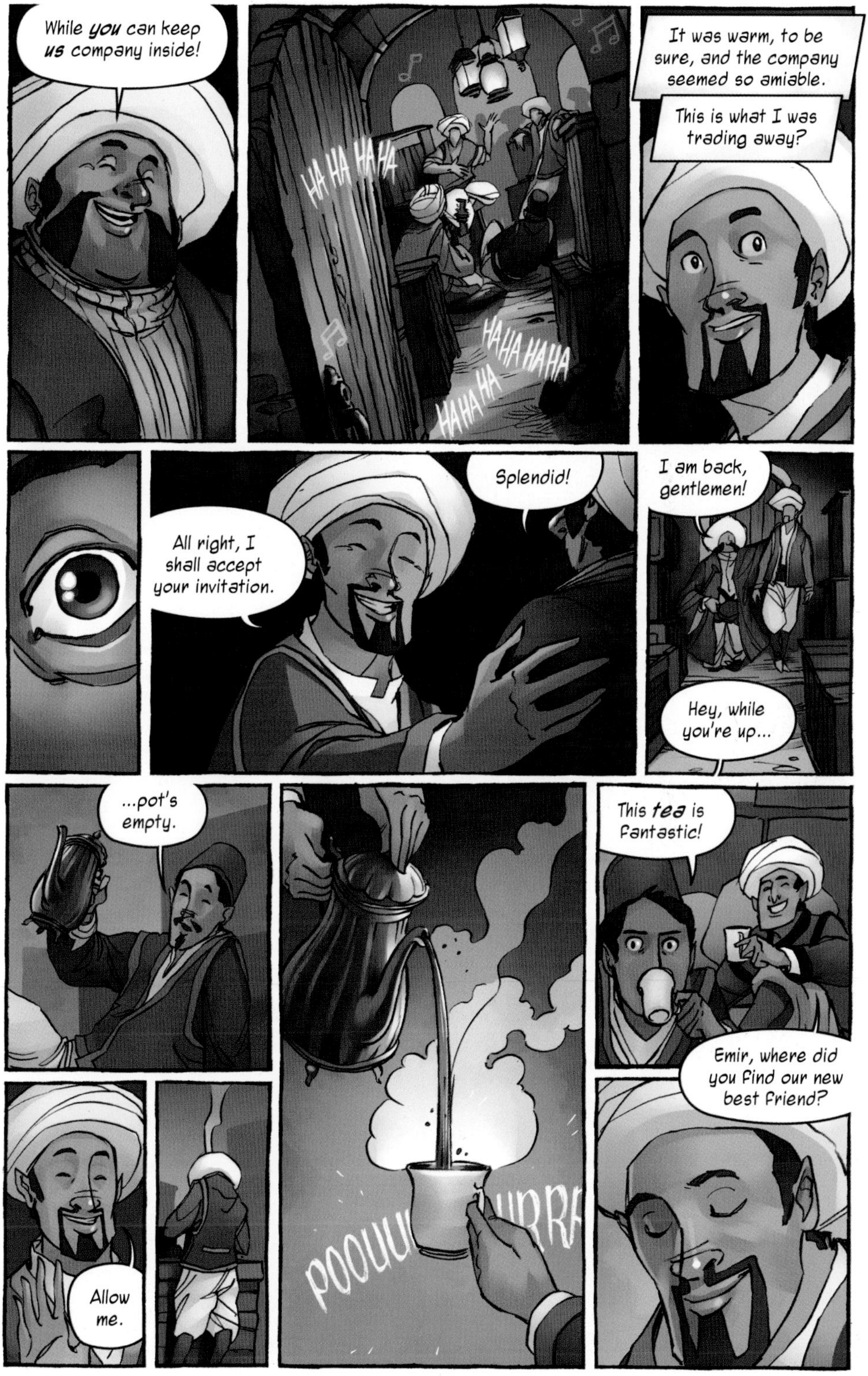
While you can keep us company inside!
HA HA HA HA
HA HA HA HA
HA HA HA
It was warm, to be sure, and the company seemed so amiable.
This is what I was trading away?
All right, I shall accept your invitation.
Splendid!
I am back, gentlemen!
Hey, while you're up...
...pot's empty.
Allow me.
POOUU
URRR
This tea is fantastic!
Emir, where did you find our new best friend?

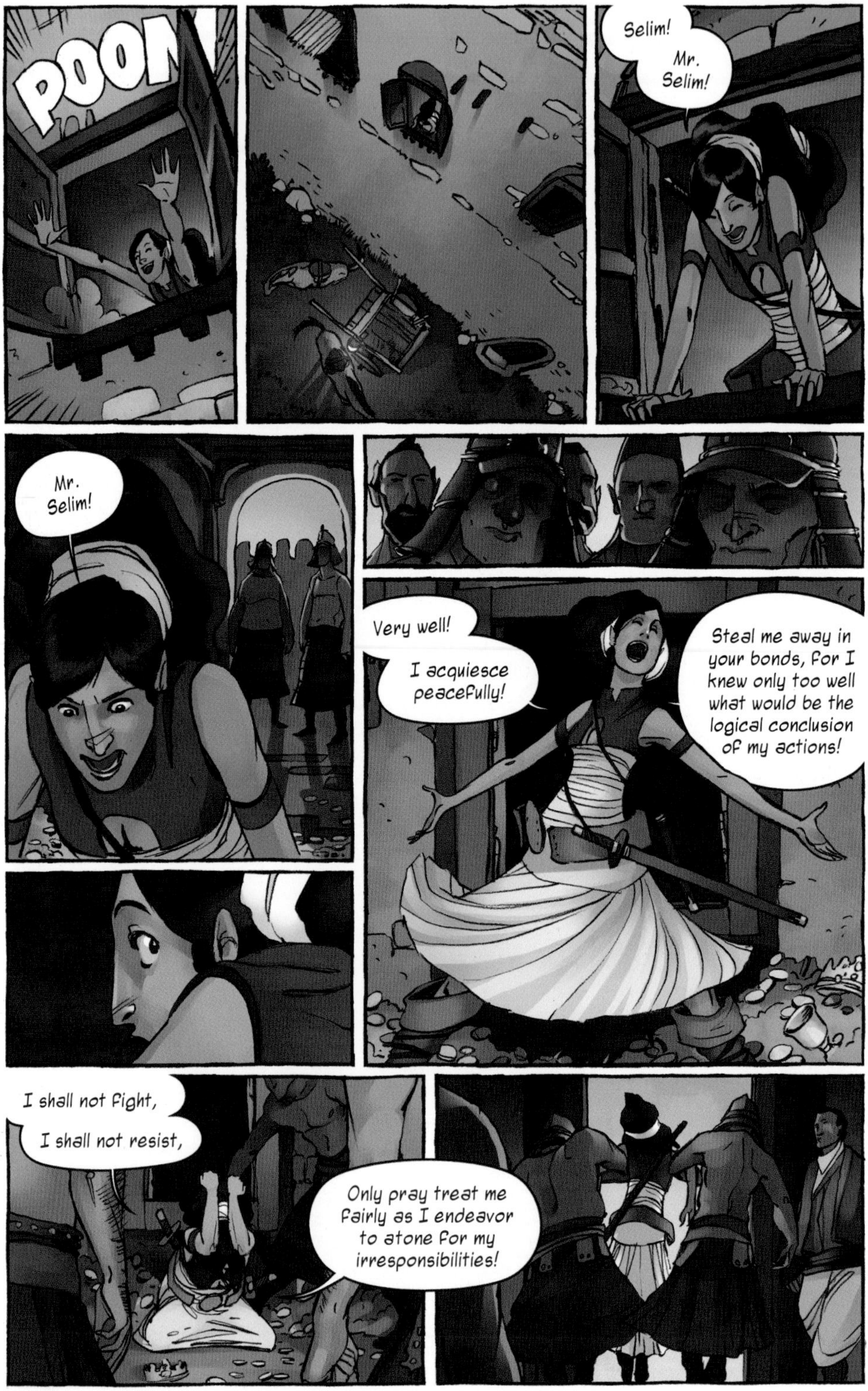
POOM
Selim!
Mr. Selim!
Mr. Selim!
Very well!
I acquiesce peacefully!
Steal me away in your bonds, for I knew only too well what would be the logical conclusion of my actions!
I shall not fight,
I shall not resist,
Only pray treat me fairly as I endeavor to atone for my irresponsibilities!

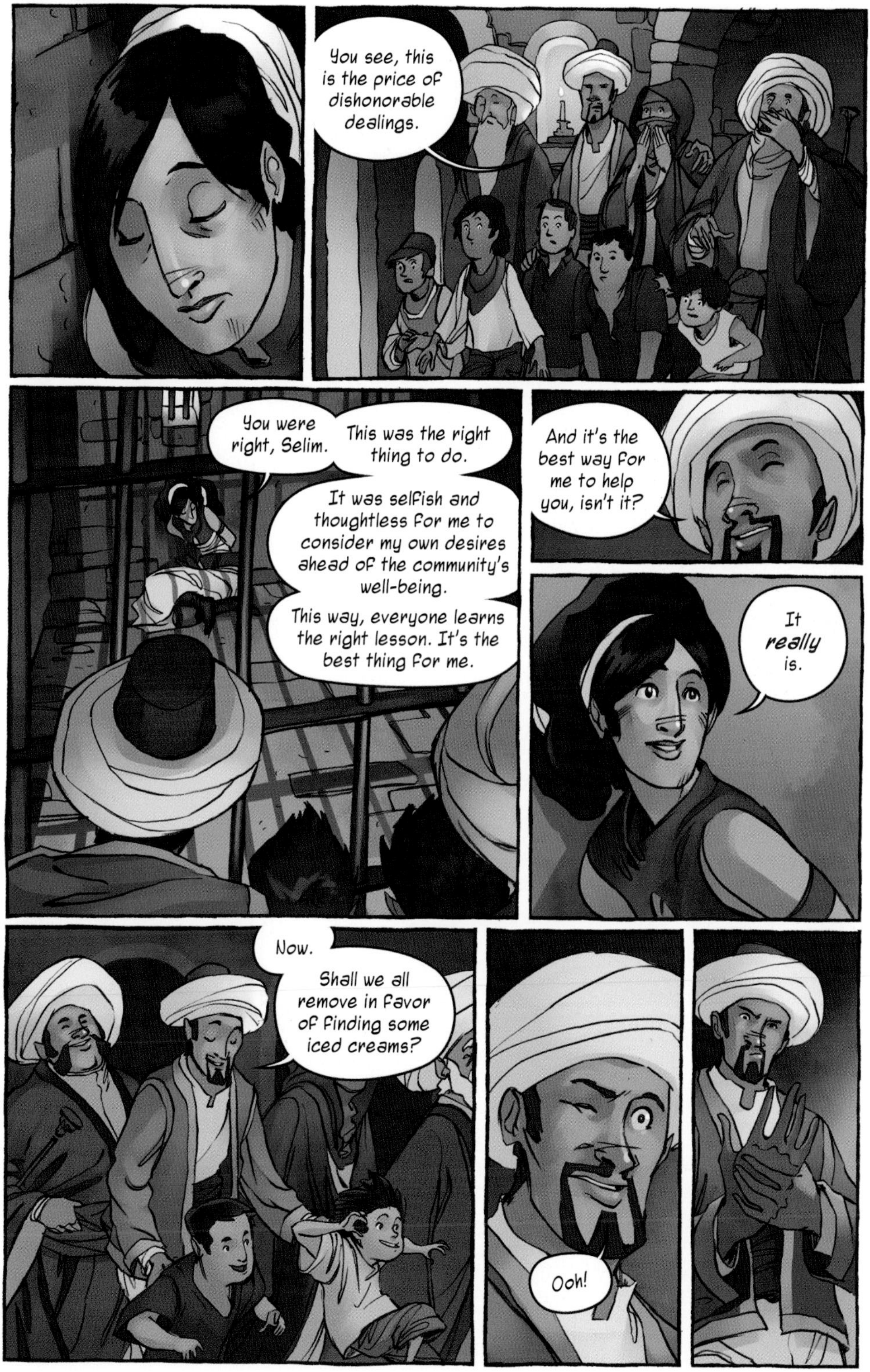
You see, this is the price of dishonorable dealings.
You were right, Selim.
This was the right thing to do.
It was selfish and thoughtless for me to consider my own desires ahead of the community's well-being.
This way, everyone learns the right lesson. It's the best thing for me.
And it's the best way for me to help you, isn't it?
It *really* is.
Now.
Shall we all remove in favor of finding some iced creams?
Ooh!

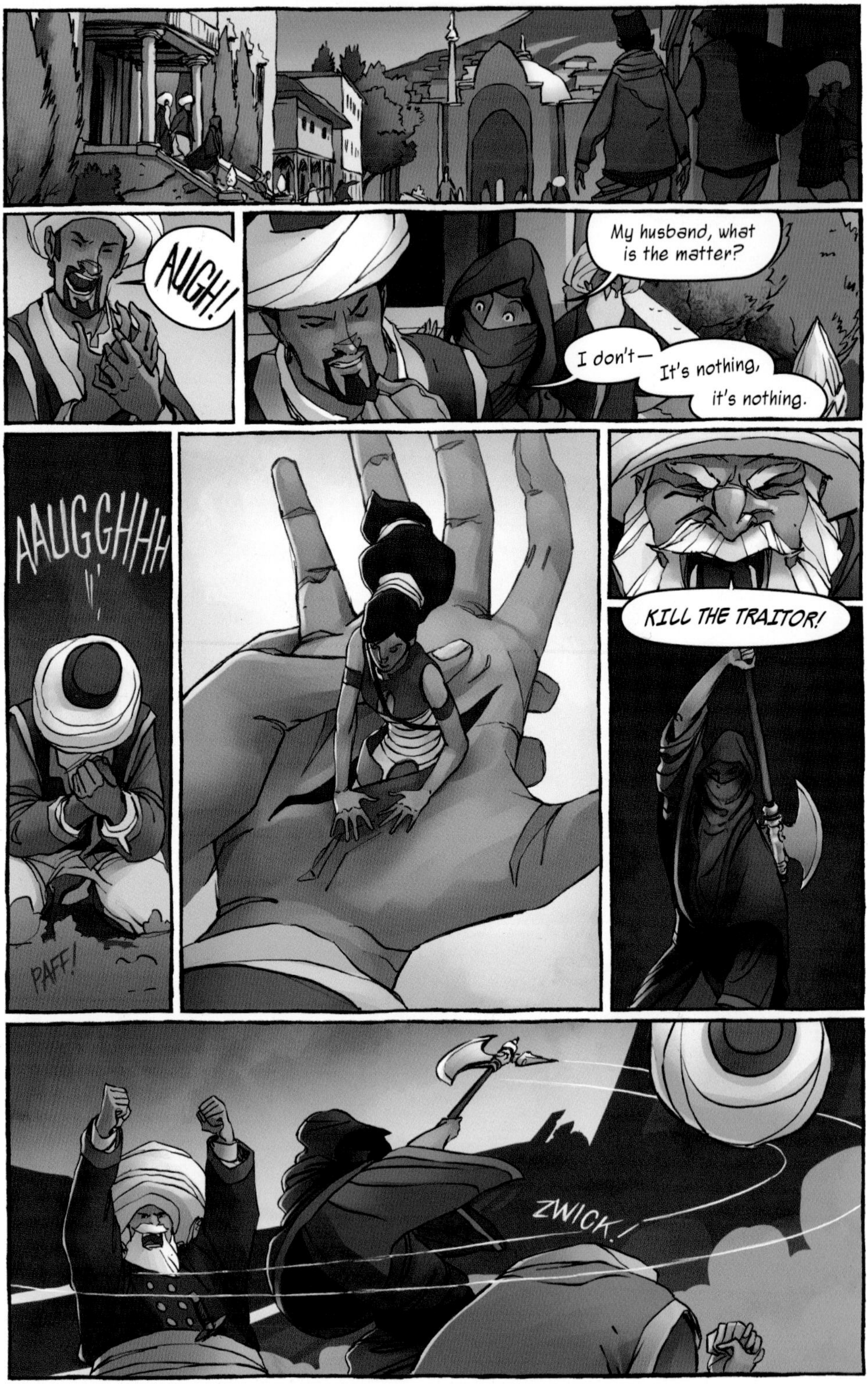
AUGH!
My husband, what is the matter?
I don't—
It's nothing,
it's nothing.
AAUGGHHH
PAFF!
KILL THE TRAITOR!
ZWICK!

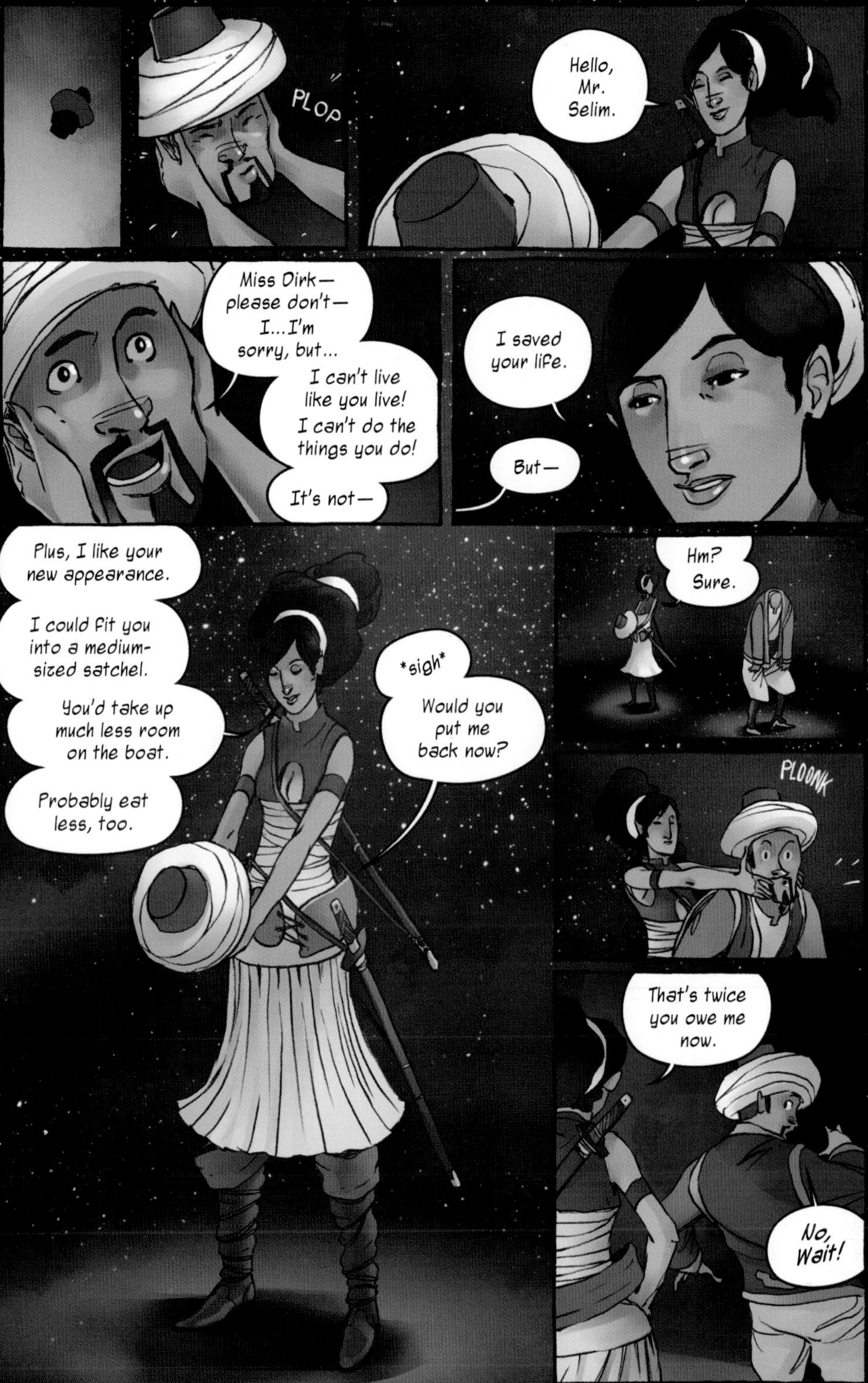
PLOP
Hello, Mr. Selim.
Miss Dirk— please don't— I...I'm sorry, but...
I can't live like you live!
I can't do the things you do!
It's not—
I saved your life.
But—
Plus, I like your new appearance.
I could fit you into a medium-sized satchel.
You'd take up much less room on the boat.
Probably eat less, too.
sigh
Would you put me back now?
Hm? Sure.
PLOONK
That's twice you owe me now.
No, Wait!

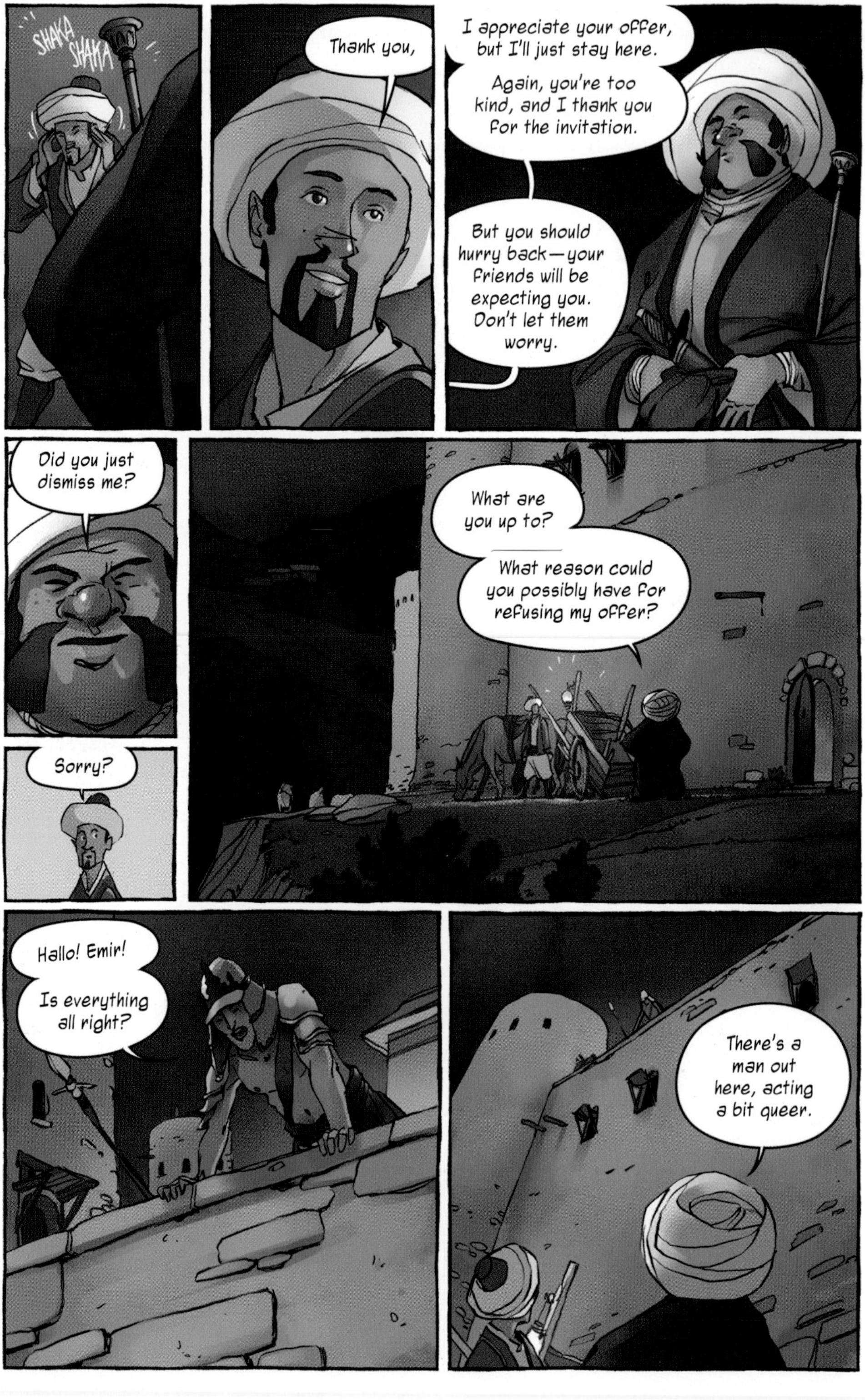
SHAKA SHAKA
Thank you,
I appreciate your offer, but I'll just stay here.
Again, you're too kind, and I thank you for the invitation.
But you should hurry back—your friends will be expecting you. Don't let them worry.
Did you just dismiss me?
Sorry?
What are you up to?
What reason could you possibly have for refusing my offer?
Hallo! Emir!
Is everything all right?
There's a man out here, acting a bit queer.

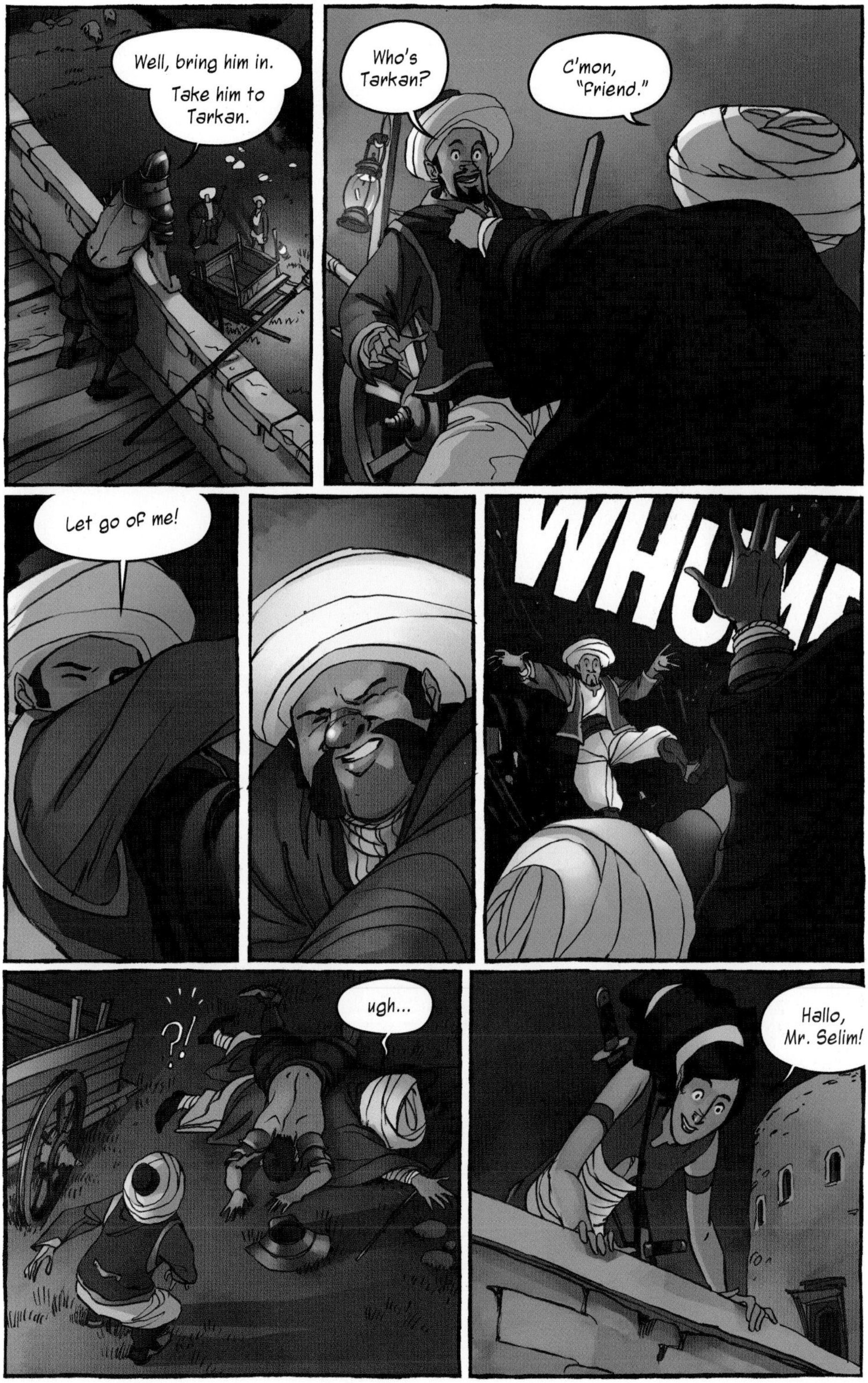
Well, bring him in.
Take him to Tarkan.
Who's Tarkan?
C'mon, "friend."
Let go of me!
WHU
?!
ugh...
Hallo, Mr. Selim!

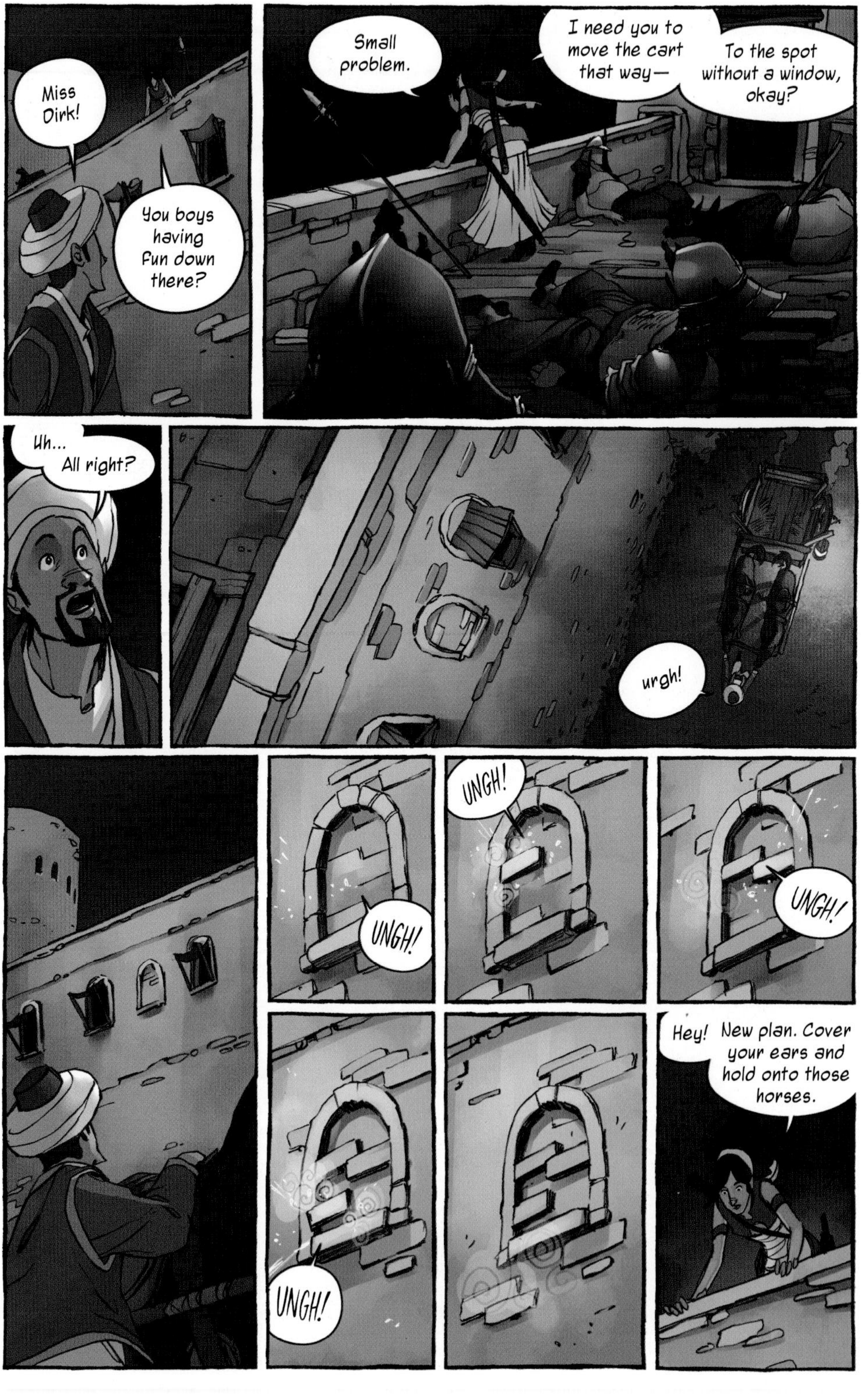
Miss Dirk!
You boys having fun down there?
Small problem.
I need you to move the cart that way—
To the spot without a window, okay?
Uh... All right?
urgh!
UNGH!
UNGH!
UNGH!
UNGH!
Hey!
New plan. Cover your ears and hold onto those horses.

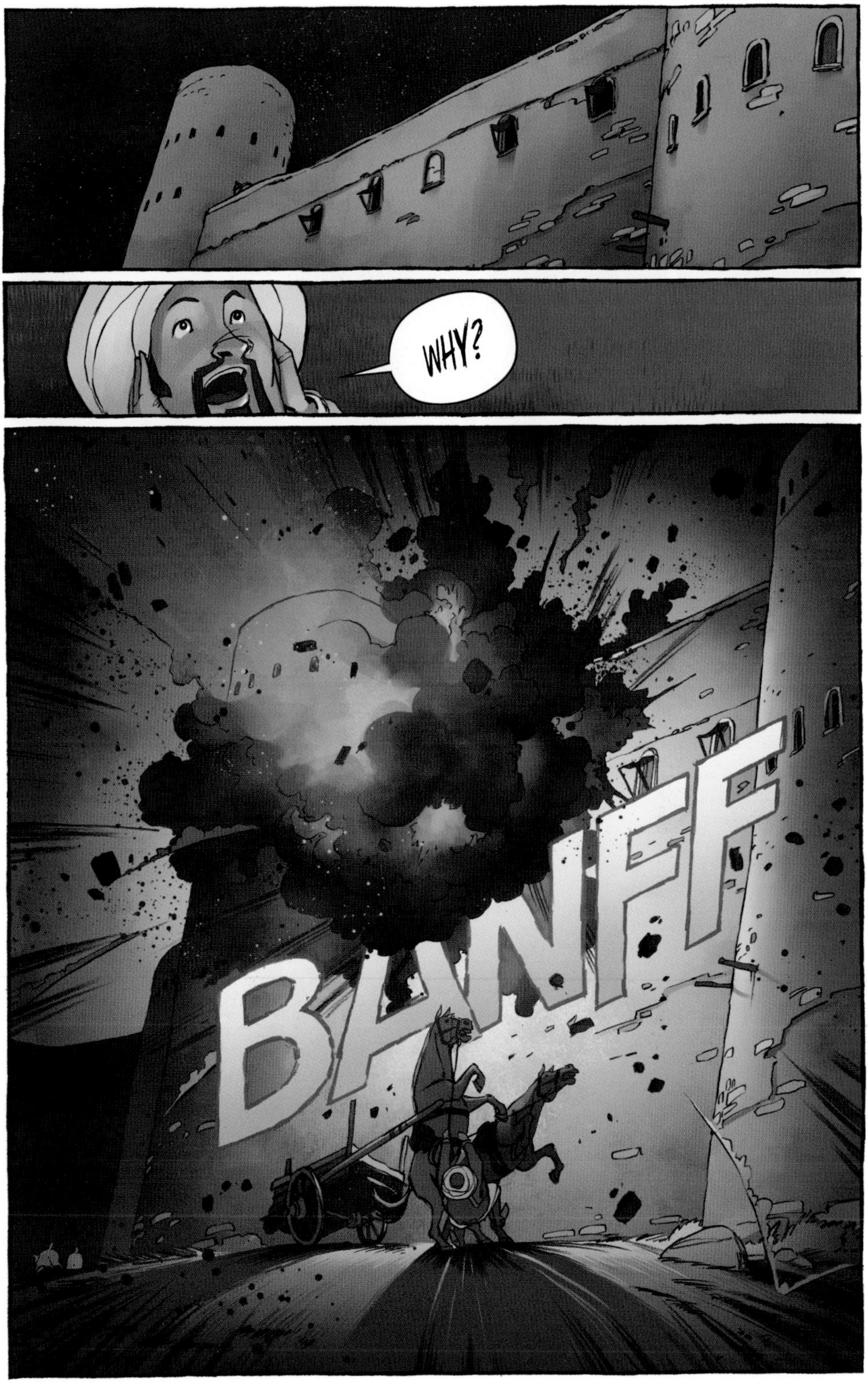
WHY?
BANFF

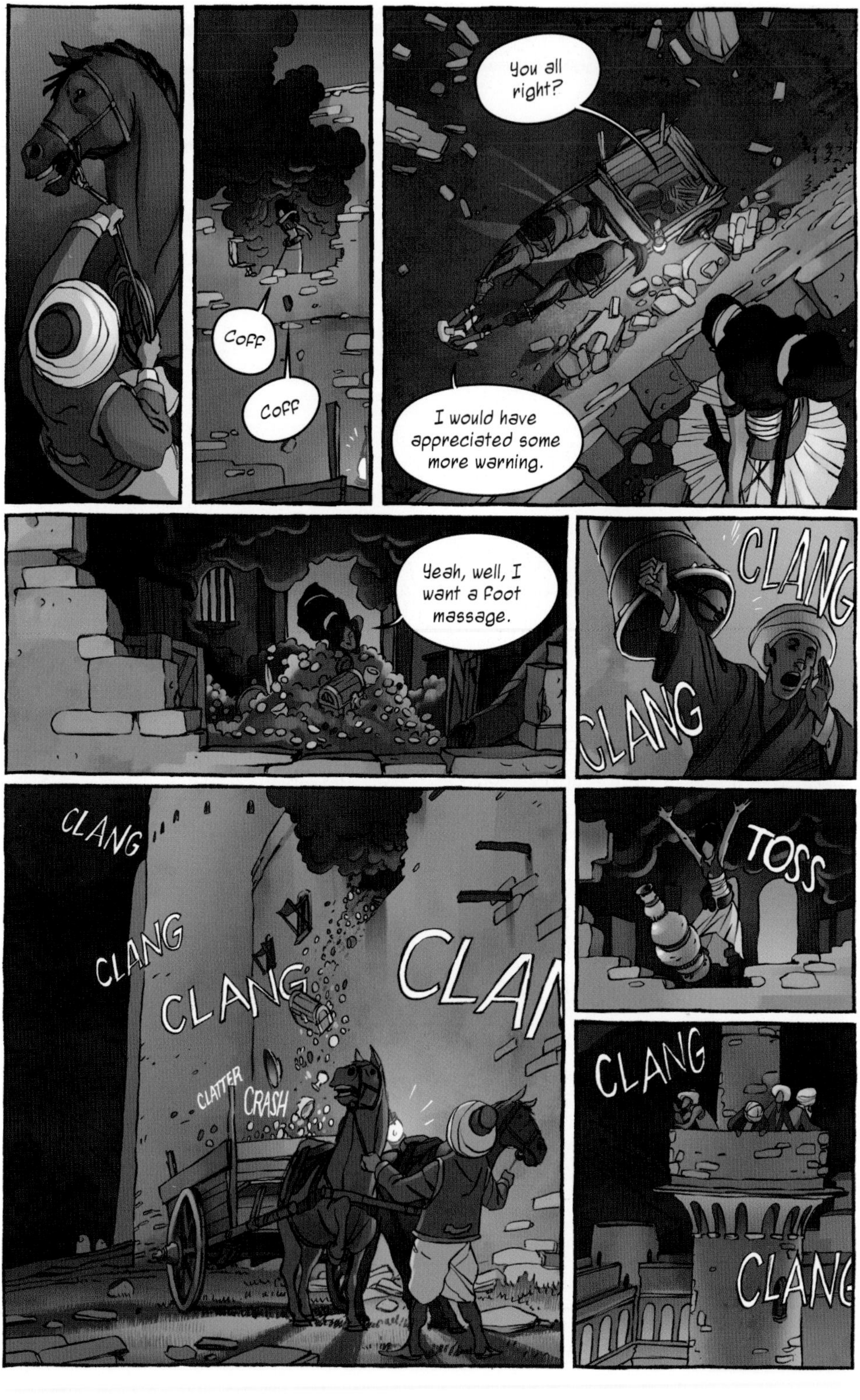
Coff
Coff
You all right?
I would have appreciated some more warning.
Yeah, well, I want a foot massage.
CLANG
CLANG
CLANG
CLANG
CLANG
CLAN
CLATTER
CRASH
TOSS
CLANG
CLANG

Time to go, Mr. Selim.

CLA[NG]

CLANG

CLANG

CLA[NG]

CLA[NG]

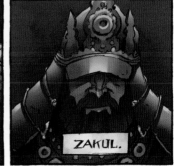

ZAKUL.

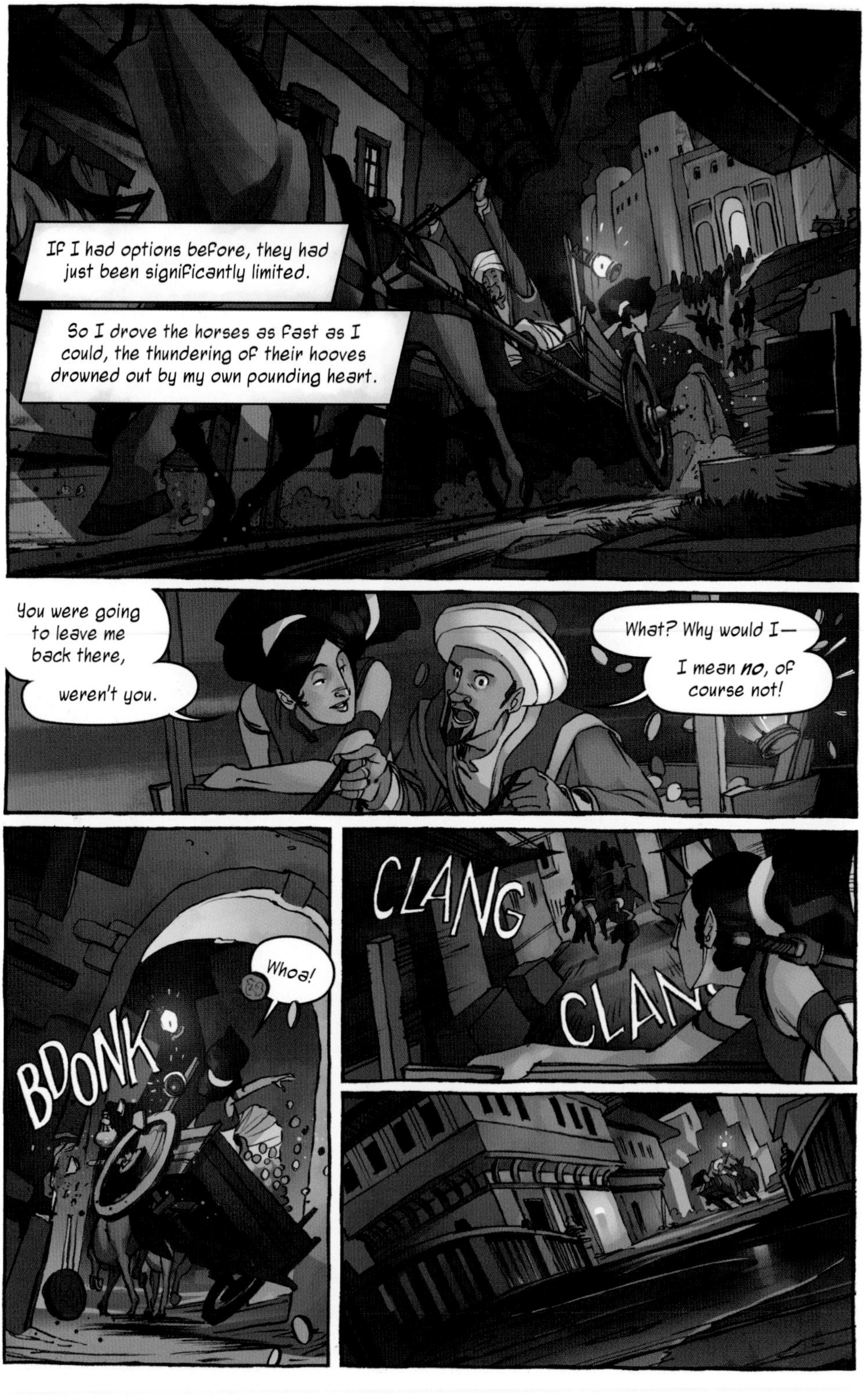
If I had options before, they had just been significantly limited.
So I drove the horses as fast as I could, the thundering of their hooves drowned out by my own pounding heart.
You were going to leave me back there,
weren't you.
What? Why would I—
I mean *no*, of course not!
Whoa!
BDONK
CLANG
CLAN

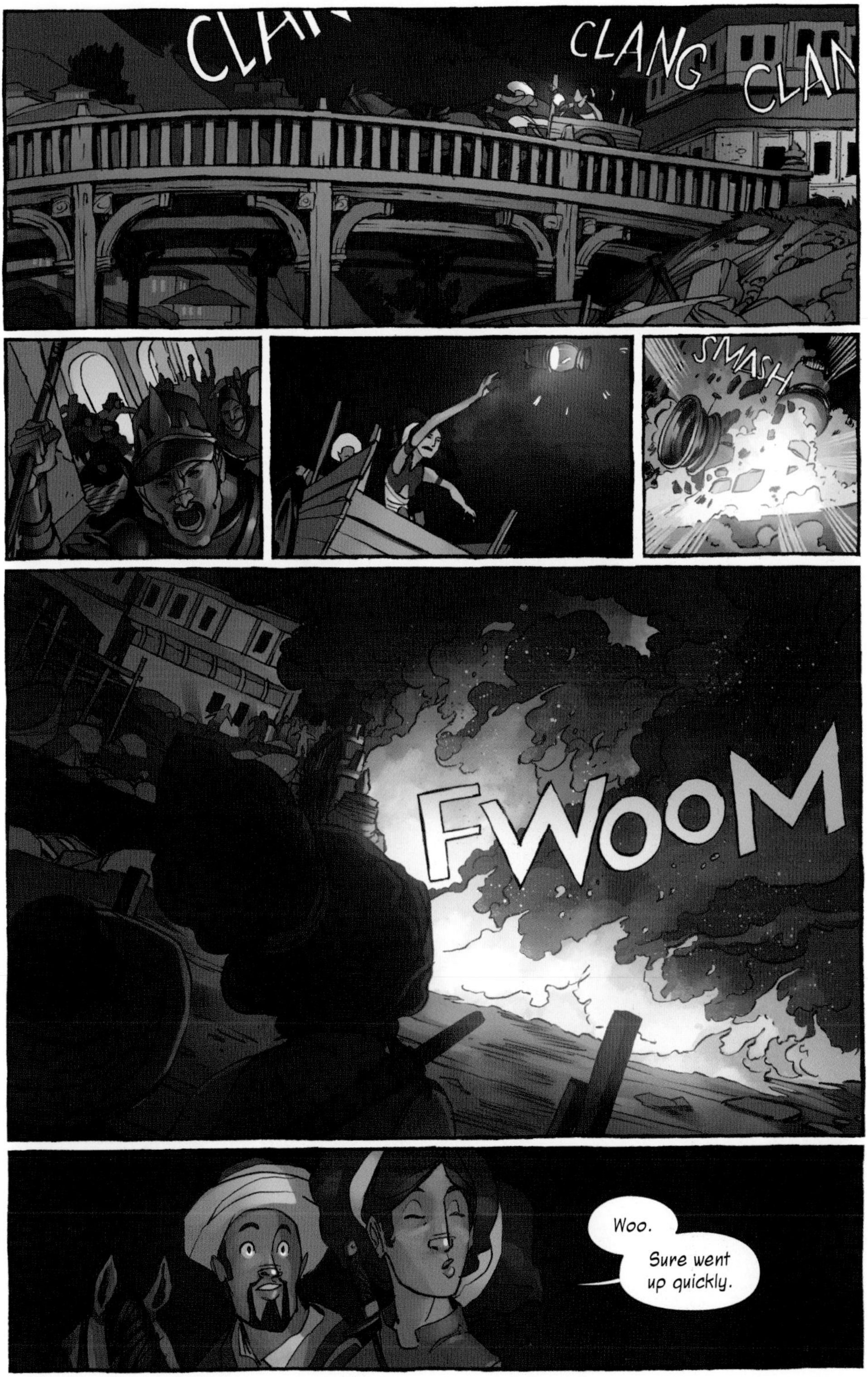
CLAN
CLANG
CLAN
SMASH
FWOOM
Woo.
Sure went up quickly.

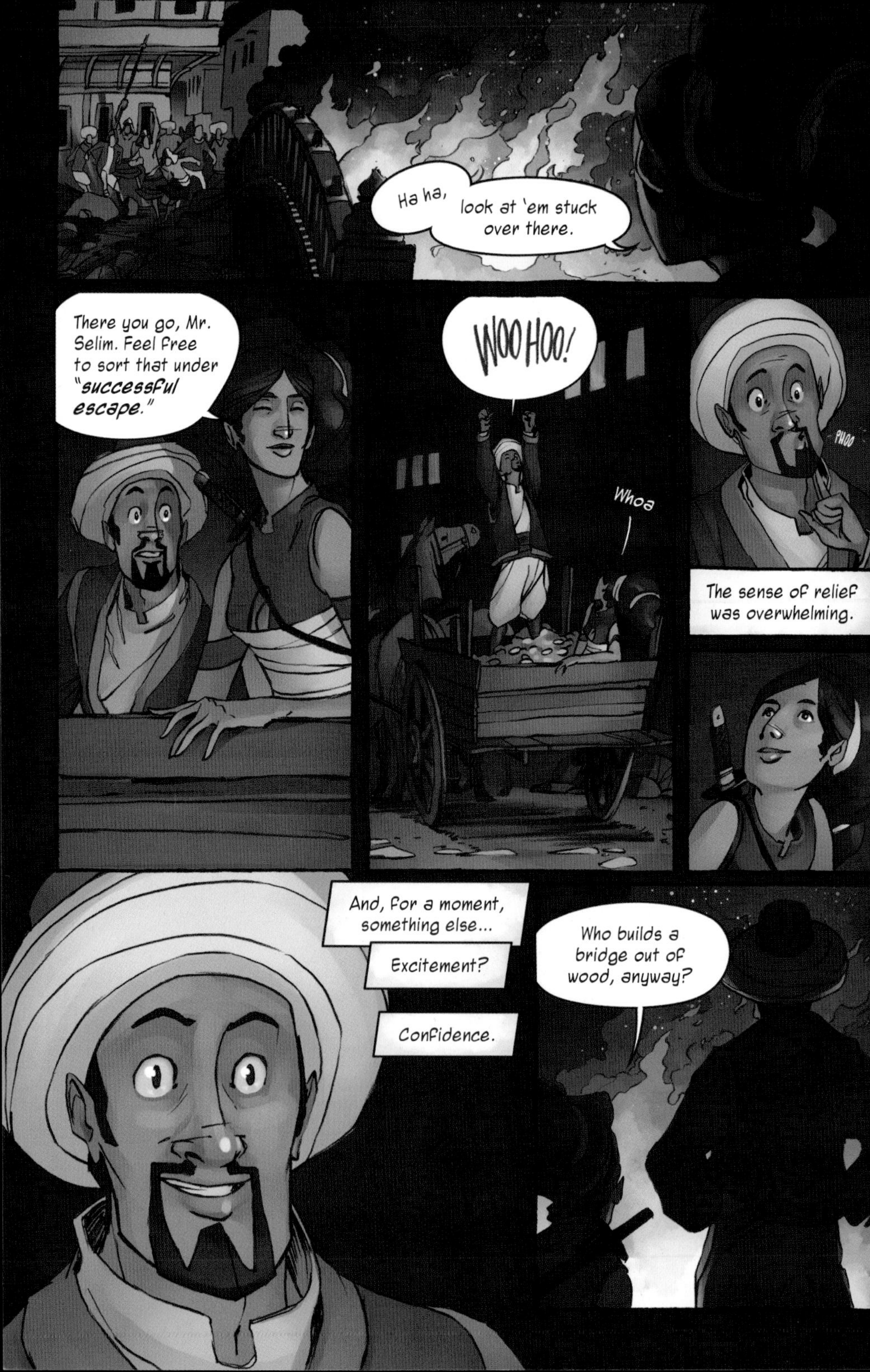
Ha ha, look at 'em stuck over there.
There you go, Mr. Selim. Feel free to sort that under "successful escape."
WOO HOO!
Whoa
PHOO
The sense of relief was overwhelming.
And, for a moment, something else...
Excitement?
Confidence.
Who builds a bridge out of wood, anyway?

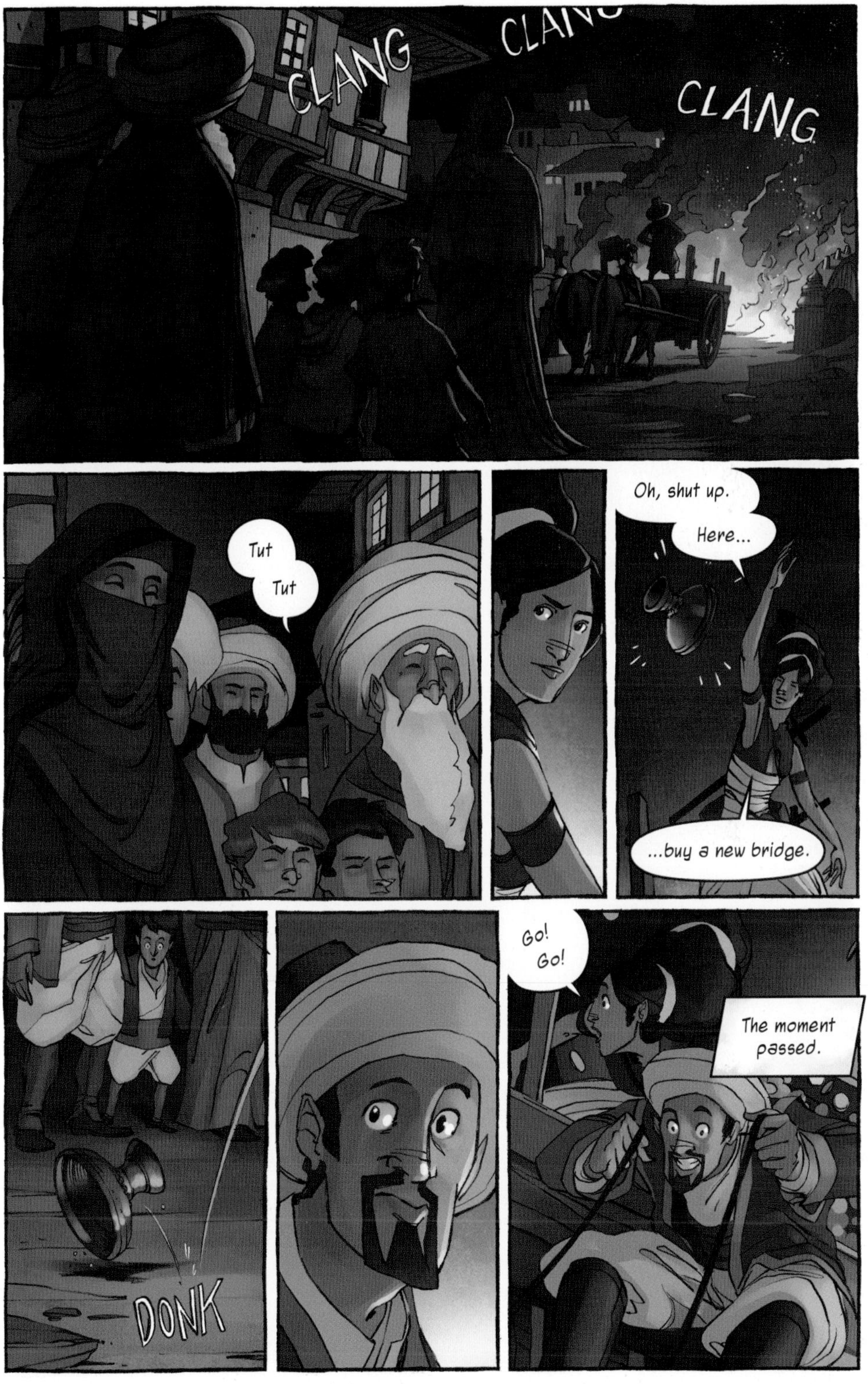
CLANG
CLANG
CLANG
Tut
Tut
Oh, shut up.
Here...
...buy a new bridge.
DONK
Go!
Go!
The moment passed.

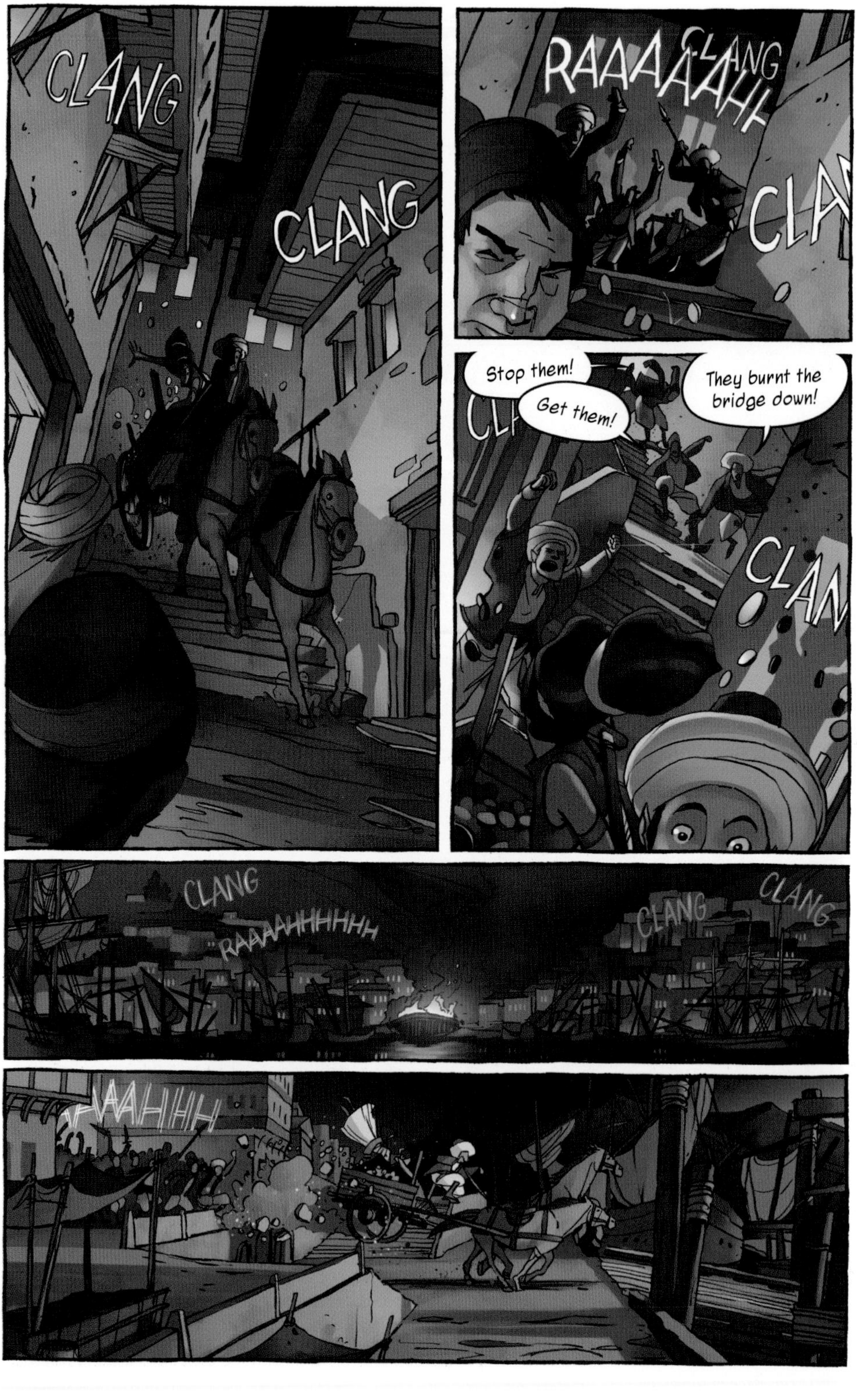
CLANG
CLANG
RAAAAAHH
CLANG
CLA
Stop them!
Get them!
They burnt the bridge down!
CLA
CLAN
CLANG
RAAAAHHHHHH
CLANG
CLANG
AAAHHHH

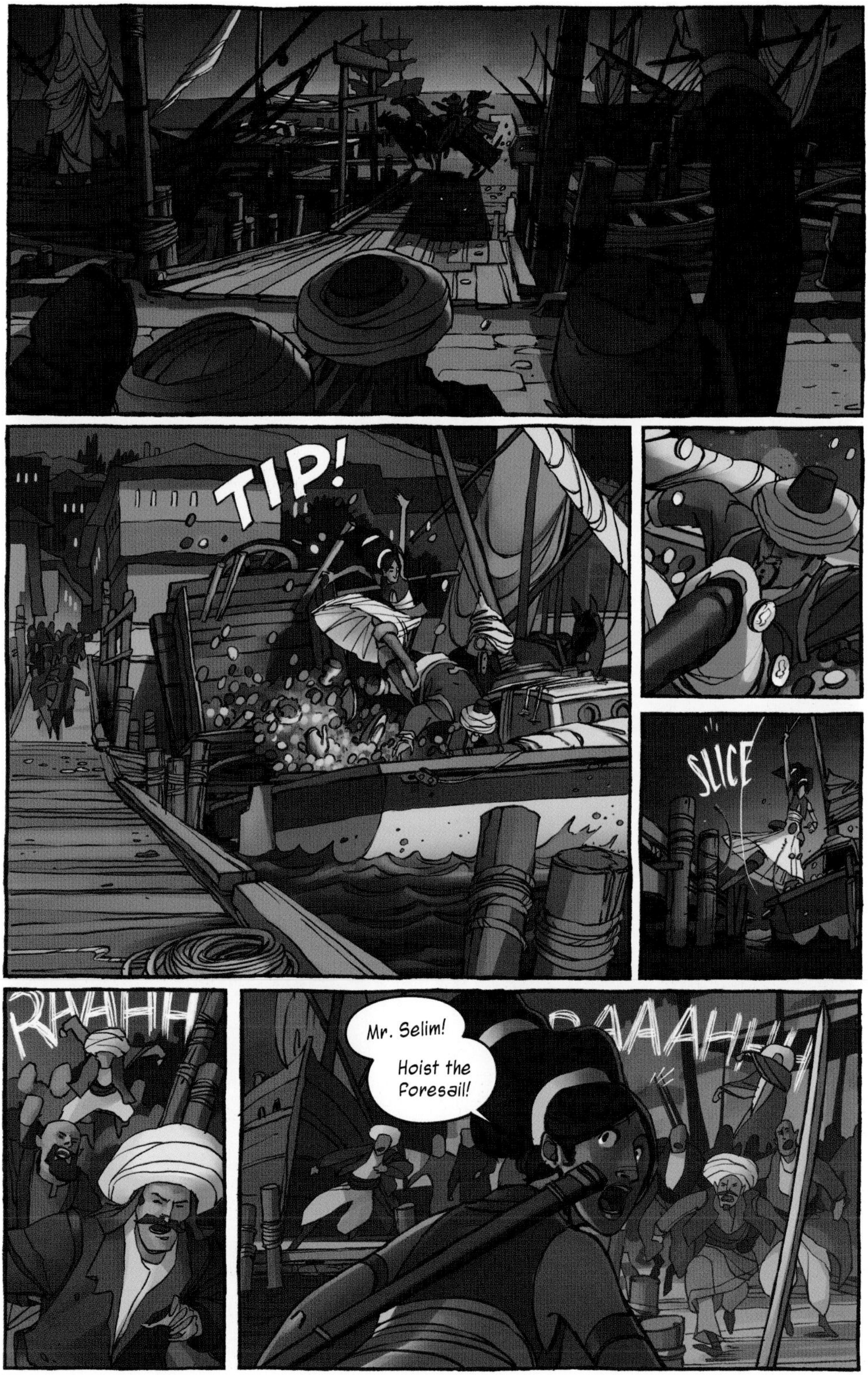
TIP!
SLICE
RHAHH
Mr. Selim!
Hoist the Foresail!

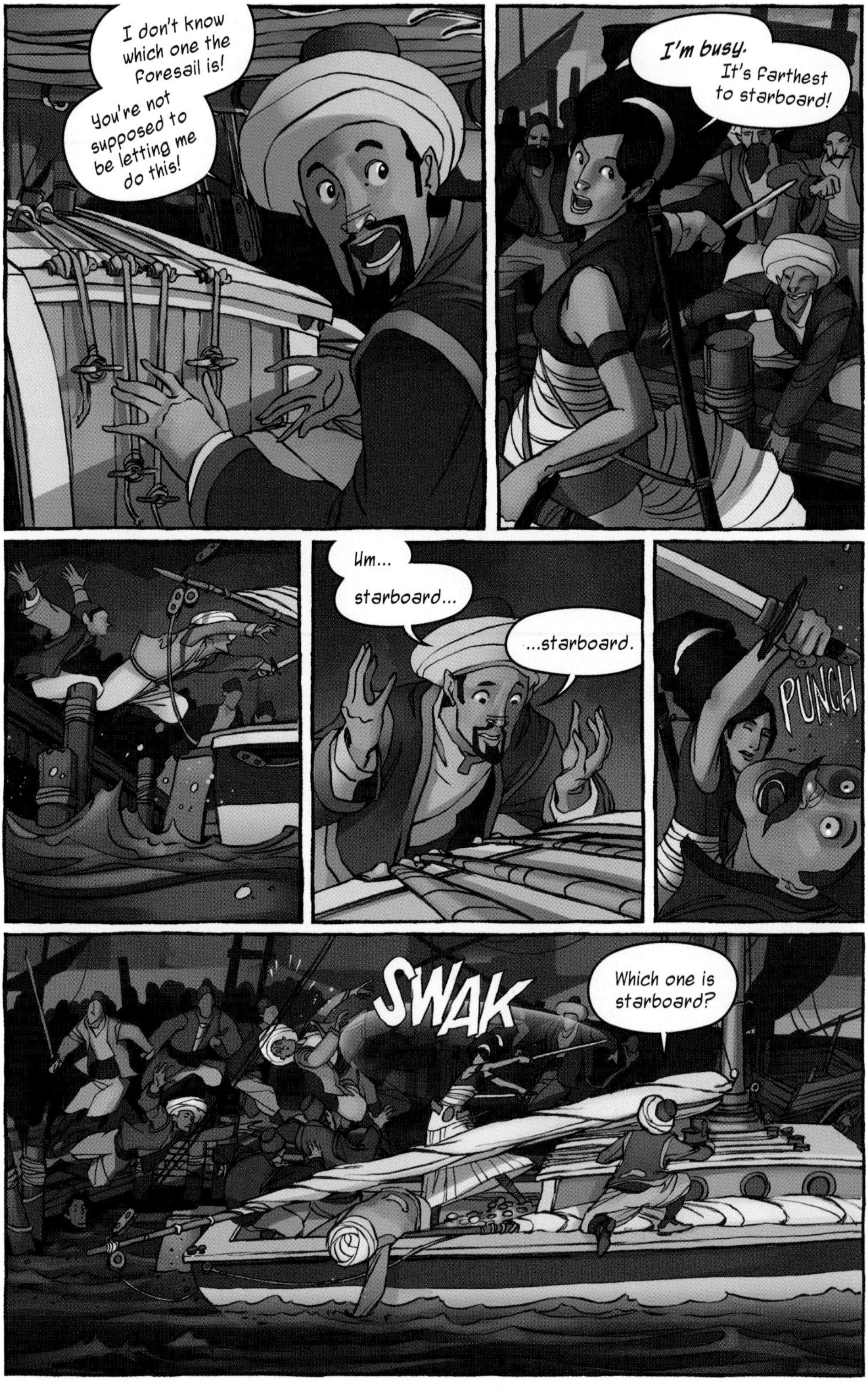
I don't know which one the foresail is!
You're not supposed to be letting me do this!
I'm busy.
It's farthest to starboard!
Um...
starboard...
...starboard.
PUNCH
SWAK
Which one is starboard?

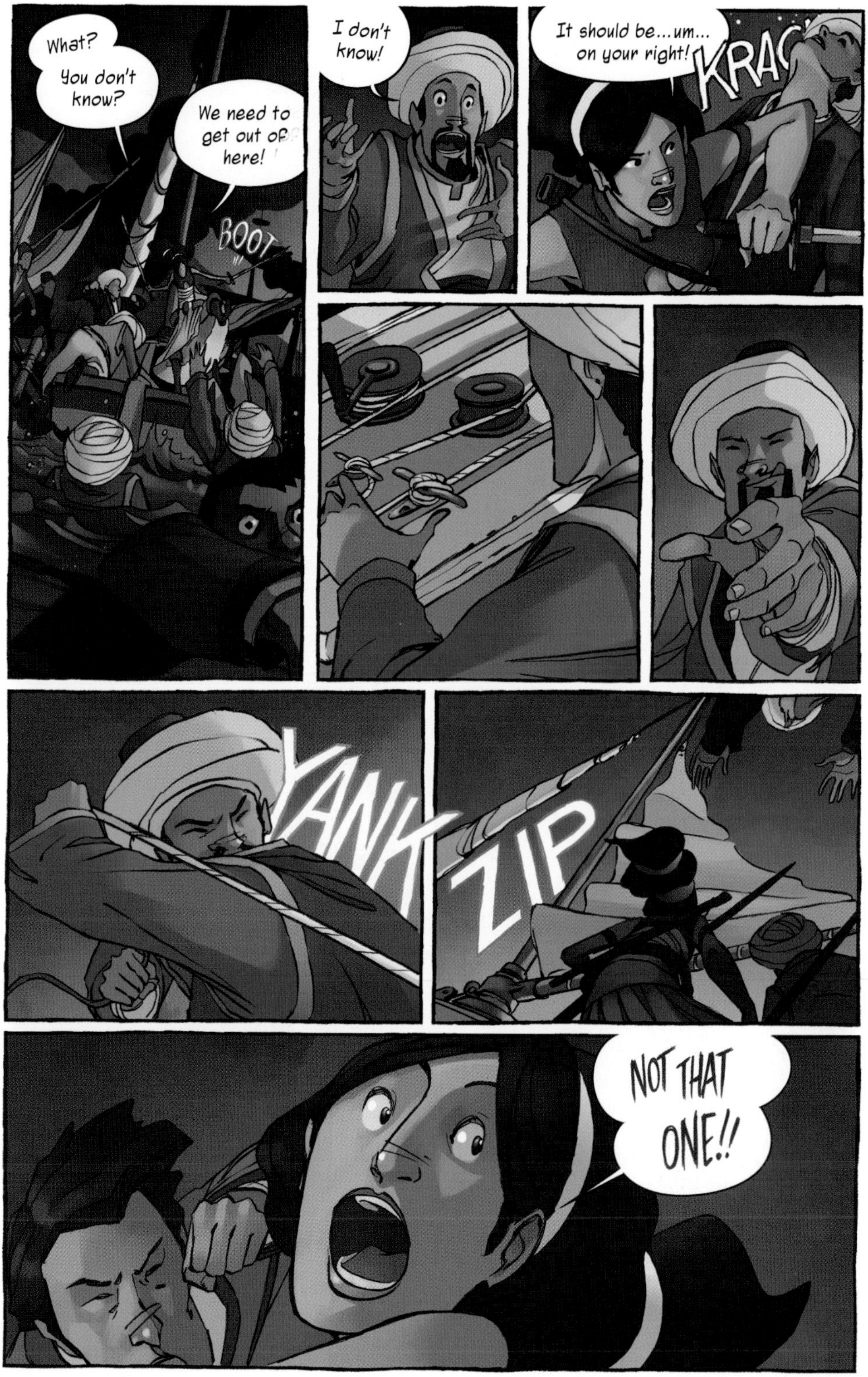
What?
You don't know?
We need to get out of here!
BOOT
I don't know!
It should be...um... on your right!
KRAC
YANK
ZIP
NOT THAT ONE!!

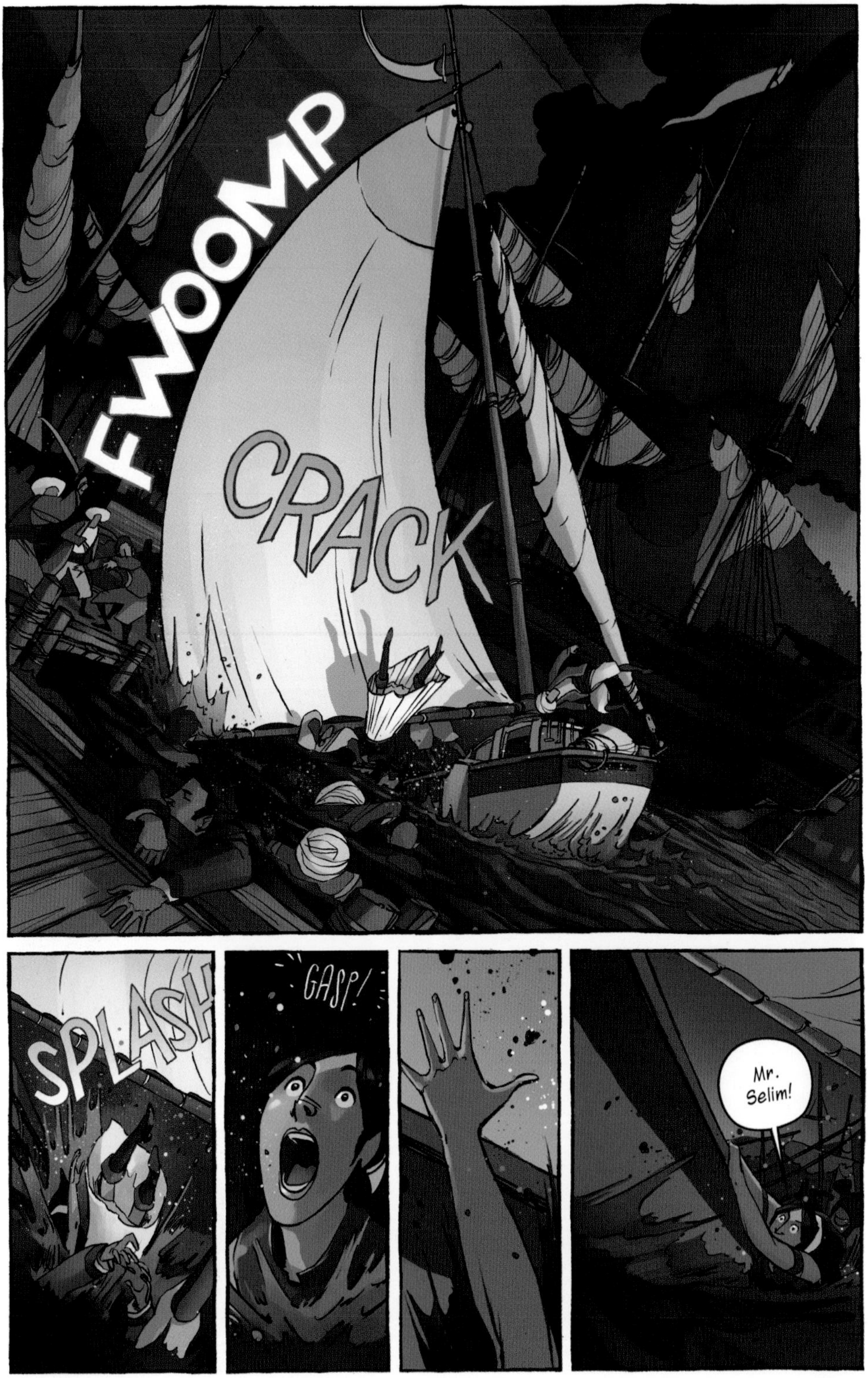
FWOOMP
CRACK
SPLASH
GASP!
Mr. Selim!

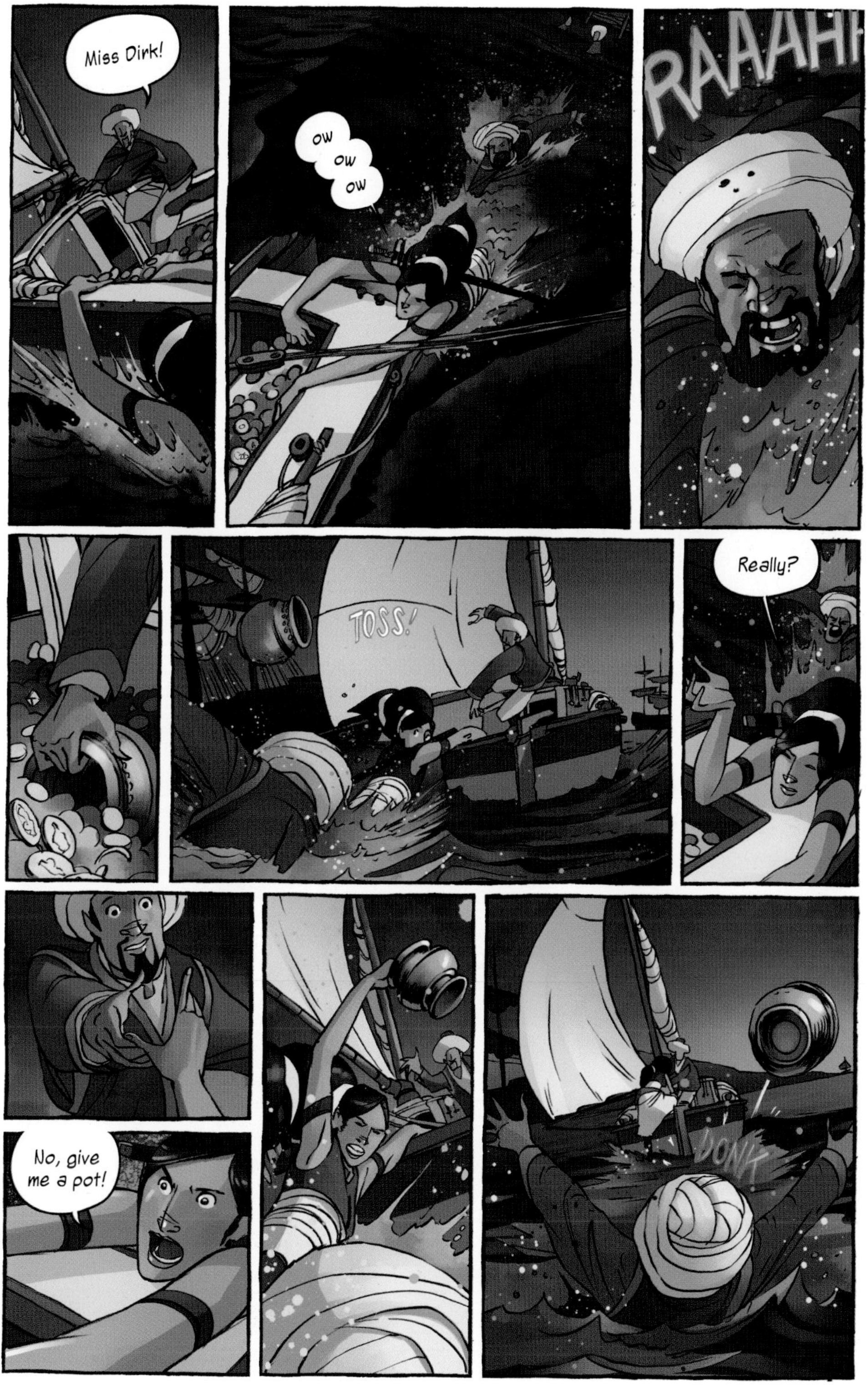

Miss Dirk!
ow
ow
ow
RAAAHH
TOSS!
Really?
No, give me a pot!
DONK

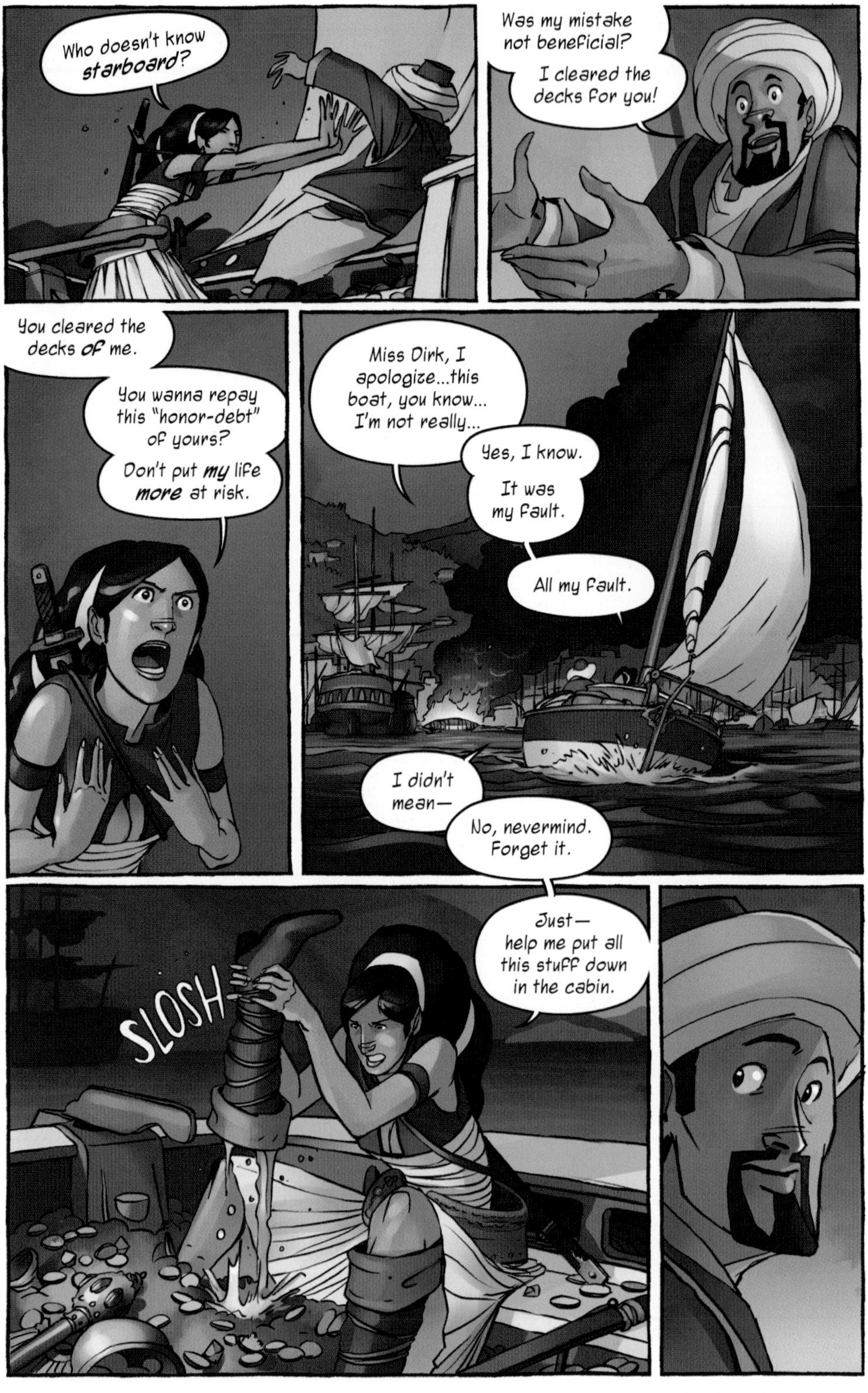
Who doesn't know **starboard**?
Was my mistake not beneficial?
I cleared the decks for you!
You cleared the decks ***of*** me.
You wanna repay this "honor-debt" of yours?
Don't put ***my*** life ***more*** at risk.
Miss Dirk, I apologize...this boat, you know... I'm not really...
Yes, I know.
It was my fault.
All my fault.
I didn't mean—
No, nevermind. Forget it.
Just— help me put all this stuff down in the cabin.
SLOSH

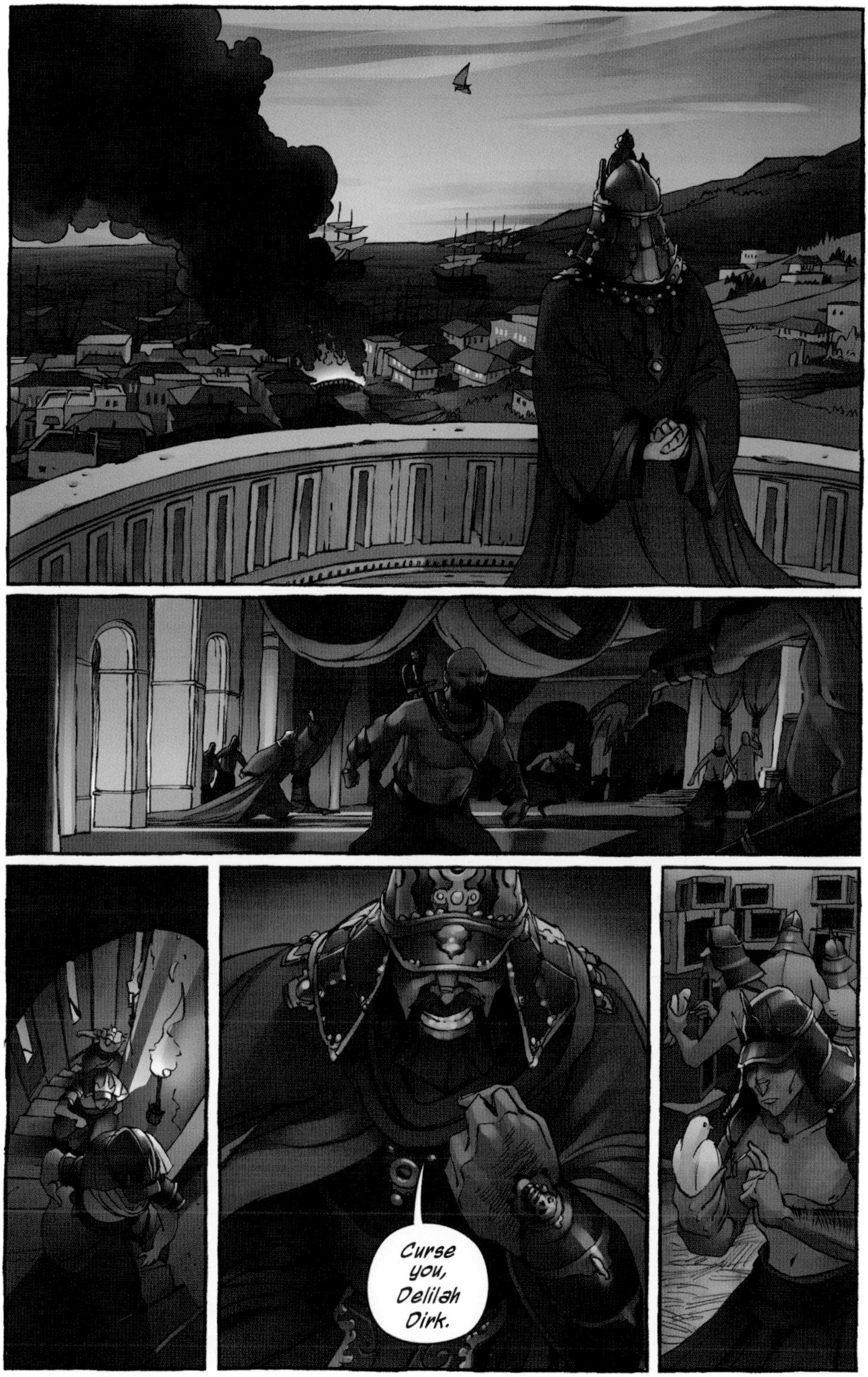
Curse you, Delilah Dirk.

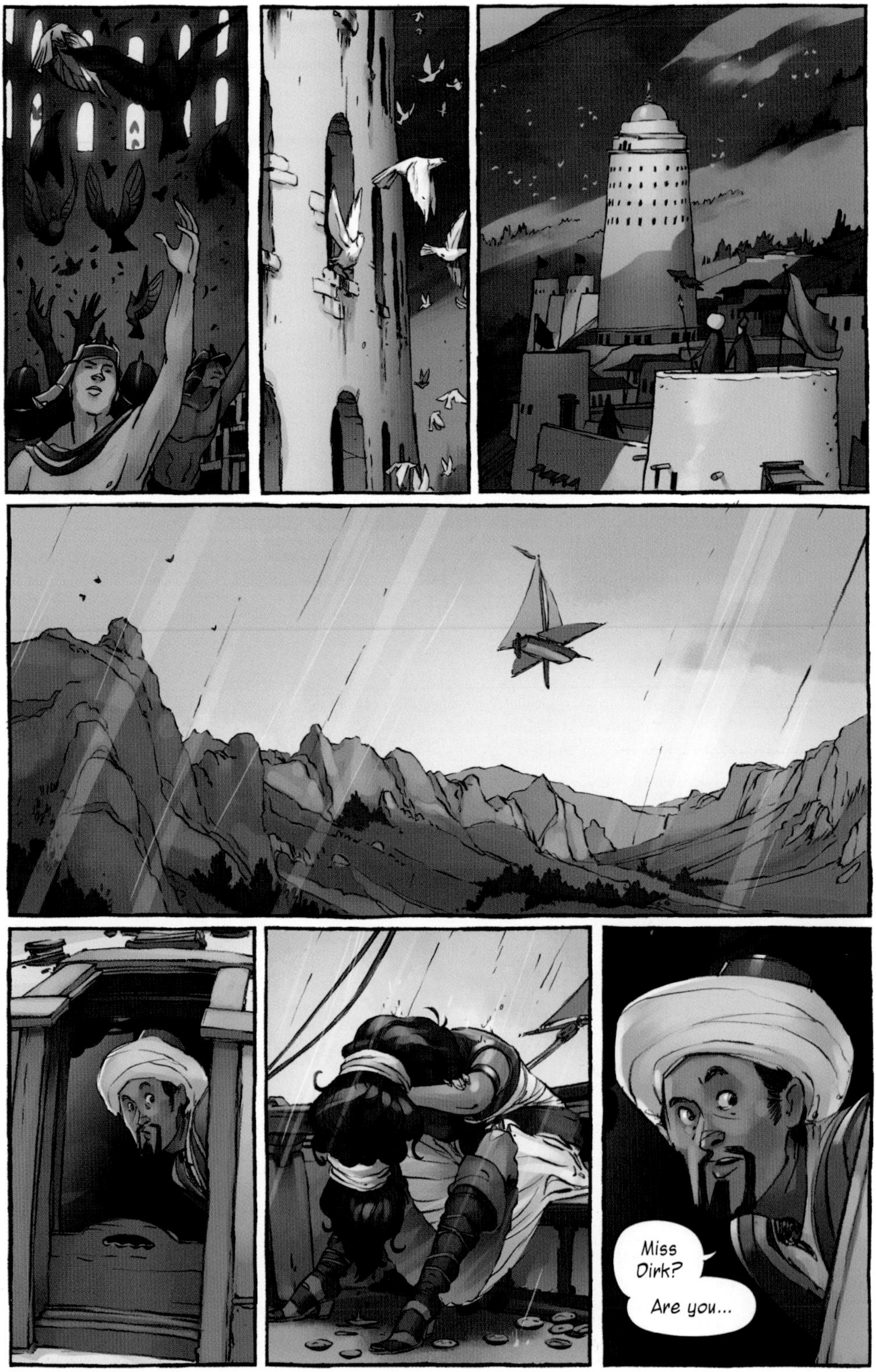
Miss Dirk?
Are you...

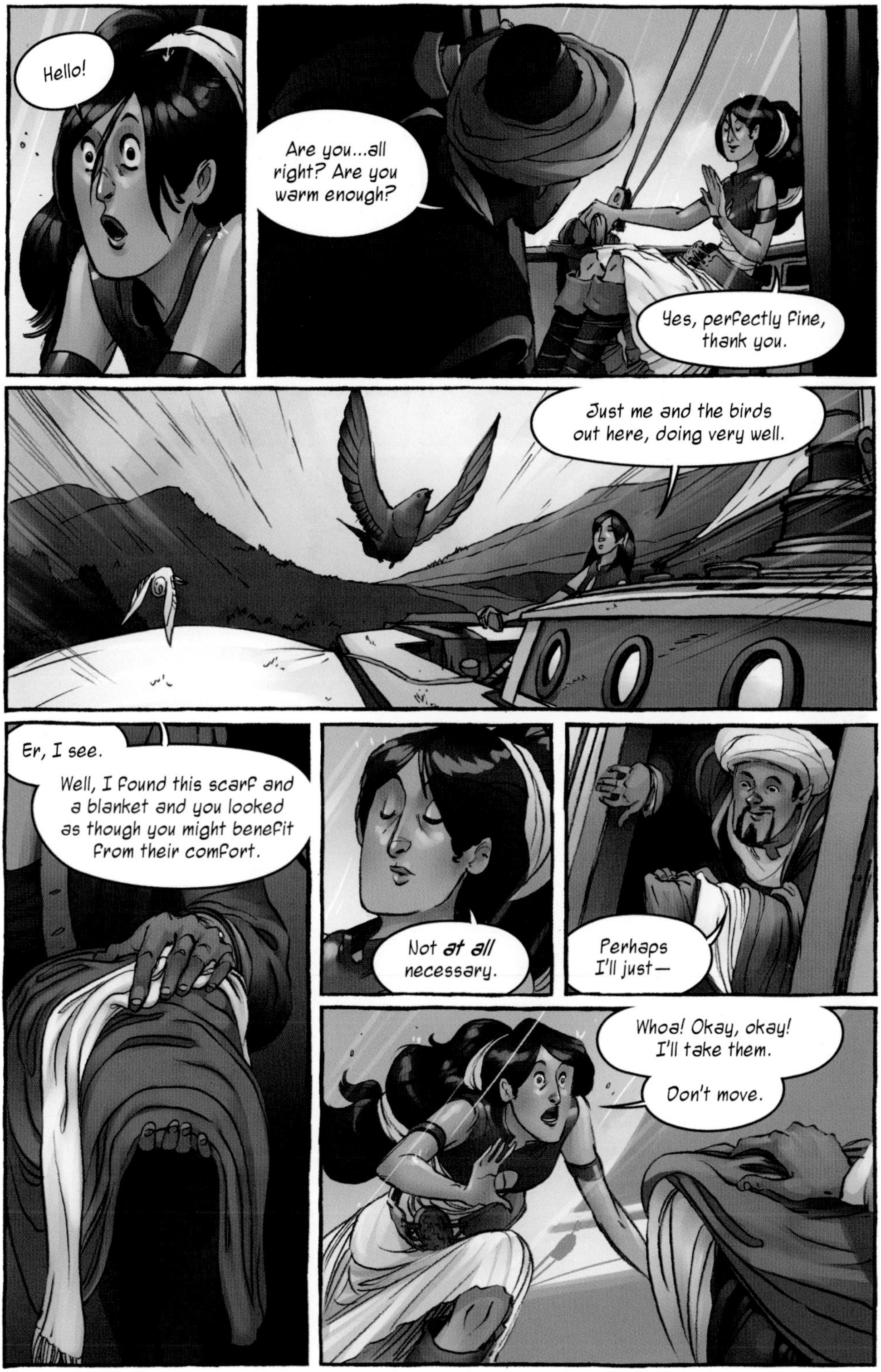
Hello!
Are you...all right? Are you warm enough?
Yes, perfectly fine, thank you.
Just me and the birds out here, doing very well.
Er, I see.
Well, I found this scarf and a blanket and you looked as though you might benefit from their comfort.
Not *at all* necessary.
Perhaps I'll just—
Whoa! Okay, okay! I'll take them.
Don't move.

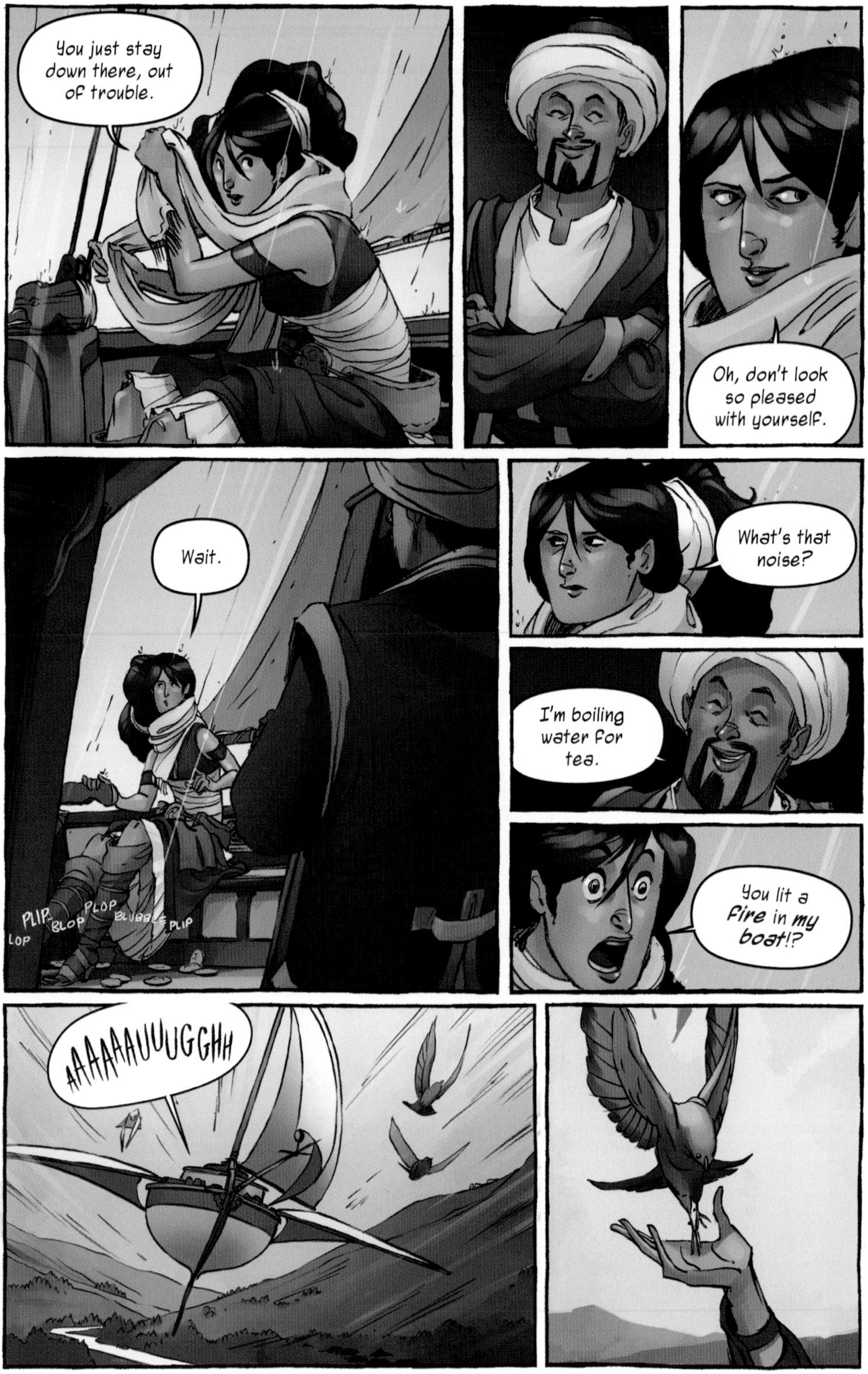
You just stay down there, out of trouble.
Oh, don't look so pleased with yourself.
Wait.
PLIP
LOP
BLOP
PLOP
BLUBBLE
PLIP
What's that noise?
I'm boiling water for tea.
You lit a fire in my boat!?
AAAAAUUUGGHH

CHAPTER 3

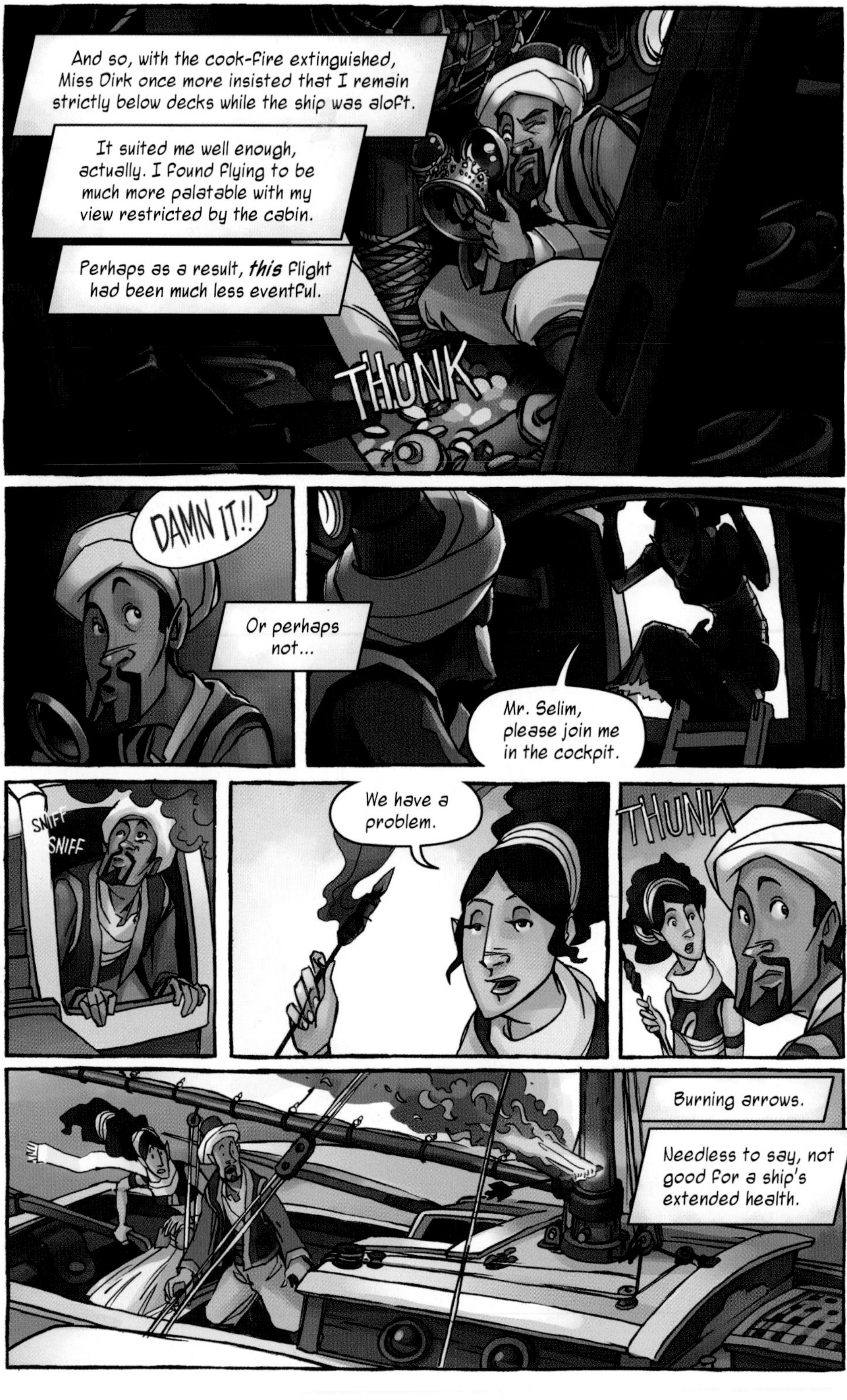

And so, with the cook-fire extinguished, Miss Dirk once more insisted that I remain strictly below decks while the ship was aloft.
It suited me well enough, actually. I found flying to be much more palatable with my view restricted by the cabin.
Perhaps as a result, *this* flight had been much less eventful.
THUNK
DAMN IT!!
Or perhaps not...
Mr. Selim, please join me in the cockpit.
SNIFF
SNIFF
We have a problem.
THUNK
Burning arrows.
Needless to say, not good for a ship's extended health.

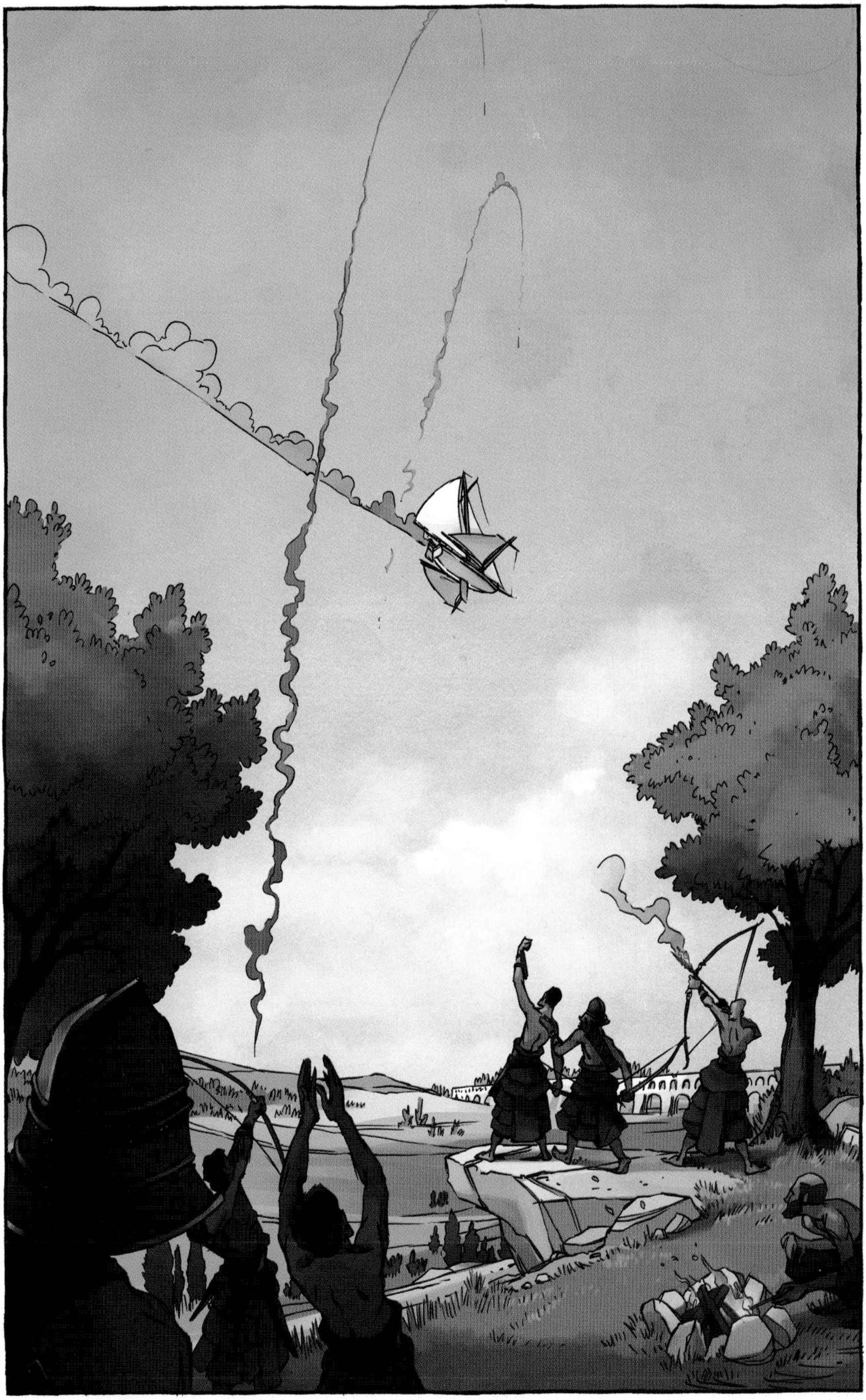

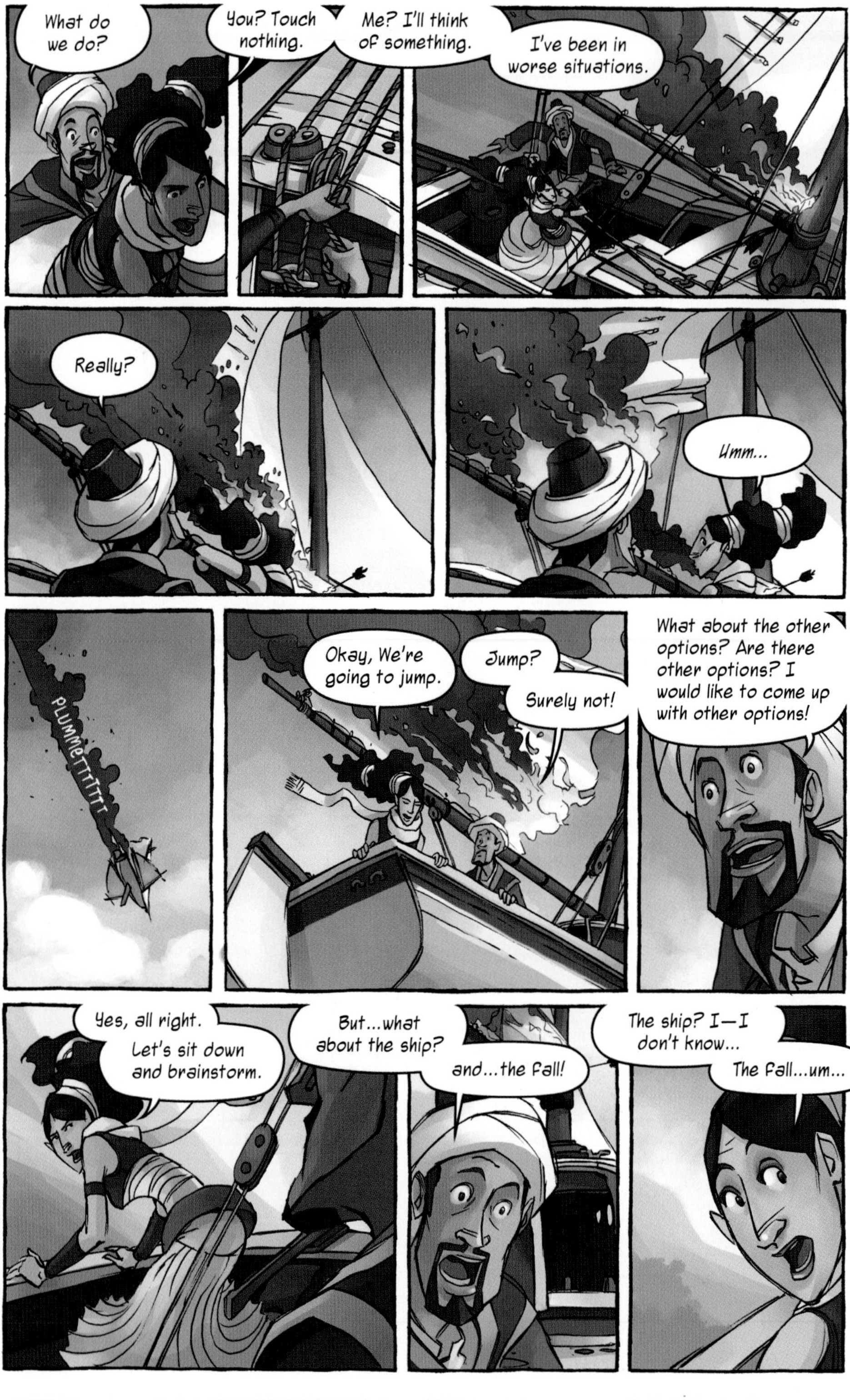
What do we do?
You? Touch nothing.
Me? I'll think of something.
I've been in worse situations.
Really?
Umm...
PLUMMETTTTTT
Okay, We're going to jump.
Jump?
Surely not!
What about the other options? Are there other options? I would like to come up with other options!
Yes, all right.
Let's sit down and brainstorm.
But...what about the ship?
and...the fall!
The ship? I—I don't know...
The fall...um...

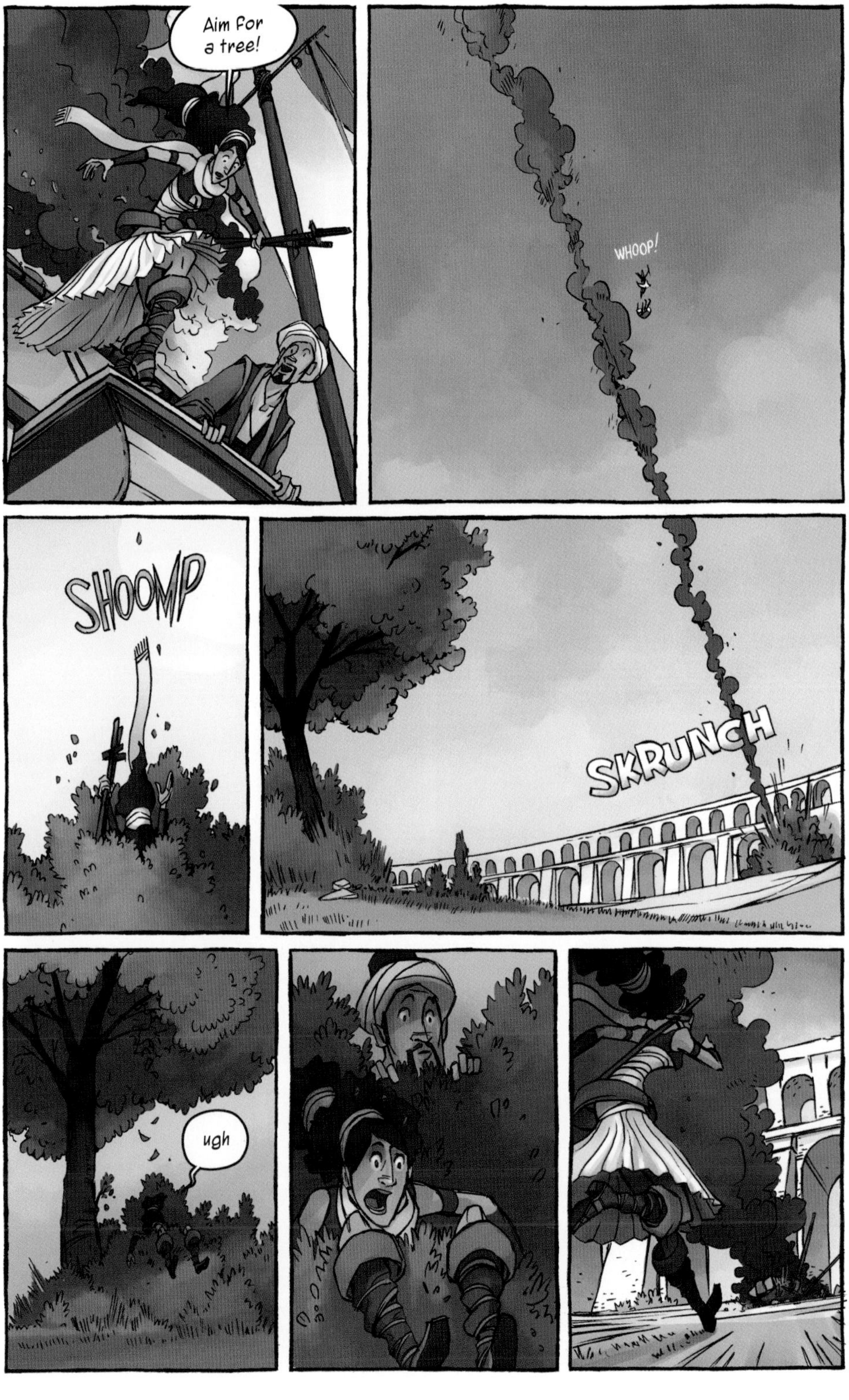
Aim for a tree!
WHOOP!
SHOOMP
SKRUNCH
ugh

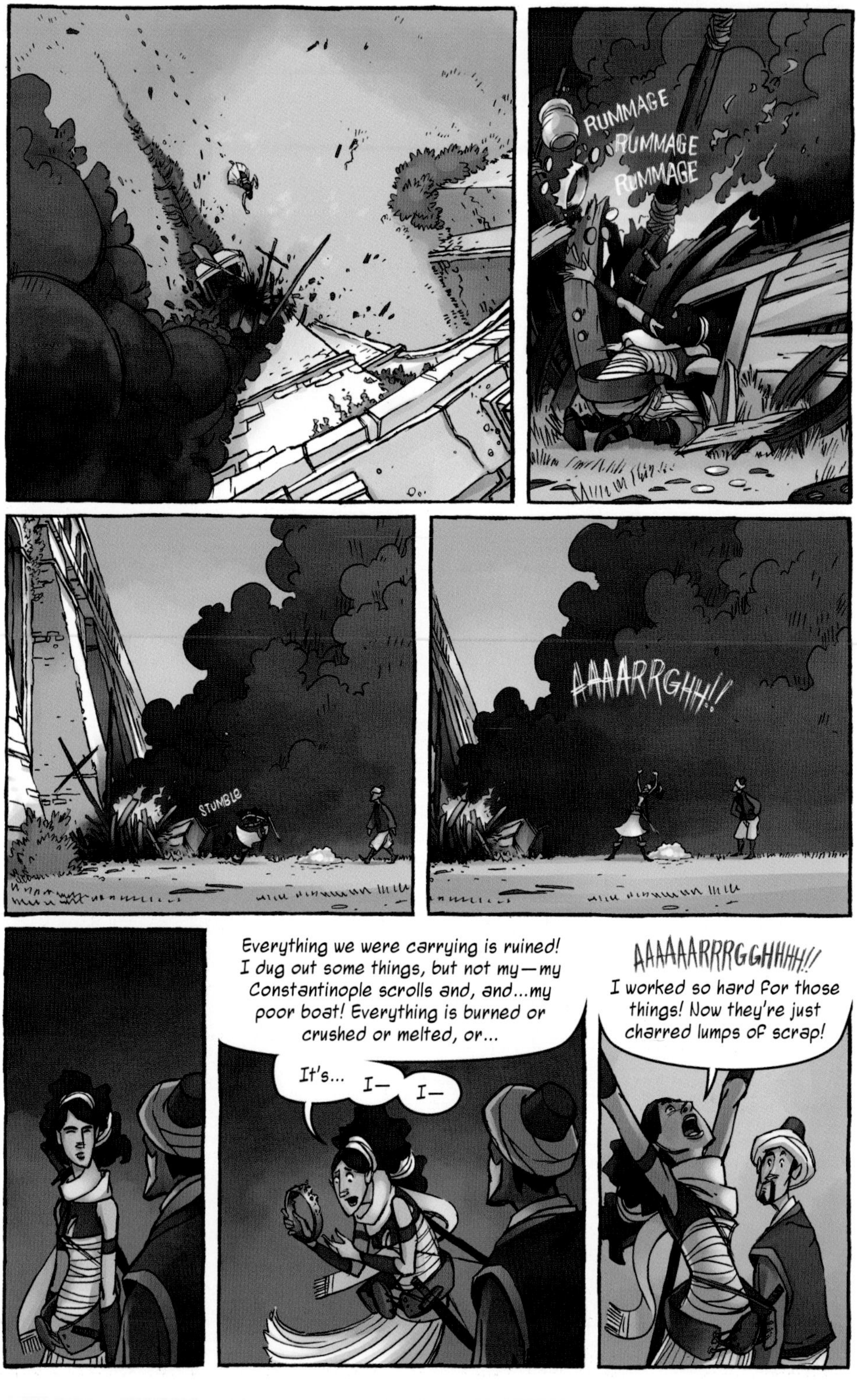
RUMMAGE
RUMMAGE
RUMMAGE
STUMBLE
AAAARRGHH!!
Everything we were carrying is ruined! I dug out some things, but not my—my Constantinople scrolls and, and...my poor boat! Everything is burned or crushed or melted, or...
It's...
I—
I—
AAAAAARRRGGHHHH!!
I worked so hard for those things! Now they're just charred lumps of scrap!

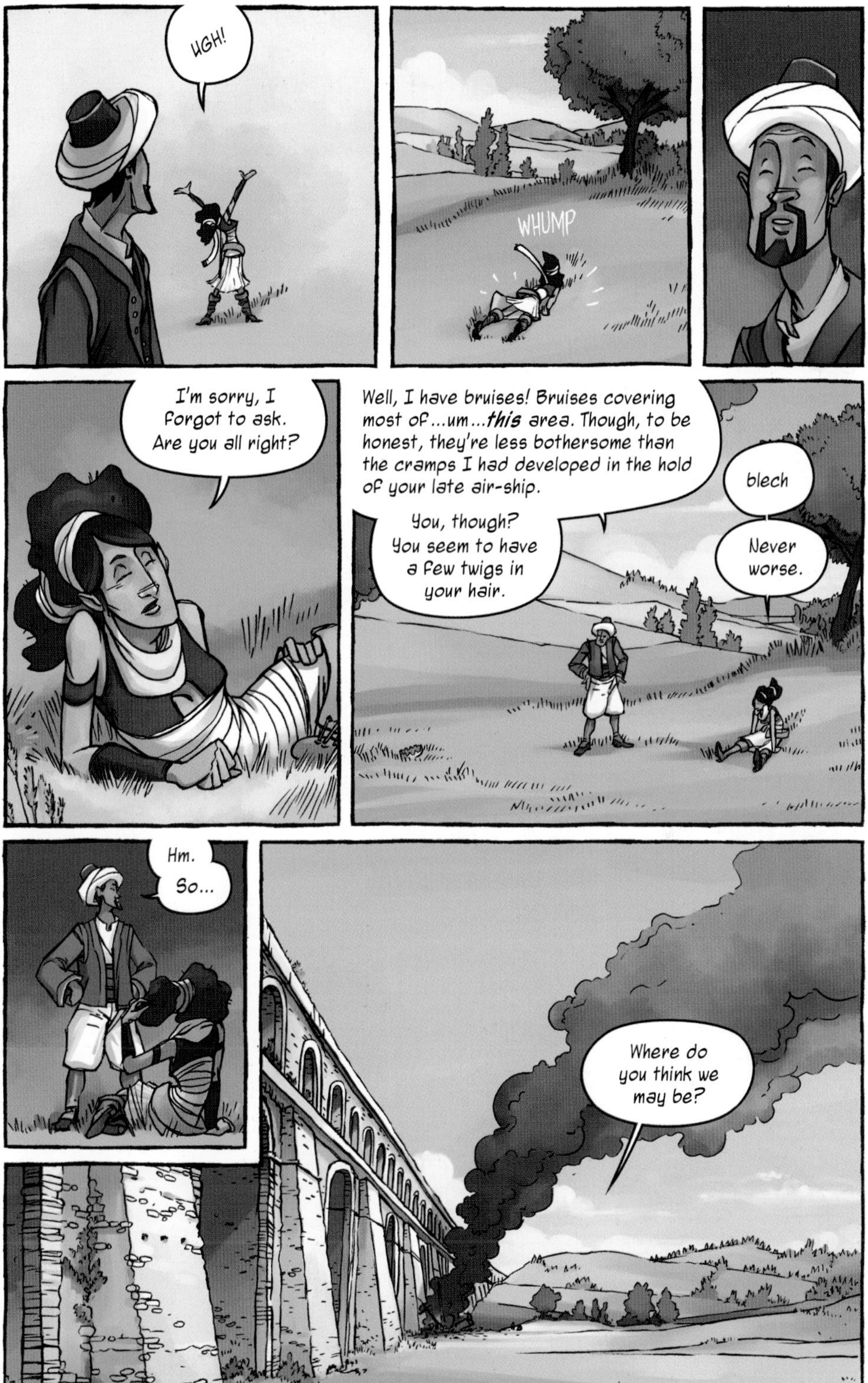
UGH!
WHUMP
I'm sorry, I forgot to ask. Are you all right?
Well, I have bruises! Bruises covering most of...um...*this* area. Though, to be honest, they're less bothersome than the cramps I had developed in the hold of your late air-ship.
You, though? You seem to have a few twigs in your hair.
blech
Never worse.
Hm.
So...
Where do you think we may be?

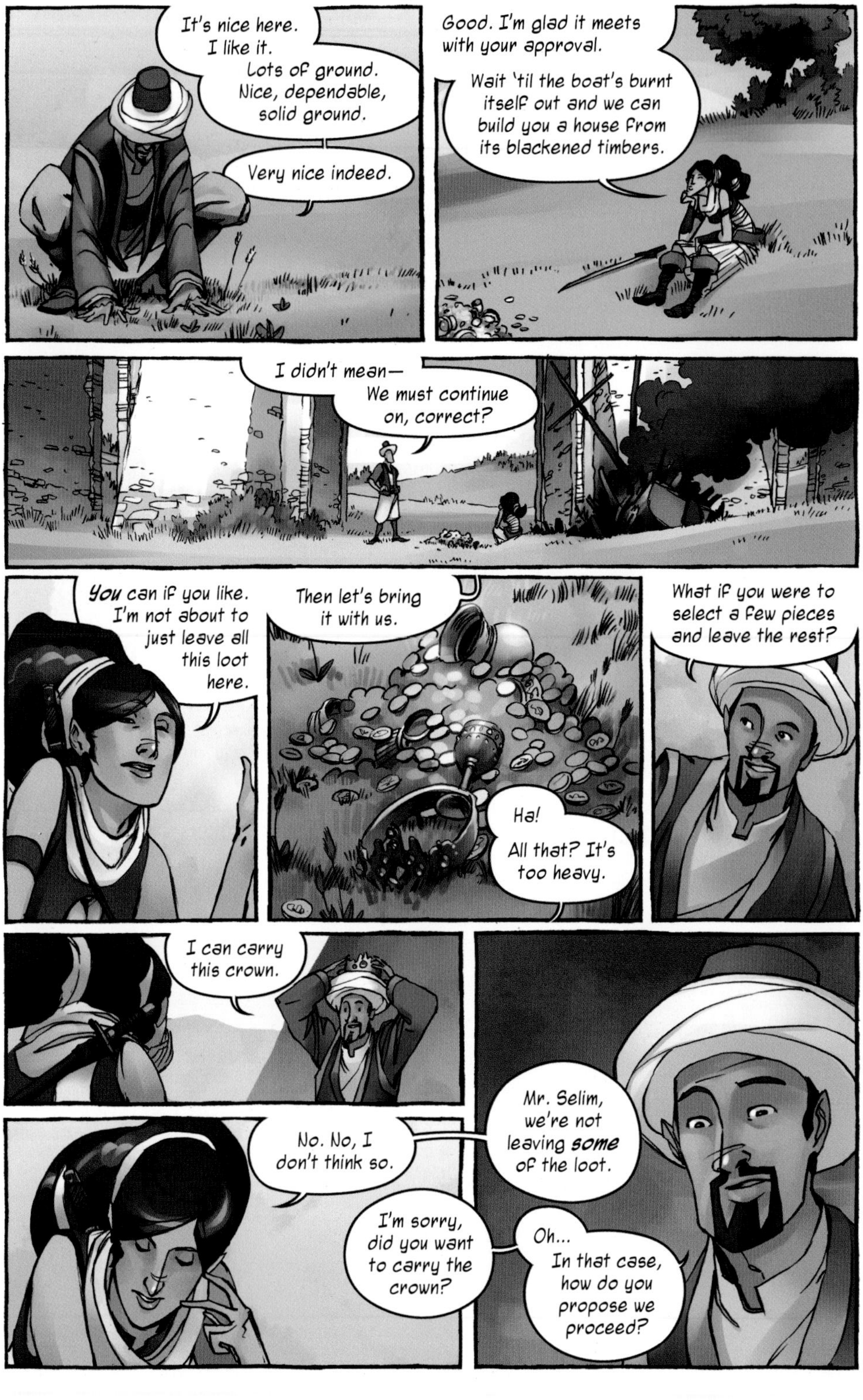

It's nice here. I like it.
Lots of ground. Nice, dependable, solid ground.
Very nice indeed.
Good. I'm glad it meets with your approval.
Wait 'til the boat's burnt itself out and we can build you a house from its blackened timbers.
I didn't mean—
We must continue on, correct?
You can if you like. I'm not about to just leave all this loot here.
Then let's bring it with us.
Ha!
All that? It's too heavy.
What if you were to select a few pieces and leave the rest?
I can carry this crown.
No. No, I don't think so.
Mr. Selim, we're not leaving some of the loot.
I'm sorry, did you want to carry the crown?
Oh...
In that case, how do you propose we proceed?

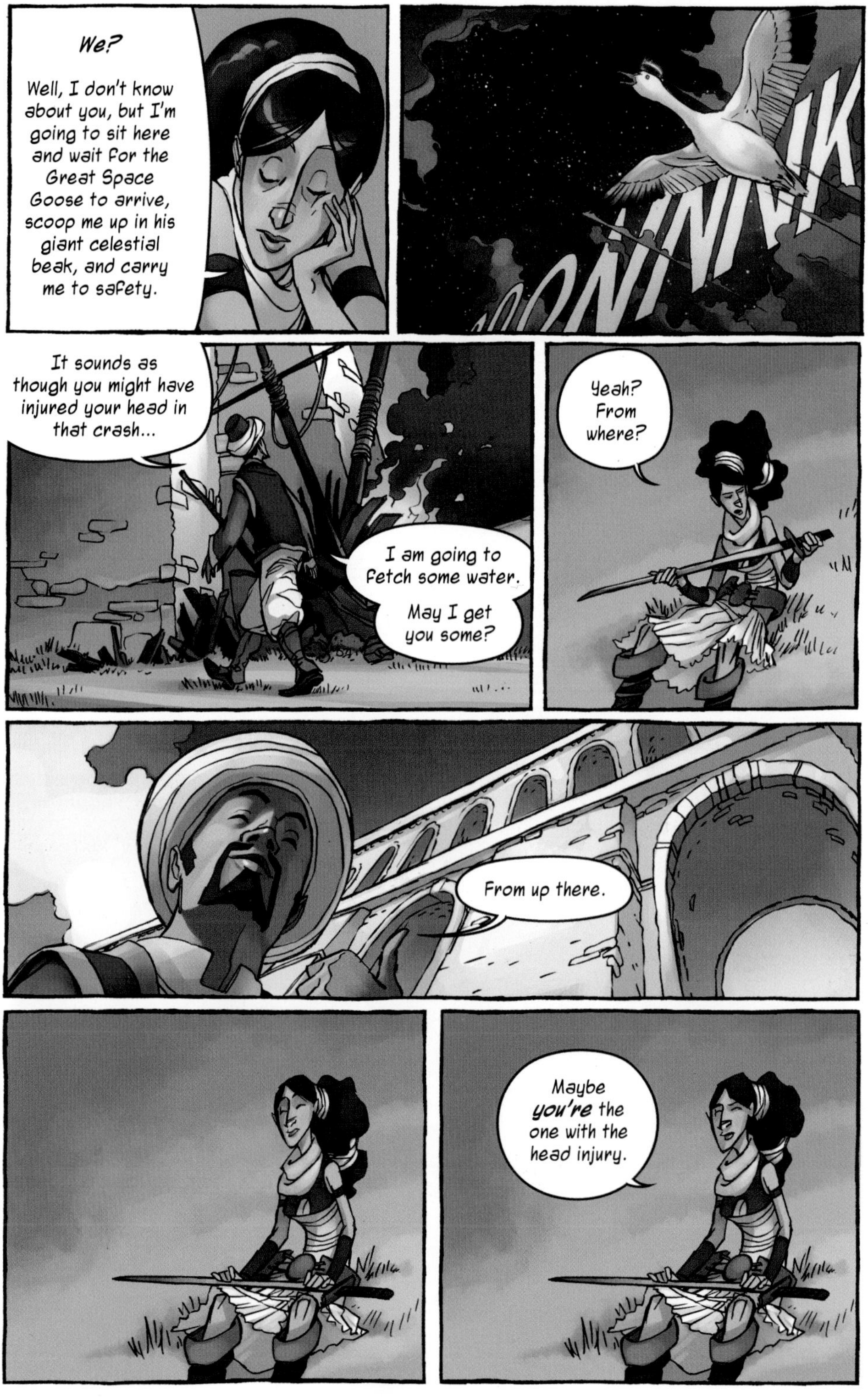
We?
Well, I don't know about you, but I'm going to sit here and wait for the Great Space Goose to arrive, scoop me up in his giant celestial beak, and carry me to safety.
It sounds as though you might have injured your head in that crash...
I am going to fetch some water.
May I get you some?
Yeah? From where?
From up there.
Maybe *you're* the one with the head injury.

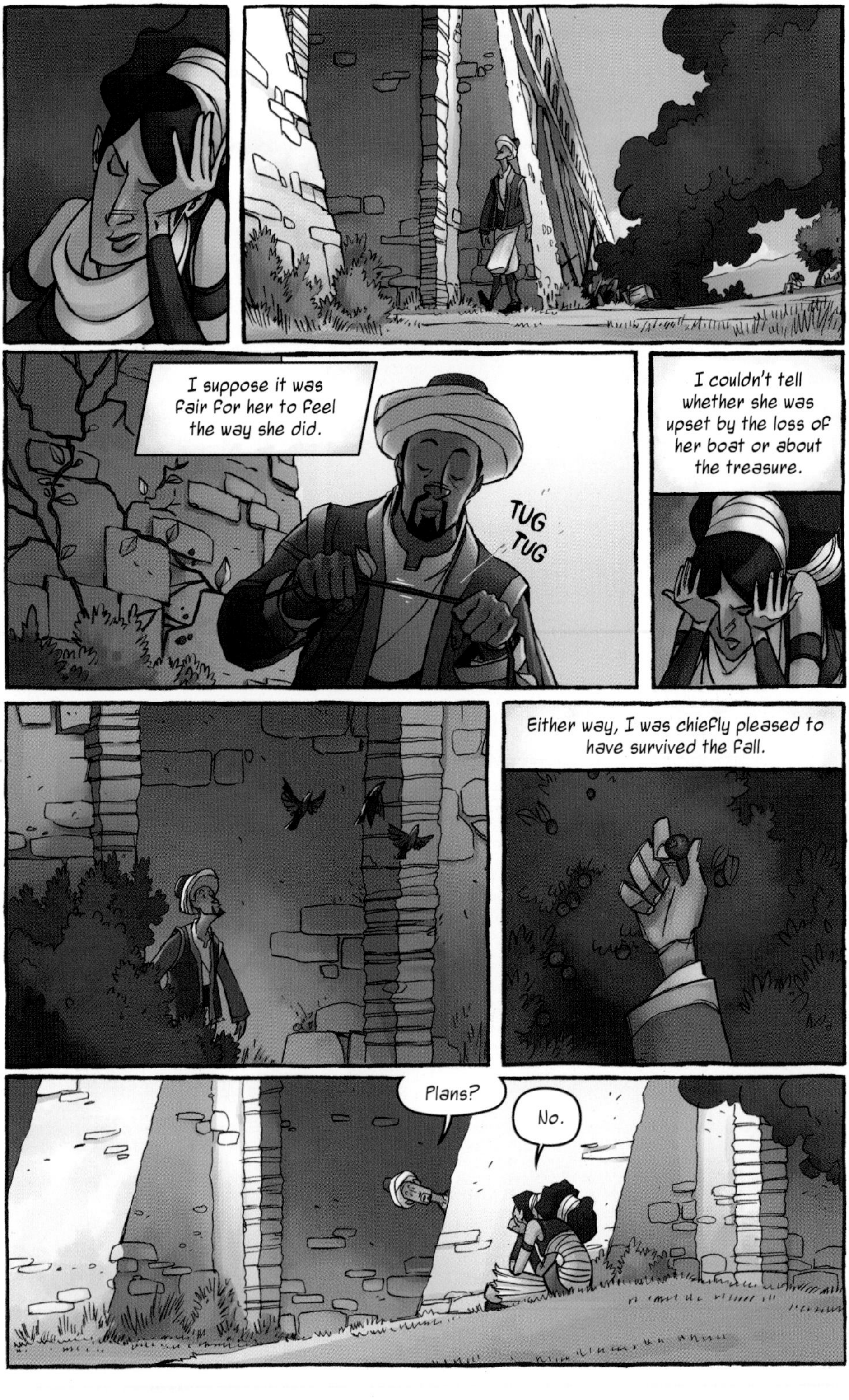
I suppose it was fair for her to feel the way she did.
TUG TUG
I couldn't tell whether she was upset by the loss of her boat or about the treasure.
Either way, I was chiefly pleased to have survived the fall.
Plans?
No.

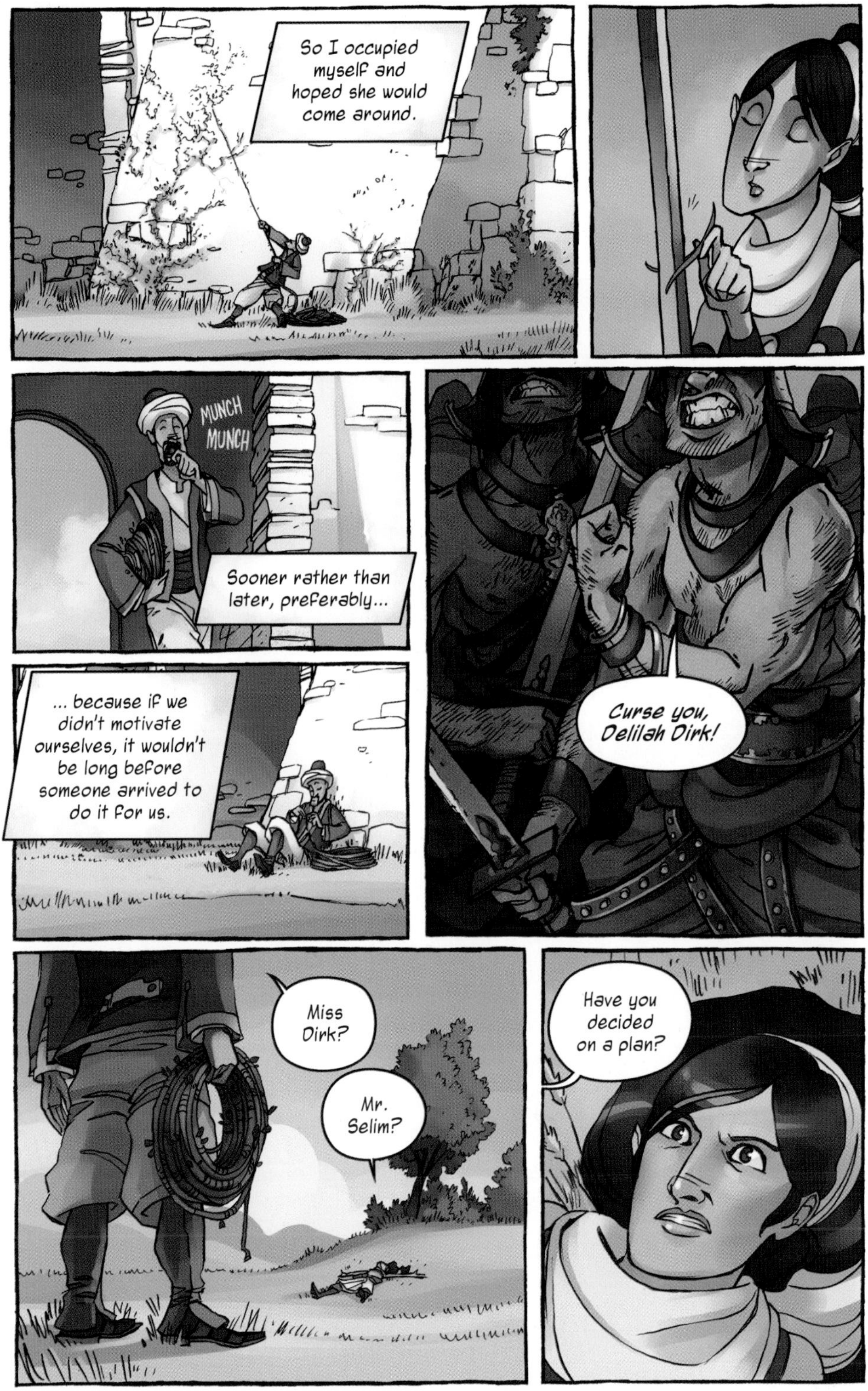

So I occupied myself and hoped she would come around.
MUNCH
MUNCH
Sooner rather than later, preferably...
... because if we didn't motivate ourselves, it wouldn't be long before someone arrived to do it for us.
Curse you, Delilah Dirk!
Miss Dirk?
Mr. Selim?
Have you decided on a plan?

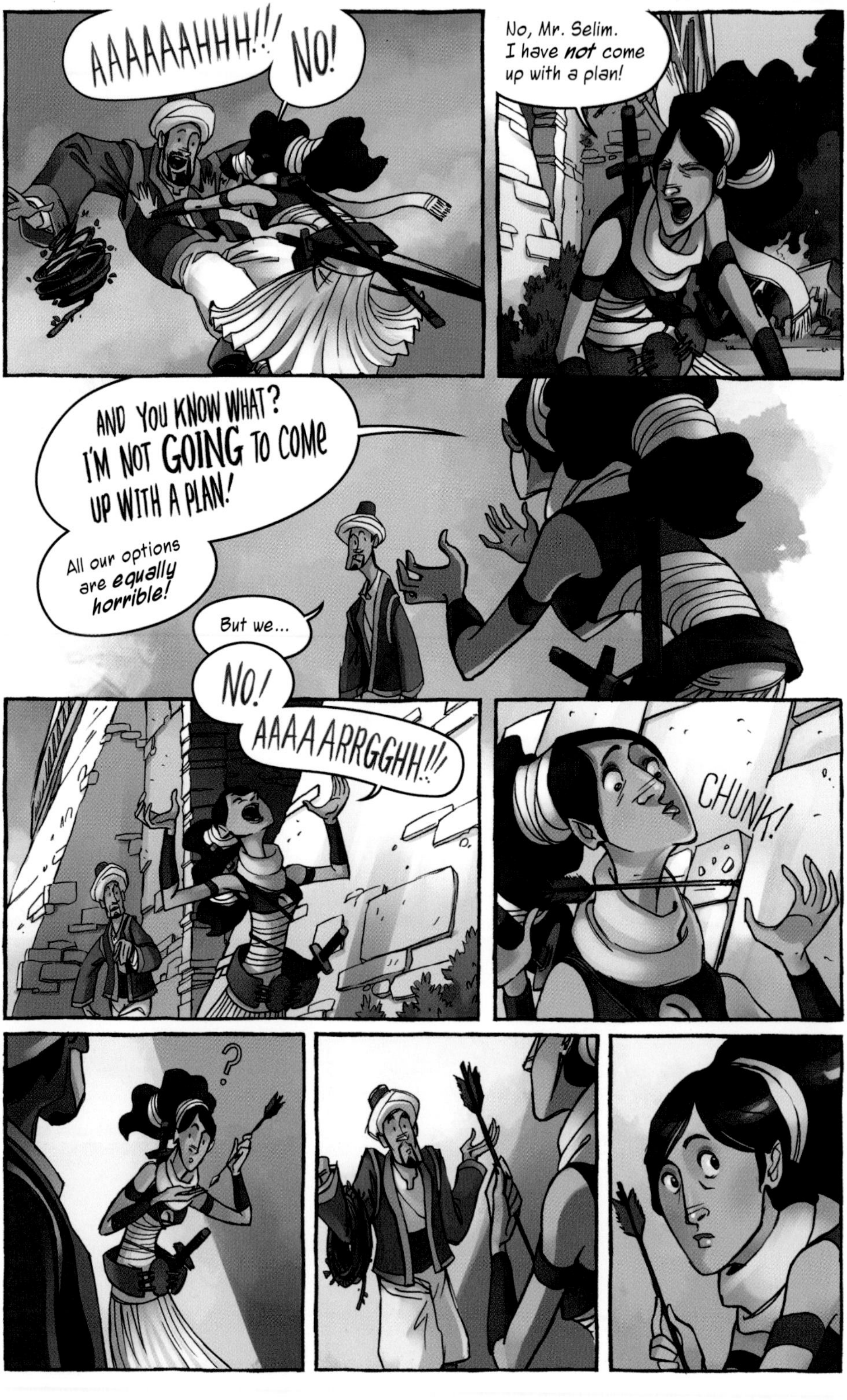
AAAAAAHHH!!!
NO!
No, Mr. Selim. I have *not* come up with a plan!
AND YOU KNOW WHAT? I'M NOT GOING TO COME UP WITH A PLAN!
All our options are *equally horrible!*
But we...
NO!
AAAAARRGGHH!!!
CHUNK!
?

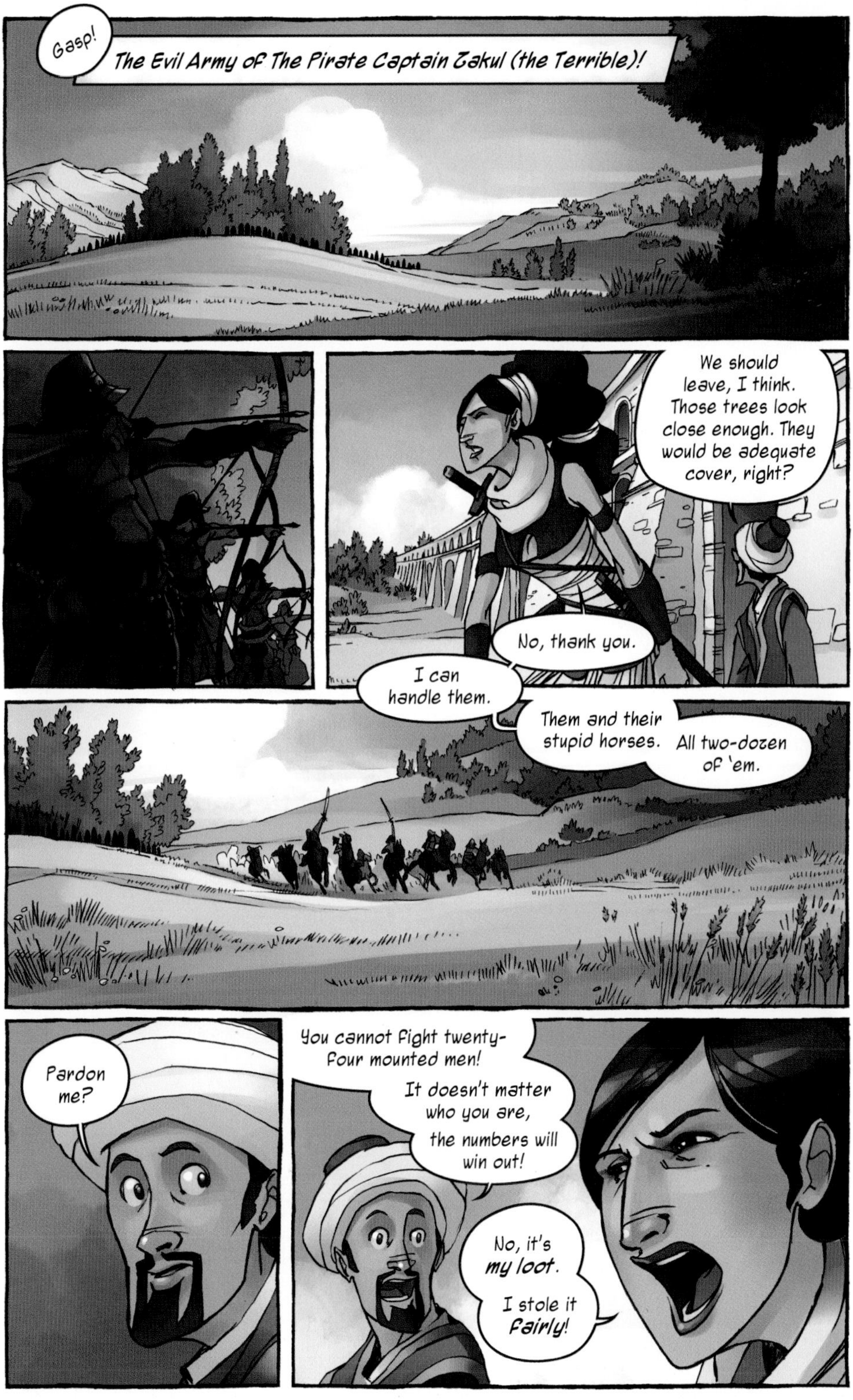
Gasp!
The Evil Army of The Pirate Captain Zakul (the Terrible)!
We should leave, I think. Those trees look close enough. They would be adequate cover, right?
No, thank you.
I can handle them.
Them and their stupid horses.
All two-dozen of 'em.
Pardon me?
You cannot fight twenty-four mounted men!
It doesn't matter who you are,
the numbers will win out!
No, it's my loot.
I stole it fairly!

So unless you have a better idea, I'm going to put up a fight over it.

If...

If we *climb*, we could buy some time...

Maybe figure out a better way to survive...

Because...maybe *you* can fight them and win...

but *I* can't.

Then she looked at me,

And it seemed as if all the fury in the world would leap from her eyes and strangle me where I stood.

But the men on horses were quite threatening, too.

Fine. Rope.

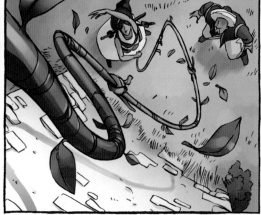

100

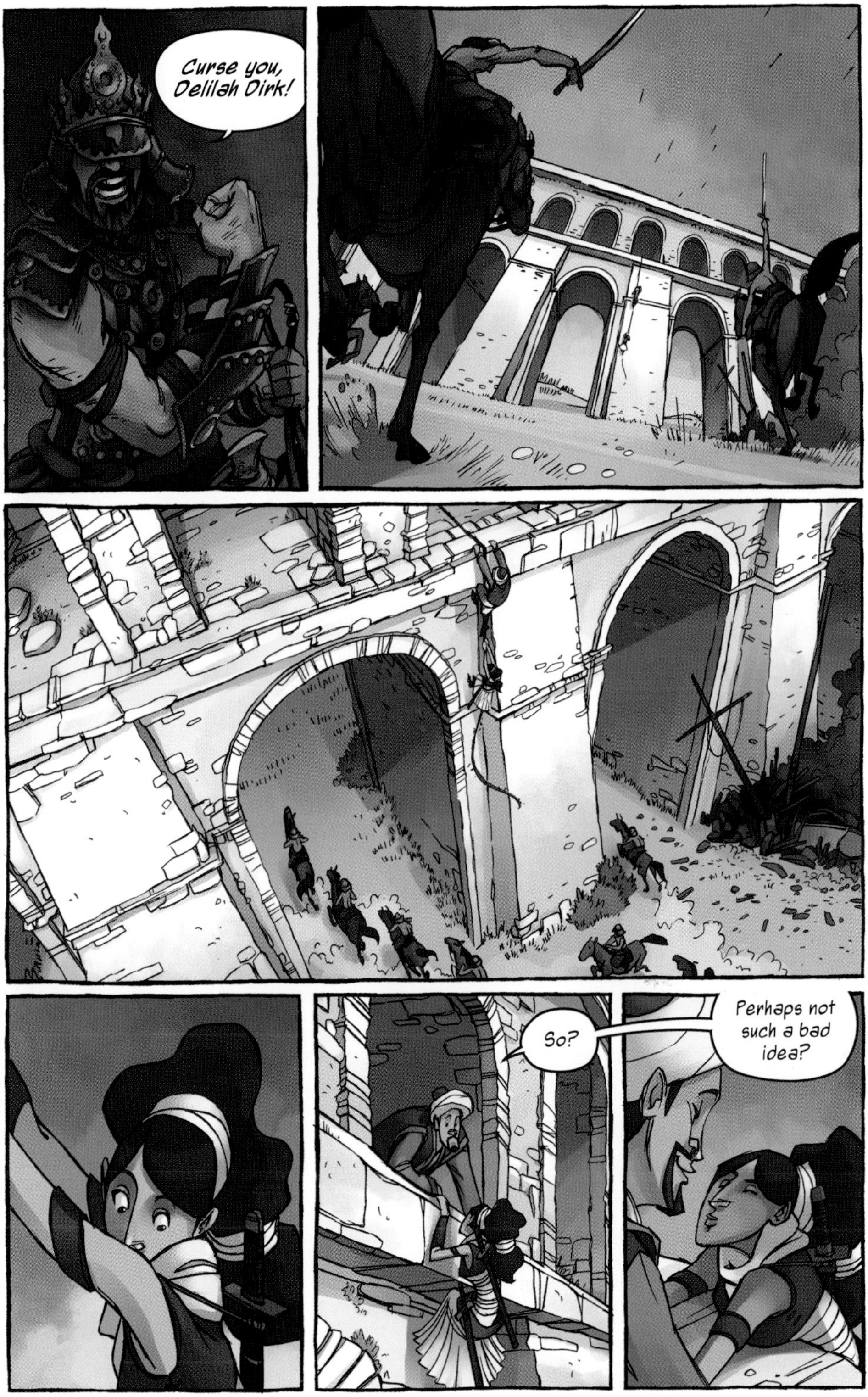
Curse you, Delilah Dirk!
So?
Perhaps not such a bad idea?

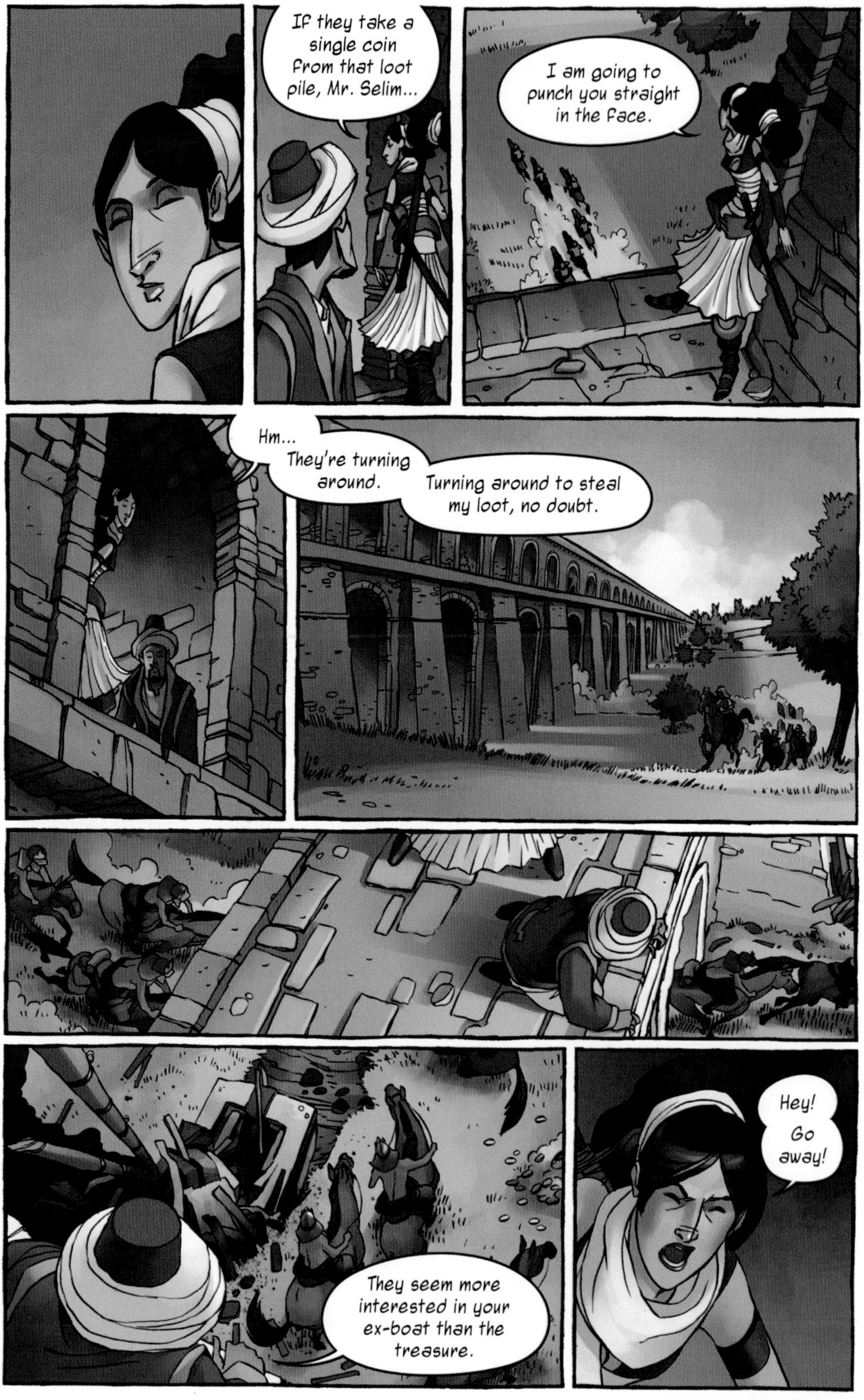
If they take a single coin from that loot pile, Mr. Selim...
I am going to punch you straight in the face.
Hm... They're turning around.
Turning around to steal my loot, no doubt.
They seem more interested in your ex-boat than the treasure.
Hey! Go away!

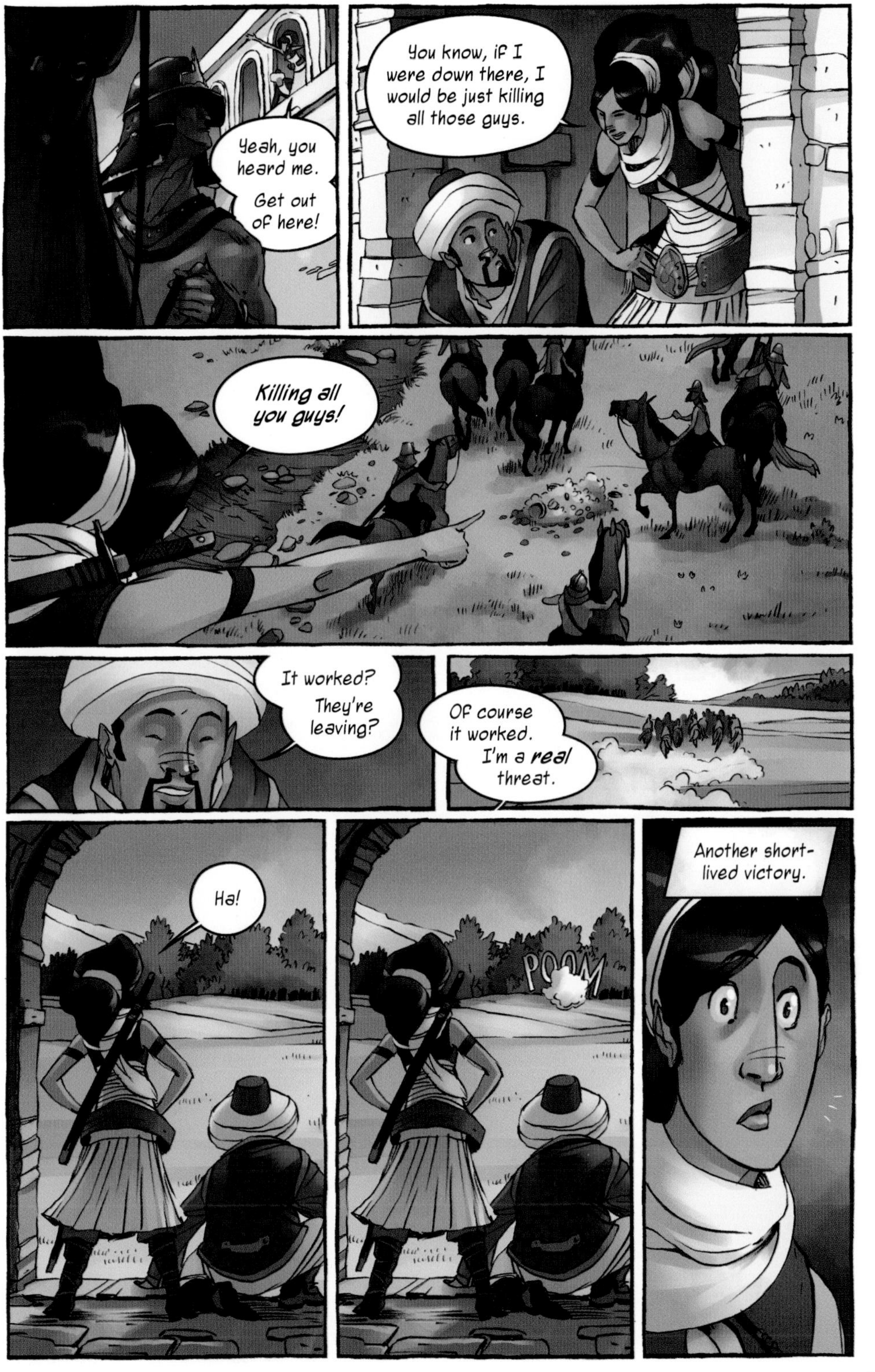
Yeah, you heard me.
Get out of here!
You know, if I were down there, I would be just killing all those guys.
Killing all you guys!
It worked?
They're leaving?
Of course it worked.
I'm a real threat.
Ha!
POOM
Another short-lived victory.

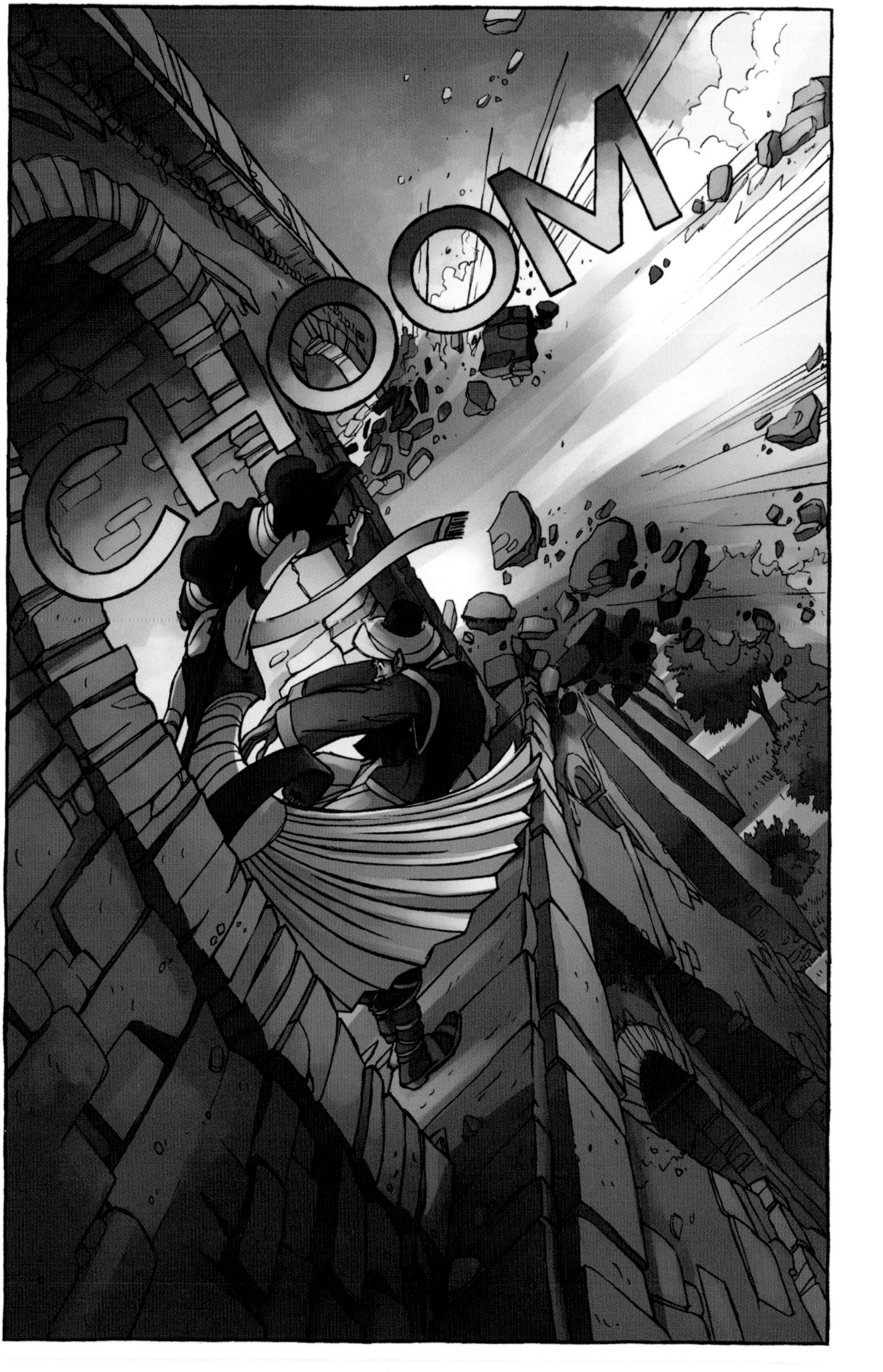
CHOOM

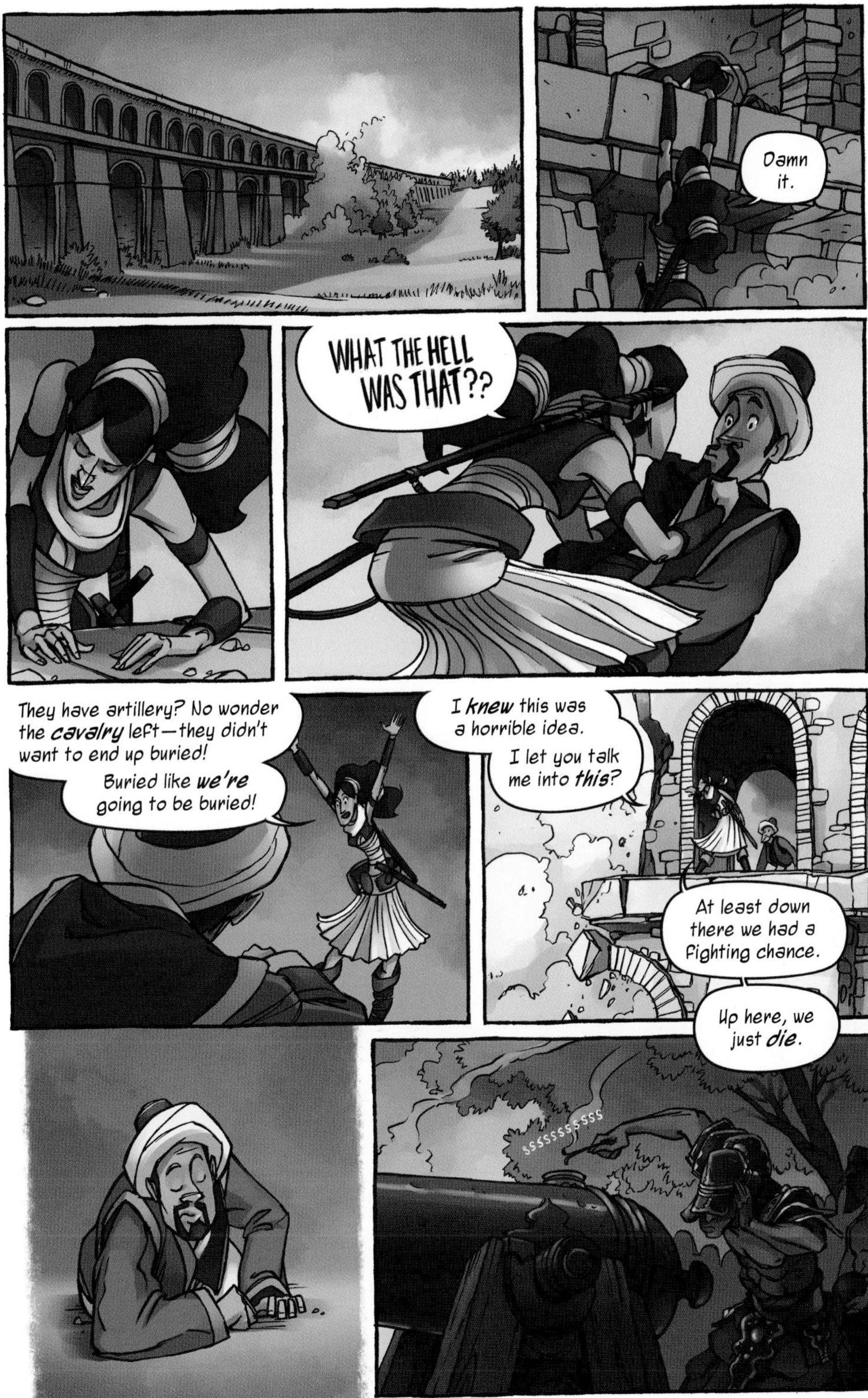
Damn it.
WHAT THE HELL WAS THAT??
They have artillery? No wonder the cavalry left—they didn't want to end up buried!
Buried like we're going to be buried!
I knew this was a horrible idea.
I let you talk me into this?
At least down there we had a fighting chance.
Up here, we just die.
SSSSSSSSSSS

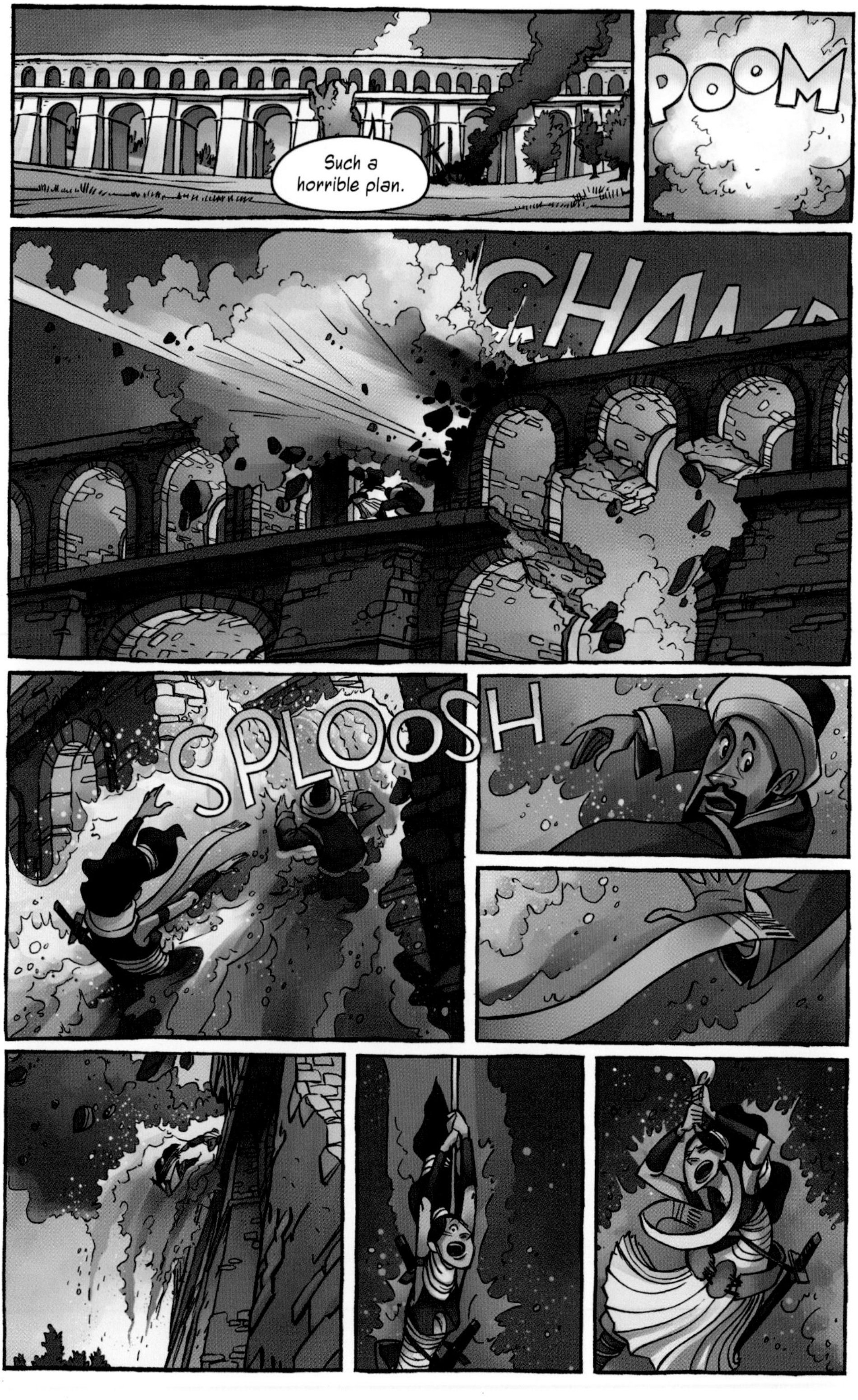
Such a
horrible plan.
POOM
SPLOOSH

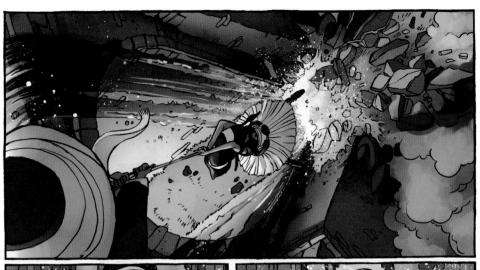

Pullmeup!
Pullmeup!
Pullmeup!

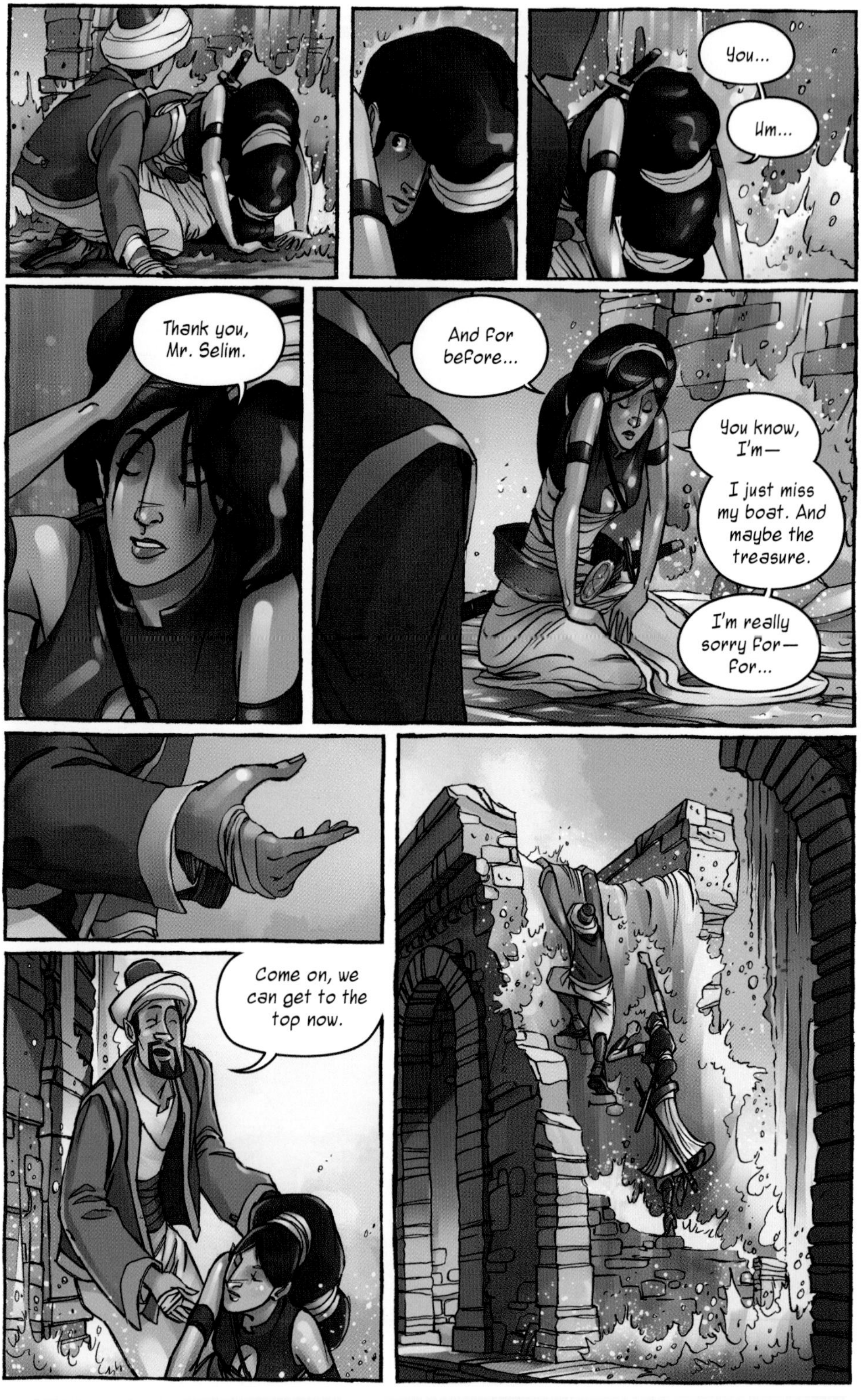
You...
Um...
Thank you, Mr. Selim.
And for before...
You know, I'm—
I just miss my boat. And maybe the treasure.
I'm really sorry for— for...
Come on, we can get to the top now.

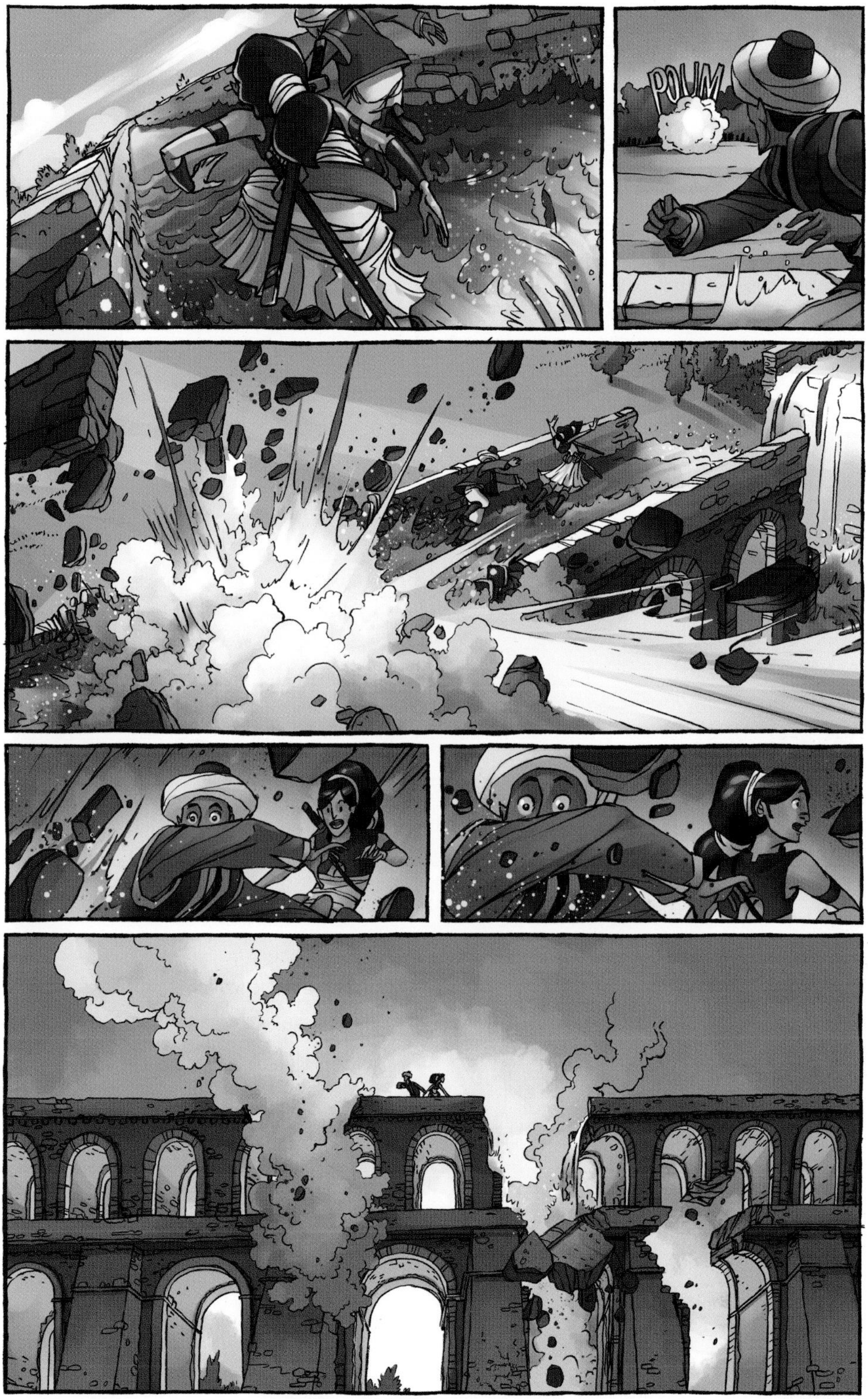
POUM

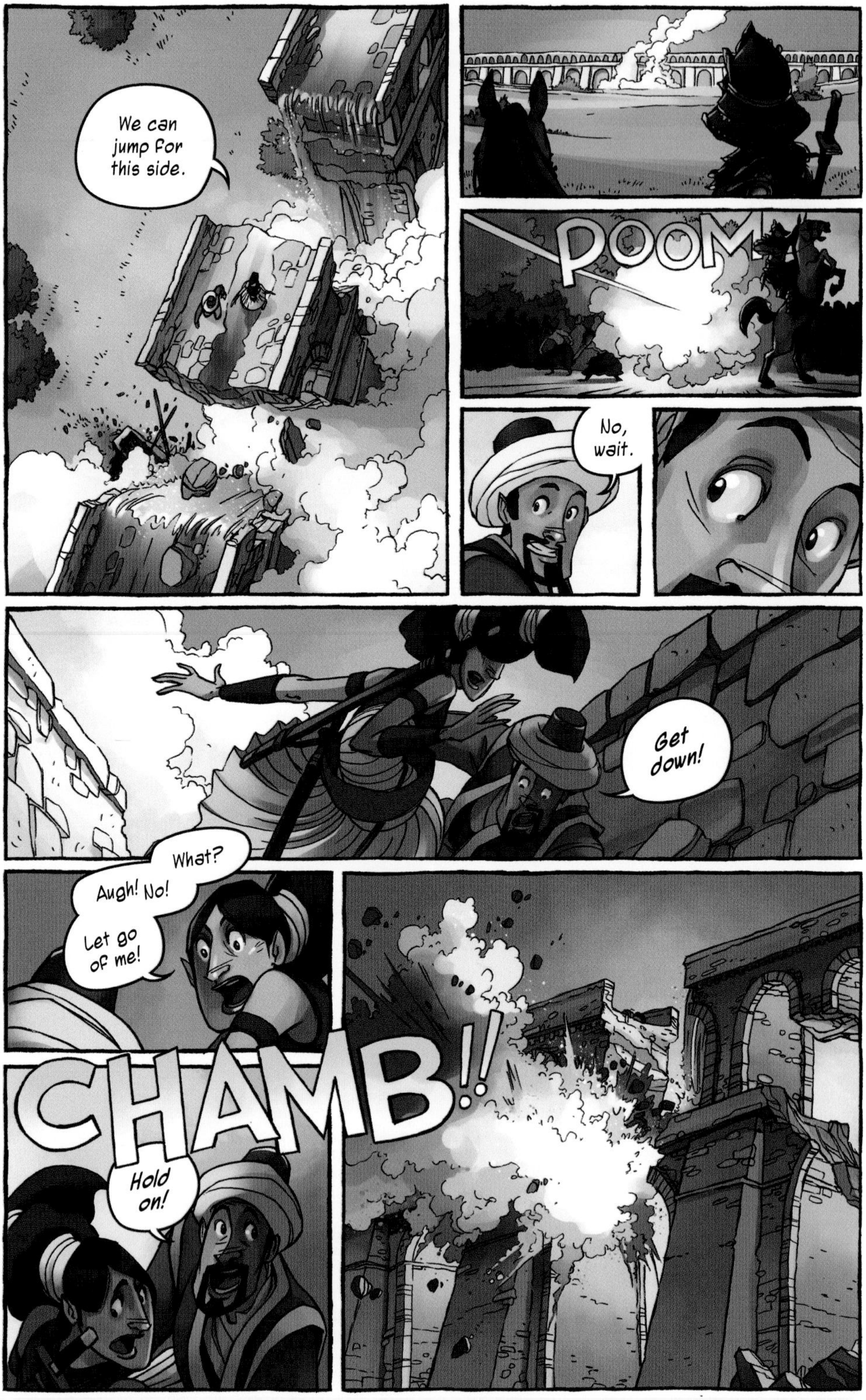
We can jump for this side.
POOM
No, wait.
Get down!
What?
Augh! No!
Let go of me!
CHAMB!!
Hold on!

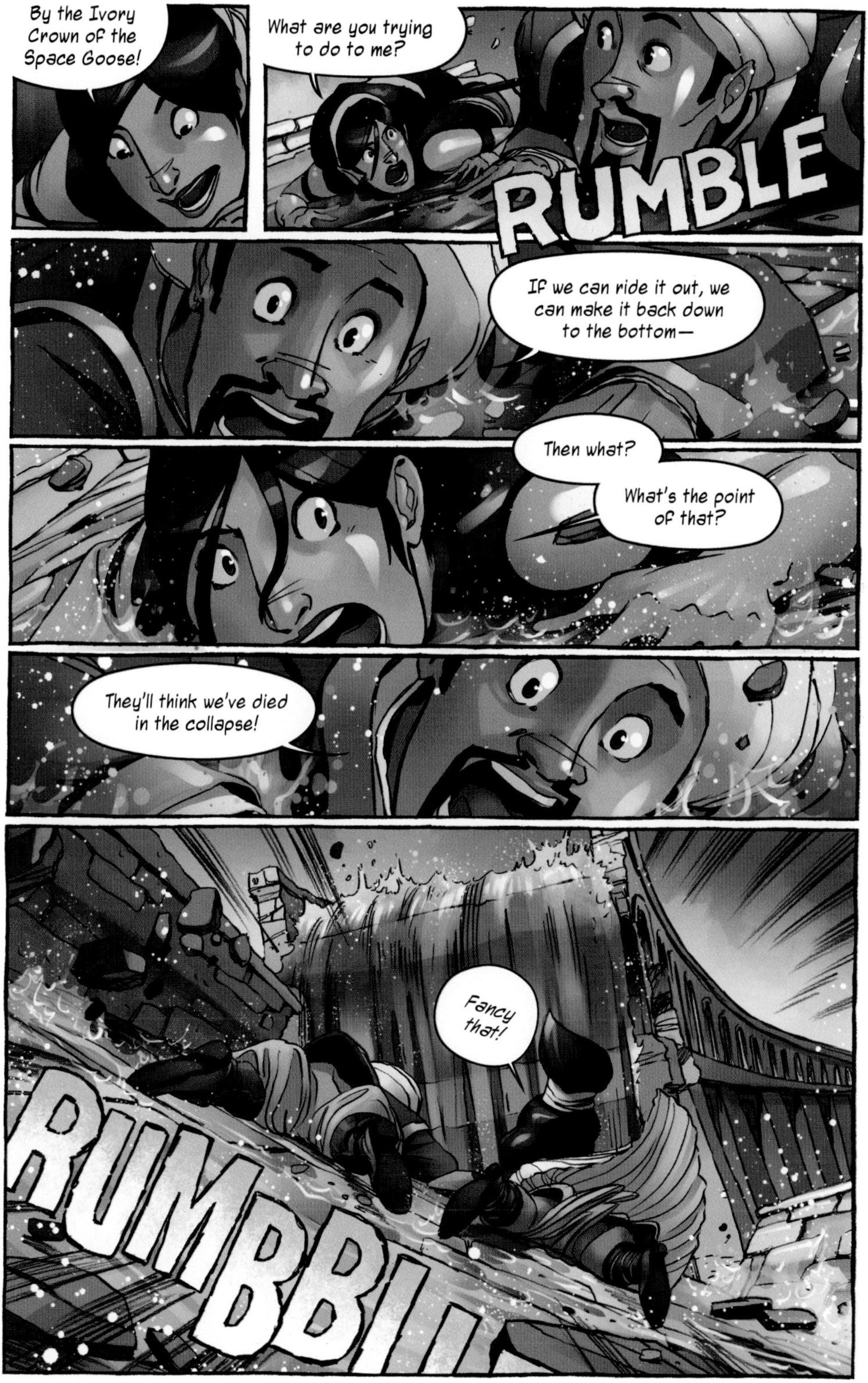
By the Ivory Crown of the Space Goose!
What are you trying to do to me?
RUMBLE
If we can ride it out, we can make it back down to the bottom—
Then what?
What's the point of that?
They'll think we've died in the collapse!
Fancy that!
RUMBBL

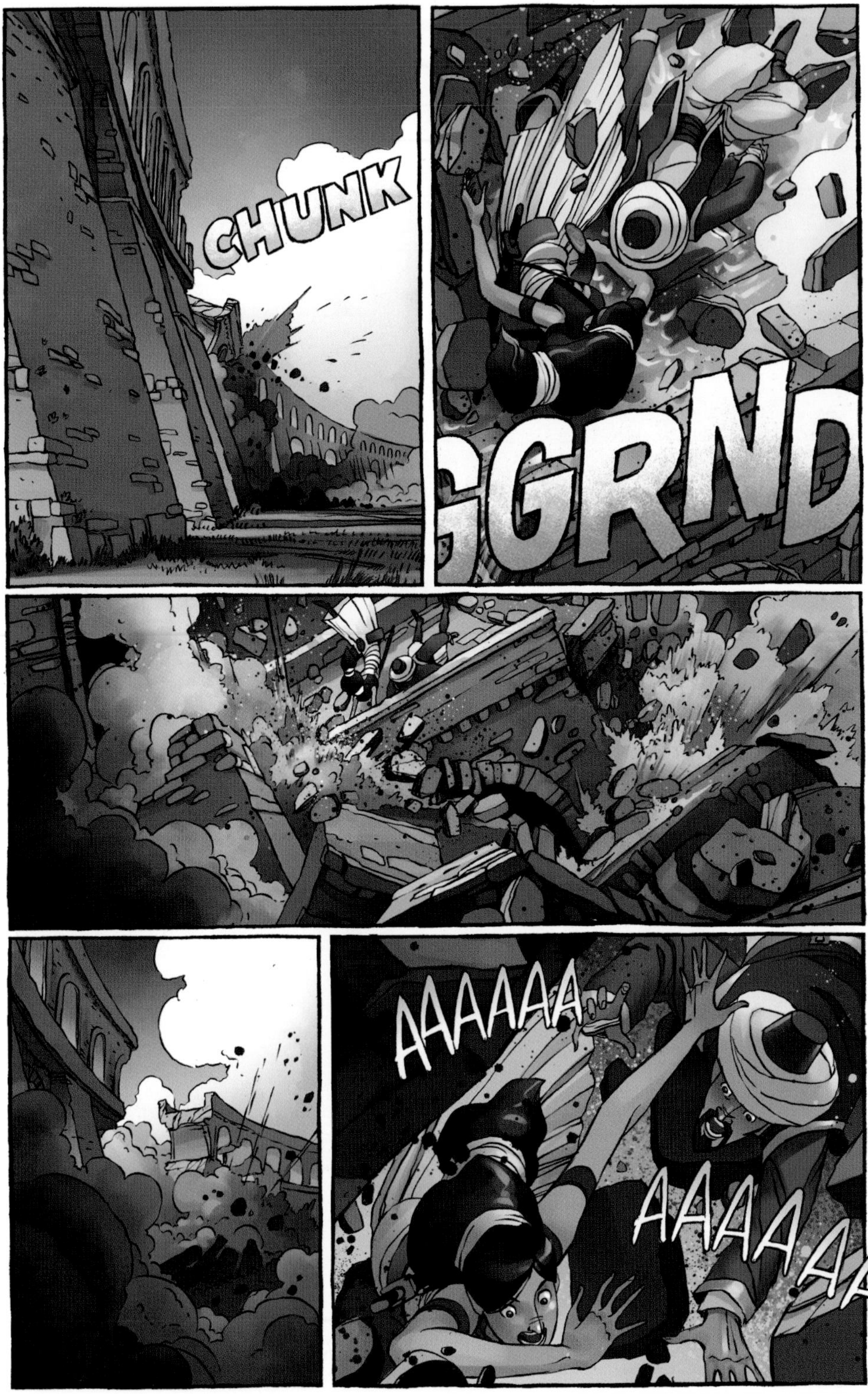
CHUNK
GGRND
AAAAAA
AAAAAAA

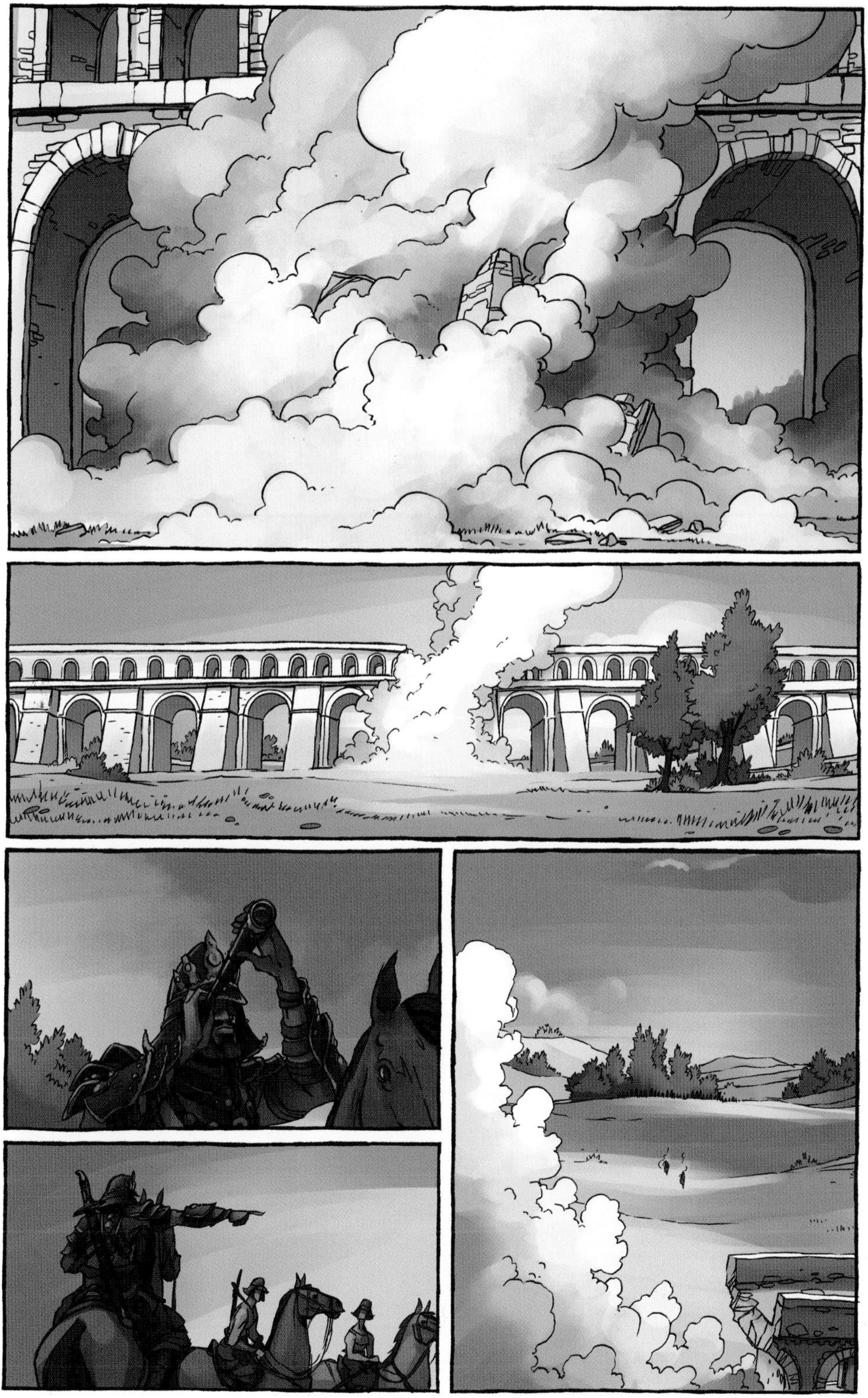

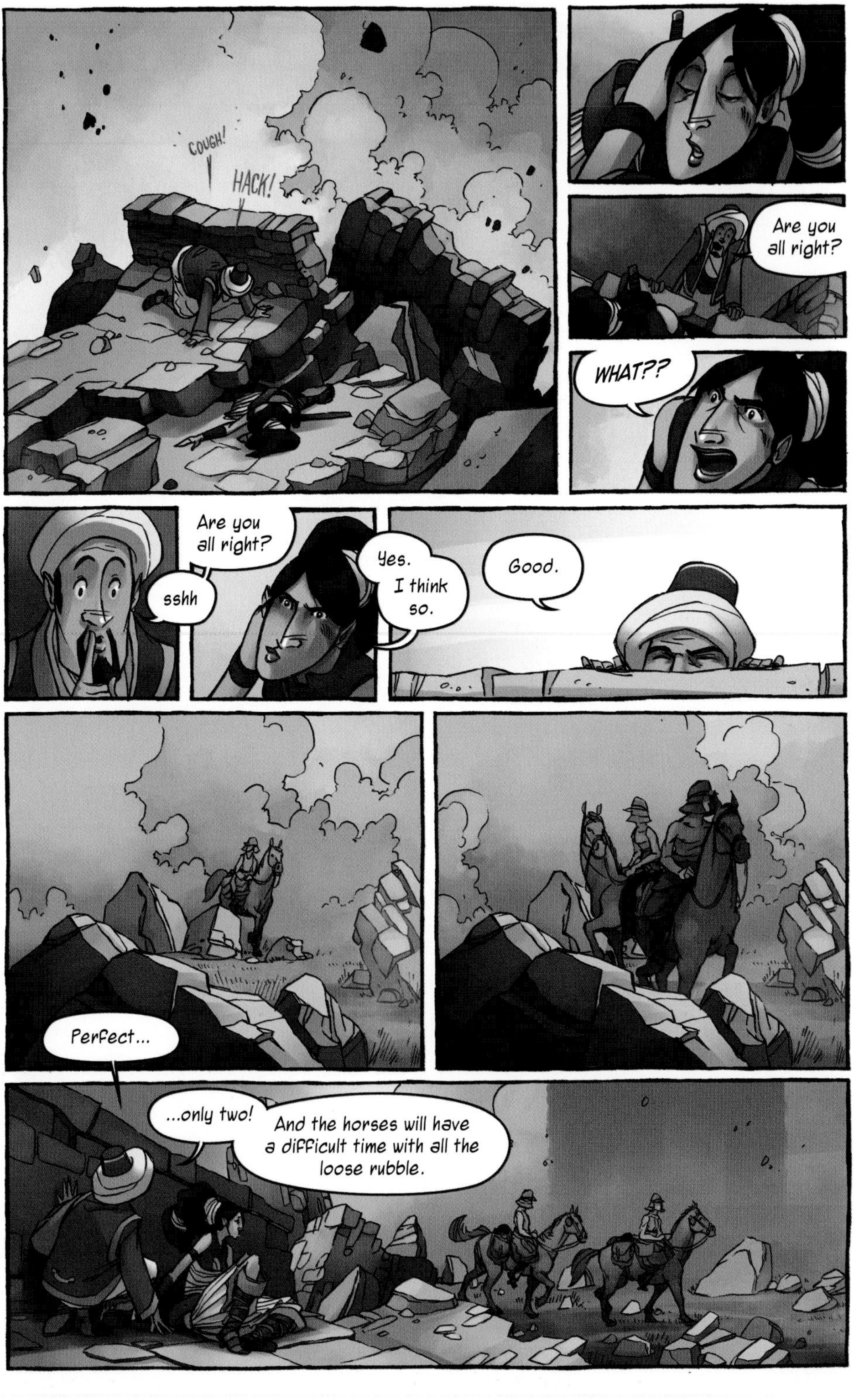
COUGH!
HACK!
Are you all right?
WHAT??
Are you all right?
sshh
Yes. I think so.
Good.
Perfect...
...only two!
And the horses will have a difficult time with all the loose rubble.

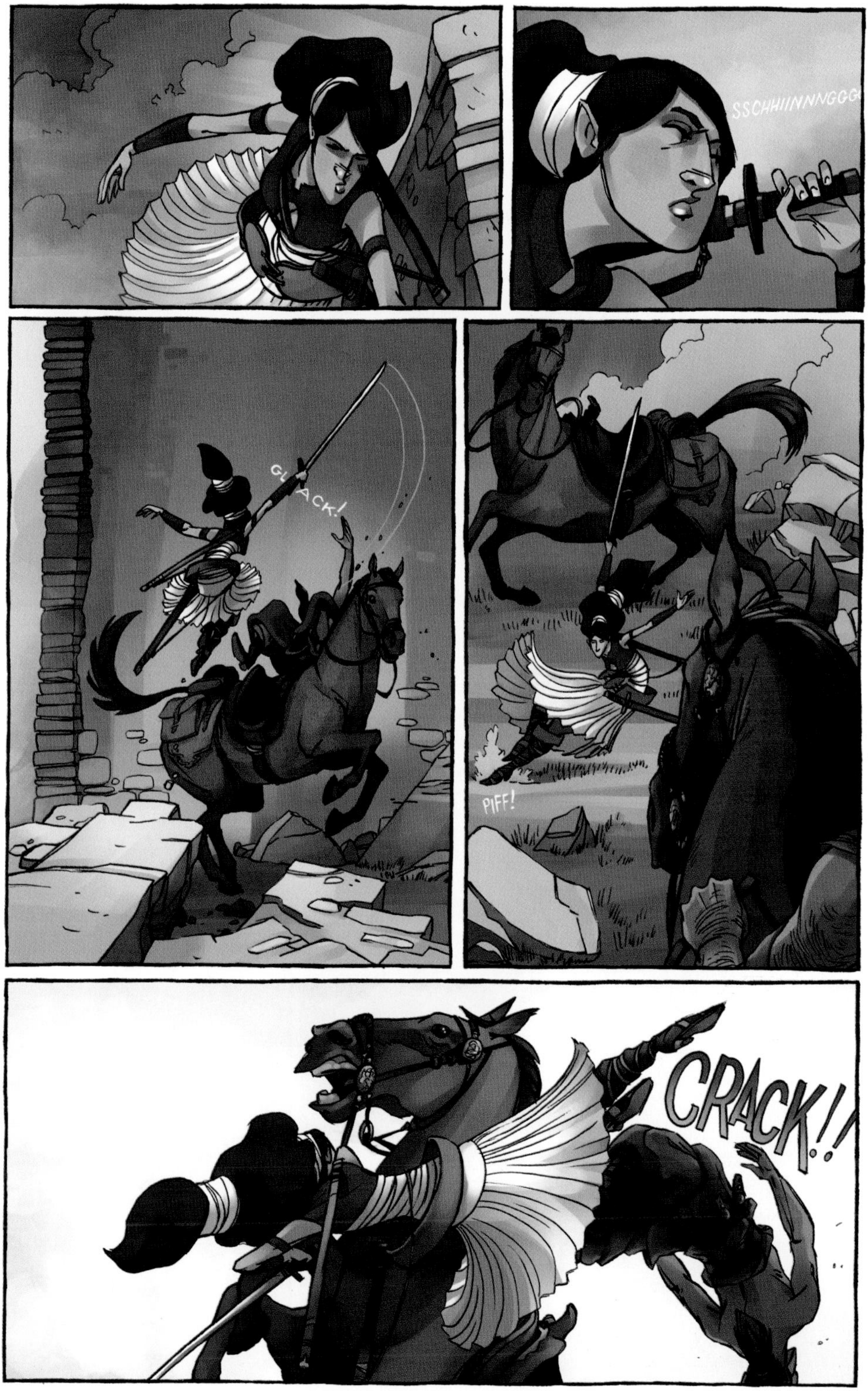
SSCHHIINNNGGG
GLACK!
PIFF!
CRACK!!

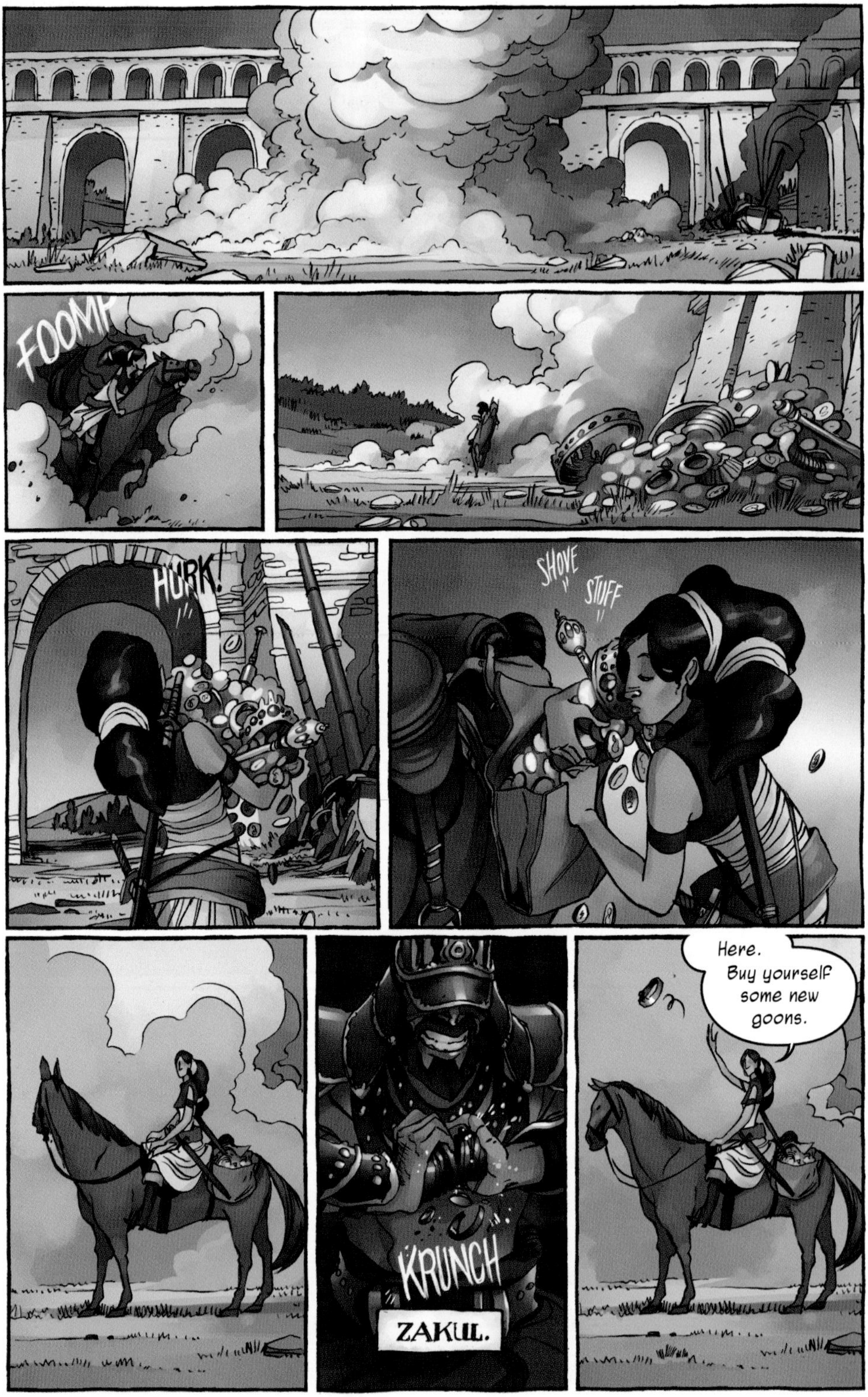
FOOMP
HURK!
SHOVE
STUFF
KRUNCH
ZAKUL.
Here.
Buy yourself
some new
goons.

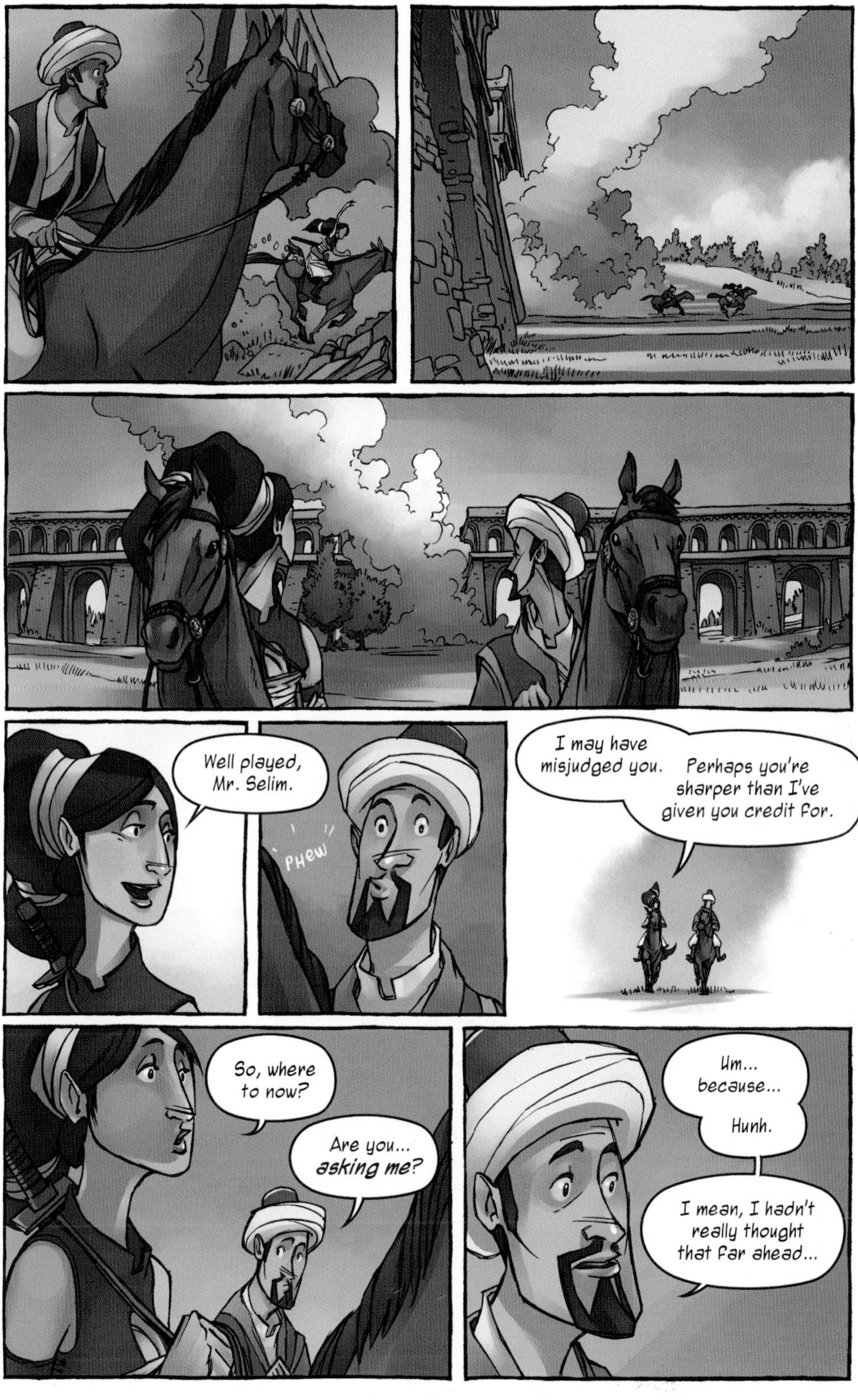
Well played, Mr. Selim.
PHEW
I may have misjudged you.
Perhaps you're sharper than I've given you credit for.
So, where to now?
Are you... *asking me*?
Um... because...
Hunh.
I mean, I hadn't really thought that far ahead...

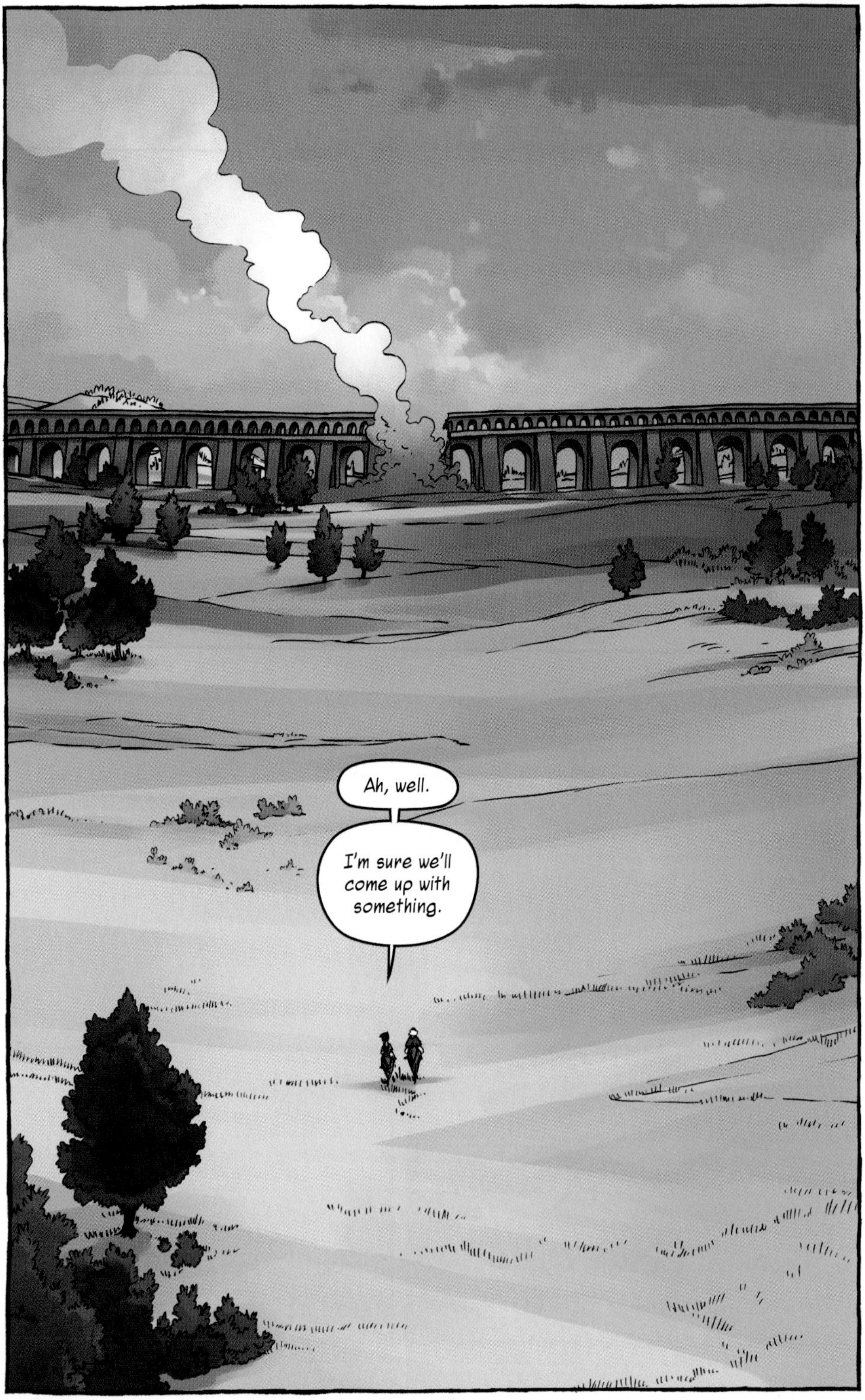
Ah, well.
I'm sure we'll come up with something.

CHAPTER 4

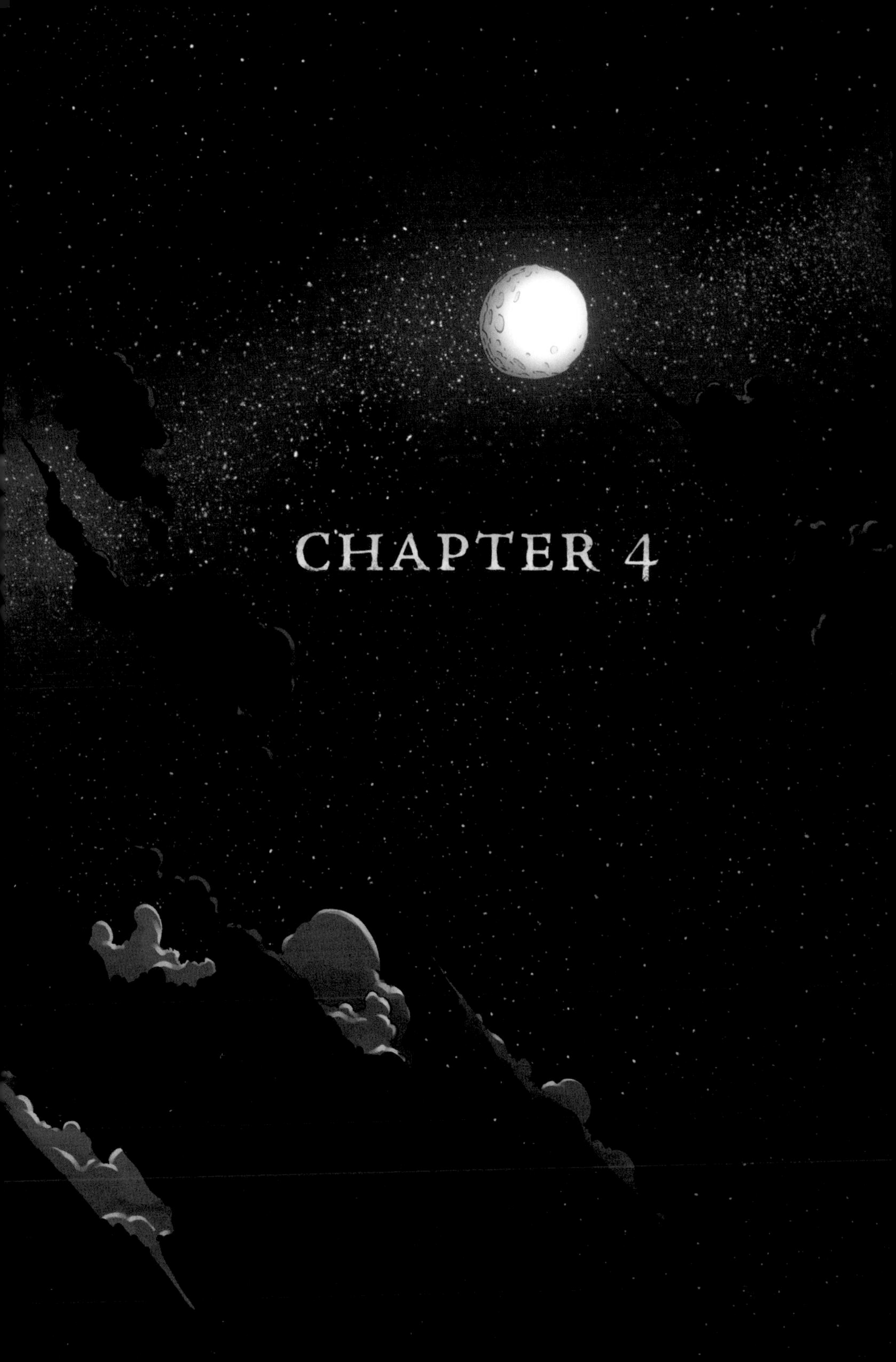

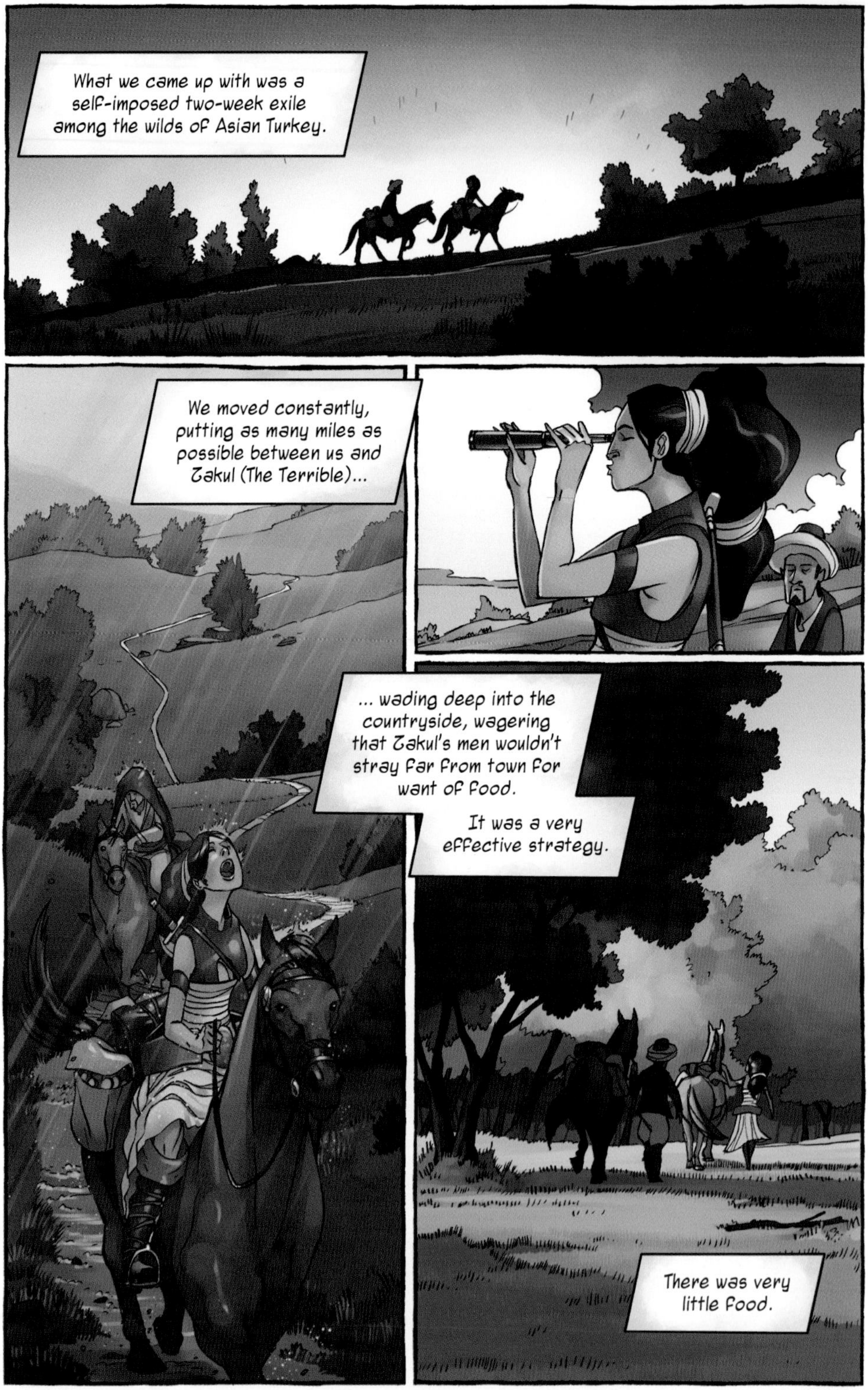
What we came up with was a self-imposed two-week exile among the wilds of Asian Turkey.
We moved constantly, putting as many miles as possible between us and Zakul (The Terrible)...
... wading deep into the countryside, wagering that Zakul's men wouldn't stray far from town for want of food.
It was a very effective strategy.
There was very little food.

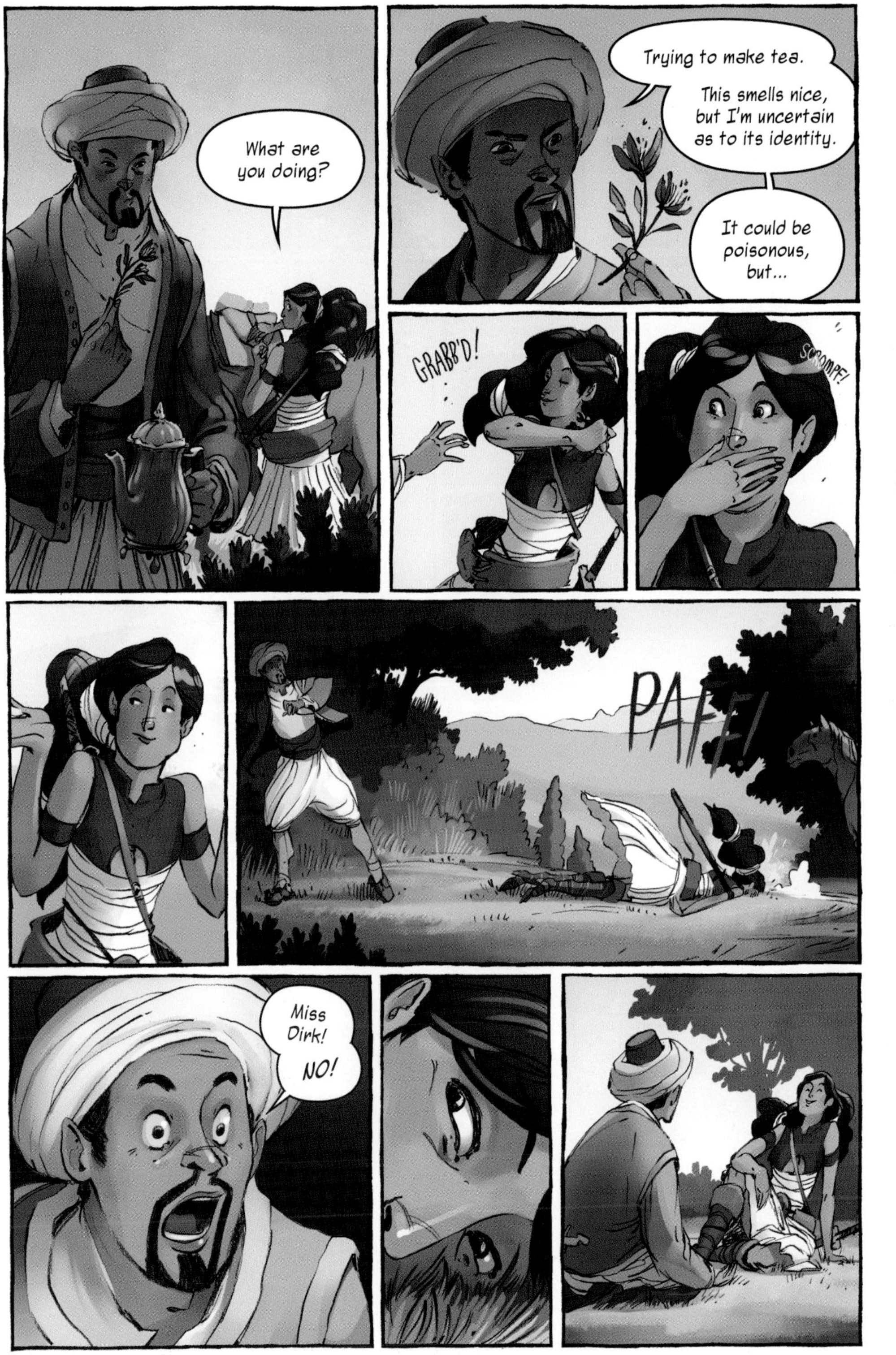
What are you doing?
Trying to make tea.
This smells nice, but I'm uncertain as to its identity.
It could be poisonous, but...
GRABB'D!
SCROMPF!
PAFF!
Miss Dirk!
NO!

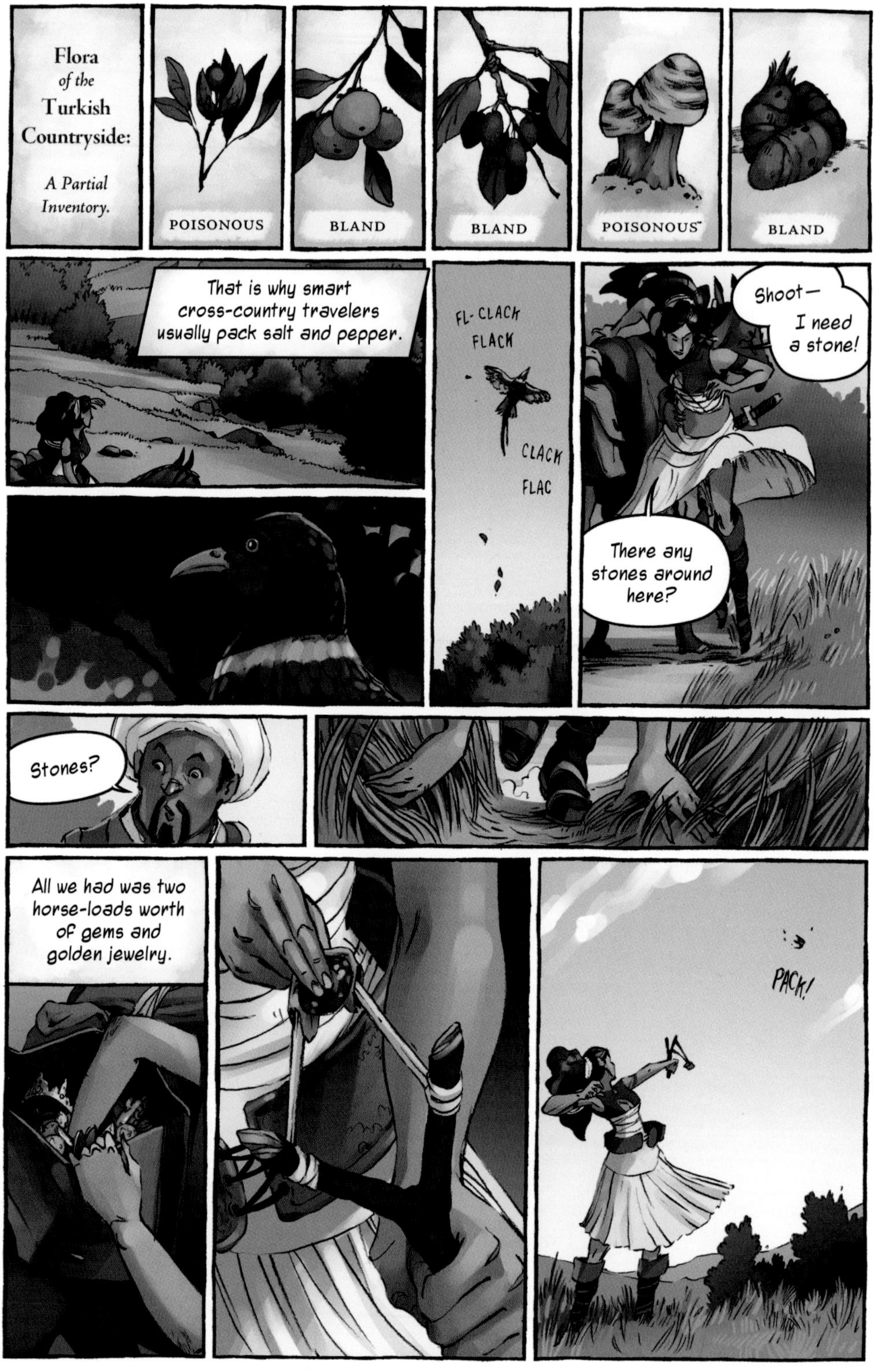
Flora
of the
Turkish
Countryside:
A Partial
Inventory.
POISONOUS
BLAND
BLAND
POISONOUS
BLAND
That is why smart cross-country travelers usually pack salt and pepper.
FL-CLACK
FLACK
CLACK
FLAC
Shoot—
I need a stone!
There any stones around here?
Stones?
All we had was two horse-loads worth of gems and golden jewelry.
PACK!

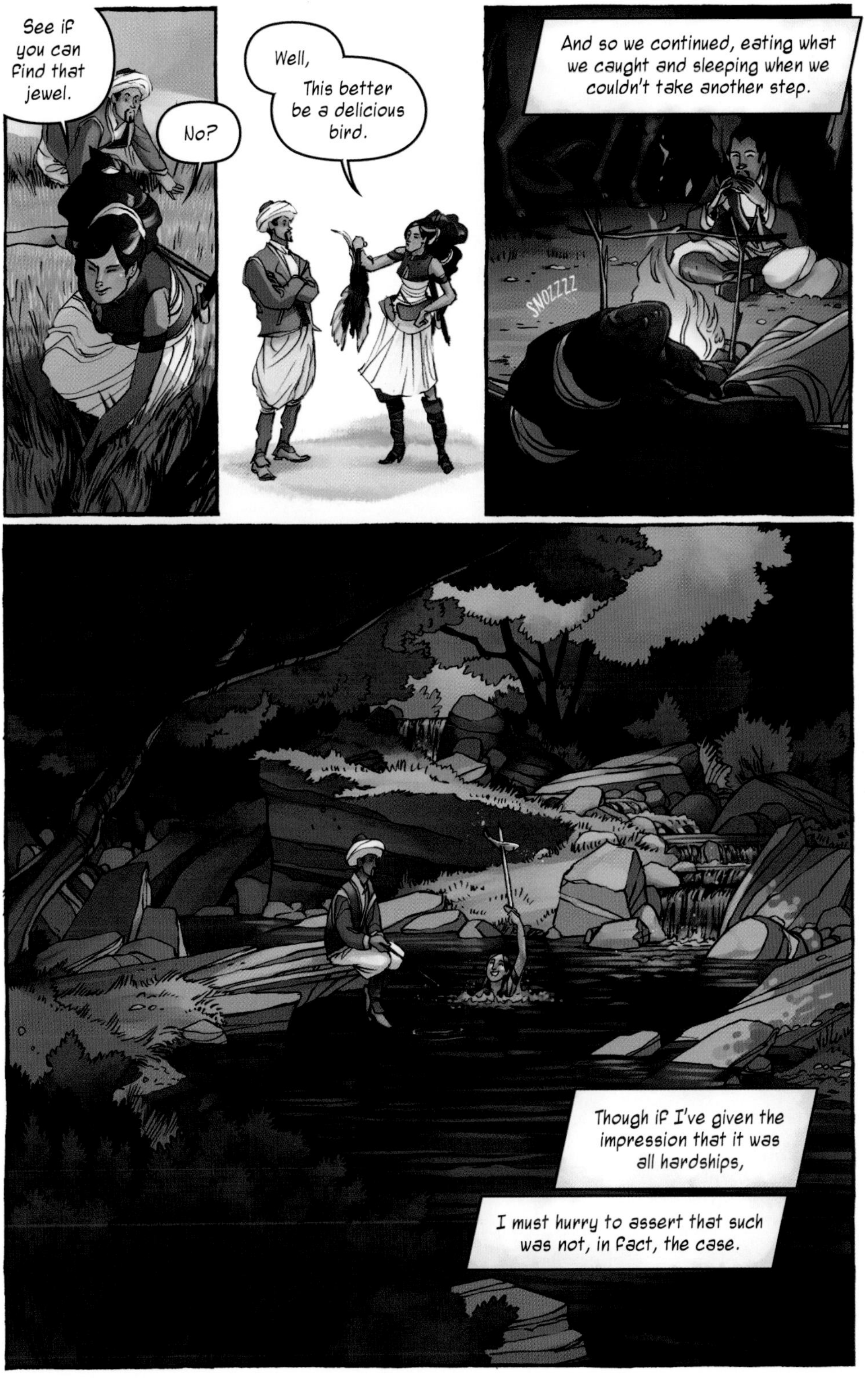
See if you can find that jewel.
No?
Well, This better be a delicious bird.
And so we continued, eating what we caught and sleeping when we couldn't take another step.
SNOZZZZ
Though if I've given the impression that it was all hardships,
I must hurry to assert that such was not, in fact, the case.

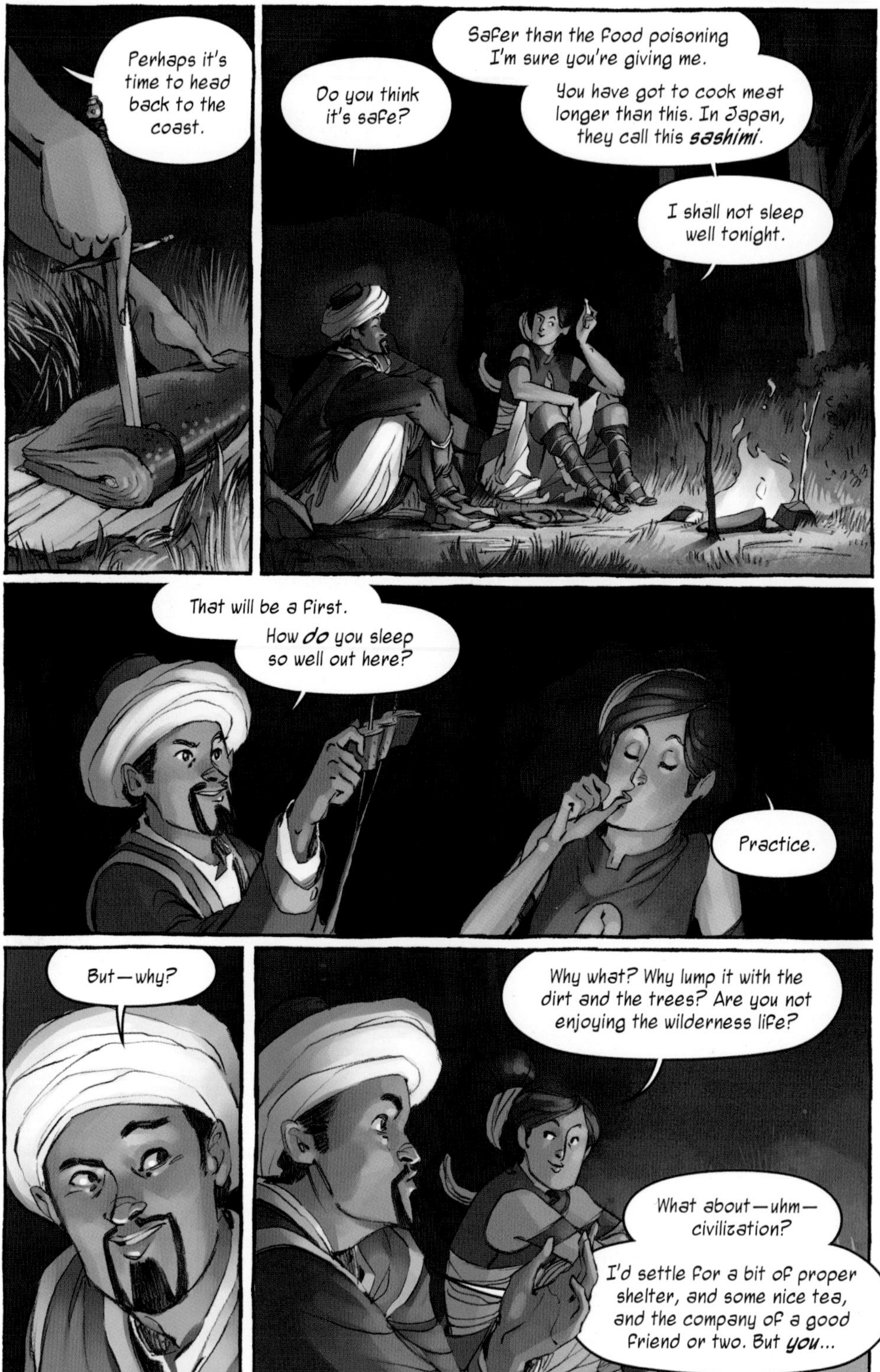
Perhaps it's time to head back to the coast.
Do you think it's safe?
Safer than the food poisoning I'm sure you're giving me.
You have got to cook meat longer than this. In Japan, they call this ***sashimi***.
I shall not sleep well tonight.
That will be a first.
How ***do*** you sleep so well out here?
Practice.
But—why?
Why what? Why lump it with the dirt and the trees? Are you not enjoying the wilderness life?
What about—uhm—civilization?
I'd settle for a bit of proper shelter, and some nice tea, and the company of a good friend or two. But ***you***...

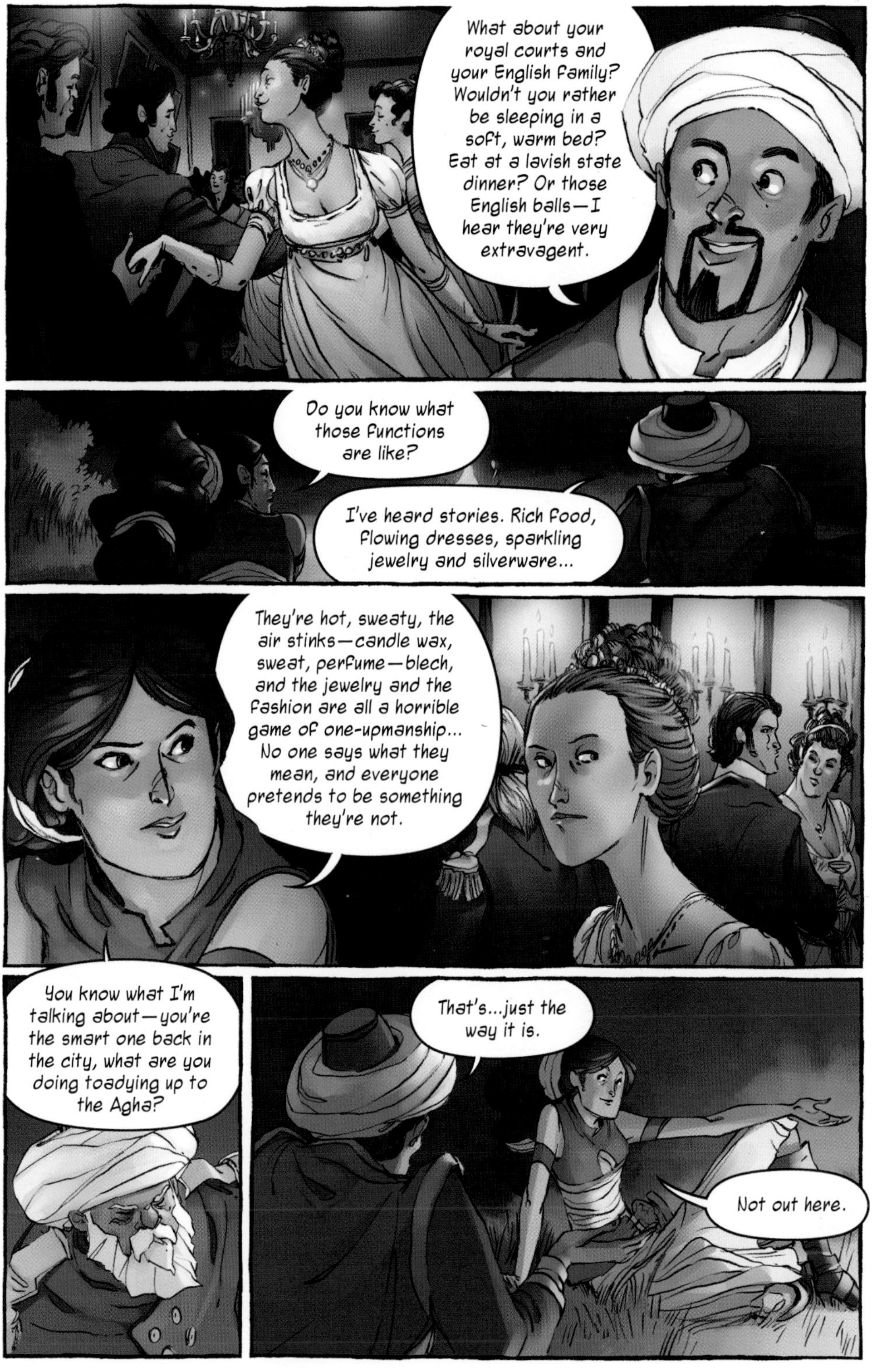
What about your royal courts and your English family? Wouldn't you rather be sleeping in a soft, warm bed? Eat at a lavish state dinner? Or those English balls—I hear they're very extravagent.
Do you know what those functions are like?
I've heard stories. Rich food, flowing dresses, sparkling jewelry and silverware...
They're hot, sweaty, the air stinks—candle wax, sweat, perfume—blech, and the jewelry and the fashion are all a horrible game of one-upmanship... No one says what they mean, and everyone pretends to be something they're not.
You know what I'm talking about—you're the smart one back in the city, what are you doing toadying up to the Agha?
That's...just the way it is.
Not out here.

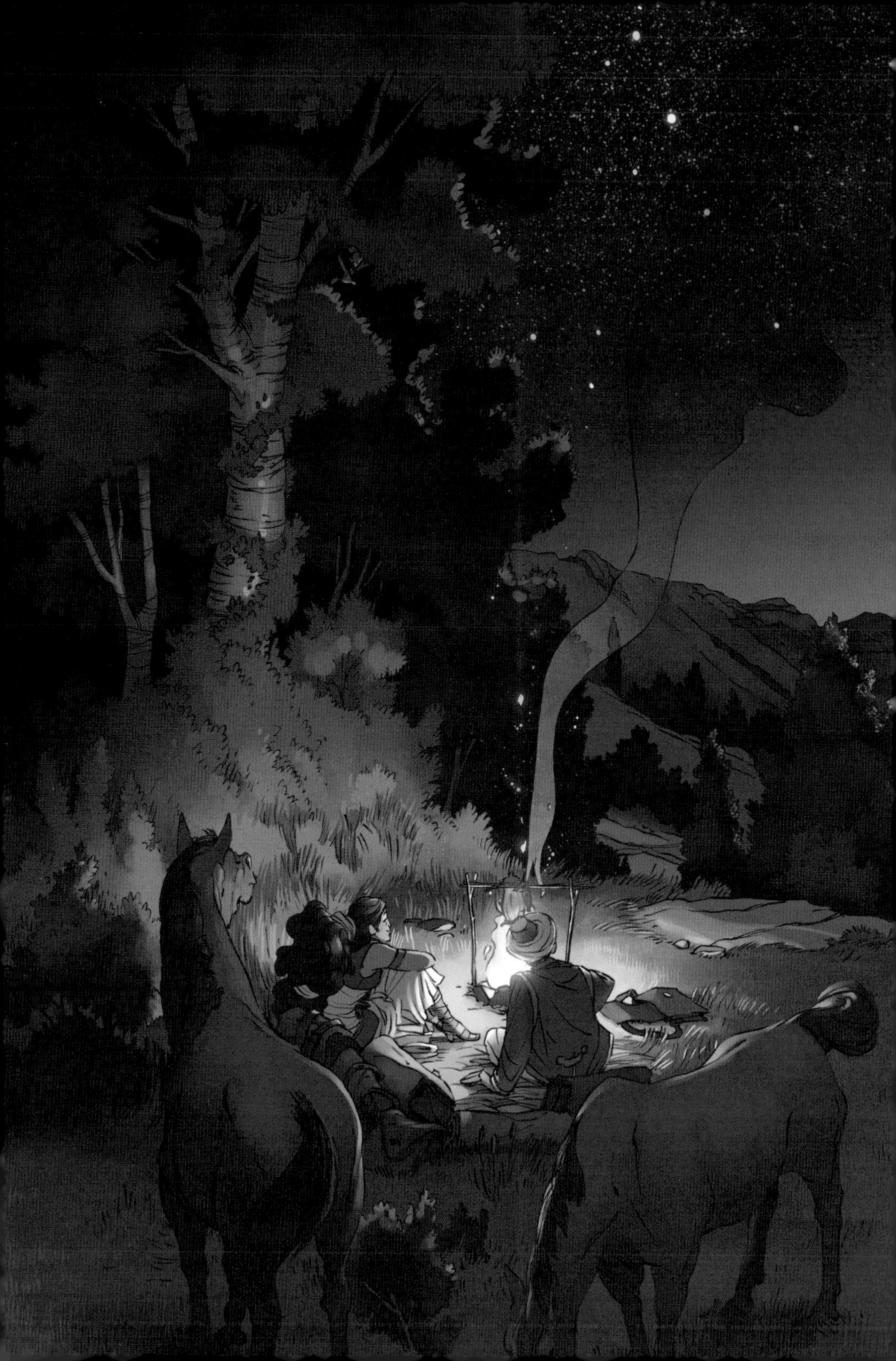

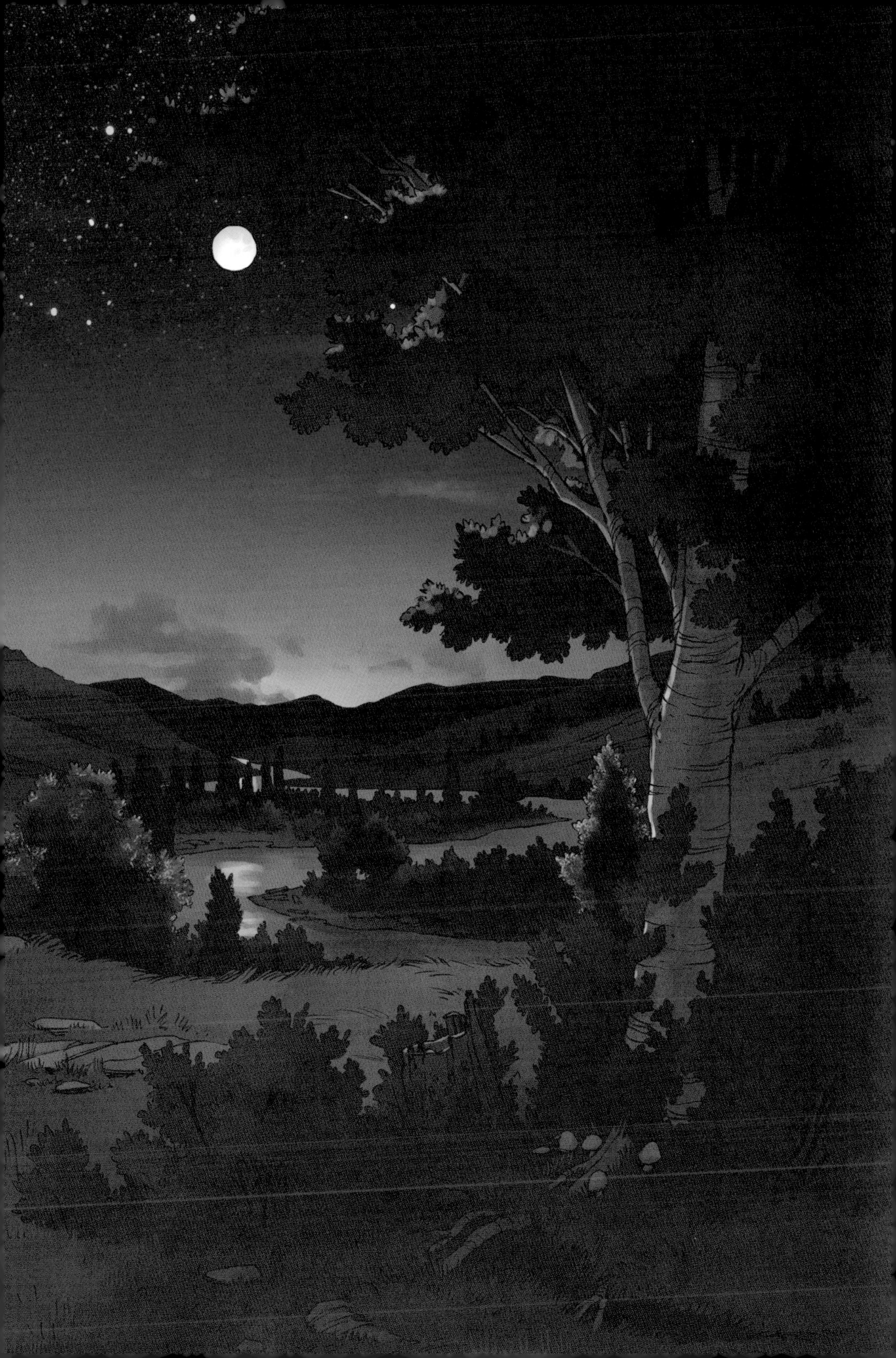

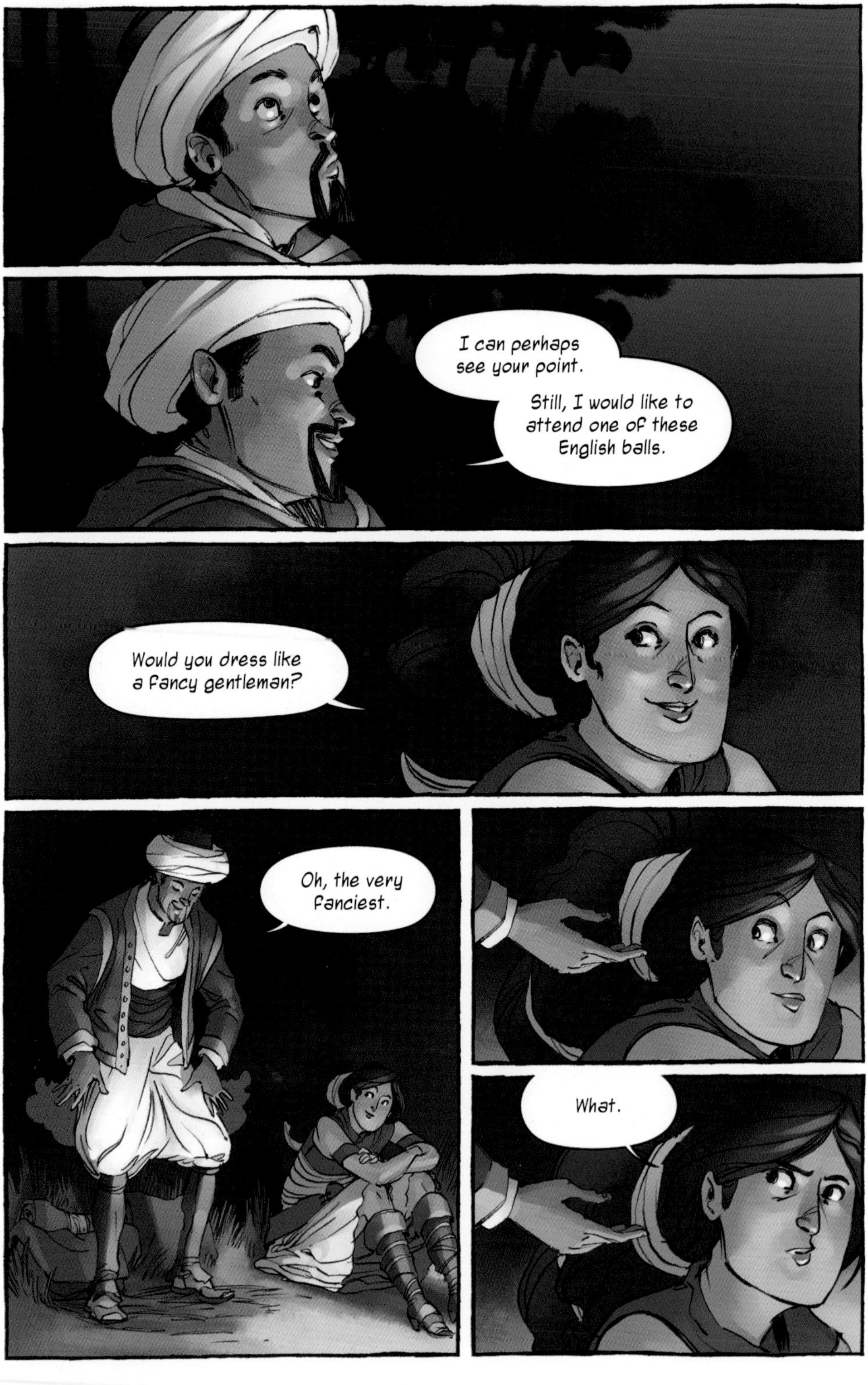
I can perhaps see your point.
Still, I would like to attend one of these English balls.
Would you dress like a fancy gentleman?
Oh, the very fanciest.
What.

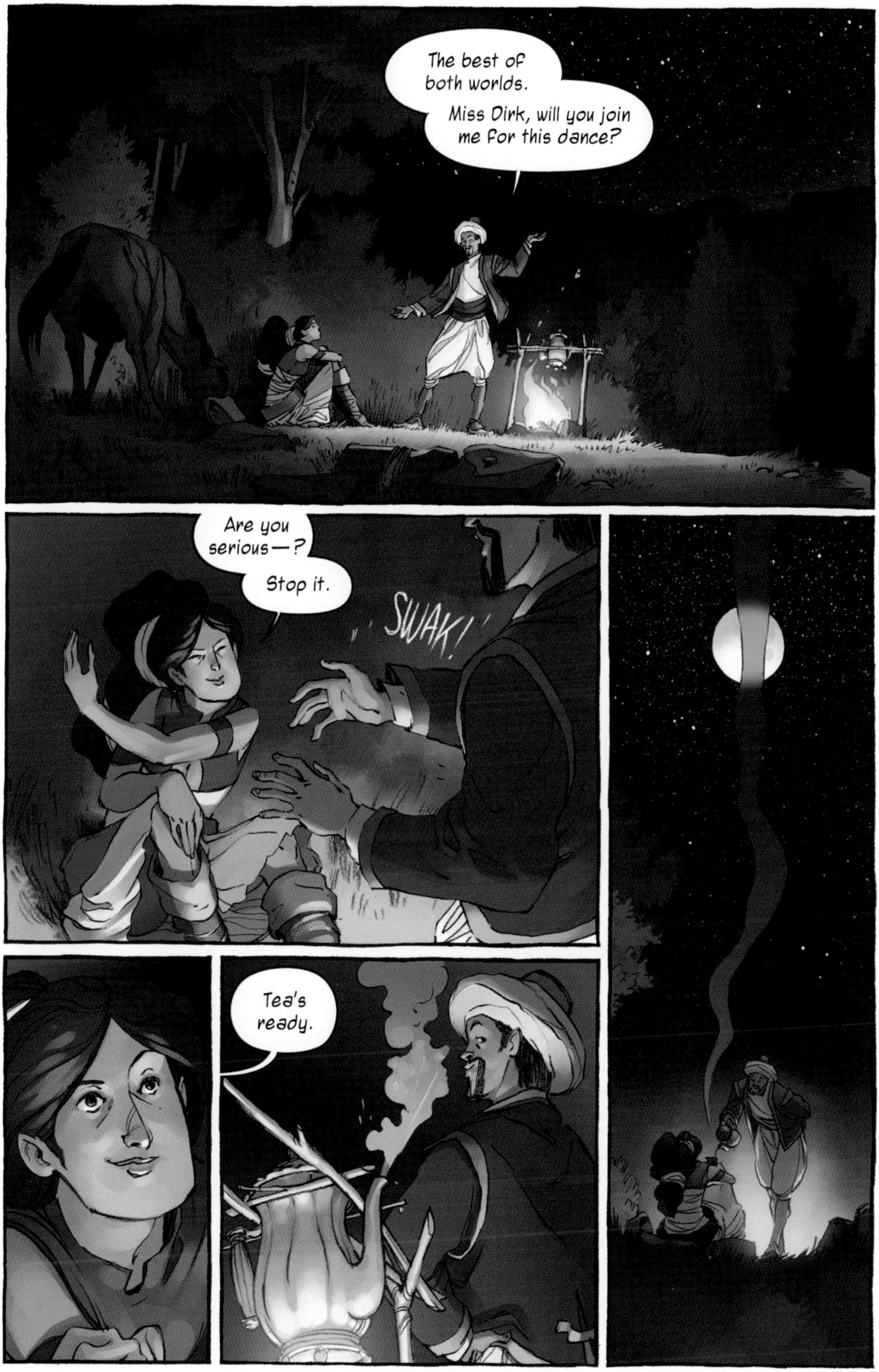
The best of both worlds.
Miss Dirk, will you join me for this dance?
Are you serious—?
Stop it.
SWAK!
Tea's ready.

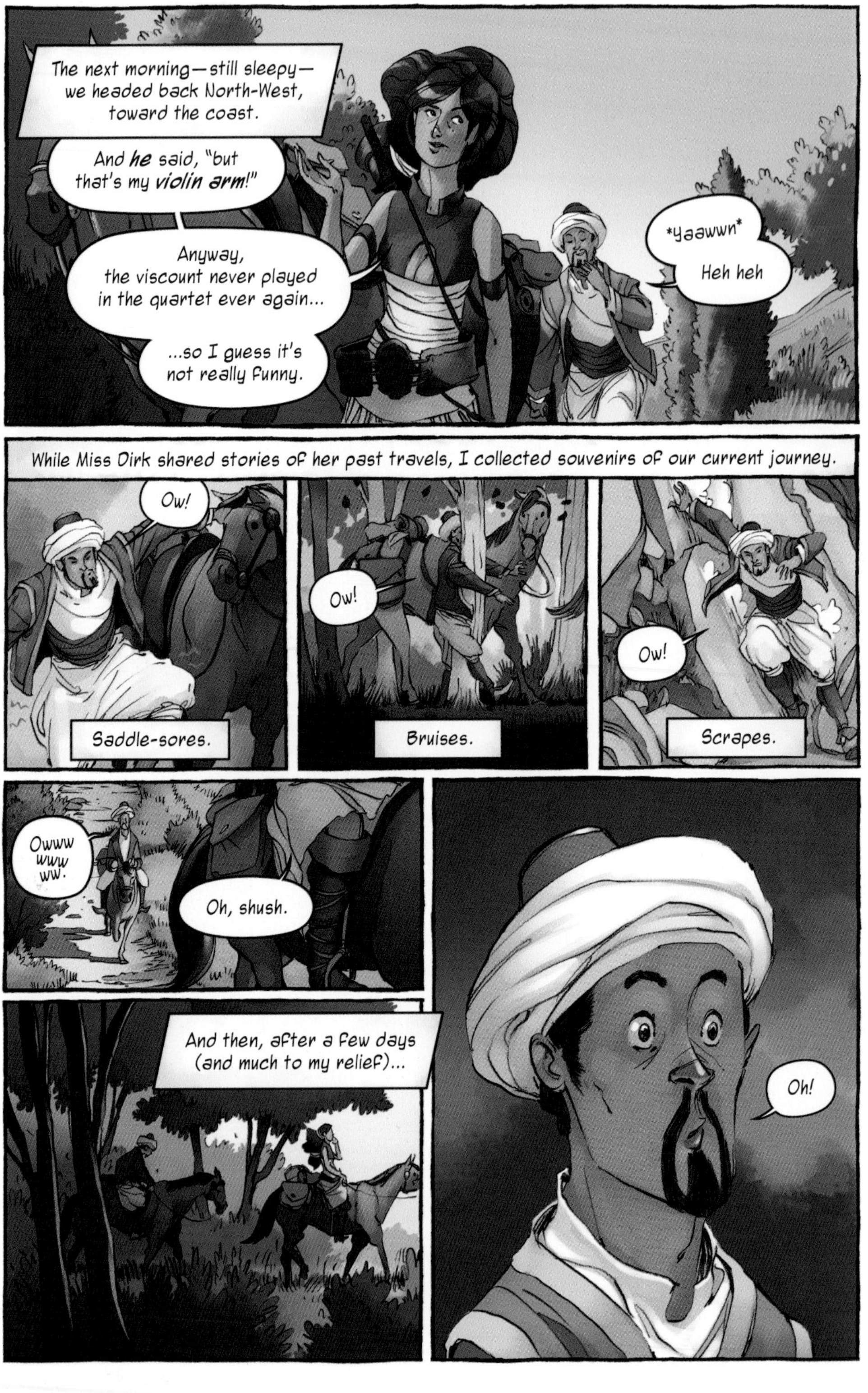
The next morning—still sleepy—we headed back North-West, toward the coast.
And **he** said, "but that's my ***violin arm***!"
Anyway, the viscount never played in the quartet ever again...
...so I guess it's not really funny.
yaawwn
Heh heh
While Miss Dirk shared stories of her past travels, I collected souvenirs of our current journey.
Ow!
Saddle-sores.
Ow!
Bruises.
Ow!
Scrapes.
Owww www ww.
Oh, shush.
And then, after a few days (and much to my relief)...
Oh!

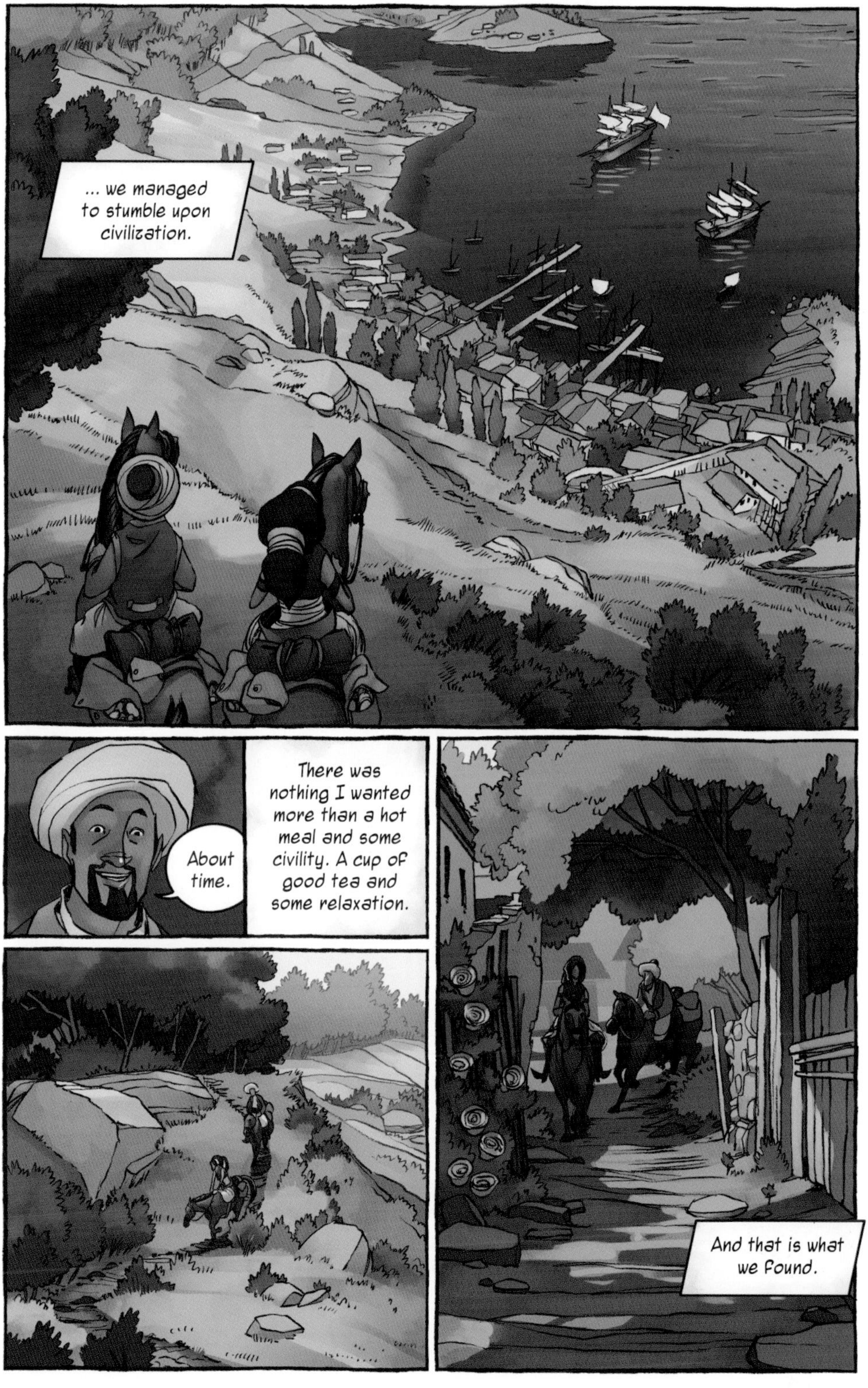
... we managed to stumble upon civilization.
About time.
There was nothing I wanted more than a hot meal and some civility. A cup of good tea and some relaxation.
And that is what we found.

Selam-un aleykum!

Ve aleykum selam, friend.

You two are not from around here!

Welcome to Kardaki!

You look like a pair of unwatered plants.

Have you been traveling long?

Yes—

No, a few weeks perhaps.

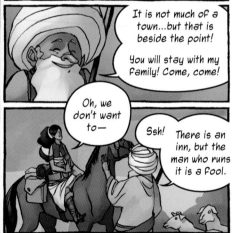

Is there somewhere in town that we might eat and rest for a day or two?

It is not much of a town...but that is beside the point!

You will stay with my family! Come, come!

Oh, we don't want to—

Ssh! There is an inn, but the man who runs it is a fool.

Thank you, you are too kind.

I am lonely!

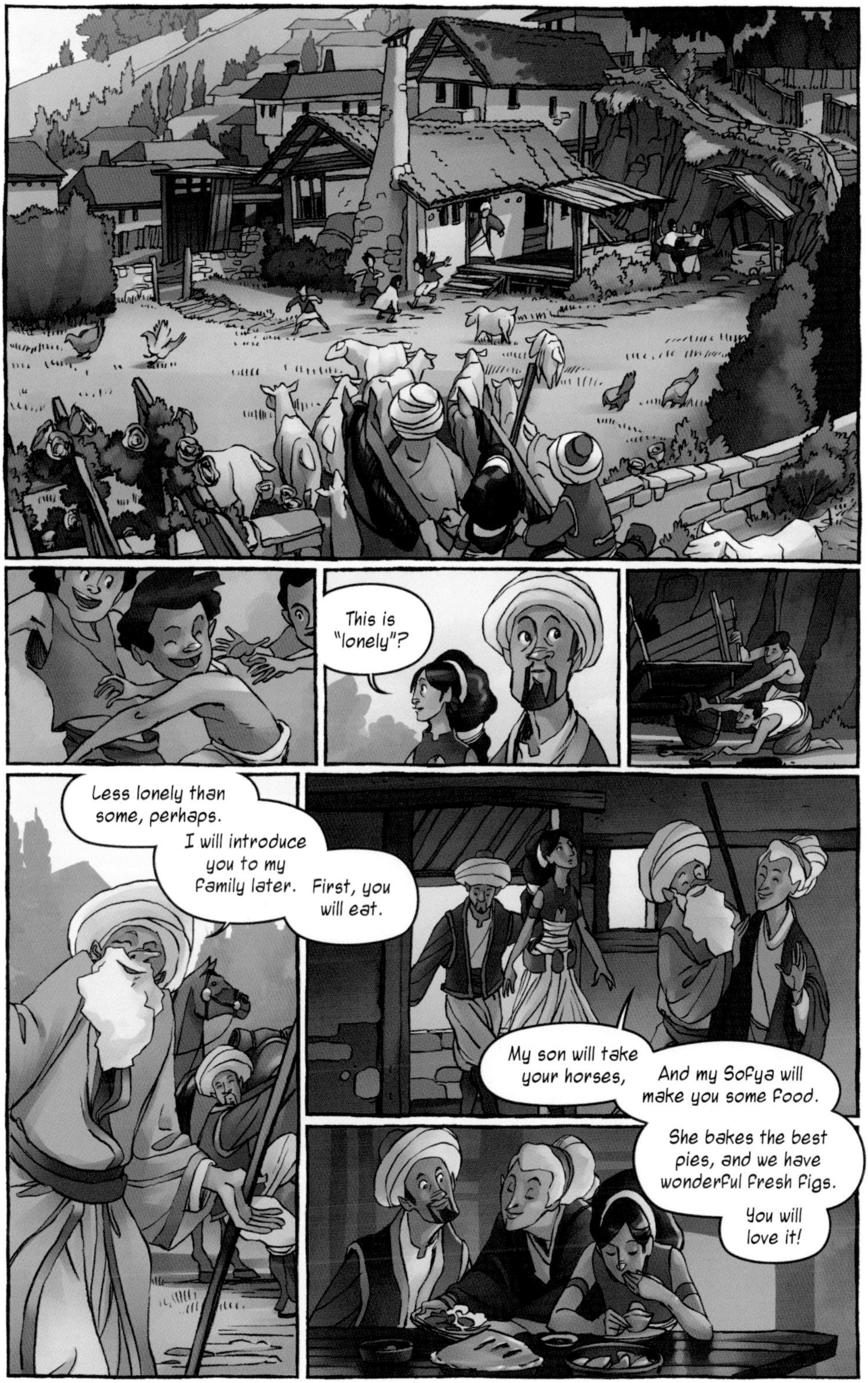
This is "lonely"?
Less lonely than some, perhaps.
I will introduce you to my family later.
First, you will eat.
My son will take your horses,
And my Sofya will make you some food.
She bakes the best pies, and we have wonderful fresh figs.
You will love it!

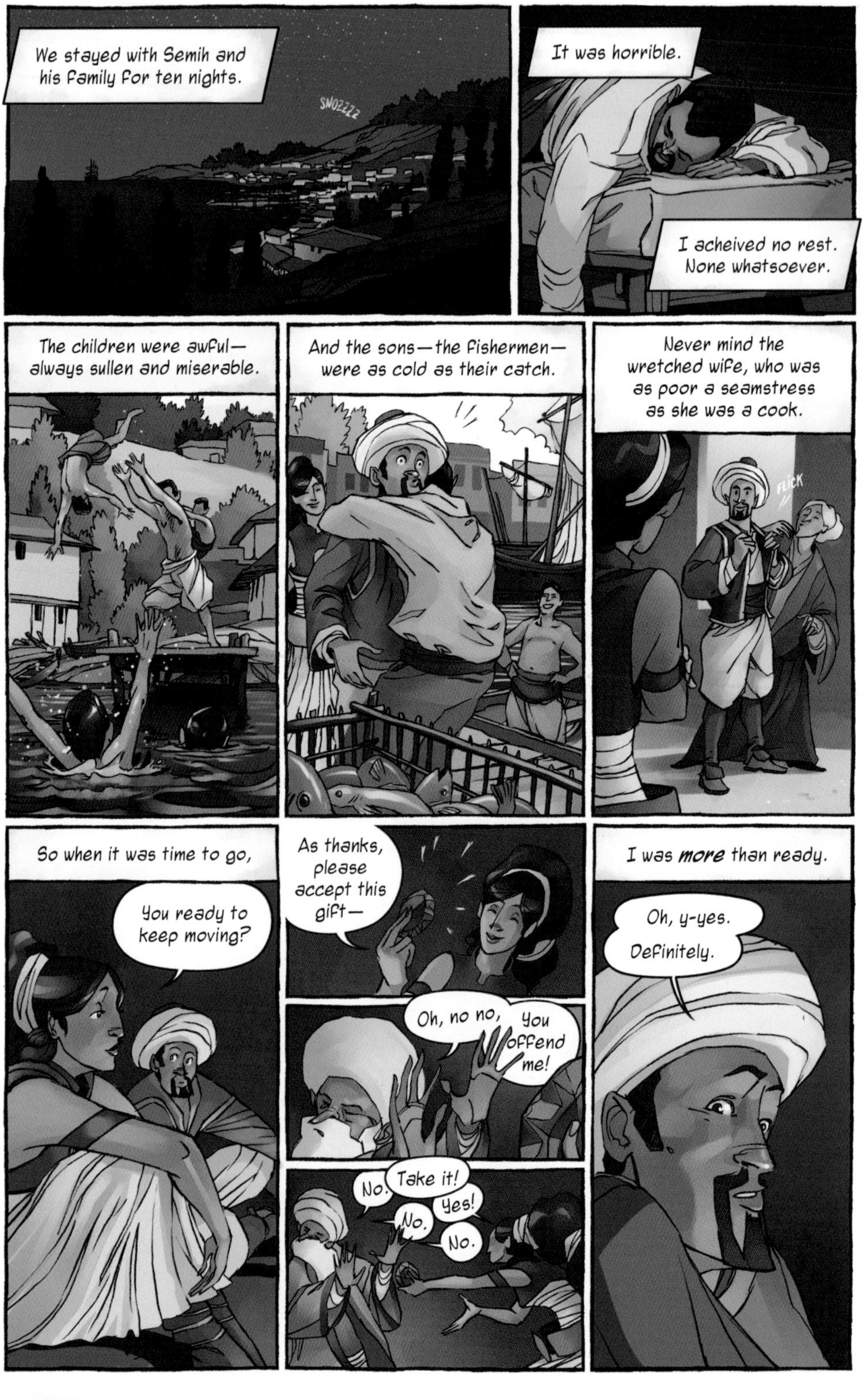

We stayed with Semih and his family for ten nights.
SNOZZZZ
It was horrible.
I acheived no rest. None whatsoever.
The children were awful— always sullen and miserable.
And the sons—the fishermen— were as cold as their catch.
Never mind the wretched wife, who was as poor a seamstress as she was a cook.
FLICK
So when it was time to go,
You ready to keep moving?
As thanks, please accept this gift—
Oh, no no,
You offend me!
No.
Take it!
Yes!
No.
No.
I was *more* than ready.
Oh, y-yes.
Definitely.

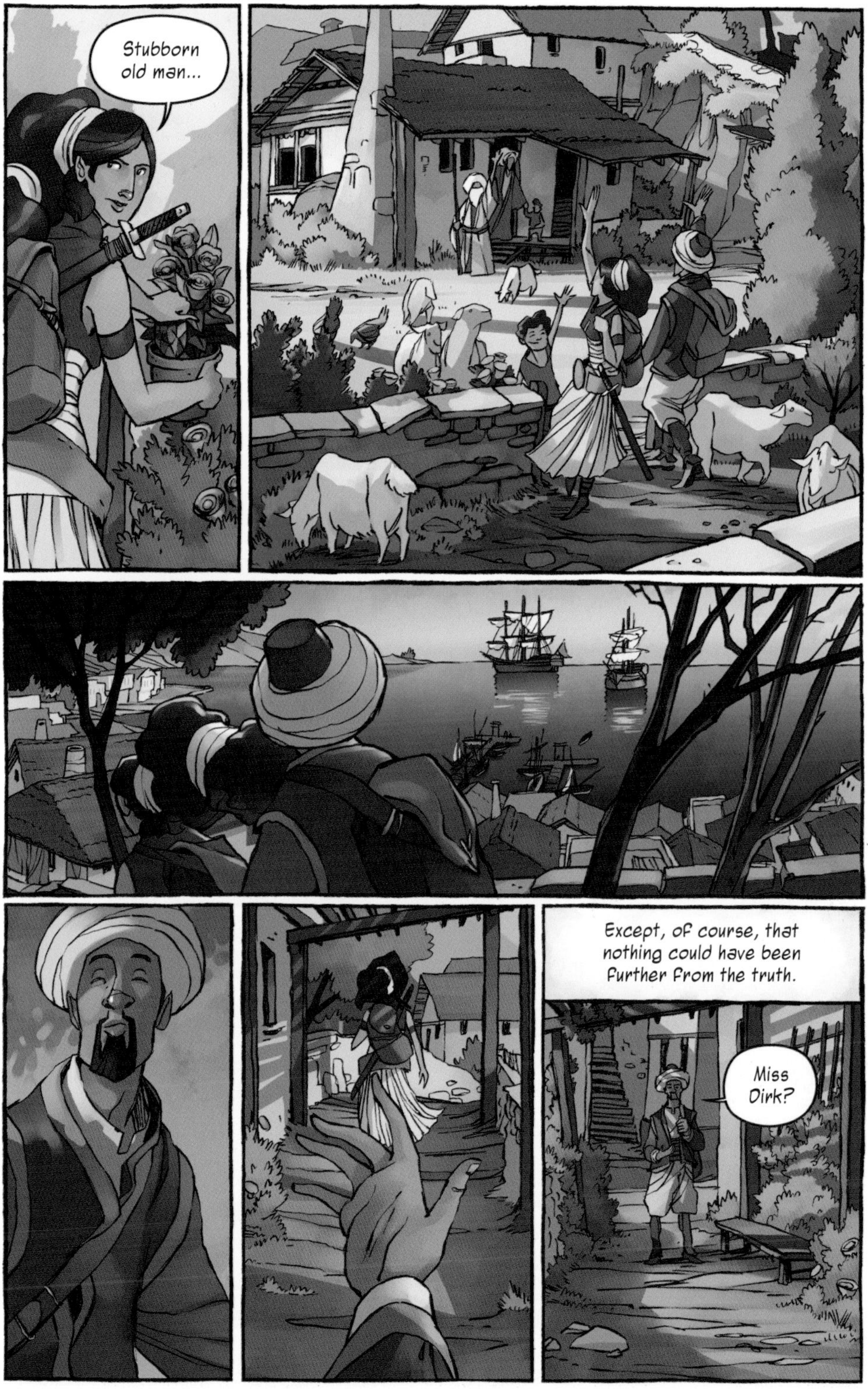
Stubborn old man...
Except, of course, that nothing could have been further from the truth.
Miss Dirk?

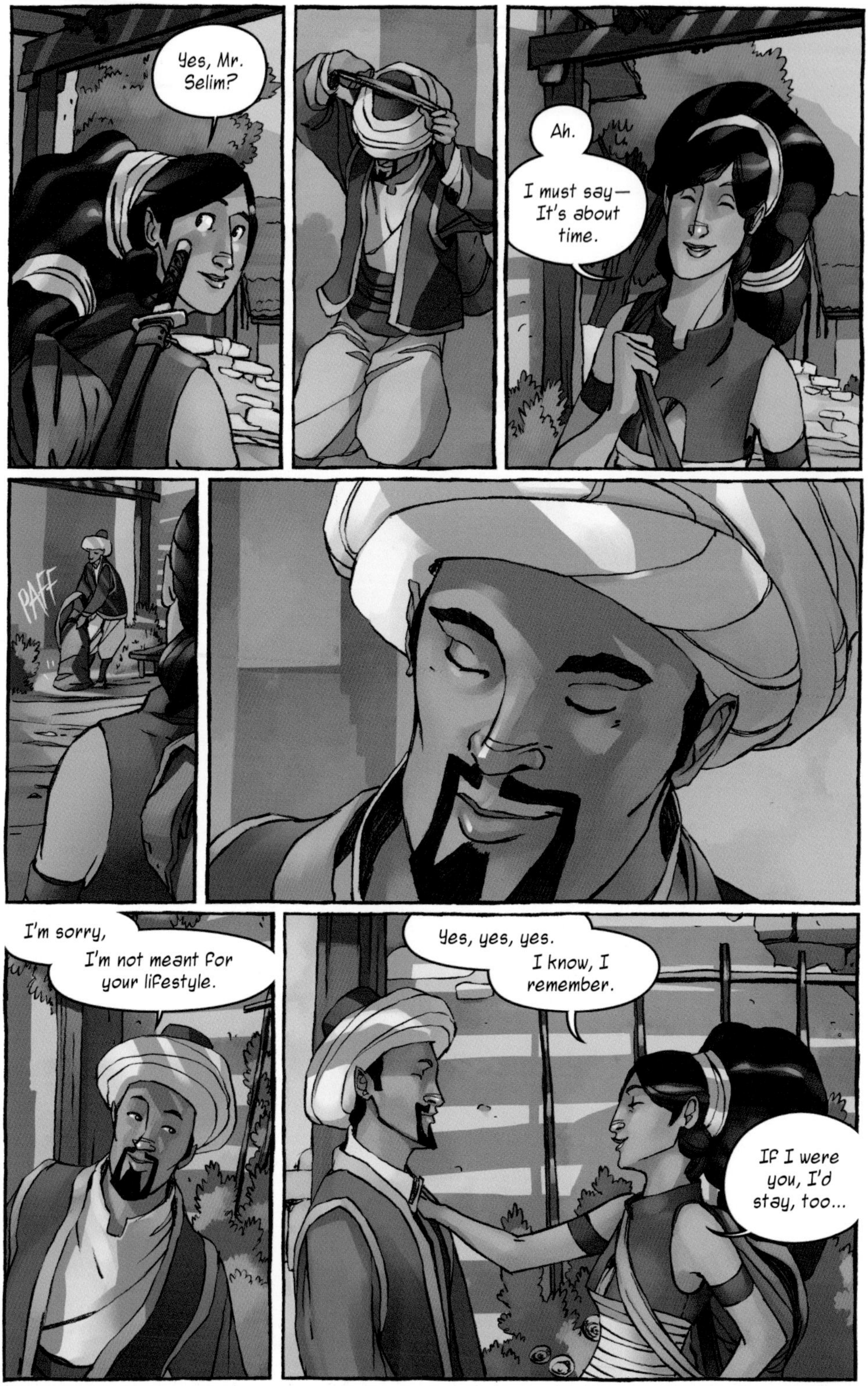
Yes, Mr. Selim?
Ah.
I must say— It's about time.
PAFF
I'm sorry,
I'm not meant for your lifestyle.
Yes, yes, yes.
I know, I remember.
If I were you, I'd stay, too...

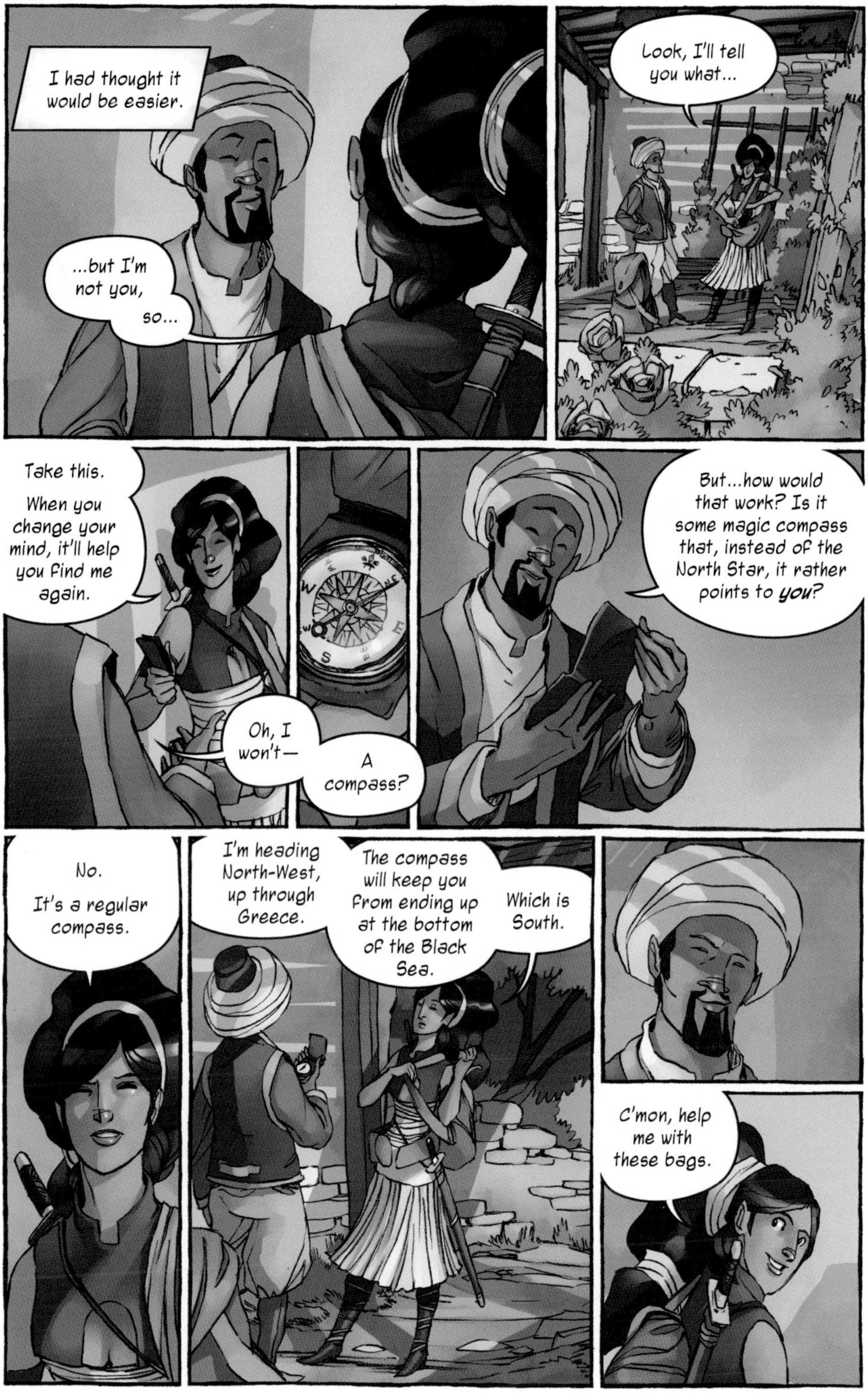
I had thought it would be easier.
...but I'm not you, so...
Look, I'll tell you what...
Take this.
When you change your mind, it'll help you find me again.
Oh, I won't—
A compass?
But...how would that work? Is it some magic compass that, instead of the North Star, it rather points to *you*?
No.
It's a regular compass.
I'm heading North-West, up through Greece.
The compass will keep you from ending up at the bottom of the Black Sea.
Which is South.
C'mon, help me with these bags.

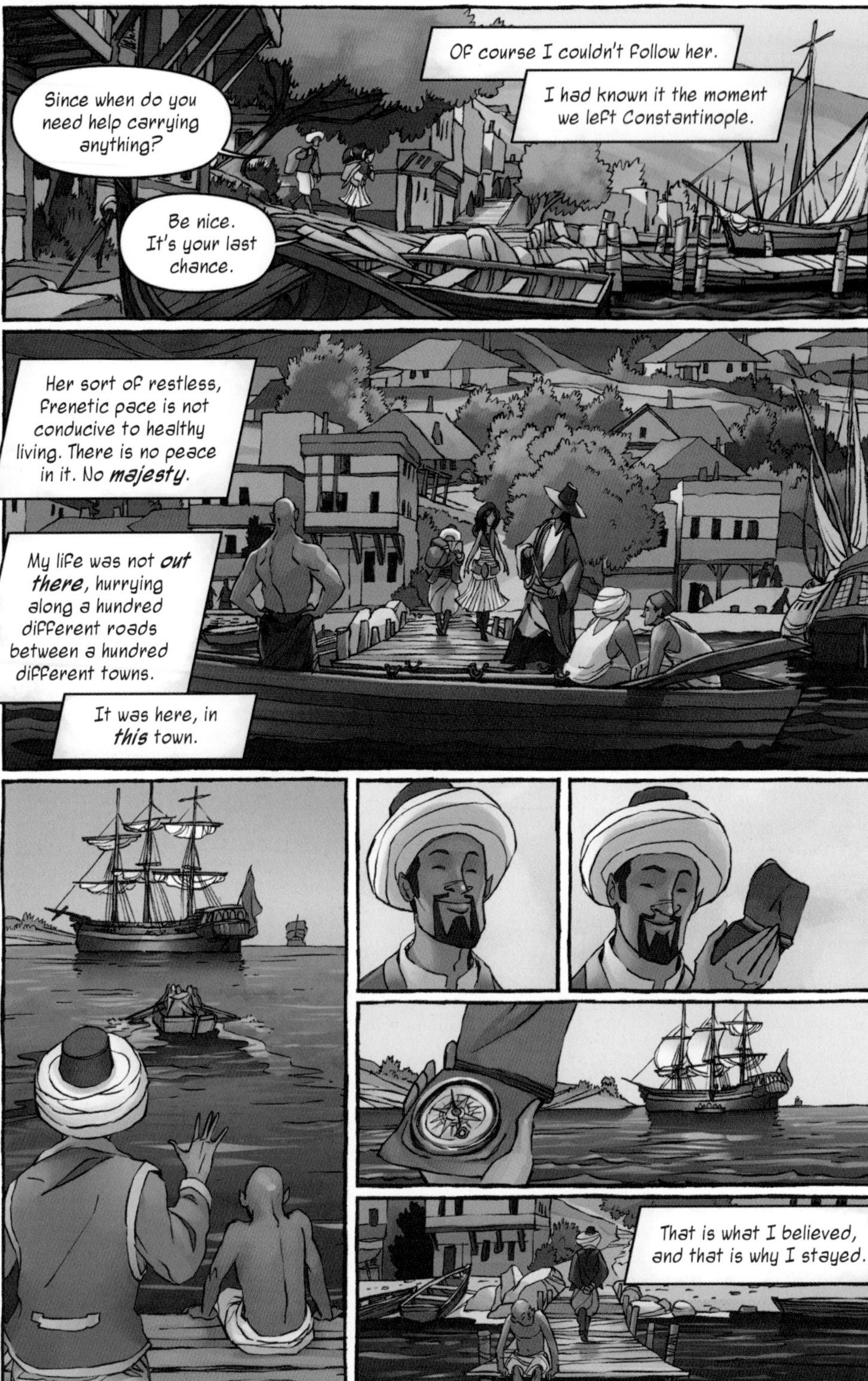
Of course I couldn't follow her.
I had known it the moment we left Constantinople.
Since when do you need help carrying anything?
Be nice. It's your last chance.
Her sort of restless, frenetic pace is not conducive to healthy living. There is no peace in it. No majesty.
My life was not out there, hurrying along a hundred different roads between a hundred different towns.
It was here, in this town.
That is what I believed, and that is why I stayed.

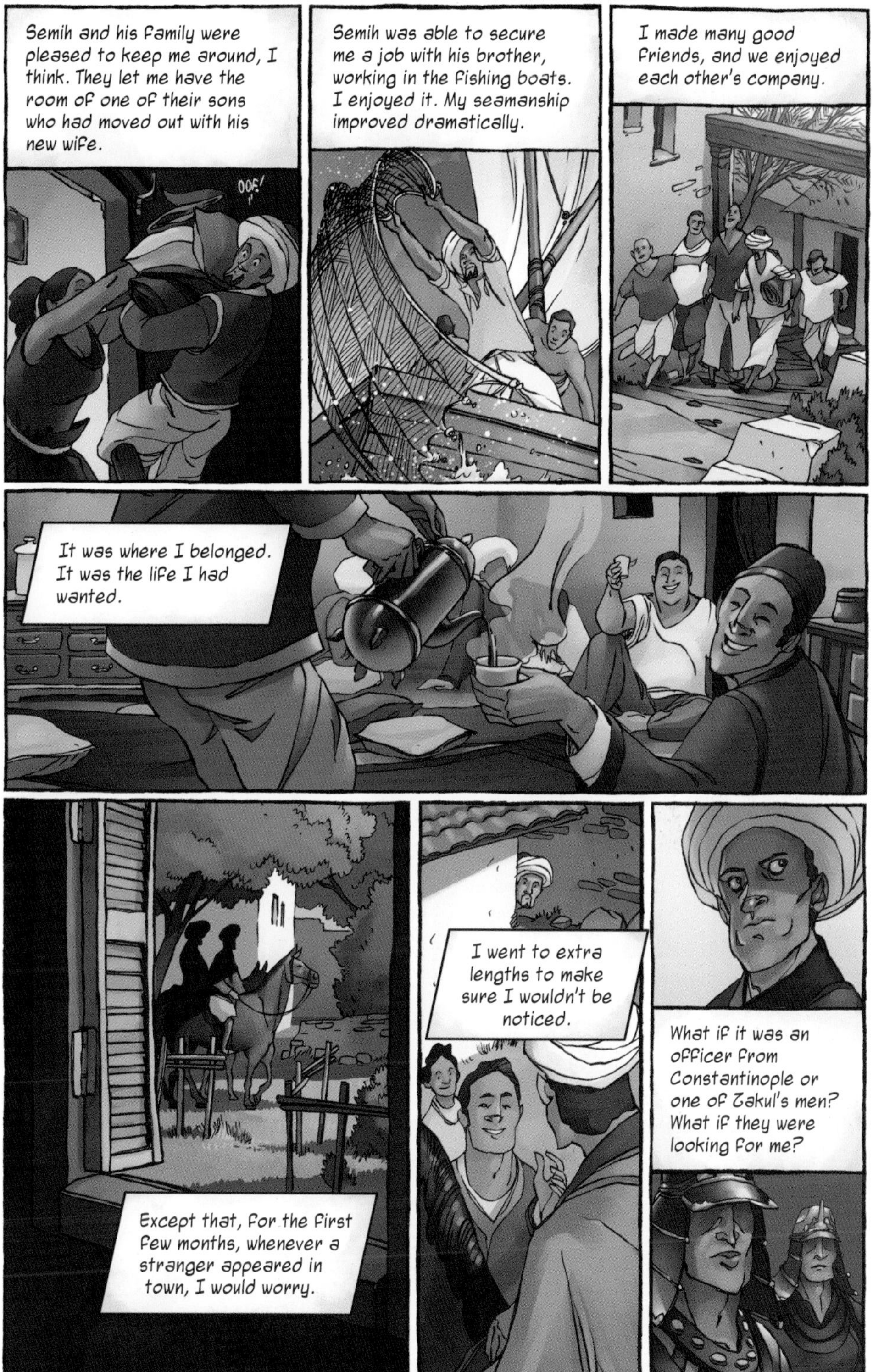
Semih and his family were pleased to keep me around, I think. They let me have the room of one of their sons who had moved out with his new wife.
OOF!
Semih was able to secure me a job with his brother, working in the fishing boats. I enjoyed it. My seamanship improved dramatically.
I made many good friends, and we enjoyed each other's company.
It was where I belonged. It was the life I had wanted.
Except that, for the first few months, whenever a stranger appeared in town, I would worry.
I went to extra lengths to make sure I wouldn't be noticed.
What if it was an officer from Constantinople or one of Zakul's men? What if they were looking for me?

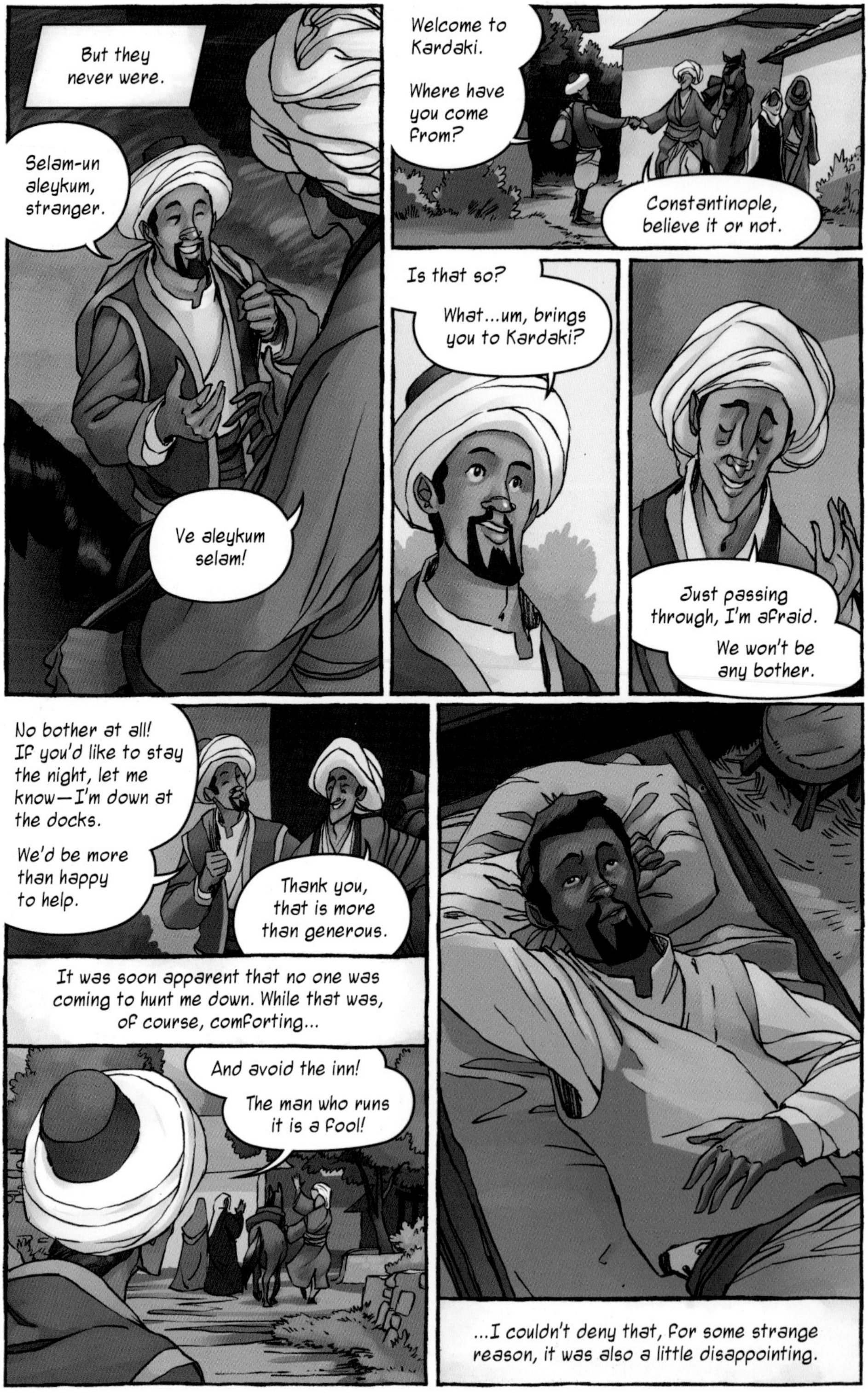

But they never were.
Selam-un aleykum, stranger.
Ve aleykum selam!
Welcome to Kardaki.
Where have you come from?
Constantinople, believe it or not.
Is that so?
What...um, brings you to Kardaki?
Just passing through, I'm afraid.
We won't be any bother.
No bother at all! If you'd like to stay the night, let me know—I'm down at the docks.
We'd be more than happy to help.
Thank you, that is more than generous.
It was soon apparent that no one was coming to hunt me down. While that was, of course, comforting...
And avoid the inn!
The man who runs it is a fool!
...I couldn't deny that, for some strange reason, it was also a little disappointing.

My friends noticed
it before I did.

I didn't intend to stop
walking with them...

I just started looking
for different paths,
different routes.

That's how, one day, I
found myself up on the
slopes above town.

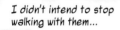

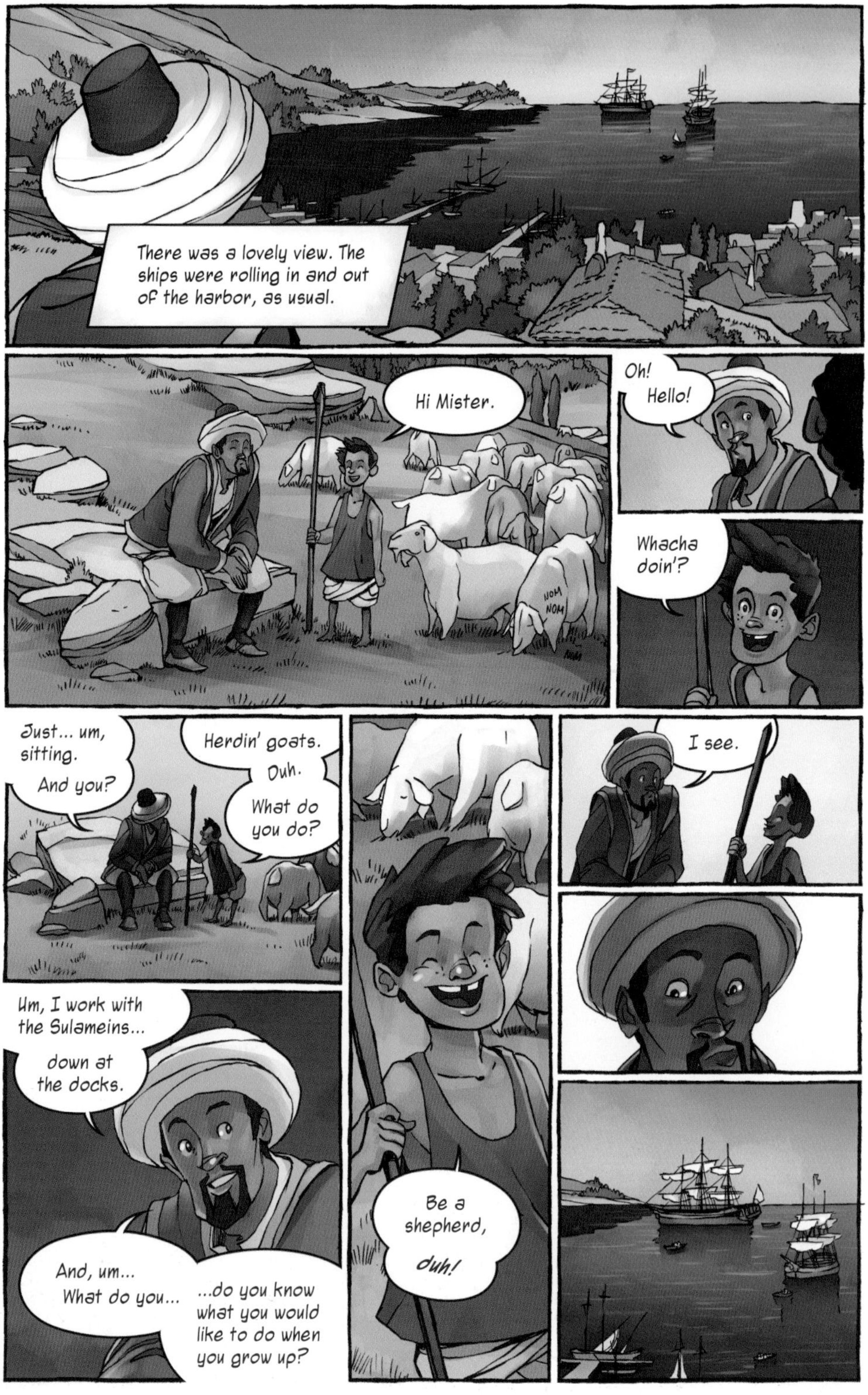
There was a lovely view. The ships were rolling in and out of the harbor, as usual.
Hi Mister.
NOM NOM
Oh!
Hello!
Whacha doin'?
Just... um, sitting.
And you?
Herdin' goats.
Duh.
What do you do?
I see.
Um, I work with the Sulameins...
down at the docks.
And, um... What do you...
...do you know what you would like to do when you grow up?
Be a shepherd,
duh!

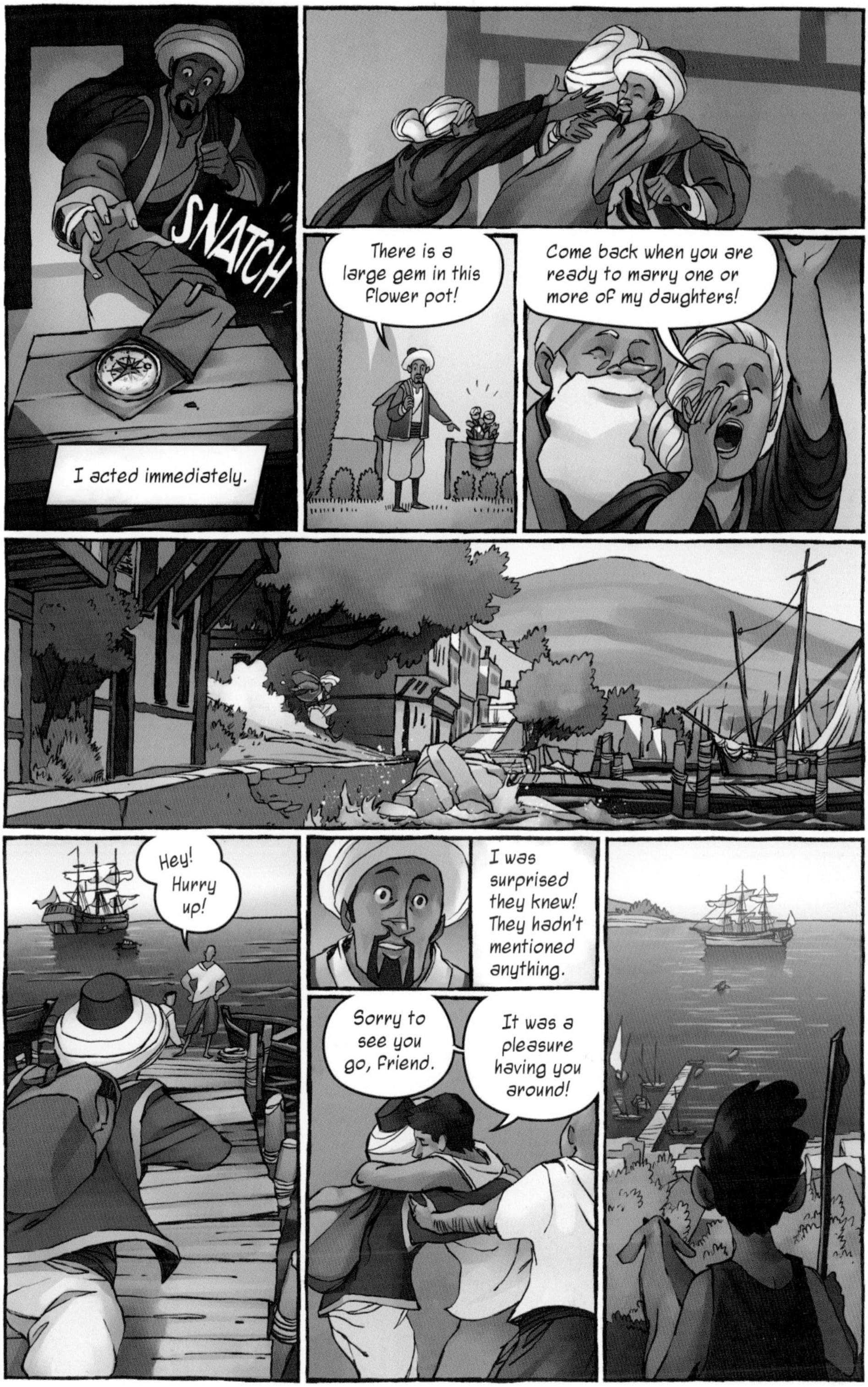
SNATCH
I acted immediately.
There is a large gem in this flower pot!
Come back when you are ready to marry one or more of my daughters!
Hey! Hurry up!
I was surprised they knew! They hadn't mentioned anything.
Sorry to see you go, friend.
It was a pleasure having you around!

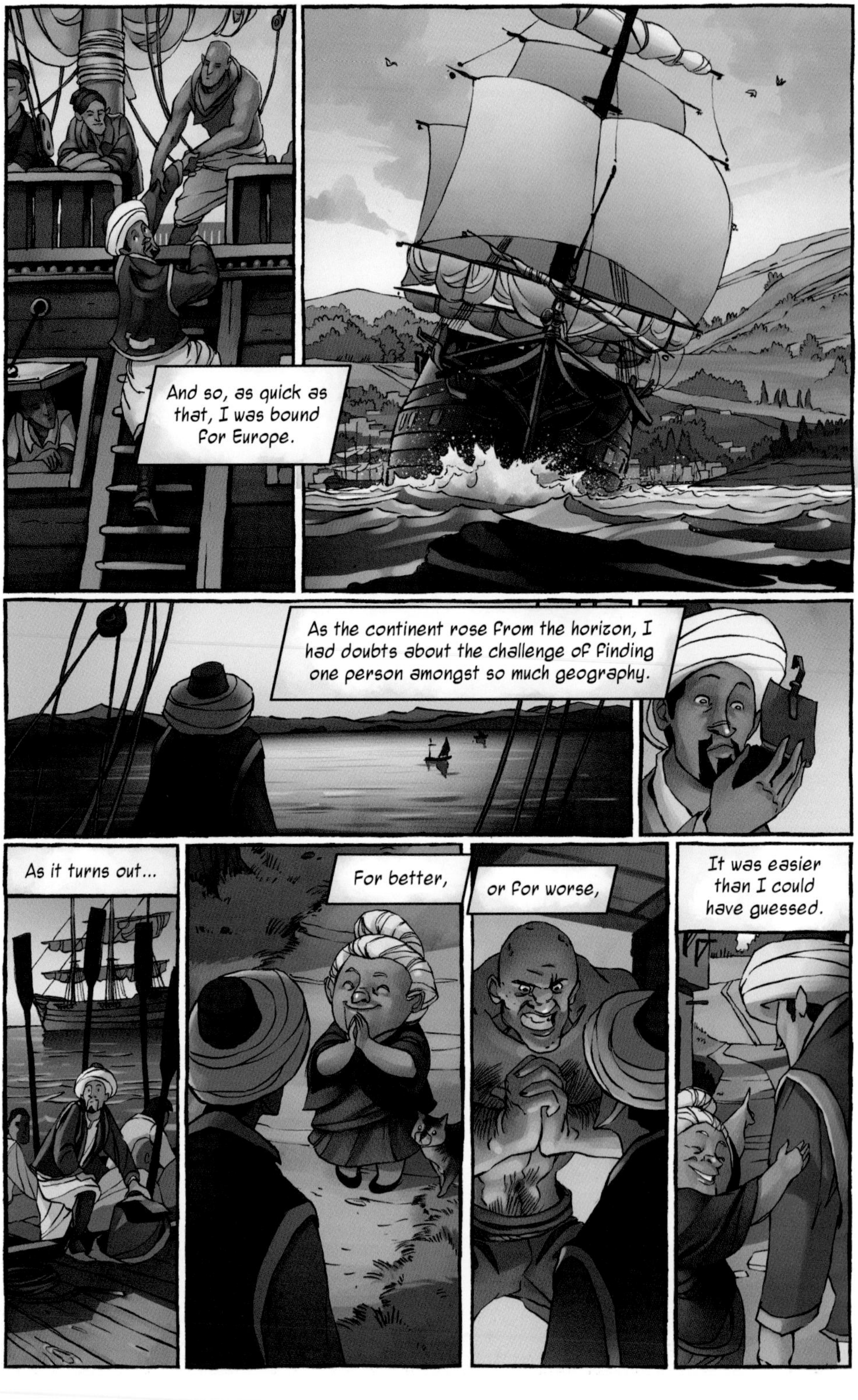
And so, as quick as that, I was bound for Europe.
As the continent rose from the horizon, I had doubts about the challenge of finding one person amongst so much geography.
As it turns out...
For better,
or for worse,
It was easier than I could have guessed.

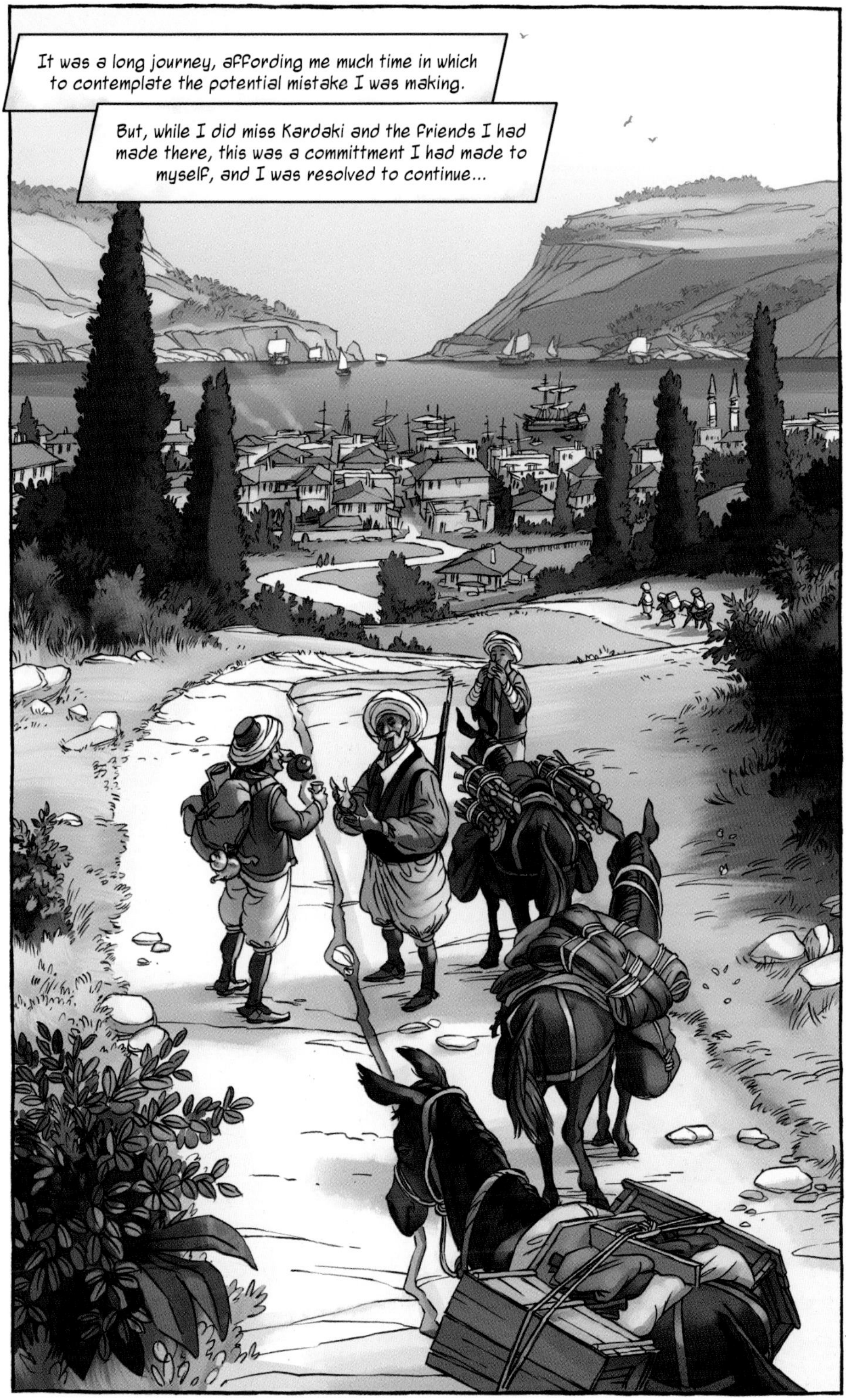
It was a long journey, affording me much time in which to contemplate the potential mistake I was making.
But, while I did miss Kardaki and the friends I had made there, this was a committment I had made to myself, and I was resolved to continue...

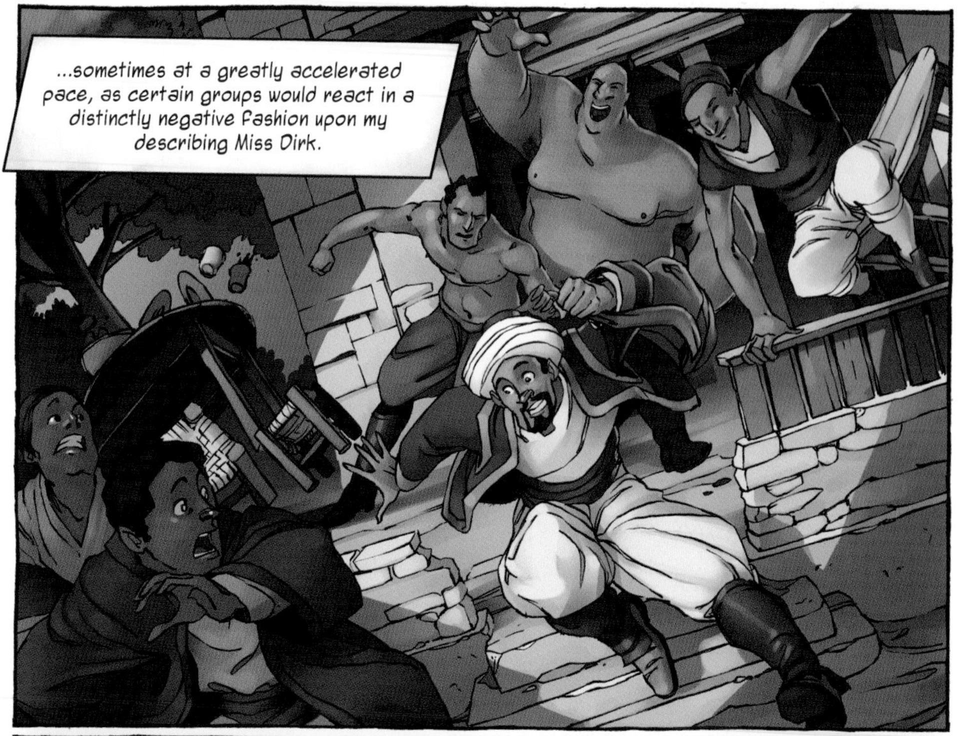
...sometimes at a greatly accelerated pace, as certain groups would react in a distinctly negative fashion upon my describing Miss Dirk.

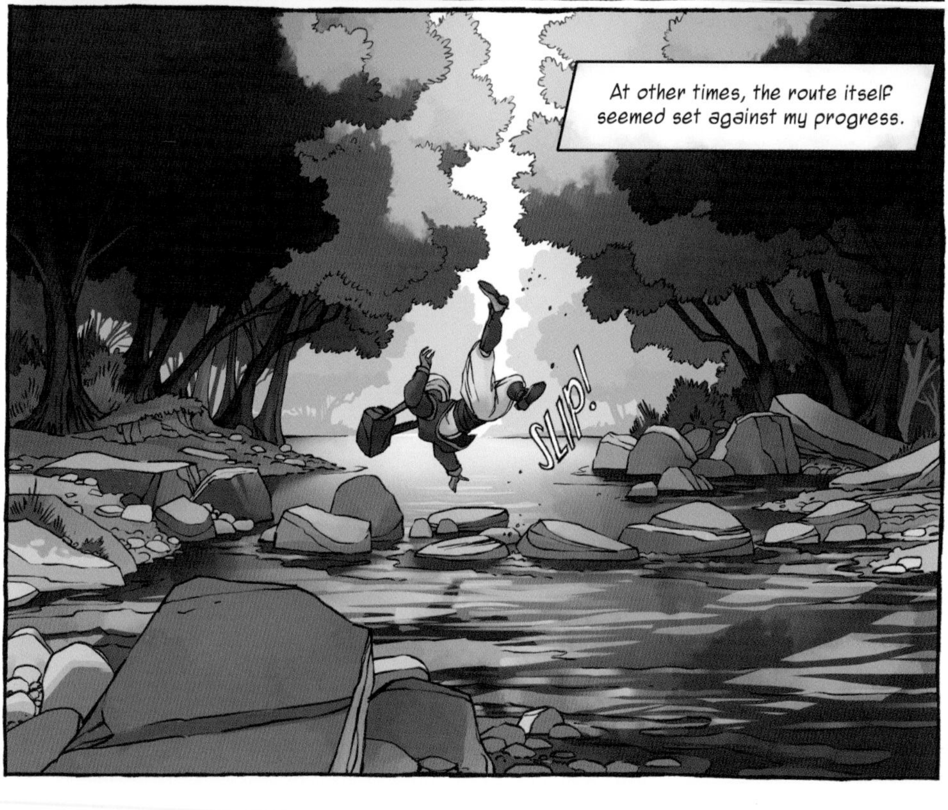
At other times, the route itself seemed set against my progress.
SLIP!

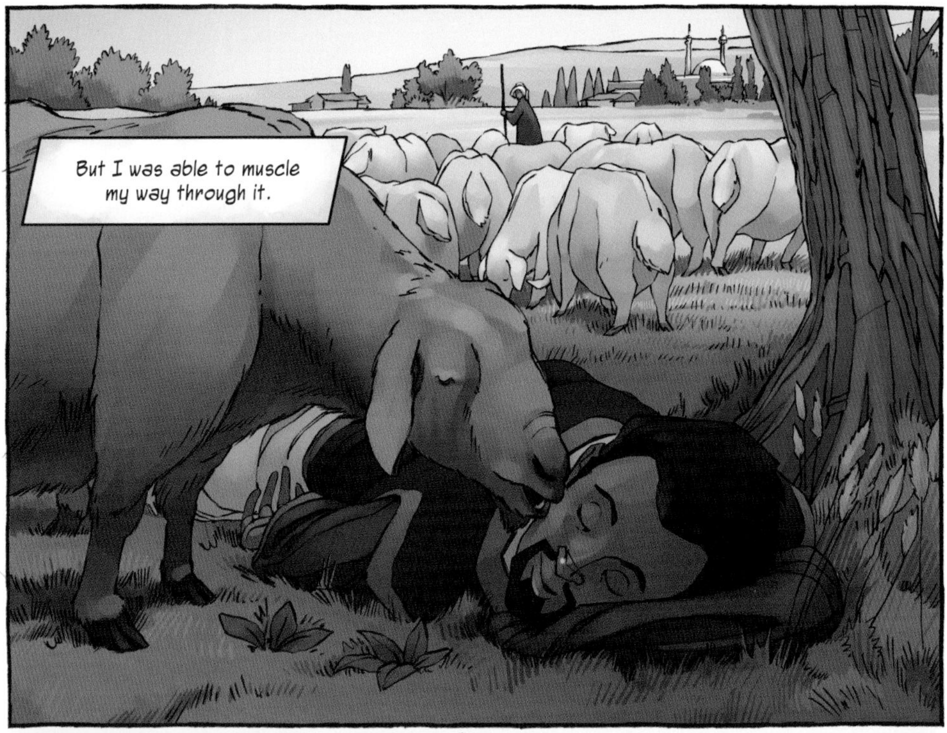
But I was able to muscle my way through it.

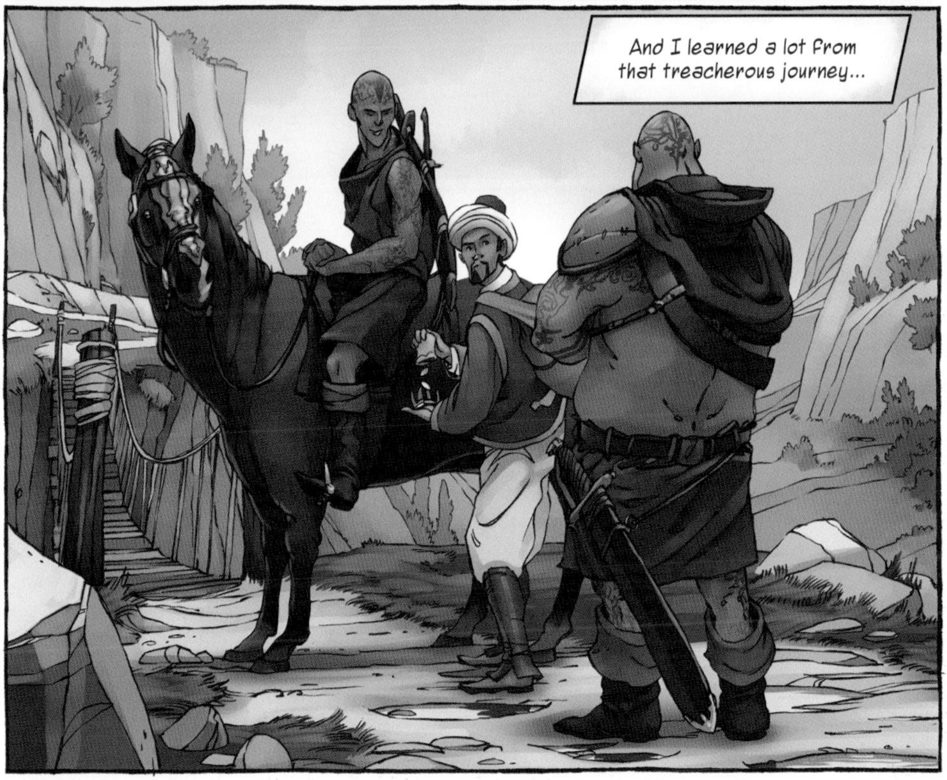
And I learned a lot from that treacherous journey...

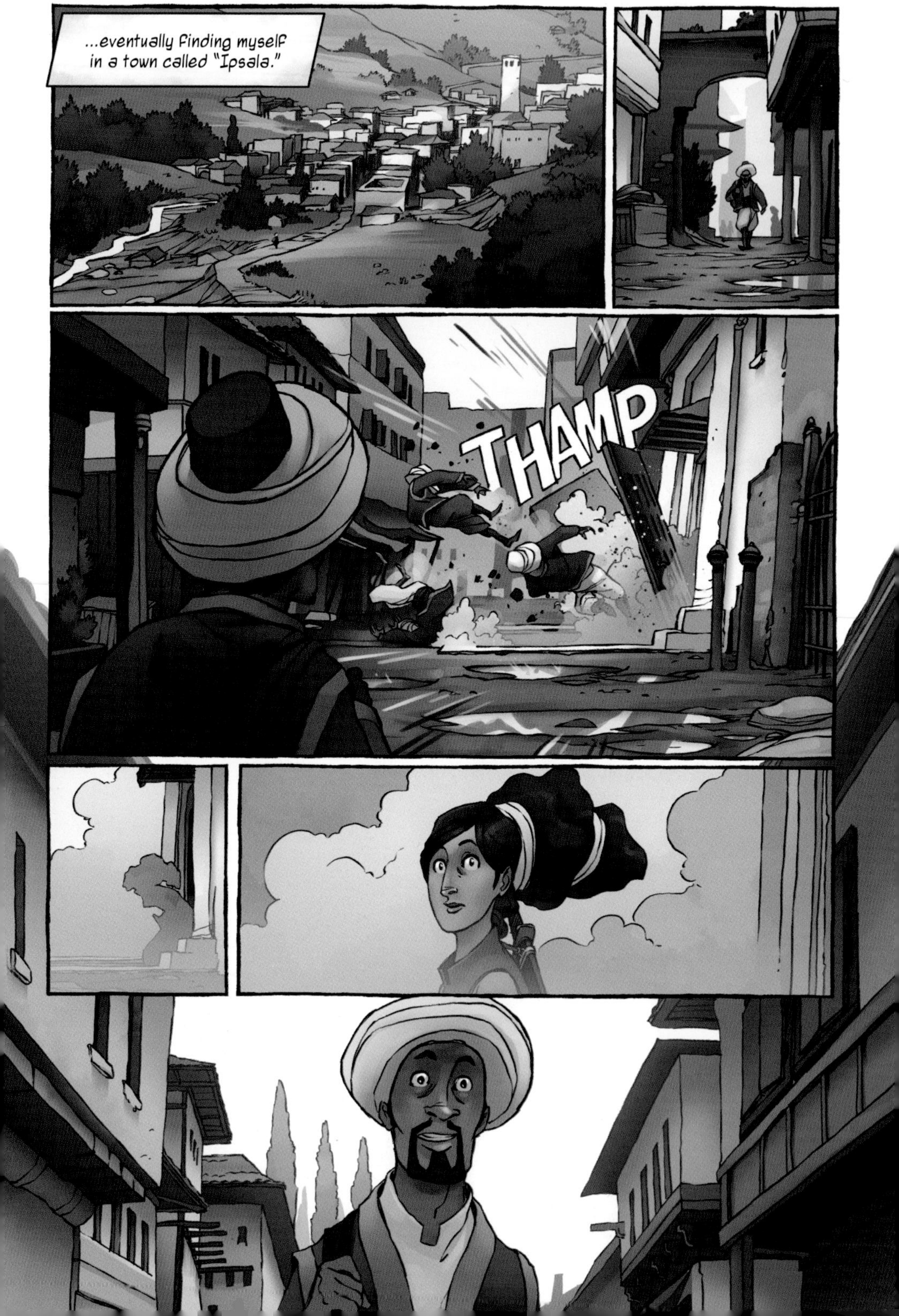
...eventually finding myself in a town called "Ipsala."
THAMP

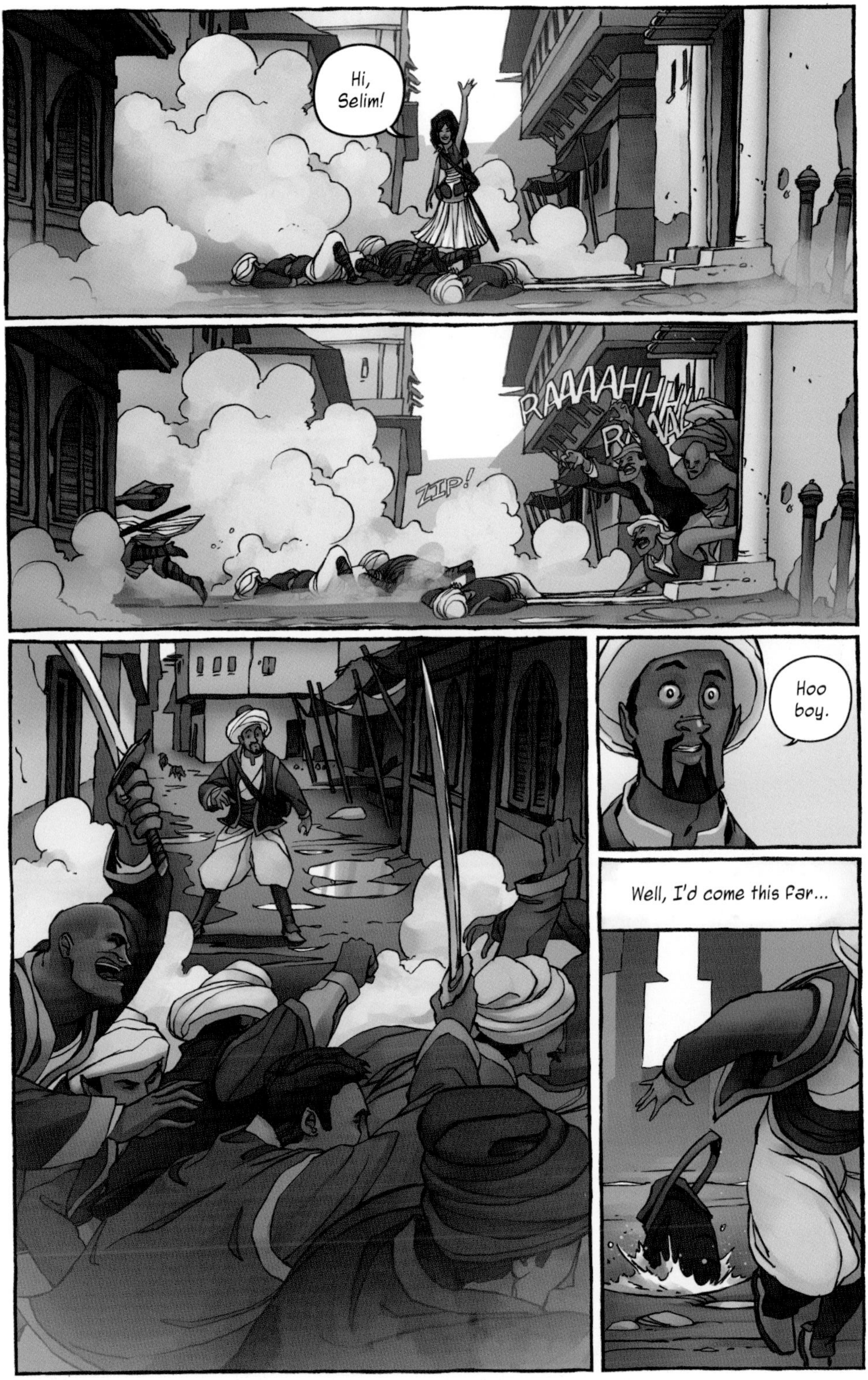
Hi, Selim!
RAAAAHHHH!
RAA
ZIP!
Hoo boy.
Well, I'd come this far...

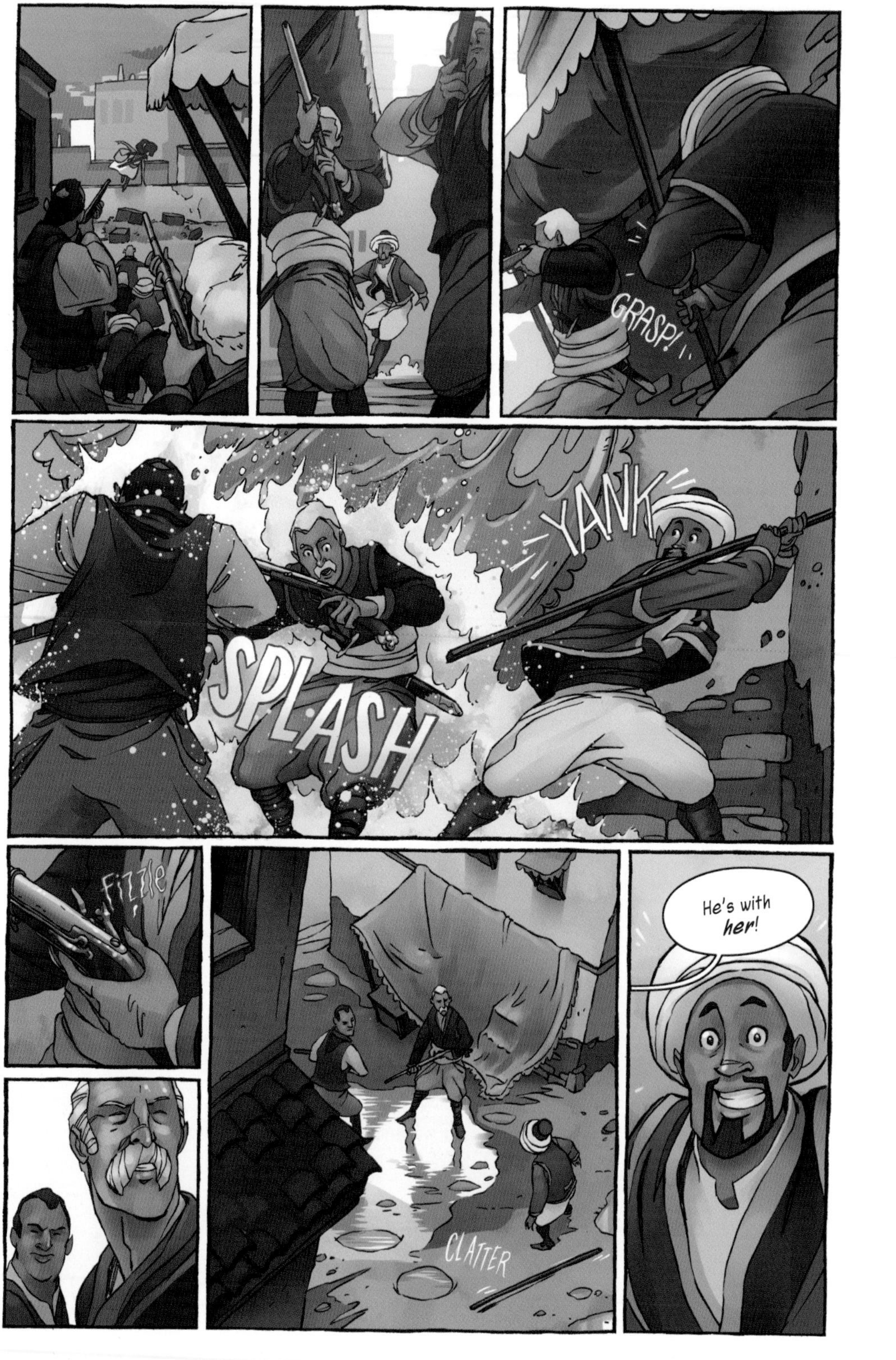
GRASP!
YANK
SPLASH
Fizzle
He's with **her**!
CLATTER

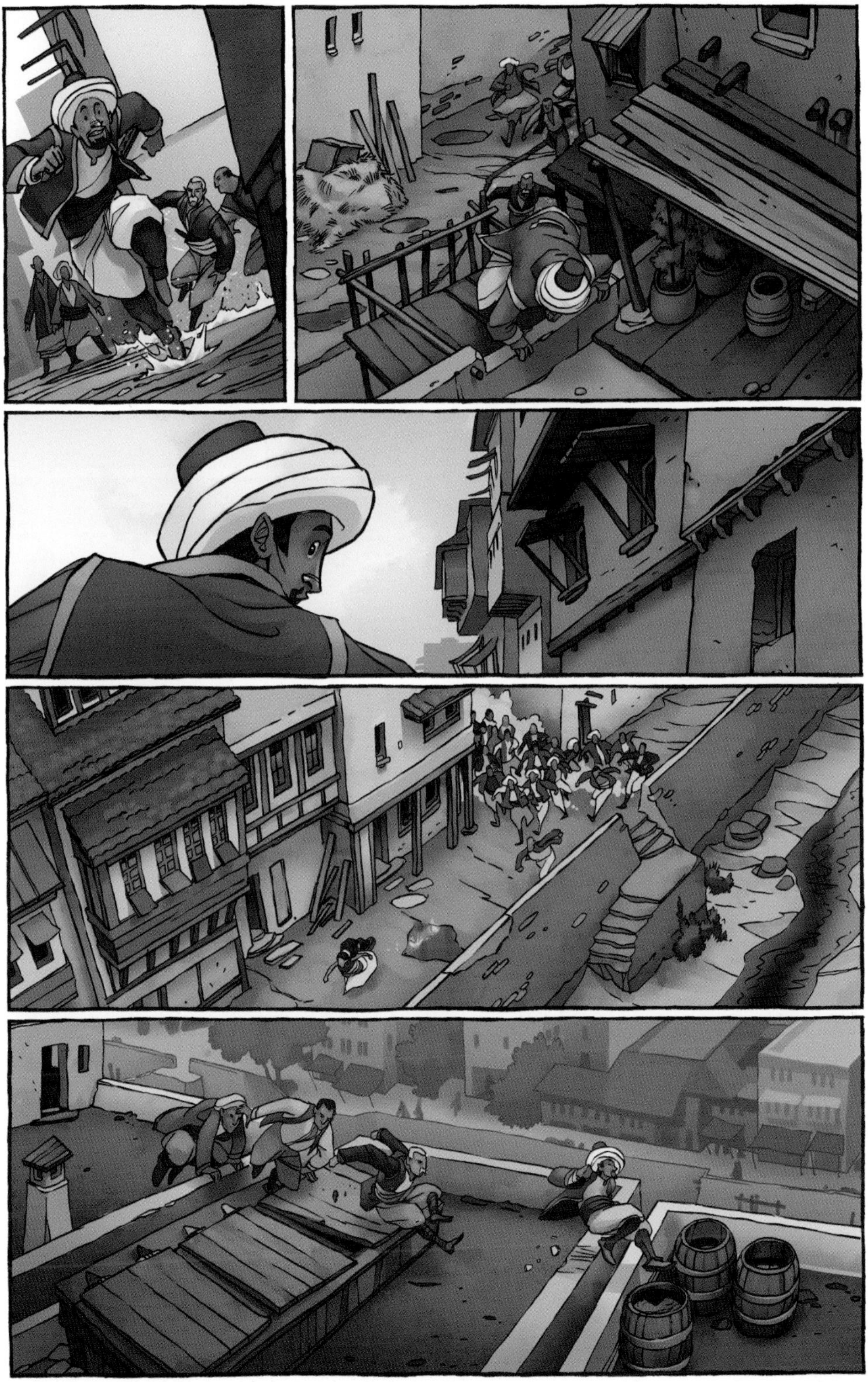

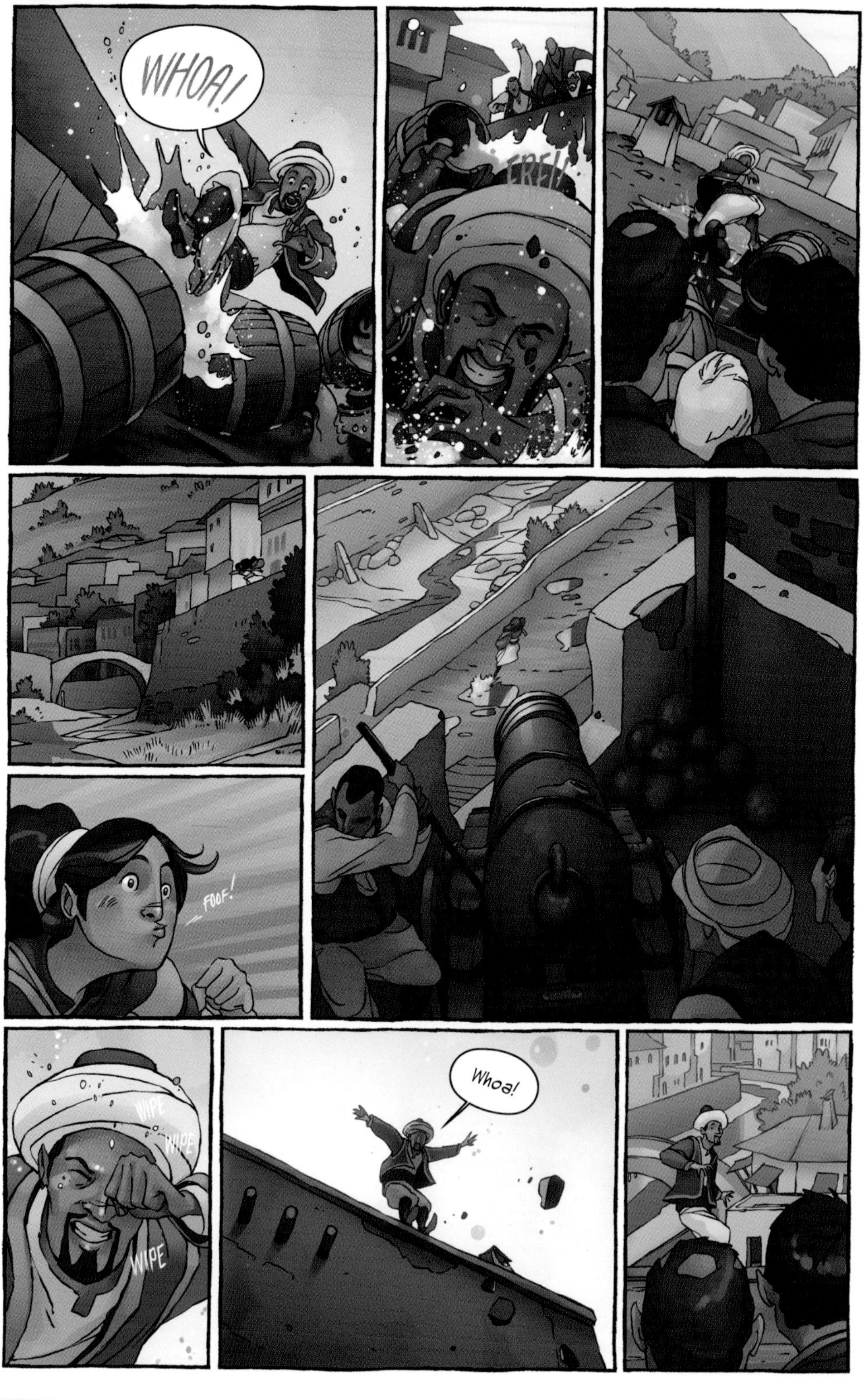
WHOA!
FOOF!
WIPE
WIPE
WIPE
Whoa!

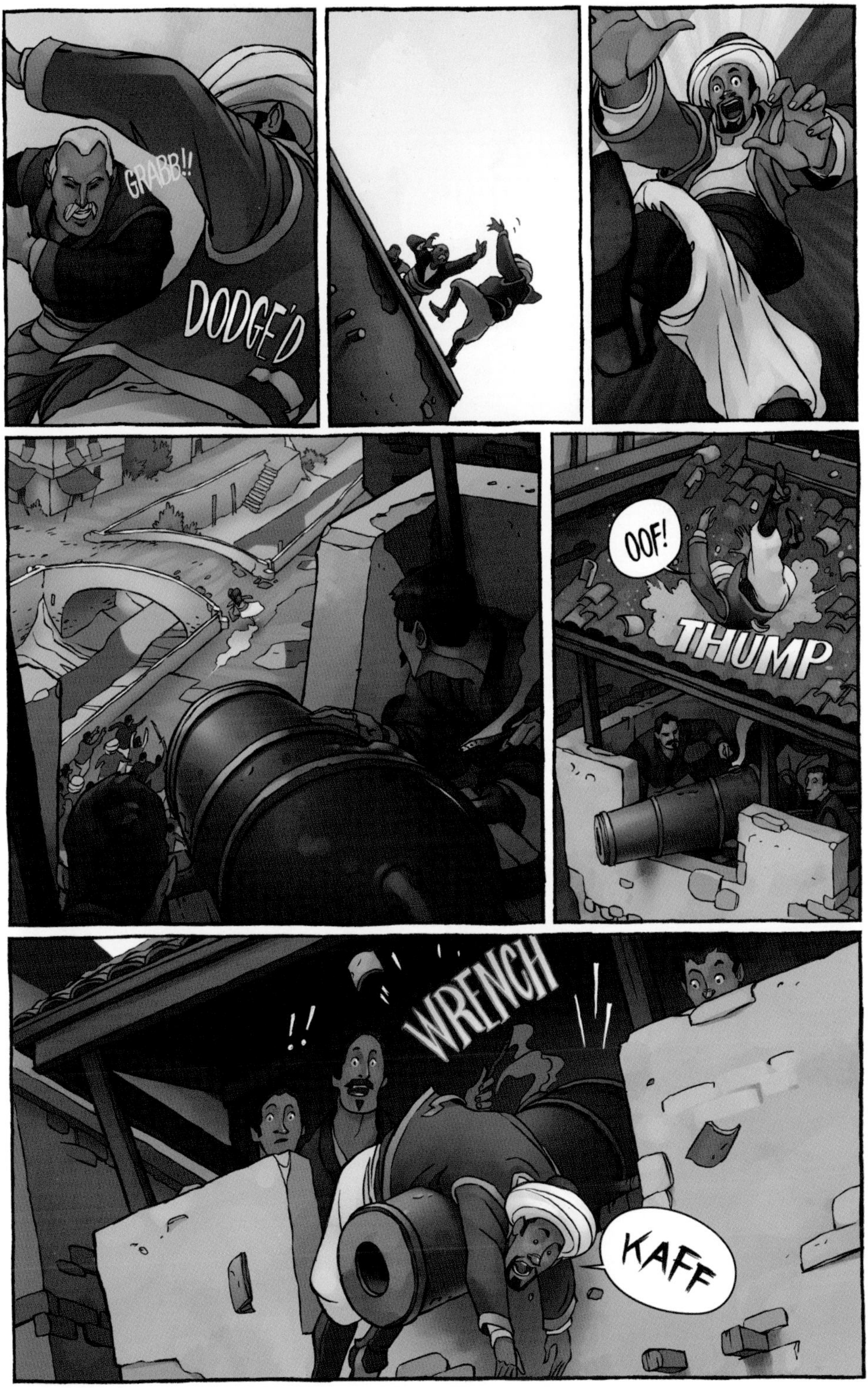
GRABB!!
DODGE'D
OOF!
THUMP
!!
WRENCH
KAFF

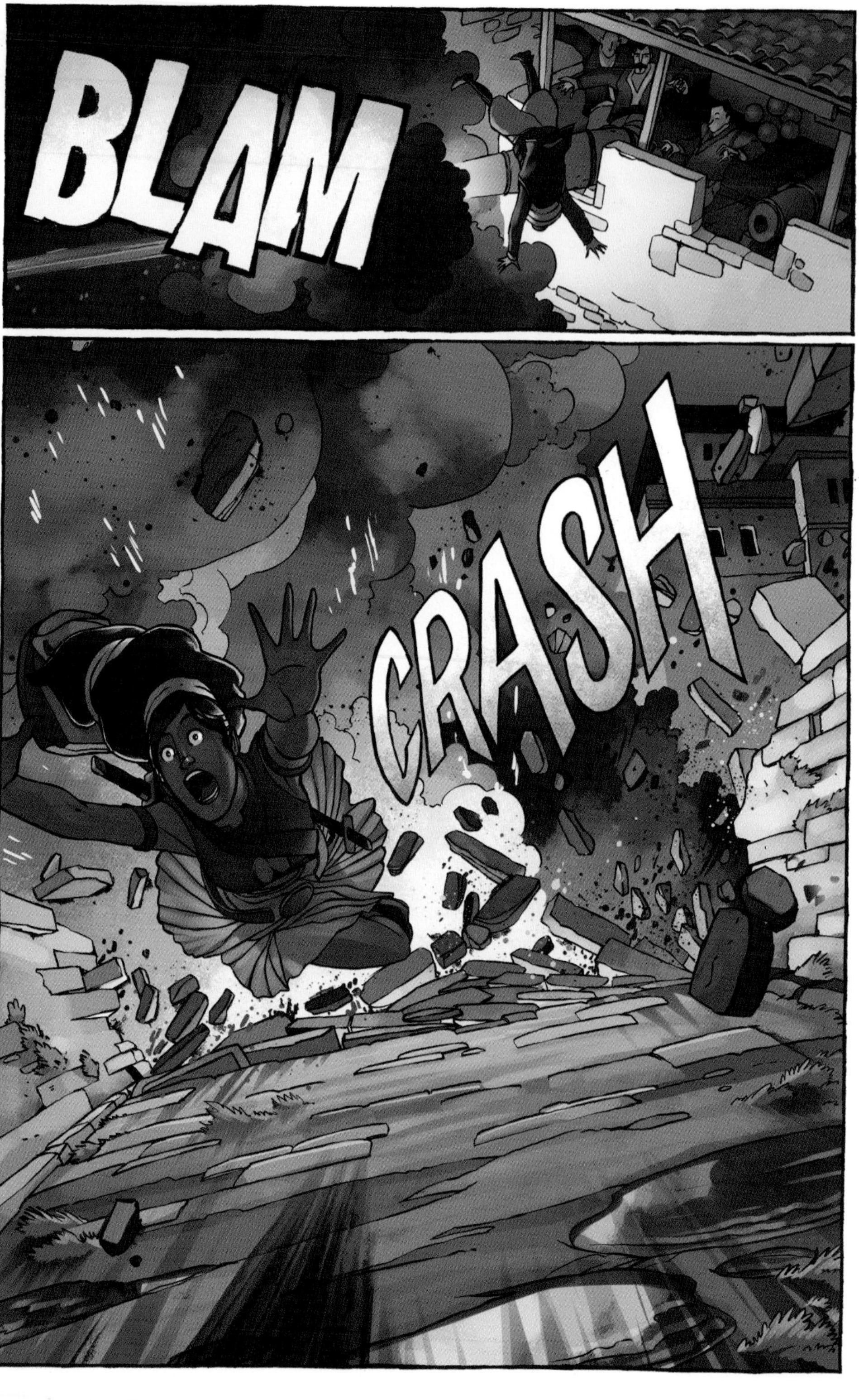
BLAM
CRASH

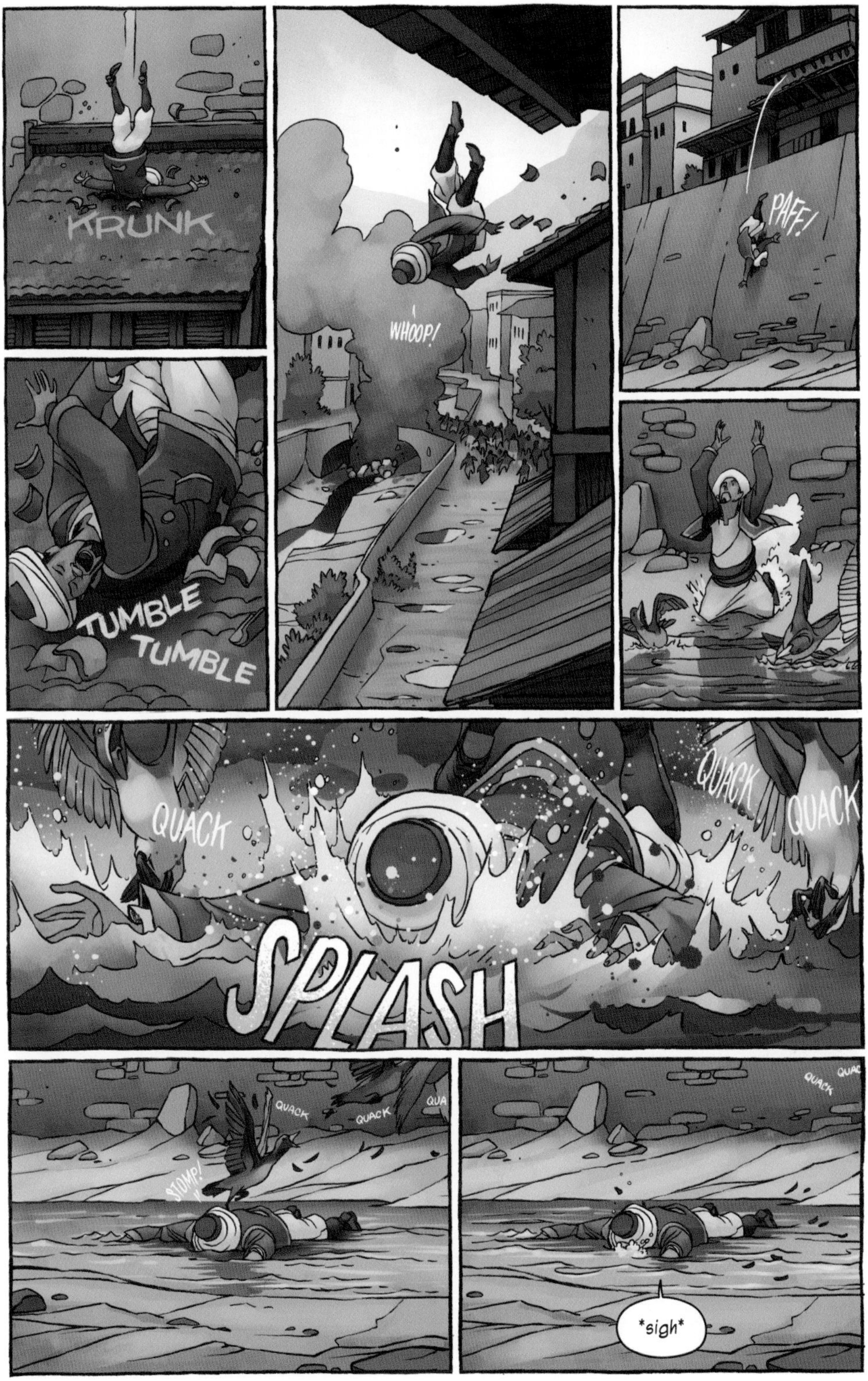
KRUNK
WHOOP!
PAFF!
TUMBLE
TUMBLE
QUACK
QUACK
QUACK
SPLASH
STOMP!
QUACK
QUACK
QUA
QUACK
QUAC
sigh

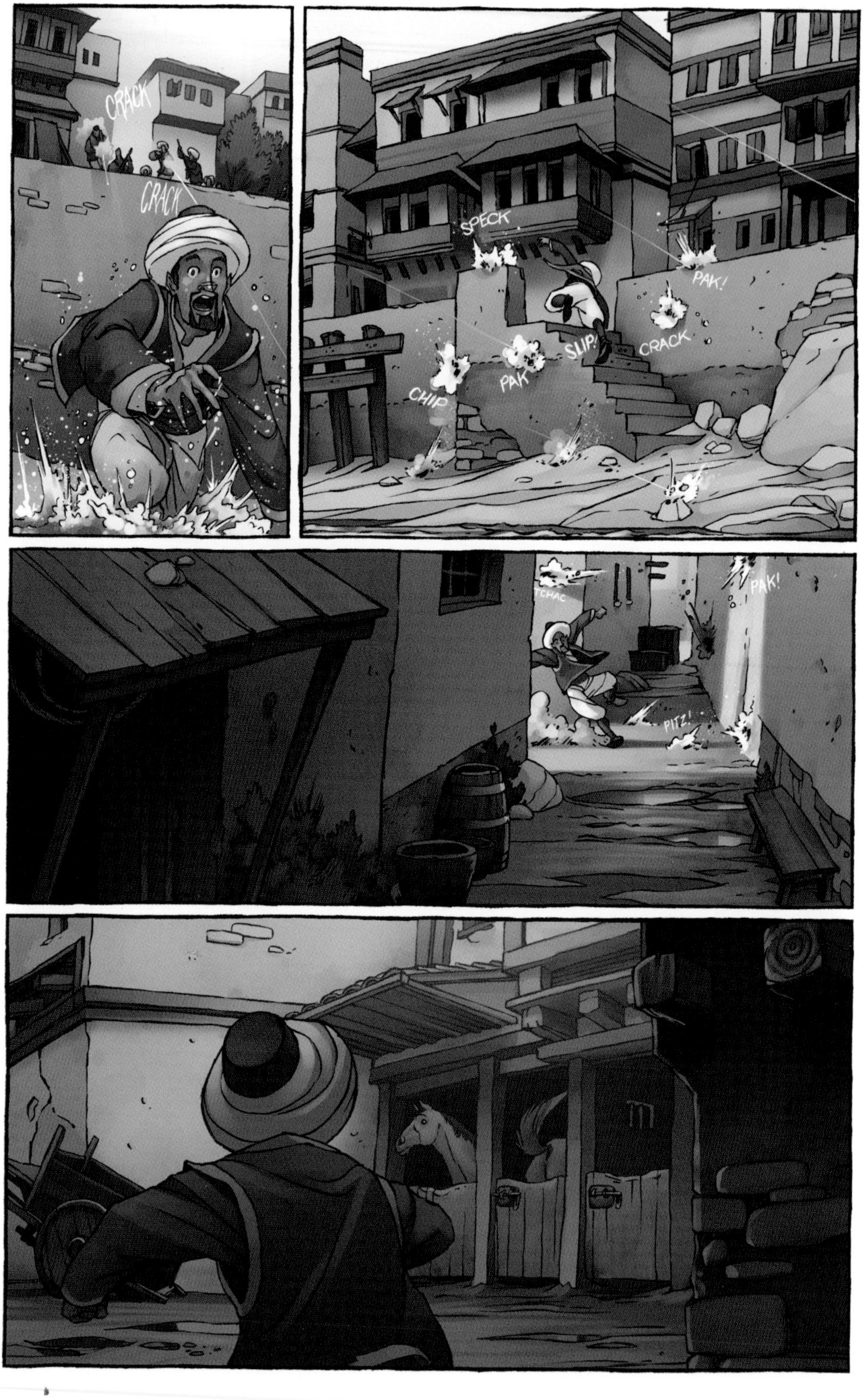
CRACK
CRACK
SPECK
PAK!
SLIP!
CRACK
PAK
CHIP
TCHAC
PAK!
PITZ!

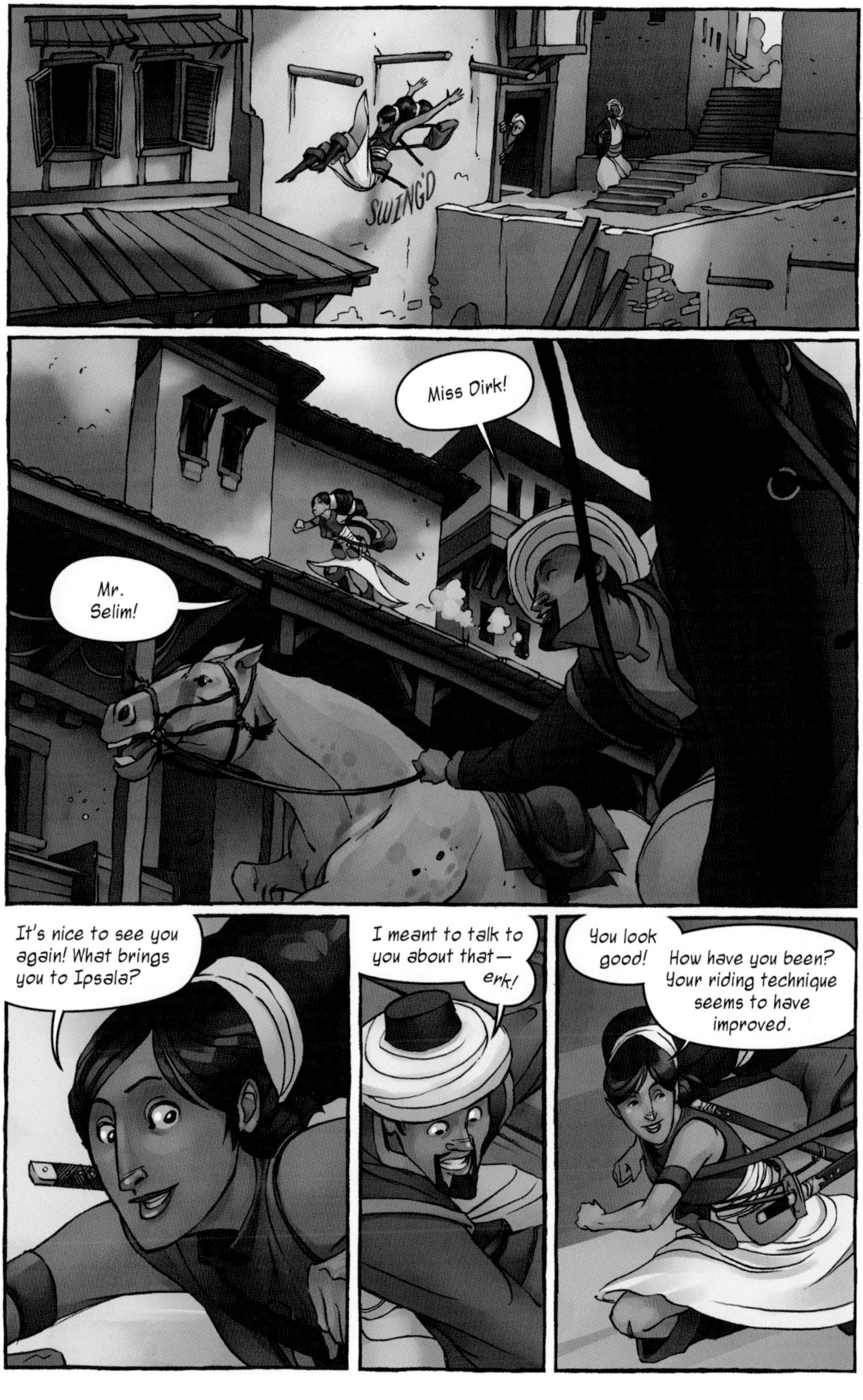
SWING'D
Miss Dirk!
Mr. Selim!
It's nice to see you again! What brings you to Ipsala?
I meant to talk to you about that—
erk!
You look good!
How have you been? Your riding technique seems to have improved.

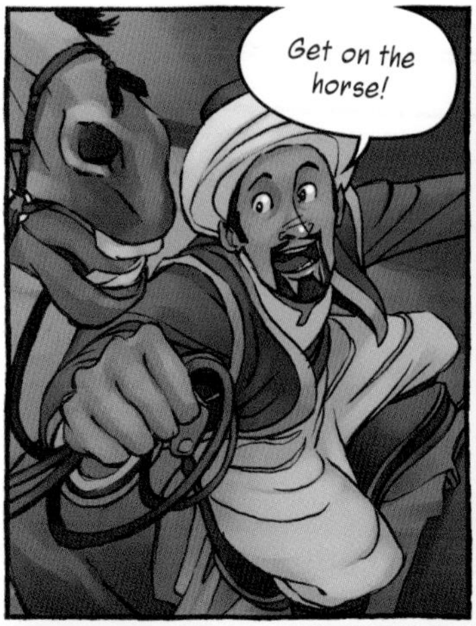
Get on the horse!

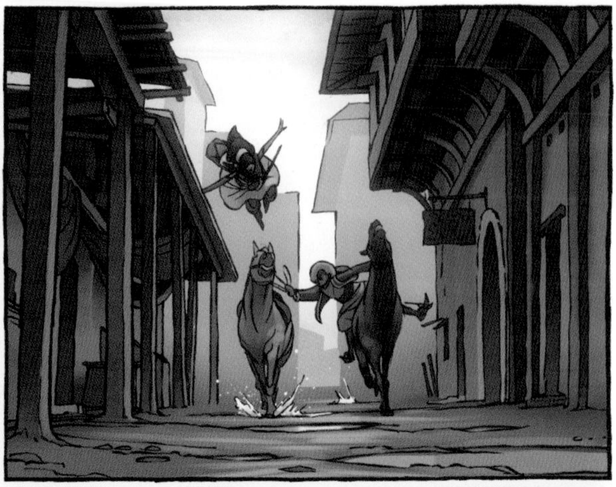

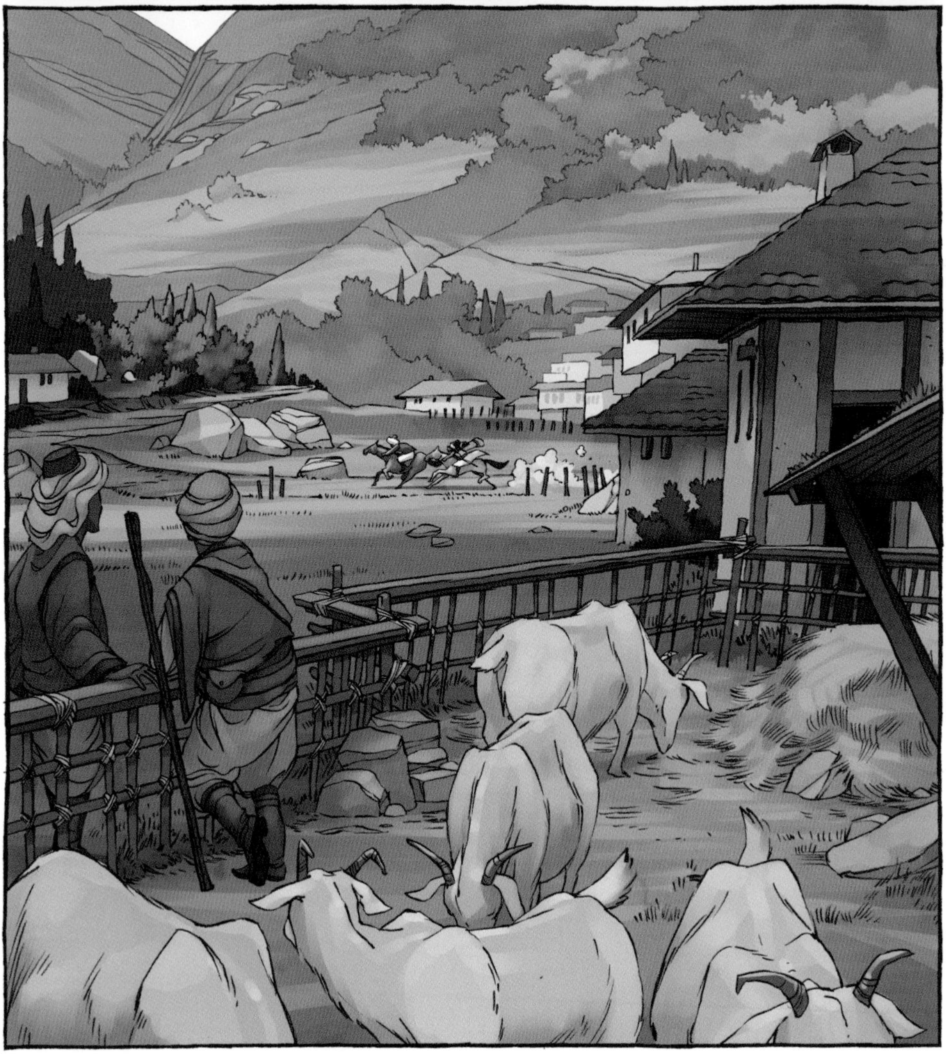

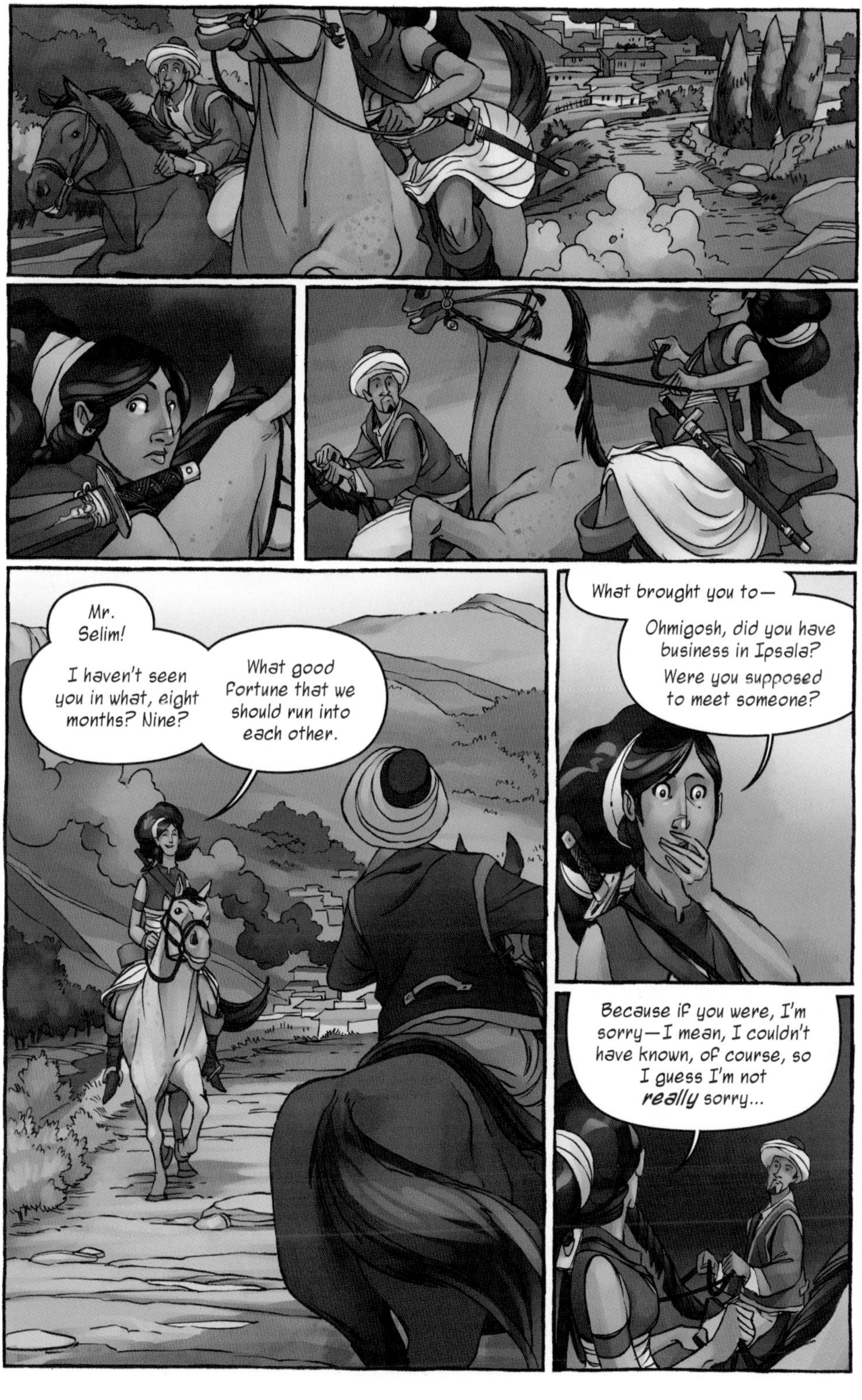
Mr. Selim!
I haven't seen you in what, eight months? Nine?
What good fortune that we should run into each other.
What brought you to—
Ohmigosh, did you have business in Ipsala?
Were you supposed to meet someone?
Because if you were, I'm sorry—I mean, I couldn't have known, of course, so I guess I'm not *really* sorry...

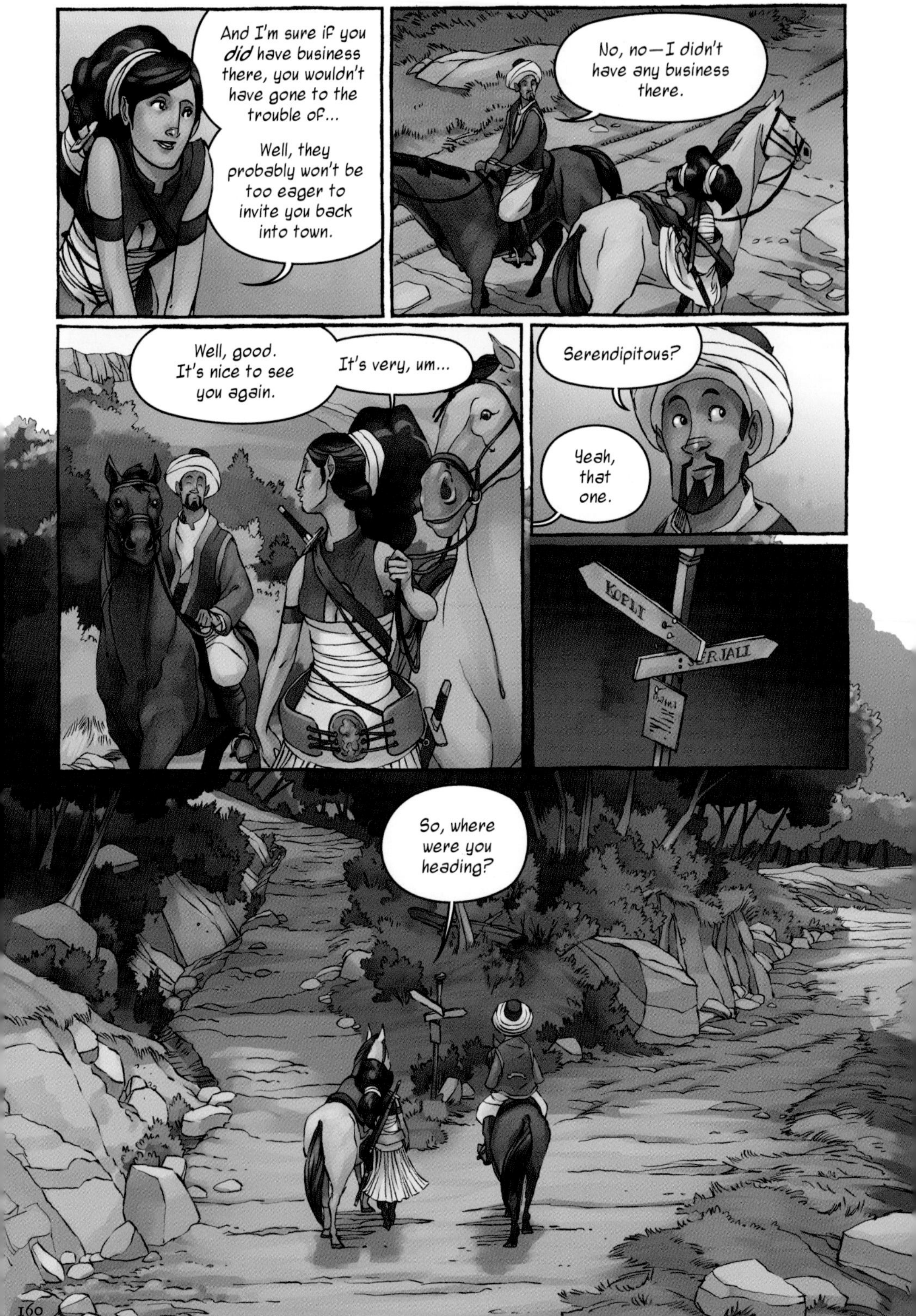
And I'm sure if you *did* have business there, you wouldn't have gone to the trouble of...
Well, they probably won't be too eager to invite you back into town.
No, no—I didn't have any business there.
Well, good. It's nice to see you again.
It's very, um...
Serendipitous?
Yeah, that one.
KOPLI
So, where were you heading?

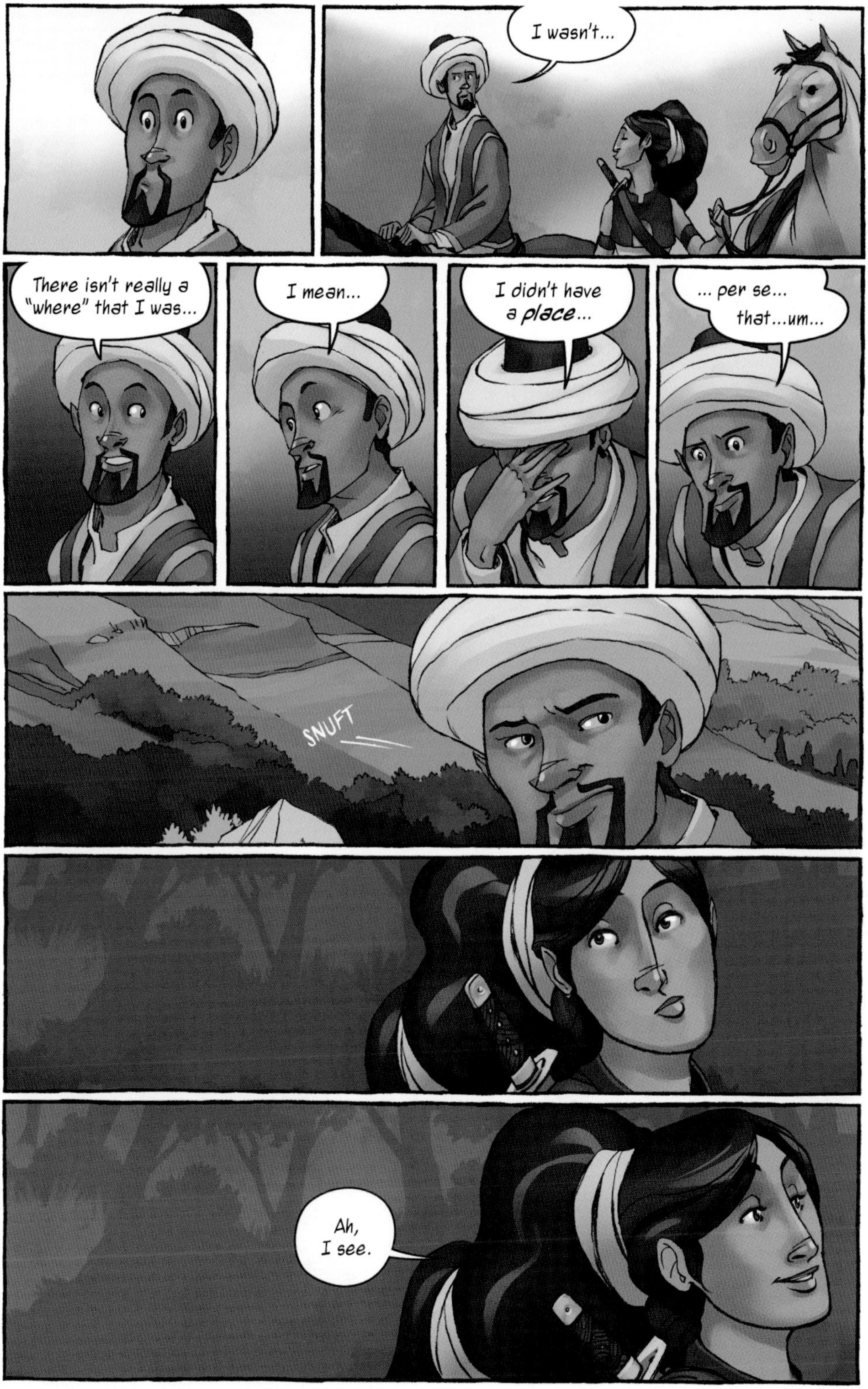
I wasn't...
There isn't really a "where" that I was...
I mean...
I didn't have a place...
... per se... that...um...
SNUFT
Ah, I see.

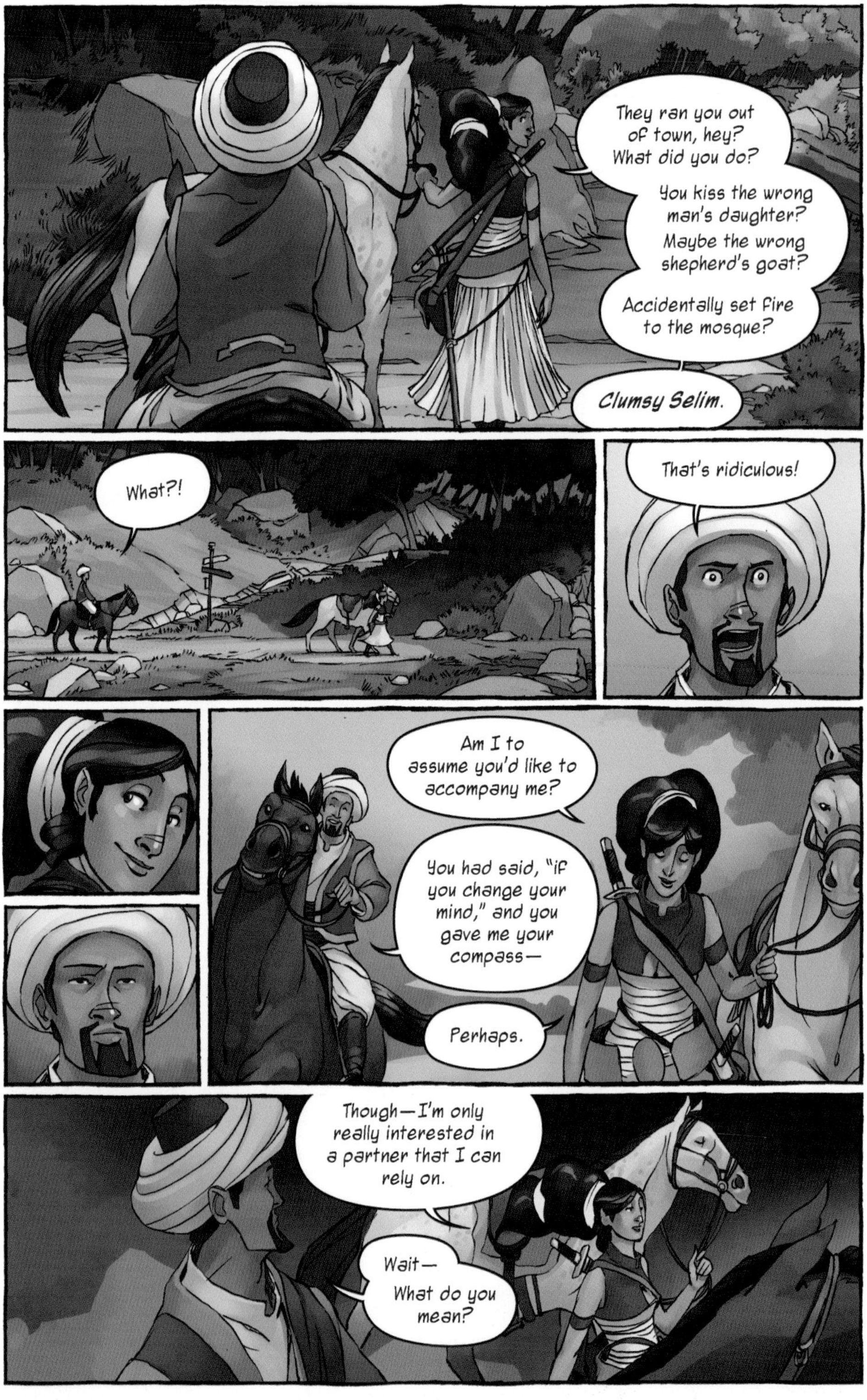
They ran you out of town, hey? What did you do?
You kiss the wrong man's daughter?
Maybe the wrong shepherd's goat?
Accidentally set fire to the mosque?
Clumsy Selim.
What?!
That's ridiculous!
Am I to assume you'd like to accompany me?
You had said, "if you change your mind," and you gave me your compass—
Perhaps.
Though—I'm only really interested in a partner that I can rely on.
Wait—
What do you mean?

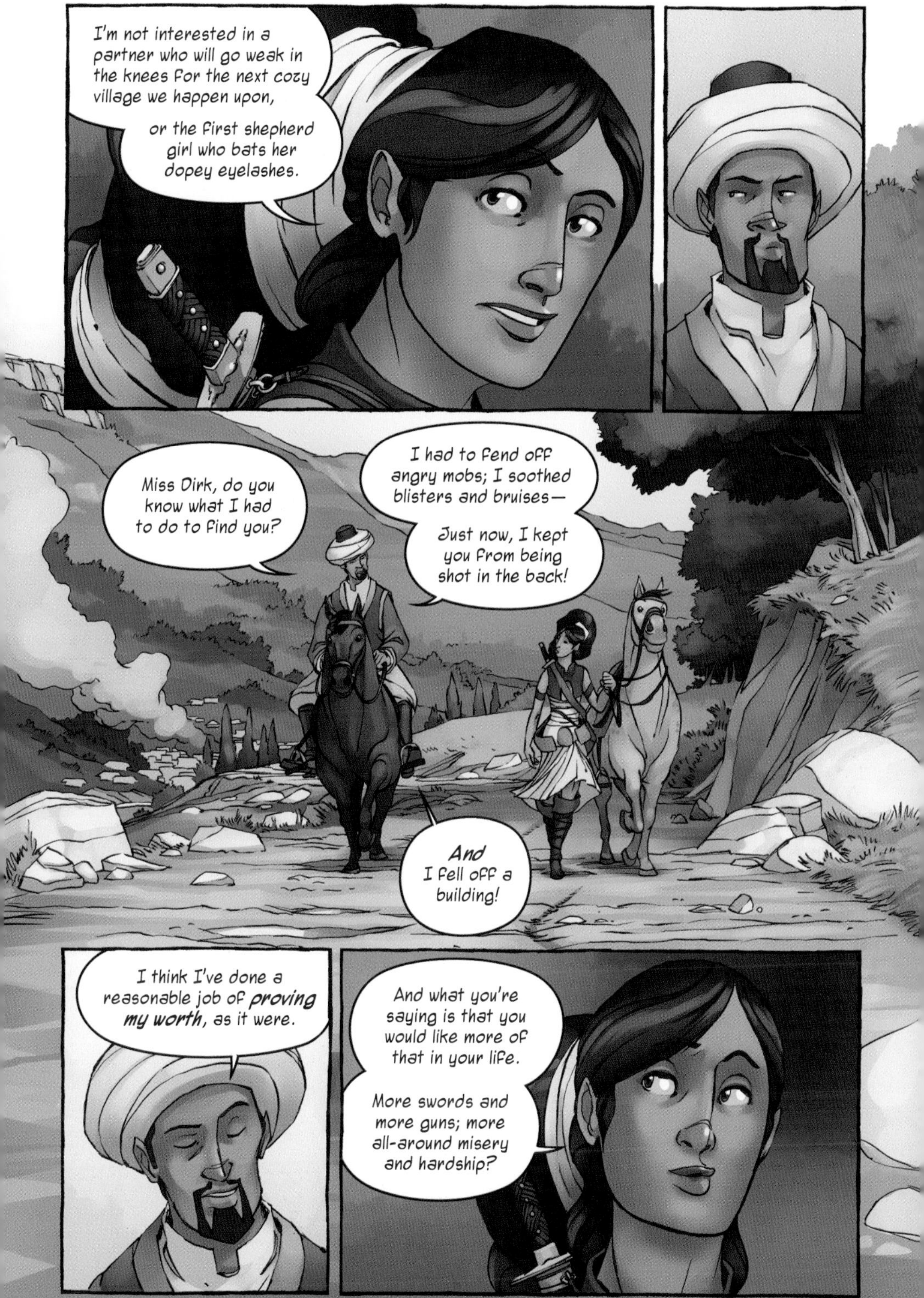
I'm not interested in a partner who will go weak in the knees for the next cozy village we happen upon,
or the first shepherd girl who bats her dopey eyelashes.
Miss Dirk, do you know what I had to do to find you?
I had to fend off angry mobs; I soothed blisters and bruises—
Just now, I kept you from being shot in the back!
And I fell off a building!
I think I've done a reasonable job of ***proving my worth***, as it were.
And what you're saying is that you would like more of that in your life.
More swords and more guns; more all-around misery and hardship?

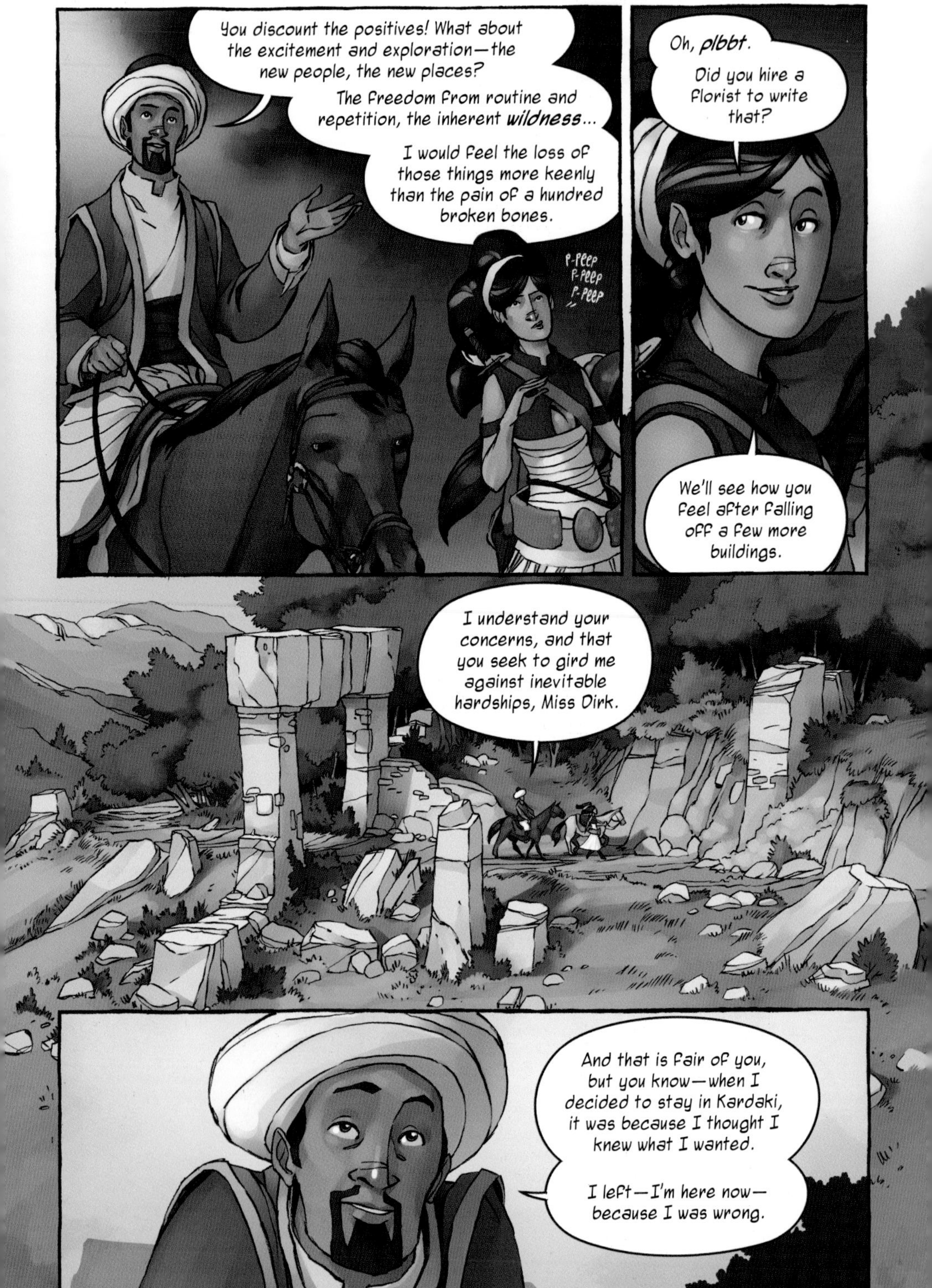
You discount the positives! What about the excitement and exploration—the new people, the new places?
The freedom from routine and repetition, the inherent *wildness*...
I would feel the loss of those things more keenly than the pain of a hundred broken bones.
P-PEEP P-PEEP P-PEEP
Oh, *plbbt*.
Did you hire a florist to write that?
We'll see how you feel after falling off a few more buildings.
I understand your concerns, and that you seek to gird me against inevitable hardships, Miss Dirk.
And that is fair of you, but you know—when I decided to stay in Kardaki, it was because I thought I knew what I wanted.
I left—I'm here now—because I was wrong.

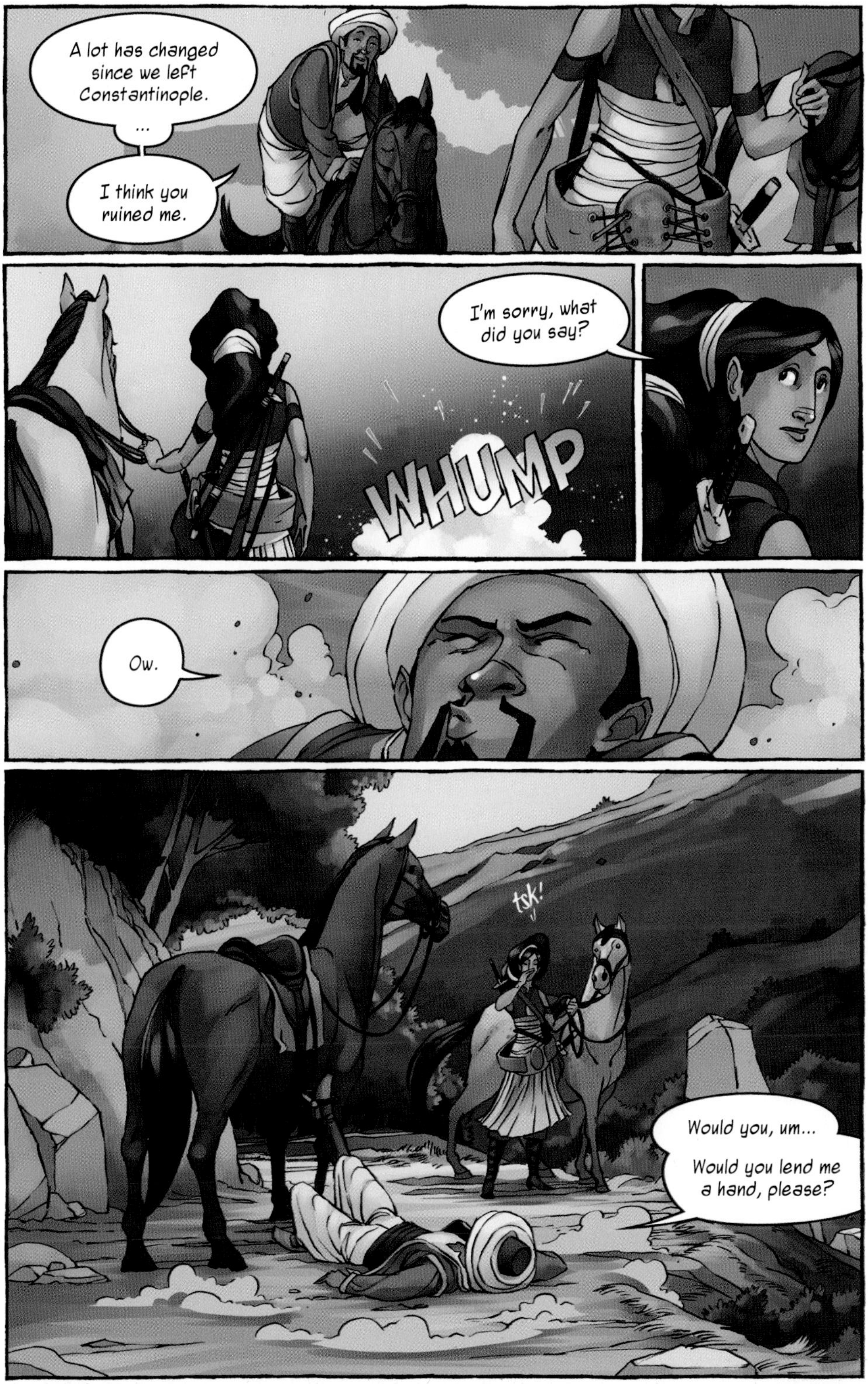
A lot has changed since we left Constantinople.
...
I think you ruined me.
WHUMP
I'm sorry, what did you say?
Ow.
tsk!
Would you, um...
Would you lend me a hand, please?

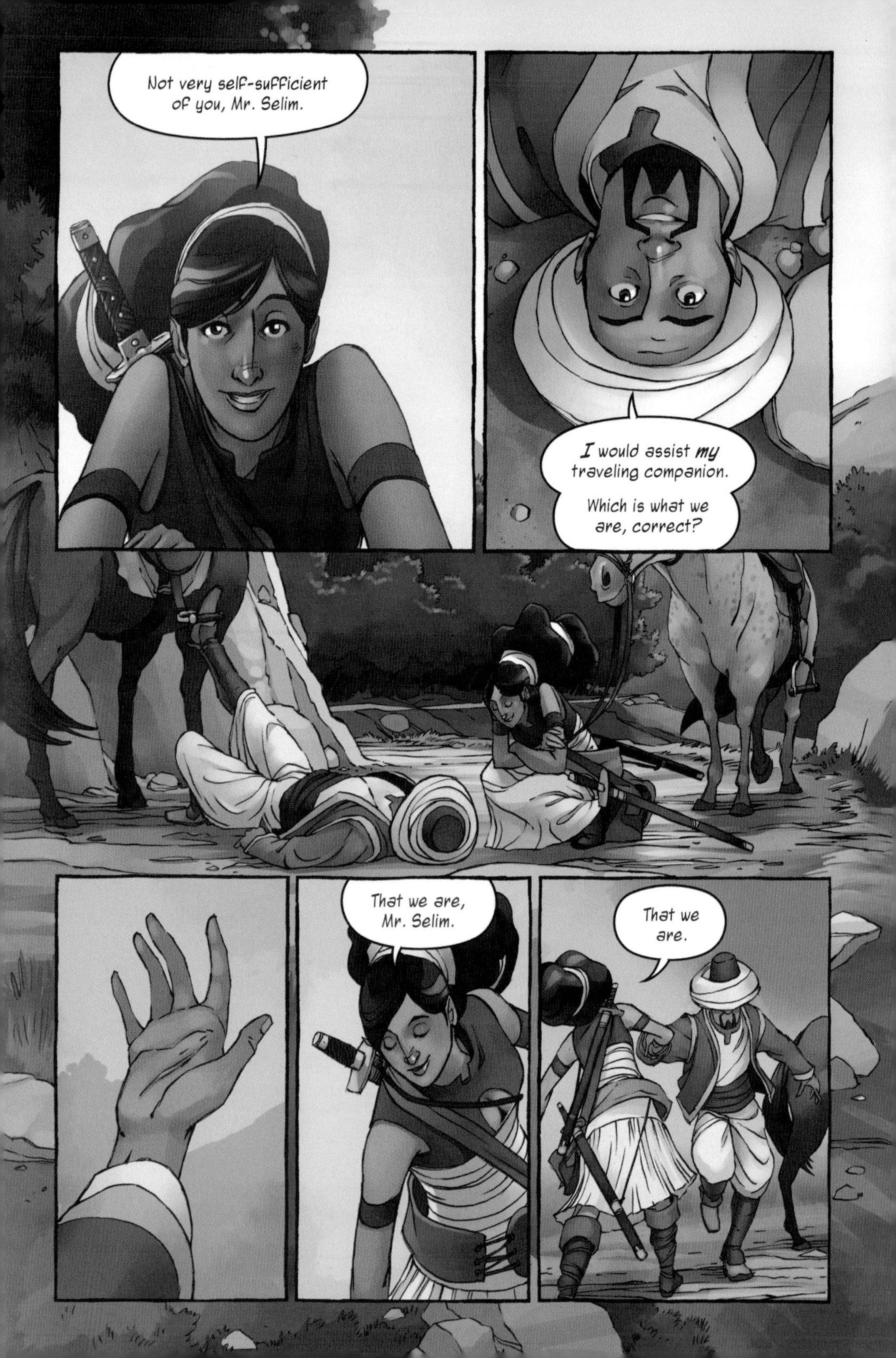
Not very self-sufficient of you, Mr. Selim.
I would assist ***my*** traveling companion.
Which is what we are, correct?
That we are, Mr. Selim.
That we are.

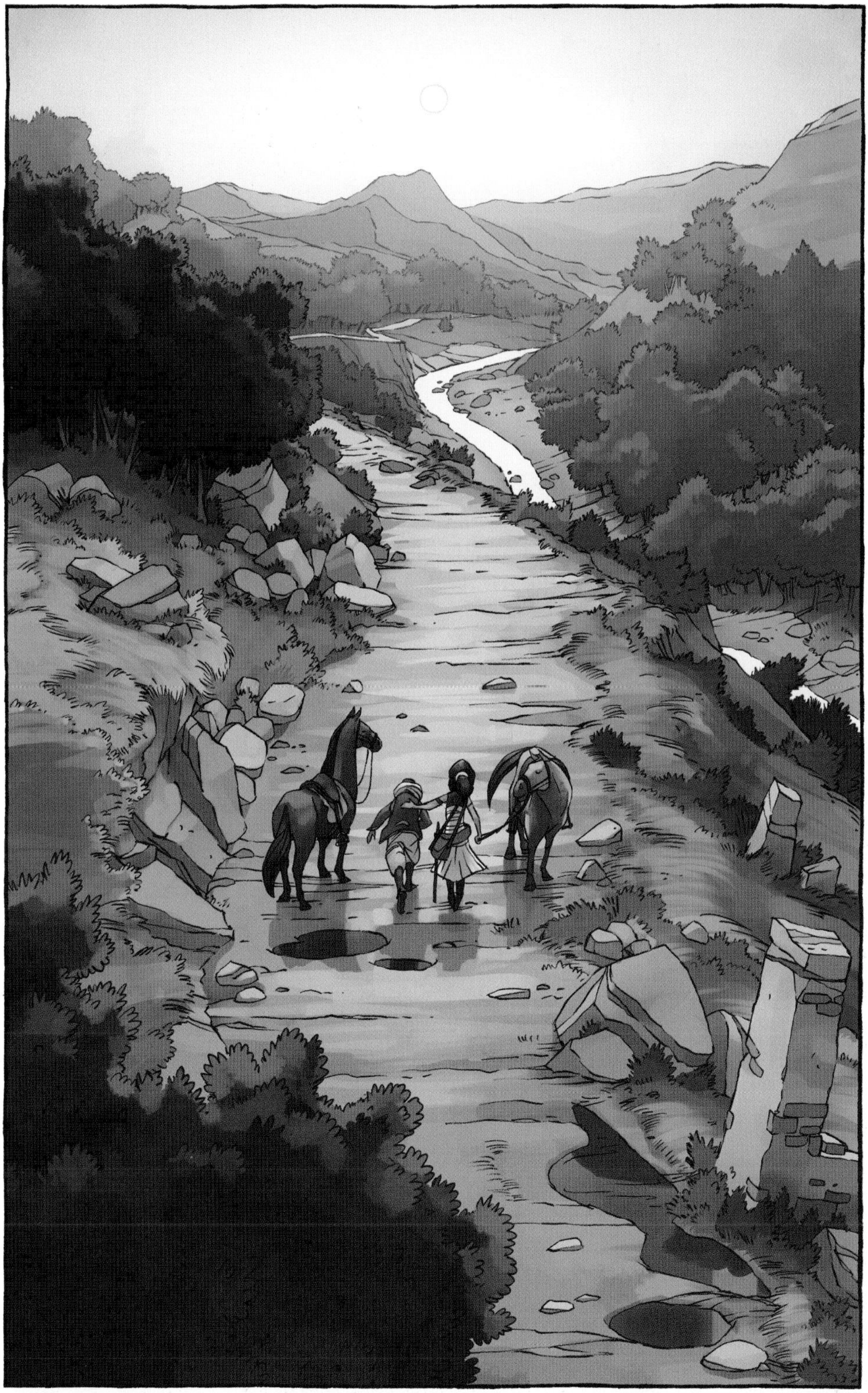

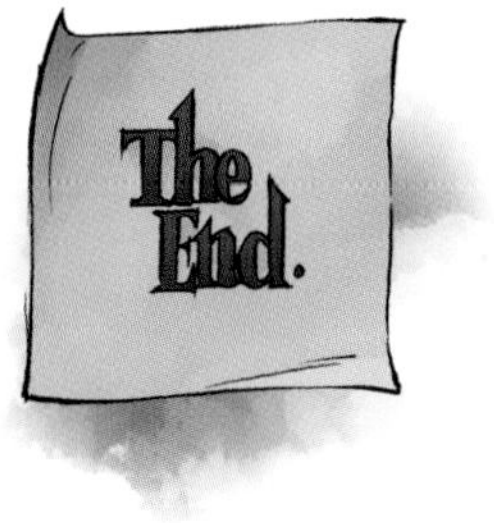
The End.

~ Acknowledgments ~

Whether they've smoothed out the process or influenced the content, *The Turkish Lieutenant* would have been much worse off if it weren't for the contributions of a few wonderful people. I extend endless gratitude to: Nicolas Bannister, Nikki Biefel, Robin Brenner, Margaret Campbell, Rebecca Dart, Chris Eliopoulos, Kevin Gamble, Colin and Gabriel Jack, Douglas Holgate, Kazu and Amy Kibuishi, Geoff Manson, Peter Millerd, Neval F. and Ahmet H. Ozturk, Kenny Park, Kean Soo, Dave Roman, Michael Swanston, Tealin, Raina Telgemeier, Hamish van der Ven, Eva Volin, the *Flight Comics* crew, and, of course, Mom and Dad. Many thank-yous and (I'm sure) overdue apologies are also due to Sarah, She of Sensible Shoes.

Thank you, too, to Calista, Colleen, Gina, and Mark for inviting Delilah into the First Second family, and to Nick Harris and Bernadette Baker-Baughman for their enthusiasm and energy.

Finally, I must also thank Delilah's readers—having spoken to or corresponded with many of you, I am certain that no author could reasonably expect as much kindness, generosity, and support as you have provided. For that I am exceedingly grateful.

— *Tony Cliff*